Scott Oden was born in Indiana, but has spent most of his life shuffling between his home in rural North Alabama, a Hobbit hole in Middle-earth, and some sketchy tavern in the Hyborian Age. He studied history and English at the University of Alabama. He is an avid reader of fantasy and ancient history, a collector of swords, and a player of tabletop role-playing games. His previous books include the acclaimed *Men of Bronze*, *Memnon* and *The Lion of Cairo*. When not writing, he can be found walking his two dogs or doting on his wife.

To find out more, visit scottoden.wordpress.com

KT-470-195

Withdrawn From Stock
Dublin Public Libraries

Acclaim for *A Gathering of Ravens*:

'Oden has done a marvellous job . . . a true triumph'
PARMENION BOOKS

'A magnificent mytho-historical saga, blending the history of 11th century Europe with Norse and Celtic mythology. A dark, grim and unrelentingly bloody tale of the last Orc and his quest for vengeance. Highly recommended'
JOHN GWYNNE, bestselling author of *The Faithful and the Fallen*

'Set in a vividly-imagined world where history and myth blur, Scott Oden's gripping and bloody tale of monsters and men carves out a fantastic new legend for this modern age'
JAMES WILDE, bestselling author of the *Hereward* series

'Everything that a Grimdark novel should be, sharp witted, dark and dangerous. Highly recommended for anyone who loves action, good characters and, you know, an amazing story. I loved it!'
JAMES A. MOORE, author of the *Seven Forges* series and *The Last Sacrifice*

'Swirling together Norse mythology with a Tolkien-esque writing style (there are even songs!) . . . if you like your fantasies with a serrated edge, this tale will be right up your alley'
OMNIVORACIOUS

'Oden has expertly weaved Norse, Saxon and Celtic mythology . . . if you're a fan of Bernard Cornwell's Saxon saga, or David Gemmell's muscular fantasy, then you would be hard-pressed to find another novel that satisfies on both fronts'
STARBURST

'Lovingly crafted . . . this fast-paced thrill ride might have been bleak or unsettling but it's rendered so lovingly . . . a satisfying saga that's as complex as an old tree's roots, and a pleasure to read'
PUBLISHERS WEEKLY (Starred Review)

'The story is imposing and dark, deftly woven by Oden to mix legend and history . . . characters appear to have stepped out of history to dance across the pages . . . Oden set out to redeem the Orc, taking pieces from Norse and Celtic mythology, from Beowulf to Balor, and he did fabulously. Highly recommended'
FANTASY-FACTION

'Right from the start this book draws you in with its evocative imagery and beautifully described landscapes . . . in *A Gathering of Ravens* the line between fantasy and historical fiction is blurred into mythology. If you like your fantasy Tolkien-esque with deep roots, then this novel is for you, and like many legends in truth, it is not exactly a story of justice or redemption, but it is a tale that must play itself out to its very end, a tale you cannot help but get drawn into'
FORBIDDEN PLANET

'I loved the prose and for me, the action sequences really brought the brutality to life . . . add to this some wonderful twists . . . a kick-ass plot . . . I was a more than happy reader. Top notch'
FALCATA TIMES

'An amazing work of fantasy with a very real touch of both humanity and the weight of history. Oden has populated his strange world with witches, monsters, Vikings, warriors, cowards and everything in between. Deft and well written'
CHARNEL HOUSE REVIEWS

'Oden taps the dark roots of 'the Northern thing'. . . mixing Norse history and mythology with fantasy and a relentless narrative drive . . . will appeal to the Grimdark crowd as well as fans of Robert E. Howard and Poul Anderson'
CHARLES R. RUTLEDGE, co-author of *Blind Shadows* and *Congregations of the Dead*

'Masterful storytelling . . . superb writing . . . . magical and lively . . . a must-read for historical fantasy lovers'
THE NERD DAILY

Also by Scott Oden

MEN OF BRONZE
MEMNON
THE LION OF CAIRO

and published by Bantam

A GATHERING OF RAVENS

SCOTT ODEN

Leabharlanna Poiblí Chathair Baile Átha Cliath
Dublin City Public Libraries

BANTAM BOOKS

LONDON • TORONTO • SYDNEY • AUCKLAND • JOHANNESBURG

TRANSWORLD PUBLISHERS
61–63 Uxbridge Road, London W5 5SA
www.penguin.co.uk

Transworld is part of the Penguin Random House group of companies
whose addresses can be found at global.penguinrandomhouse.com

Penguin
Random House
UK

First published in the United States of America in 2017 by
Thomas Dunne Books, an imprint of St Martin's Press

First published in Great Britain in 2017 by Bantam Press
an imprint of Transworld Publishers
Bantam edition published 2018

Copyright © Scott Oden 2017

Scott Oden has asserted his right under the Copyright,
Designs and Patents Act 1988 to be identified as the author of this work.

This book is a work of fiction and, except in the case of historical fact, any
resemblance to actual persons, living or dead, is purely coincidental.

Every effort has been made to obtain the necessary permissions with
reference to copyright material, both illustrative and quoted. We
apologize for any omissions in this respect and will be pleased to
make the appropriate acknowledgements in any future edition.

A CIP catalogue record for this book
is available from the British Library.

ISBN
9780553819847

Typeset in 10½/13pt Sabon by Falcon Oast Graphic Art Ltd.
Printed and bound by Clays Ltd, Bungay, Suffolk.

Penguin Random House is committed to a sustainable
future for our business, our readers and our planet. This book is made
from Forest Stewardship Council® certified paper.

MIX
Paper from
responsible sources
FSC® C018179

1 3 5 7 9 10 8 6 4 2

For Steve Tompkins
and Miguel Martins,
shield-brothers.

All fled, all done, so lift me on the pyre;
The feast is over and the lamps expire.

— ROBERT E. HOWARD

He knew himself a villain – but he deem'd
The rest no better than the thing he seem'd;
And scorn'd the best as hypocrites who hid
Those deeds the bolder spirit plainly did.
He knew himself detested, but he knew
The hearts that loath'd him, crouch'd and
dreaded too.
Lone, wild, and strange, he stood alike exempt
From all affection and from all contempt.

– LORD BYRON, *THE CORSAIR*

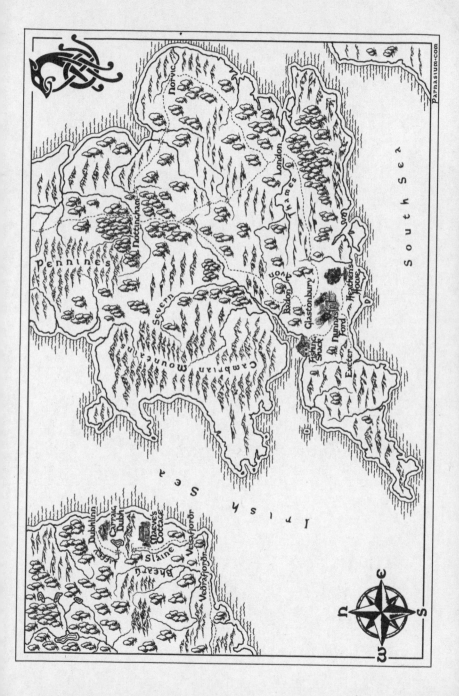

BOOK ONE

THE ISLAND OF SJÆLLAND, THE DANEMARK

THE YEAR OF OUR LORD 999

I

The storm howled out of the west like the terrible voice of God, shouting down the heretics who doubted the coming Apocalypse. The autumn had been warmer than it should, and Njáll son of Hjálmarr – who in the last year had forsworn the whale-road so he might carry the banner of the White Christ – knew he should not have trusted it would hold. The priest back in Jelling, that scrofulous bastard who preached conversion with the sword rather than the psalter, had warned him that this *oväder* – this un-weather – was of the Devil's making; that the fumes of Hell warmed the world of Man, and soon the armies of God would strike from the Gates of Heaven to set the balance right.

A year ago, before his conversion, Njáll would have dismissed the priest for a fool. He would have seen the heathen hand of Thor in the deafening crash of thunder and the jags of lightning crackling across the night-black sky; heard the false laughter of Rán in the pelting hail and the sheets of rain soaking him to the bone. And he would have sacrificed and called out to Odin for succor. But, like the blessed apostle Paulos, the scales had fallen from Njáll's eyes and he could see the truth laid out before him: the power of the old gods was breaking, and the world's end was nigh – and not the treacherous lie that was Ragnarok, with its false promises of glory and slaughter without end, but the Day of Judgment when the White Christ would return and scour the earth clean of heathens and apostates and deniers of the Lord.

And Njáll Hjálmarr's son counted himself blessed to have received the gift of salvation so close to the end . . .

Thunder shook the heavens. Njáll kept a tight grip on the halter of their donkey. The beast shied and threatened to bolt with every step, its eyes rolling in fear. Only the strength in his great shoulders, a legacy of the days he had gone raiding with Norway's king, Olaf Tryggve's son, kept the animal from plunging off the path and into the undergrowth, where wind-stripped leaves faded from orange and red to a muddy brown in silent testimony to the coming winter. The path, hardly better than a cow trail, led inland from the beach at Seal Reef. Roskilde was their destination; once there, his companion, Aidan, would take service with old Father Gunnar and Njáll would . . . would what? Simply await the End of Days?

Water sluiced from Njáll's salt-and-pepper beard as he hauled on the rope lead; he tried to drag the blasted donkey but the effort only gouged furrows in the mud. His feet slipped on wet rock; he nearly fell. Njáll railed at the animal, his voice lost to the roaring wind. 'Damn you, you miserable beast! I swear if we reach Roskilde I'm going to skin you and make a pair of boots from your flea-bitten hide!'

For a moment, Njáll considered backtracking to the beach, to ride out the storm in the moss-grown ruins of the old stone tower there – a relic of the days when the kings of the Shield-Danes ruled over Sjælland. But Seal Reef was a good two hours or more behind, while Roskilde was a day, perhaps two, ahead. No, they needed shelter here, now.

There was a lull in the rain; the echo of thunder rolled

from horizon to horizon. Njáll glanced about, seeking Aidan. The irrepressible young Briton, who for the last year had helped guide the Dane through the darkness and into the light of the Christ, was ahead of him, clambering up the rock and scrub of the hillside. Njáll frowned. 'Aidan!'

Aidan turned. The gale snatched off his cowl, revealing a shock of hair the color of dark copper and not even a hint of a beard. He bent into the fierce wind; his black woolen mantle flapped like vestigial wings as he pointed to something a short way up the slope.

There, partially hidden by hawthorn and bramble, was the yawning mouth of a cave.

Njáll waved him back. Though secure in his newfound faith, the Dane had not lost the superstitions of his heathen kin. He had learned from a young age that a cave like that might shelter any number of fell creatures, beyond bears or wolves. Witches could meet there in conclave, to weave the songs that wrought the doom of good men; trolls, wights, and goblins might lurk in the shadows, ready to seize unwary travelers. The spreading Word of God might keep the evils of a forgotten world at bay, but it could not destroy them completely . . .

Njáll shouted at the younger man, cold dread seeping into his bones. 'It's not safe!'

'Safer than walking in this wrack!' Aidan replied, his voice high and sharp, like that of a castrato. Before Njáll could respond, Aidan scrambled up the slope, slipped behind the hawthorn thicket, and vanished into the mouth of the cave.

Njáll reeled off a long – and very un-Christian – litany of curses. He did not dare leave the donkey to its own devices. One sharp crack of thunder and they would not see their belongings again until they reached Roskilde, if

5

then. Njáll's curses redoubled as he manhandled the beast up the slope; despite the chill and the rain soaking him to the bone, sweat dripped from his brow by the time he reached the stand of hawthorn. The God-cursed animal balked at entering the cave, so Njáll compromised: he tied the donkey's lead rope as tightly as he could to the thickest branch he could find. Pausing to dig a bearded axe with a short oak haft from his gear – the *skeggox* he had carried on the whale-road – Njáll charged in through branch and bramble, half-expecting to see nothing left of Aidan but bloody shreds.

But Njáll's war cry died on his lips, his charge to death and glory arrested by a distinct lack of foes. Indeed, the slender young man stood whole and unscathed inside the mouth of the cave. He looked over his shoulder at Njáll, blue eyes daring the wet and bedraggled Dane to reprimand him. Though Aidan's cheeks were ruddy and windburned, his features were as fine and delicate as any woman's. Njáll might have marked him for a lesser son of nobility had he not known better.

'God loves a fool,' Njáll muttered, breathing hard. 'That's the only reason I can fathom why you're not dead yet.'

Aidan grinned. 'God also helps those who help themselves, which is why we now have shelter from the storm.'

Caves were a rarity on Sjælland, and this one, Njáll could see, was rarer still. It was gigantic. It could easily have held the burial mound of Gorm the Old, back in Jelling. The cave entrance hung like a ledge in the wall of a mine shaft; gray light and rain trickled down from a scrub-choked fissure twenty feet over their heads, the water dropping down to pool in a corner of the cave floor, some thirty feet below them. A trio of stunted hawthorn trees grew at the edge of the pool, branches still festooned with autumn leaves; a fourth, nothing but a dead husk, stood like a naked caricature of its brothers. How far back the cave stretched Njáll could not apprehend, for its farthest reaches lay cloaked in darkness. He wondered if this might be the lair of the dragon that slew and was slain by old Bödvar, the Geat who made himself king of the Shield-Danes? Though given over to the Christ, Njáll felt his once-heathen blood stir at the thought of testing the edge of his axe against the scales of a great wyrm. *That would be a good death!*

Aidan shuffled close to the edge and peered down at the pool. 'Why doesn't it flood?'

'Drains out through chinks in the rock, I'd wager.' Njáll sniffed the air. It was damp and musty, with a faint metallic-animal reek that reminded him of a badly tanned leather jerkin worn beneath a chain hauberk.

To the right of the entrance, a series of rock shelves like stair steps carved by dwarves led down to the cave floor. Njáll tested them. They were slick with moisture but solid. The Dane descended first, axe held loosely in his fist. His free hand brushed the cave walls. Under his fingers, he could feel scratches and grooves.

'Runes,' he said, his voice echoing.

Aidan looked closer. 'Here's a word in Latin, I think.'

'What does it say?'

The youth tilted his head this way and that, rising on his toes as he tried to get a better view of the faint inscription. ' "*Or-Orcadii*," perhaps? Maybe '"*Orcades*"?'

'Orkney?'

Aidan shrugged. 'Hard to tell. Could be . . .'

Jags of hard white light flashed from overhead; in answer, thunder seemed to shake the very ground. By the time they reached the last step, a fresh deluge was pouring from the fissure. Chains of lightning made bright the gloom of the cave; by their brilliant flares Njáll saw another sigil chiseled deep into the wall: an eye, its slitted pupil like that of some monstrous serpent. The giant Dane shuddered.

'What bandit's lair is this?'

'Does it matter?' Aidan replied. 'God has granted us a dry place of respite from the storm. Would you turn up your nose at a gift from the Almighty?'

Njáll glared up at the eye; the crude savagery of its carving left him uneasy, like a memory of something – some whispered warning – from his childhood. He glanced around, half-expecting a fork-tailed devil to leap from the shadows. 'Satan's own front porch is no gift.'

Aidan chuckled, shaking his head. 'Come, turn your axe on that dead tree so we can get a fire going. I'll see to our poor donkey. I think you will better appreciate the Lord's generosity with dry clothes, warm feet, and a hot meal in your belly.'

Njáll grumbled, but in short order the two had built a small campsite against the cave wall, near the rising steps. No amount of coaxing, however, would convince the donkey to move deeper than the relatively dry cave mouth. Taking pity on the trembling beast, Aidan unloaded their possessions – two woven reed panniers, their contents wrapped in seal skin – and left the donkey hobbled and tied by the cave entrance, along with a measure of oats and a bucket of water drawn up from the pool below.

The fire crackled to life, lending warmth and a little light to their corner of the cave. While Njáll busied himself with setting a hank of salted pork to roast over the flames, Aidan took his spare clothing and moved off to the far side of the cave – out of sight – to change. When he returned, he laid his wet garments out to dry. Njáll followed suit, a ritualized sort of modesty that seemed natural between the two of them. While Njáll was gone Aidan fished some bread and cheese and a handful of dried apples from their gear, along with a flask of watered mead, and prepared them each a plate of food. The smell of roasting pork, and the sizzle and pop of fat, made Aidan's mouth water. Stirring the fire, he felt a faint breeze coming from deeper in the cave, like the exhalation of some great beast. He was staring at the darkness behind them when Njáll came back. 'How deep under the earth do you think this cave goes?' he asked the Dane, who knelt and spread his own wet clothes out alongside Aidan's.

Njáll glanced at the rear of the cave and shrugged. 'Only God knows.'

'We should investigate it.'

'Not until I have the warm feet and bellyful of food you spoke of.'

Njáll sat on the lowest step; Aidan handed him a plate, and both men bowed their heads as Aidan recited the Lord's Prayer, his mixed accents, English and Danish, mangling its Latin phrases. At the end, both of them muttered, 'Amen.' And with a nod, they fell upon their food.

'Who made that, you think?' Aidan asked, jerking his narrow chin at the eye sigil. 'And what does it mean?'

'An ogre, like as not,' Njáll said around a mouthful of pork. 'My grandfather told me caves like this were hacked out of the earth by the sons of Ymir, foul beasts who drink the blood of good Christians.' Njáll paused. He swallowed and then fixed Aidan with an iron-hard stare. 'Are *you* a good Christian? They will ask you this, once we reach Roskilde. They will ask how you came to be here. They will ask you about your home, your people, and why you left a place as sacred as Glastonbury to join a wretched little church that's two hairs shy of the asshole of the world. And they will ask if you cleave to our Lord's commandments. How will you answer?'

Aidan didn't flinch; this was an old game between them,

preparation for taking up a life of holy service when truth and circumstance did not match one another precisely. 'I will answer with alacrity,' Aidan replied, 'and silently implore God to forgive the lies that must escape my lips. I will tell them the tale of Red Njáll Hjálmarr's son, who captured me in the sack of Exeter and forced me into a life of vile servitude. I will tell them how the power of the Redeemer turned Njáll from his heathen ways and how I, because of my upbringing at Glastonbury, helped set that once-vicious reaver's heart upon the path of the One True God. And I will tell them that, with the End Times upon us, I came east with you so we might help spread the Gospel among your godless kin.'

Njáll nodded. 'But, what if they discover your true nature? What if you fall in love with one of your brother monks and he rejects your advances? What then?'

'I . . . I don't know,' Aidan said with an exasperated sigh, weary all of a sudden. He rose and took Njáll's empty plate. 'I don't care for such things, not at Glastonbury, certainly not at Exeter, and not now. I only know this: I won't live as I did before, and I want to serve the Lord in what time remains to us. Nothing else matters.'

Njáll nodded. 'Pray that will be enough.'

Aidan carried their dishes to the pool and rinsed them in the stream of rainwater falling from above. He heard rumbles of muted thunder as distant lightning yet cast its white glare over the hillsides. Aidan peered up through the fissure; outside, night had fallen and a chill had settled on the land. By dawn, it would be frigid. Aidan turned and shuffled back toward their fire.

The youth looked longingly at the hinterlands of the cave, its shadow-cloaked mystery crying out for resolution. *Maybe a little exploration before bed.* A flare of lightning cast its glare . . .

And as Aidan watched, the light illuminated a figure – etched it against the darkness with startling clarity. Something shaped like a man, savage and barbaric. Something that moved.

'Jesus, Mary, and Joseph!' Aidan dropped the plates; he trod on the hem of his robe, tripping and scrabbling over the rock in his haste to get back to the fire. 'Christ Almighty!'

Aidan's cry startled Njáll, who had settled against the now-warm wall with his eyes closed. He lurched to his feet and hefted his axe. 'What ails you?'

The youth gestured toward the darkness at the rear of the cave. His voice, when he found it, was a terrified hiss. 'We . . . We are not alone! There's someone back there! I swear it! A man, surely . . .'

Njáll's eyes narrowed. 'Stay behind me.' He reached down, drew a brand from the fire, and held it aloft. Wood crackled and sparked; embers drifted on the faint breath of air.

Njáll, too, saw something move. His makeshift torch revealed a glint of iron, the swirl of a wolf pelt, and then . . . nothing. He tensed, ready for the rush of a foeman. His axe felt once more like an extension of his arm. 'If I say run, you run. Do you hear?' he muttered to Aidan, who nodded. Njáll drew himself up to his full height and bellowed into the darkness: 'Who goes? If you be a thief, we are but poor sons of Christ! We have nothing! Show yourself!'

The echo of Njáll's challenge died away. He strained to hear some sound, a clink of metal on stone, a hissed breath, something. But there was nothing, save for the dull rumble of thunder and the splash of rain. He was on the verge of calling out again when a voice answered from the gloom – a voice as hard as knapped flint that spoke the tongue of the Danes with an accent Njáll could not place. 'You have food, poor sons of Christ.'

11

'Aye. Little enough for our own needs, but what we have we will share with you.'

'At what price?'

'We ask nothing in return. Our charity is the charity of Christ,' Njáll said. 'My brother, here, will fetch you a plate. Aidan?'

Njáll heard a snuffling sound, followed by harsh laughter. '*Brother*, is it?' There came a derisive noise, just then – halfway between a growl and a cough. '*Faugh!* I'll play your little game, poor son of Christ. I have crossed paths with many a Dane in my day. Spear-Danes and Shield-Danes, Bright-Danes and Ring-Danes, West-Danes and South-Danes . . . but never a *Christ*-Dane.' The voice filled that epithet with a sense of scorn. 'Do you *Christ*-Danes still follow the ancient laws of hospitality?'

'We do,' Njáll replied.

'And did I sneak past you like a thief in the night, *Christ*-Dane?'

Njáll ground his teeth. 'No.'

'I don't understand,' Aidan said. The youth shot Njáll a confused glance.

'Then understand this, little fool.' The voice grated like iron on a whetstone. 'This cave is mine! I have marked it with the Eye! You trespass, disturb my rest, drink my water, and cut down my trees, and you have the spleen to call me *your* guest?'

'We . . . We meant no offense,' Aidan said. 'We did not know this cave belonged to you.'

Still cloaked in shadow, the figure laughed once more. There was no humor in his voice. 'Aye, claim ignorance and blindness, for is that not your way? Keep your Nailed God's charity. I will trade you my hospitality for your food. Do we have a bargain?'

Njáll considered the offer. In the past, he would have

simply trusted his axe to win the day and taken what he needed as spoils of battle. But those days were over. He was a man of peace, now. Perhaps this was a divine test of his patience, of the strength of his new faith? Surely he could pass a night with a surly heathen in exchange for warmth, shelter, and the blessings of the Lord. Slowly, he let his axe fall to his side and nodded. 'We have. I am Njáll son of Hjálmarr. My companion, here, is Aidan of Glastonbury. We are bound for the church at Roskilde. How are you called?'

The figure moved nearer to the circle of light cast by the travelers' fire. The thunder had faded; the rain was a soft hiss. Weak flares of lightning revealed little more than a twisted silhouette, gnarled limbs bulging with muscle and sinew. 'I am called many things, Christ-Dane. Corpse-maker and Life-quencher, the Bringer of Night, the Son of the Wolf and Brother of the Serpent. I am the last of Bálegyr's brood, called Grimnir by my people.'

Aidan backed over to the panniers and drew out some bread and cheese. A bit of pork remained, as well as an apple, wrinkled and sweet. He glanced up as he worked, curious as to what kind of man this Grimnir was. 'Who . . . who are your people?'

But what stepped from the shadows was not human. The flickering firelight threw Grimnir's features into sharp relief. While his face had the same construction as a human face, its planes and angles were long and sharp, vulpine in the half-light of the cave. Coarse black hair, woven with gold beads and discs of carved bone, framed eyes like splinters of red-hot iron, set deep into a craggy brow. He was broad of chest and long of arm, slouch-backed in his posture, with tattoos in cinder and woad snaking across his swarthy hide. Grimnir was clad in antiquated splendor: a sleeveless hauberk of iron rings sewn onto black leather,

13

a kilt of poorly tanned horsehide cut from the flanks of a dappled roan, a cloak of wolf skins, and arm rings of gold, silver, and wrought iron. One black-nailed hand rested on the worn ivory hilt of a long seax.

Aidan was taken aback, but Njáll reacted as though he had been struck. He brought up his axe. No longer was he a man of peace in the service of God; rather, he was a Dane facing an ancestral enemy. 'Christ's mercies! *Skrælingr,* I name you! Back, child of Satan!'

'You would forget our truce, *Christ*-Dane?' Grimnir's voice was full of cold menace; he shifted his weight, balancing on the balls of his feet like a predator ready to spring.

'There can be no truces with an enemy of God!'

'Bugger your god!'

But before Njáll and Grimnir could come to blows, Aidan thrust himself between the two, with no thought for his own safety. 'Stop! Both of you! Is it not written that we should love the sinner though we despise the sin?'

Njáll hesitated. 'This is no mere sinner, Aidan! It is not even a man! It comes from a race of traitors and oath-breakers and defilers of corpses!'

'And so? Were not your people once described in no less despicable terms? How runs the prayer, brother? It was once on the lips of every God-fearing man from Britain to Byzantium. Do you recall it?'

The stinging condemnation in Aidan's voice dampened Njáll's anger. 'Aye. "Deliver us, O God, from the savage race of Northmen."' Njáll lowered his axe, teeth grinding with the effort; though he might struggle with it every day until the End of Days, he was a man of God, now, and not some blood-mad heathen. Not any longer. When he spoke again his voice was constrained. 'Thank you for reminding me. You are wise beyond your years, and a Christian without equal, brother. Forgive me, Grimnir. We are ill guests to abuse your hospitality so. Will you not join us?'

Grimnir's narrowed eyes slid from man to youth and back again. He was plainly suspicious of them, but with an agonizing slowness he nevertheless took his hand from the hilt of his seax. 'Tonight we eat, and you will sleep in peace. But, come the dawn, I might just split your miserable skull, *Christ*-Dane.'

Njáll picked up the plate of food and held it out to Grimnir. 'Fair enough,' he replied. 'If that is God's will, so be it.'

With a fierce grin, Grimnir accepted the food and joined the two travelers by the fire.

2

The world beyond the cave had grown silent with the fullness of night. A wind moaned inland from the sea, driving a shoal of fallen leaves before it and rattling the branches of the hawthorn trees. The clouds overhead shredded to reveal the gleaming lamps of Heaven, closer and brighter now that the Ending of the World drew nigh.

Inside the cave Njáll and Aidan knelt on the cold stone floor before a small cross carved from the old spruce oar of a dragon ship. The youth led them in prayer, reciting the words by rote even as his mind dwelled on the creature whose cave they shared. Grimnir had squatted on his haunches, his hair a stringy veil from which rust-red eyes gleamed suspiciously; he sniffed at each bite as though he expected it to be poisoned. Aidan had a thousand questions for the – what had Njáll called him? *skrælingr?* – but all that had been forestalled when the older man declared he needed to pray before taking his rest. Grimnir had snarled and spat when Aidan brought out the cross, as though the sight of it pained him; he loudly and profanely cursed their faith as mummery and wanted no part of it. Aidan could hear him even now, relieving himself beyond the hawthorns screening the mouth of the cave and, if Aidan's ear could be trusted, *singing*. Grimnir's flinty voice filtered down, tuneless and unlovely:

Brothers shall strive and slaughter,
Sisters shall sin together;
Ill days among men:
An axe-age, a sword-age,
Shields shall be cloven;
A wind-age, a wolf-age,
Ere the world totters.

He heard Njáll mutter 'Amen' and quickly added his own. The Dane stood; while Aidan carefully wrapped their carved cross and stowed it in their gear, Njáll went over and stoked the fire. He rubbed his eyes.

'That song he sings,' Aidan said, crouching by the panniers. 'Do you know it?'

'Aye, it is a song the heathens sing of Ragnarok,' Njáll replied, frowning. 'What my people call the end of the world.' The older man resumed his place against the cave wall, his axe beside him. Aidan passed him a blanket then set about preparing a place where he would sleep. Smoke coiled and drifted out of the fissure as Grimnir's song faded.

The End of Days weighed heavily on Aidan's mind. Somewhere in the world beyond, on this very night, the Antichrist stalked the earth, sowing the seeds of its destruction and drawing all things of evil nature and intent to him. In his mind, Aidan knew this to be true, for was it not written in Revelation? And did not the blessed Abbot Ælfric of Eynsham determine this year to be the Great Year, the year of the Last Judgment? Why, then, did Aidan not feel in his heart the jubilation that surely must come from the nearness of the Lord? The Christ would return by year's end, but Aidan could not sense anything special about each day that passed. The wars had not increased in number, nor had tribulations grown more than what was

17

each man's lot to bear. Lands where crops had failed suffered famine while their neighbors might fill their larders and barns nigh to bursting with the bounty of the Lord. Aidan saw neither rhyme nor reason to this. He could accept the idea that perhaps the learned abbot of Eynsham was wrong in naming this as the Great Year, but surely not the *Revelation to John*. It was infallible, was it not?

Aidan stirred from his reverie. 'I did not know heathens believed in the End Times, too.'

'Aye, they do,' Njáll replied. 'Though it is not like ours. They believe Ragnarok will be a time of glory and endless war, when the gods issue forth from Ásgarðr to battle the *jötunn*, their sworn foes. Their struggle will break the world. It is an ancient tale.'

'You know,' Aidan said after a moment, 'this Grimnir reminds me of your old shipmates. He has that same godless exuberance.'

'We Danes can at least find redemption. His folk are beyond even that.'

Aidan's brow furrowed. 'Surely there is no man who is beyond redemption?'

'I told you, that thing is no man.'

'I thought so, too, when I first saw him. He looks like' – the youth struggled to find the words – 'like no man I've ever seen, but he does have two arms, two legs, and a head as we do. He breathes as we do, eats as we do, drinks, spits, laughs and curses as we do. If we judge him on his appearance, alone, then I would concede your point. But *how* is he not a man? And this name you have for him, *skrælingr*? I've never heard it.'

'I expect not. It is as old as Ragnarok. But, there is a word in your tongue, '*orcnéas*.' Have you heard that one? It describes a monster of great evil, an ogre who stalks fen

18

and marsh, and eats the flesh of the dead. They are one and the same.'

Aidan looked at the older man as though he had gone daft. 'Aye, I know that name. *Orcnéas* were enemies of God, children of Cain who fought long against the Almighty. Grimnir can't be one of those! God banished them from His sight. Honestly, Njáll! What game is this? You name him something he cannot be!'

'It is no game,' Njáll replied. 'You say these *orcnéas* strove against God and were banished? So it was with the *skrælingar*. My grandfather told me many times about these wolves of the North, these children of Loki, who rebelled against Odin and were cast down here, to Miðgarðr, to plague the sons of Men.'

'Banished from the sight of God?'

Njáll nodded.

'So, we will tell the monks at Roskilde that, as we journeyed, we passed a night in a cave with a creature of legend? A *monster*?'

The older Dane smiled, though even Aidan could see it was forced – the smile of an adult indulging a child's whim. 'You will find if you live as long as I have that even the most outlandish tales have a tiny grain of truth at their heart, and from that grain the minds of men can make fabulous pearls. When we first looked upon this cave, a part of me wondered if it might be the lair of the dragon slain by old King Bödvar of the Shield-Danes. No doubt the monks at Roskilde would laugh at me for this, since they surely believe dragons to be the bailiwick of children, skalds, and fools. But I am no addle-headed poet. I've seen the skull of a great wyrm – at Borghund; it was harder than stone and brimming with knifelike teeth – so they must have existed. Likewise, I've never laid eyes upon one of the *skrælingar* till now, but I have seen their bones and heard

19

the tales of my kin, so I know this one for what he is.

'Grimnir's folk were the bane of my people for a dozen generations and more. They raided our villages, striking at night while we slept, killing our men and our children and making off with our women and our possessions. An old chieftain named Hróarr made the Danes fight as one people, and they finally broke the *skrælingar,* though it cost Hróarr his life. In truth, it's been many long years since anyone has seen one. My grandfather thought them gone from this land.'

Grimnir's voice caught them both off guard. So quiet was he that neither man had heard his approach. 'Hróarr? That old swine got what was coming to him.' He rose from a crouch, where he'd been listening to their conversation, and descended to the cave floor. He made a hissing noise and fixed Njáll with a belligerent stare. 'And you . . . you yammer on about things beyond your reckoning, *Christ*-Dane. The *kaunar* were not born of the Sly One. Ymir is our sire and the black blood of Angrboða runs hot in our veins.'

Njáll ignored him; Aidan glanced between the two, his brow furrowed. 'Forgive me,' he said after a moment, 'what is *kaunar?*'

'To you, I am *orcnéas*. To the Dane, I am *skrælingr*. The blasted Irish would name me *fomórach,*' Grimnir said, then smote his breast with one black-nailed fist. 'But I am *kaunr*! Do you understand now?'

Aidan flinched at the vehemence in Grimnir's voice. He nodded. 'And . . . And are there many of y-your people left?'

'*Nár,* I am the last.' Grimnir snatched up his cloak, wrapping the old wolf skin around his shoulders, and then sat just outside the ring of firelight with his back to the pool. His eyes gleamed like red coals. 'I made the death song for old Gífr, who was my mother's brother, back in that bastard Charles Magnus's day. Not seen another of my kind since. When I am gone . . .' Grimnir trailed off.

'But . . .' Aidan cleared his throat. 'But Charles Magnus ruled the Franks nigh upon two hundred years ago. Forgive me again, but just how old do you claim to be?'

Grimnir shrugged. 'How do you reckon your age?'

Aidan ducked his head, his cheeks coloring. 'I . . . I do not rightly know,' he replied. 'The monks at Glastonbury say I was left upon their doorstep one snowy Yule. I have seen my twentieth year, to be sure. Perhaps more.'

'A foundling, eh?' Grimnir shifted his baleful gaze to Njáll. 'And you, *Christ*-Dane?'

'I am hard upon my fiftieth year.'

'Striplings, the lot of you.' Grimnir's nostrils flared. 'I first drew breath at Orkahaugr, in the Kjolen Mountains, in the last days of the Peace of Frodi.' His lips skinned back, revealing a fierce, serrated grin. 'My birth was a harbinger of strife and shield-breaking!'

'Impossible!' Aidan barked. 'Our host is playing us for fools, brother. Frodi's Peace lasted as long as our Lord Christ's stay on this earth. That would make our friend, here, at least a thousand years old!' Aidan expected protestations from the giant Dane, scoffing laughter, something. Njáll, however, remained silent. Aidan saw not even a shadow of doubt darken his bearded visage. 'You believe him?'

Grimnir leaned forward, his eyes glittering with a dangerous light. 'You call me a liar?'

'A liar?' Aidan said quickly, holding up his hands to forestall Grimnir's anger. 'No. I did not mean it like that. It's just . . . while I will concede you are not like us, a man descended from the loins of blessed Adam, to believe you are over a thousand years old is something else, entirely. Only Christ is immortal.'

21

'*Man,* eh?' Grimnir chuckled. Like a spring uncoiling, he settled back. 'Believe what you will, little foundling. It matters nothing to me. Have you any more of that cat piss you call mead?'

Aidan handed him the near-empty flask; he watched as Grimnir drained it. Njáll leaned back against the wall, his eyes closed, one fist tight around the haft of his axe – though by the laws of hospitality he should be as safe this night as if he slept under the roof of his kin. Aidan lowered his voice. 'We are bound for Roskilde, to spend what time we have left preparing for the End of Days. And to spread the message of our Lord and Savior, Jesus Christ, to those poor souls among the Danes who yet kneel before pagan gods. Is this your home?' Aidan indicated the cave with a jerk of his head.

Grimnir stared into the fire, as though reading an omen in its crackling heart. 'For the winter, aye. I came south from Skaane, seeking an old enemy, a worm who owes me weregild.'

Though on the verge of sleep, this nevertheless caught Njáll's ear. He raised an eyelid. '*Revenge is mine,* the Lord says, *and I will repay them in due time.*'

Grimnir's wolfish face twisted into a mask of malevolence, lips peeling back in a snarl of contempt. 'Your paltry little god best keep his hands off what's mine. Especially this one. Wretched maggot who calls himself Bjarki. Bjarki Half-Dane! May the Serpent twist his guts! He hides from me, but I will find him. And when I do – *Nár!* That filthy oathbreaker will pay.'

'Bjarki Half-Dane, eh?'

Grimnir's eyes snapped up. 'You've heard of him?'

Njáll shifted to a more comfortable position. 'More than that. I know him. Ugly bastard, and too smart for his own good by far. Before I gave my life to Christ, I took the whale-road with Olaf Tryggve's son. Bjarki sailed with us.'

Aidan listened as Njáll told Grimnir of the raids he had made under Olaf's banner – the same Olaf who was now Norway's king. For years, Red Njáll had slaughtered, plundered, and traded from Frisia to the Hebrides and down to the coast of Wessex in England, where he sacked the rich town of Wareham and put its lord, Prince Eothred, to the sword. This Bjarki, Aidan heard, fought alongside them until the Scilly Isles, off the coast of Cornwall.

'That's where Olaf broke with the Old Ways and became a Christian,' Njáll said. 'Now, Bjarki thought of himself as our *goði,* our priest, and he took Olaf's conversion hard. They'd sworn a pact to Odin. Bjarki claimed Olaf broke it when he repudiated the Allfather. The rest of us tried to broker peace between them. But, harsh words often lead to harsher blows. Bjarki came against Olaf one morning before sunrise and dealt him a grievous wound before we could drive him off. He escaped by the skin of his teeth – him and a small crew. That was . . .' The Dane did a quick sum on his fingers. '. . . four, maybe five years back, and he's not been seen in the North since, not with King Olaf nursing a grudge.' Njáll yawned. 'I left the whale-road last year, after the sack of Exeter, and became a Christian, myself. As far as I know, Bjarki still haunts the waters off the English coast, somewhere between the tip of Cornwall and the mouth of the Thames.'

'He does, eh?' Grimnir spat into the fire. 'I'll find him.' He glanced sharply at Aidan, red eyes boring into him. 'You're English. You know the lay of the land and speak the tongue better than I do. You come with me.'

Aidan's face hardened at the mention of returning to his native land; he met Grimnir's gaze with blue eyes as cold and bitter as hoarfrost. 'A Jew will sit on Saint Peter's throne before ever I touch English soil, again. Perhaps a guide can be found for you in Roskilde.'

Grimnir sucked his teeth, the corner of his mouth curling up in a sneer. 'Roskilde? *Bah!*'

'Then may God bless your journey,' Aidan said. He looked to Njáll, who had dropped off to sleep. 'It is late. We must arise early and take to the road. We thank you for your hospitality.'

Grimnir grunted; he pulled his wolf-skin cloak tighter and rolled over, his back to the fire. Aidan shrugged, fed the flames another bundle of dry hawthorn branches, and stretched out, head cradled in his arm. It only took a few moments for the youth to drop off, his measured breathing joining with the snores ripping from the giant Dane.

Unseen by either man, the *skrælingr* raised his head. He looked back at Njáll and Aidan, then up to the cave's entrance, where their donkey shifted and stamped; he nodded to himself. Sinking back down, he stared – gimlet-eyed and cruel – up through the fissure at the star-flecked sky and mimicked the deep breath of sleep.

3

*Aidan wakes to the sound of iron nails clawing on stone.
He lies in darkness, unmoving; the faint light that filters
down into the heart of the cave is gray and cold. He hears
it again, something heavy, pulling itself along the floor.
Aidan raises his head slightly. A shape moves in the gloom
at the back of the cave. Something gnarled and blighted,
its black-nailed fingers scrabbling for purchase on cold
stone. The stench of putrefaction runs before it like the
gale before a squall. Through eyes half open, not daring
to breathe, he watches the thing creep into the light – an
impossible thing, a thing that should not be: gnarled limbs
and a bloated belly, knifelike teeth gleaming from a black
thatch of beard woven with thorn and bramble; lifeless
eyes, hollow and accusing, pierce Aidan to his core.*

*'You cannot hide,' the thing hisses, its voice familiar to
Aidan. It is the voice of a man from Exeter, a hateful man
who has been dead for more than a year, now. Godwin. 'You
cannot hide, my sweet little whore. Come back to me.'*

*Aidan screams as the thing's hard-nailed fingers close
around his ankle . . .*

The youth bolted awake, gasping, a name and a prayer
both half formed on his lips. 'God!' Wild-eyed, he cast
about for the thing that had menaced him.

Aidan sat on the frigid cave floor, his breath steaming;

morning sunlight lanced down from the overhead fissure to sparkle on the surface of the pool. Pain lanced down his spine and he could yet feel the skin of his ankle tingling where the dream thing had grabbed him. The youth ran a hand through his short coppery hair. Their fire had burned down to a bed of embers. On the other side of it, Njáll lay under his blanket, still gently snoring. Aidan fought the urge to wrap his own blanket back around himself and snatch another hour's sleep. But it was surely time to be up and about. He stretched and turned . . .

. . . and saw Grimnir staring at him from the shadows. *An impossible thing, a thing that should not be.* He had his seax drawn and was tending to the rune-etched blade with a whetstone.

'How long has the sun been up?' Aidan muttered.

Grimnir stropped the stone along the blade's edge, a slow and precise rasp – *the sound of iron nails clawing on stone*; when his inhuman eyes flickered over to the youth, Aidan felt the skin on the back of his neck crawl. The previous night's conviviality was gone. Now, there was a hatred in his gaze that Aidan could not fathom.

'An hour,' he hissed. 'Maybe less.'

Aidan gave a nervous chuckle. 'Aren't we a pair of lay-abouts? I'll build up the fire and make a bit of breakfast, then rouse Njáll. Hot food—'

'Best go catch your beast, first.' Grimnir gestured up at the cave mouth with the point of his seax. The donkey was gone. 'It chewed through its halter and headed off down the road.'

Aidan clapped a hand to his forehead. 'God's teeth! That animal will be the death of me!' He sprang up and headed up the stairs. An ugly thought burst full-grown into his mind; he paused. 'Could you not have stopped it from escaping?'

Grimnir shrugged. 'I could have.'

'For the love of God, why didn't you?'

The *skrælingr* smiled; there was humor in the gesture, but it was not good-natured or well-meaning. Rather, Aidan got the impression he was playing a malicious prank upon the travelers. 'Keep talking, little fool,' Grimnir said. 'Your ass will be in Roskilde long before you.' Laughing, he returned his attention to his seax; Aidan bit back a reply and hurried up to the entrance of the cave. Sparing no thought for the length of rope that remained, Aidan pushed through the screen of hawthorn and out into the frigid morning light.

4

Grimnir heard him call the animal's name, the young fool's voice fading as he skidded down the slope to the road. Then, with a final susurration of stone on steel, he stood; Grimnir wiped his blade on his kilt, sheathed it, and fixed Njáll's sleeping form with a look that could curdle milk.

He walked over and kicked the Dane's feet. 'Ho, there, you miserable sluggard. Up! We have business, you and I.' Njáll mumbled a curse. Grimnir kicked him again. 'Up, damn you.'

'God rot your bones, *skrælingr*!' Njáll muttered. 'Touch me again and I'll twist your pox-ridden head off!'

'Try it, you fat-bellied hymn-singer! Up, you lout!'

Njáll pulled himself into a sitting position; he rubbed his eyes and glanced about the cave. Suddenly, he stiffened. 'Where's Aidan?'

Grimnir laughed, a sound like stones sliding into the grave. 'I sent your little whore outside. A smart bastard, you are. Very smart, hacking off her hair and making the slut wear the rags of a poor son of Christ. Almost fooled me. Where are you bound for, in truth? Do you take her to the slave markets to the East, or back to your steading? Does she know what you have in store for her?'

'You're addled!' Njáll said. He stood and pushed past Grimnir, shuffling along to the pool, where he knelt and splashed ice-cold water in his face. 'Aidan's a good man, destined to join the Order of Saint Benedict, and we are bound for Roskilde, like he said.'

'Liar! She bleeds. Her moon is upon her. I can smell it.' Grimnir's voice became an unctuous purr. 'Come, I have good silver. I will buy her from you.'

Njáll straightened, damp beard bristling; there was righteous fury in his eyes as he towered over Grimnir. The latter did not quail. 'You profane little wretch! God-forsaken piece of filth! She is a child of the Lord, not chattel to be traded! She—'

'*She?*' Grimnir hissed.

Njáll dropped any pretense at hiding the truth. Aidan *was* a woman. 'Aye, *she*! We go to Roskilde, she and I. Once there, she will serve the Church as best she can, and none will be the wiser! It is God's will!'

'And what will they do to her when they find out her little secret, eh?'

'That's none of your concern!'

'What will *you* do, Christ-Dane? That's the question . . . will you raise your axe against them, when they come for her? And they will, you know it in your bones. I can smell the fear you carry for her. It rots your faith, you filthy oathbreaker. Repent to your Nailed God and give the girl to me. I'll keep her safe.'

'Shut your mouth, you poisonous little worm!' Njáll rounded on the *skrælingr*. Only the ancient bonds of hospitality kept his hands from Grimnir's throat. 'Go back to the shadows and pray to your foul gods that the next time we meet you don't leave this world with my axe buried in your miserable skull! She is my charge, and I will do everything I can to keep her safe! And I will die before I allow harm to come to her!' Njáll shouldered Grimnir aside.

Grimnir snarled. 'So be it!'

Quick as a snake, he lashed out and kicked the Dane in the back of the left knee; that leg crumpled. The blow pitched Njáll off balance. Before he could recover – before he could so much as react – a second kick caught him between the shoulder blades and drove him forward, onto his face. Air *whuffed* from Njáll's lungs.

The Dane gasped. He struggled to draw breath even as he struggled to rise, to fight back. Grimnir gave him no opportunity. Disdaining his seax, he leapt full upon Njáll's broad back, straddling him and driving his head into the stone floor of the cave. Cartilage crunched; blood spurted from the Dane's crushed nose. Tear-blind and roaring with rage, Njáll thrashed like a wounded beast and lurched upright. He clawed at Grimnir. If he could but get his hands on him . . .

Grimnir, though, was a relentless foe. He clung to the Dane's back and hammered blow after blow into the side of his head. Njáll twisted. He staggered, blowing a bloody froth through his mashed lips. Grimnir's horny fist connected once more, crushing his eye socket and bruising the soft flesh of his temple. Njáll crashed to his knees and in that instant Grimnir gained both purchase and leverage. Iron fingers closed around the Dane's throat and choked off his bellow of agony.

5

After the previous day's storms the morning that came to Sjælland was crystalline. The woman who called herself Aidan – for indeed she was a woman who did a masterly job of passing herself off as a rosy-cheeked young man – shaded her eyes and looked back down the road, the way they had come the day before. She imagined she could almost see the combers breaking on the beach at Seal Reef, where a ship bound for the island of Borghund in the Baltic Sea had put them ashore. Ahead of her, through the scrub and the trees, a glittering blue fjord cut into the heart of Sjælland, and to the south – on her left – the hills rose a few hundred more feet before dropping down into a shallow wooded valley. On the horizon, she could see smudges of smoke that marked villages and steadings.

The wind was unseasonably cold; shivering despite the brilliant sunlight, she skidded down the hillside to the rutted trail. Puddles from yesterday's rain still stood, their edges crusted with ice. She found a fresh hoofprint in the mud and discovered that, by an act of Providence, the donkey had not strayed far.

The animal stood near a thicket, its rope lead tangled in the thorns. The donkey's ears twisted and flattened as she approached. It was wary. Scared. She purposely kept her voice low, cooing and speaking as to a child rather than with the thundering hellfire and brimstone that the stubborn beast deserved. It allowed her to take its headstall. Working the lead free of the thorns, she noticed a curious thing about it. The lead did not look frayed, as from chewing, but rather it looked cut – and cleanly, at that. So, too, were the donkey's hobbles.

Immediately her suspicions lit upon Grimnir. She recalled him sitting there, smugly honing his seax. But why? Why would he try to drive off their donkey? It made no sense . . .

She heard it, then, over the keening wind: an agonized roar, like the voice of a wounded beast.

Already skittish, the donkey took fright at the sound and bolted from her grip. It knocked her off balance; unable to recover, she fell to her hands and knees on the frosty trail bed. Stones bored into her palms. She watched as the donkey galloped off in the direction of Roskilde. Another cry, choked off at its crescendo, drew her eyes up to the cave mouth; the blood left her face as she recognized the voice. 'Merciful God,' she muttered. Scrabbling to her feet, she ran back up the slope and ducked under the hawthorn boughs.

'Njáll?'

It took a moment for her eyes to adjust to the gloom. She pressed on recklessly, one hand on the cave wall as she flew down the stairs.

'Njáll!'

But what she saw there in the shadows by the pool drew a gasp from her. Grimnir straddled Njáll, his black-nailed hands looped around his throat, choking the life from him. And the look on the *skrælingr*'s face was one of savage exultation.

'Lord God Almighty! No!'

Even as she reached the cave floor, though, she knew

she was too late. Grimnir's muscular arms shook and convulsed; he slammed Njáll's face into the ground, using the momentum to propel himself to his feet. Grimnir snatched Njáll by the shoulder and flung him onto his back. The woman calling herself Aidan cried out at the sight of the Dane's bloody face, his nose mashed and his eye socket deformed. Most of all, she cried out when she saw the distended tongue, like that of a hanged man, and the fixed, bulging eyes. She cried because she knew, in that moment, that Njáll was dead.

Grimnir threw his head back and gave a terrible howl of triumph – a godless barbarian gloating over his kill. As the echo of that hideous sound died away, his gleaming red eyes turned toward her.

'Foundling,' he hissed.

Her legs trembled beneath her and gave way. Why run? Where would she go? Who would defend her from this beast if trusty, fell-handed Njáll could not? *Trust in God*, a voice murmured in the back of her mind. *Trust in the Lord, most high*. There, on her knees, she made the sign of the cross and bowed her head.

'I . . . I am the wheat of God, and am g-ground by the teeth of the wild beasts . . . I long after the Lord, the Son of the true God and Father, Jesus Christ. I . . . I am e-eager to die for the sake of C-Christ—'

Two steps brought Grimnir to her side; she squeaked in terror as he caught her up by the throat and slammed her into the cave wall. His grip choked off her cry; lights danced before her eyes. 'You hymn-singers are all so eager to meet death. Do that Nailed God you love a favor and meet death on your feet. Make that bastard work for his supper!' With his free hand, Grimnir groped under her robes. She twisted away from that probing hand, fighting and clawing. She felt sickened as he touched her sex. But

33

he did no more. He brought his hand away and held his fingers up before her eyes. The tips were wet with blood. Her blood. The blood of her cycle. 'So we understand each other,' he growled, using his red-smeared fingers to sketch the sigil of the Eye on her forehead. 'I know what you are. I have marked you like I marked this cave, little fool. I killed your protector. You belong to me, now. What's your name, eh? Your real name.'

'E-Étaín,' she said. 'My name is Étaín.'

Grimnir nodded and turned her loose; she slid to the cave floor, where she lay, wiping her forehead and sobbing, while he went over and rooted through the panniers holding their belongings as if they were the spoils of his victory. He set their food to one side, pocketed what little coin he found wrapped in one of Njáll's old shirts, and smashed the carved cross to kindling. He flung books and scrolls carelessly about and scattered a sheaf of fine vellum meant as a gift to Father Gunnar at Roskilde, but carefully put the two small pottery jars of ink down beside the food.

Étaín stifled her sobs. *You're a servant of God,* she muttered to herself, *not some weeping victim! Get up!* Her jaw set and resolute, she rose to her feet on unsteady legs and staggered over to where Njáll lay. She knelt beside him. Fresh tears cascaded down her cheeks without recrimination; he had been first her captor, after the sack of Exeter, then her protector, and finally her companion in Christ. And in the small hours of the night, when her sins grew too large to bear, Njáll had been the father she never knew – taking her in his arms and comforting her, singing to her as one might to a child. She closed his eyes, arranged his limbs. 'God our Father,' Étaín whispered, making the sign of the cross, 'Your power brings us to birth; Your providence guides our lives, and by Your command we return to dust.'

'Why do you weep, foundling? Is he not sitting at your Nailed God's right hand, now? Ha! I did that oath-breaking swine a favor.'

'He broke no oaths!' she replied. 'Not like you! You offer us hospitality and then murder us when it suits you! May my God and yours curse you!'

'My hospitality ended with the sunrise,' Grimnir said, kicking the now-empty panniers over. 'And I'd wager when that one was born his idiot father pledged him to the service of that tyrant, Odin – an oath he likely renewed when he sailed with that fool, Olaf. What happened to that oath when he took up with your White Christ?'

'An oath to a false god is no oath!'

'False, eh? You're sure?' Grimnir turned in a circle, his arms held wide. The bone discs and silver beads woven into his long hair clattered as he threw his head back and shouted to the heavens: 'I struck down your sworn man, you cross-hanging bastard! Where's your swift and terrible vengeance? Here I am! Do you fear me?' The echo of Grimnir's challenge faded away. 'Ha! Just like I thought.'

Étaín stood, fists balled at her side. Her eyes were the cold blue of a glacier. 'What about your precious Odin! Where is he? Will he not defend his name? Will he not strike—?'

Without warning, the back of Grimnir's hand cracked across her mouth; she staggered and would have fallen had he not pressed closer and seized her jaw in his black-nailed fingers and dragged her close – close enough to smell his rank breath. Red eyes bored into blue. 'There, you see? Insult your Nailed God and nothing happens. But, insult the gods of the North and their vengeance is swift, little fool!'

He shoved her away; she caught herself before she could fall. Grimnir vanished into the shadows at the back of the

35

cave only to emerge moments later bearing his own gear – a satchel of age-blackened leather hung with all manner of fetishes: strings of wolf and bear teeth; human finger bones carved with runes; red-and golden-haired scalps with shriveled strips of skin still hanging off them. The satchel bore a painted eye sigil, but beneath that, stamped into the leather, were the faint emblem of a bull's head and the Latin letters LEGIO XIX.

Étaín watched him stow the things he'd taken from her own and Njáll's possessions in various places, then slide Njáll's axe through the thongs that tied down the satchel's flap. He worked quickly. Once finished, he knelt there and stared hard at her. She could see the mechanisms of thought grinding away behind that wolfish face.

'Will you kill me, now?' she said, after a moment. 'Or do you plan on selling me to the heathen?'

'You're English,' he replied, rising.

She apprehended his meaning. 'I will not go with you. I must . . . I must bury Njáll and b-be on my way.' Étaín knelt once more beside Njáll's corpse, as if expecting him to protect her now as he always had. 'They . . . They're awaiting us in Roskilde.'

Grimnir's hand dropped to the worn hilt of his seax. 'Oh, you'll do this and you'll not do that, eh? That's enough from you. The only question is do you walk or do I truss you like a pig and drag you to England?'

Étaín sat with her head bowed, eyes closed in prayer. Was this to be her lot in life? To return to a land she hated, as much a captive now as when she left it, perhaps more so? She asked God for a sign, but the only answer was the soft *click-click-click* of Grimnir's fingernail as he tapped impatiently on the pommel of his seax.

'Well?'

Finally, Étaín opened her eyes. 'I will come quietly,' she said, 'if first you help me bury him.'

Grimnir looked from her to the corpse and back again. 'Your word. Swear it by your Nailed God.'

'I swear it,' she said.

Before she could even so much as move, Grimnir had crossed the space between them and knotted his fingers in her copper hair. He hauled her to her feet and bent her head back at a cruel angle. She gasped. 'You break your oath,' he hissed, 'and my hand will be the weapon of your wretched little Christ's retribution as easily as it was the weapon of Odin's. You understand?'

Étaín nodded. Suddenly, she found herself praying for the End of Days . . .

6

If Étaín thought Grimnir would go out, hack a hole in the stony ground, and help her lower Njáll's body into it, she was mistaken. Instead, he took the Dane's axe off his pack and attacked the dead tree, felling it in no time at all. He worked effortlessly, shearing off branches and sectioning the gnarled trunk with blows powerful enough to split an iron-rimmed shield. She watched and wondered. And then it hit her. She had a horrified image in her mind of Njáll laid out on a pyre like his heathen ancestors. *He was going to burn him!*

'No!' she cried. 'He must be buried! Buried in the ground, his body whole and unburned! His head must face east, so he might look upon the rising sun and witness the coming of Christ on Judgment Day!'

Grimnir paused in his effort. He spat. For an instant, he looked as though he might argue with her, but then he cast his gaze up and around. Something he saw satisfied him. He motioned to her. 'Arrange his limbs, then. Make him pretty for the coming of your Nailed God.' He sank the axe in the dead wood and sat on the stump.

Étaín frowned at him. But she went to where Grimnir had scattered their possessions and gathered a few things: his blanket, a flask of water, two squares of fine linen that had protected the strewn vellum, a slender codex with stained leather covers – an incomplete recension of the Gospel of Saint John, which she'd been using to teach him Latin – and pieces of the broken cross. The sight of those fragments tore a sob from her breast. He'd been so proud of it. Now, to see his loving handiwork wrecked was almost too much to bear.

She brought these things to his side. His body was still warm, the joints pliant as she reverently put his feet together and brought his arms to his sides. She straightened his head. Moistening one of the linen squares, she cleaned the blood from his face as best she could. Étaín used the other square to shroud Njáll's proud visage; she wrapped his blanket around him and laid the codex with the splinters of their cross on his chest.

'East is that way,' Grimnir muttered, pointing at the back of the cave.

'He must face east once he's in the earth,' she snapped. 'There must be good ground nearby, perhaps down by one of the beaches on the fjord.'

Grimnir stood and walked over to where Njáll's body lay. Étaín moved aside. Reaching down, he grabbed the Dane by the ankles and dragged him round to where his feet pointed east.

'He's in the earth,' Grimnir said flatly. 'No sense lugging his carcass around. Gather what you need and let's be off. You've wasted enough time.'

'You mean leave him here? You vile wretch! You said you would help me bury him!'

'Aye. And we have – in a barrow fit for a king.'

'Barrow?' said Étaín. 'This is no barrow! It's nothing but—'

Grimnir cut her off. 'It's a barrow if I say it's a barrow! If you don't like it, we can burn the useless bastard! Choose!'

There was no choice, really. Étaín knew it – and she was half convinced the *skrælingr* knew it, too. Burning the body was anathema. Without a body, how could poor Njáll rise from the dead to be reunited with his soul when Judgment Day dawned? No, his tomb must be this cave in the wilderness; a tomb no less humble than that of the Redeemer himself. Étaín sighed. She crouched beside Njáll's body and gently put his limbs back in order. Leaning down, she kissed his brow through the linen shroud. 'Our journey is at an end, my beloved friend,' she whispered. 'Go with God, and dwell forever in the magnificence of the Lord.'

But as she made to stand, something happened. Something that filled her with equal measures of hope and dismay: a low moan escaped Njáll's lips. The sound caused her spine to go rigid; she cast a surreptitious glance over her shoulder to see if her captor had heard it. Grimnir, though, was busy rooting once more through the detritus of their belongings. He had taken it upon himself to gather a few things he deemed to be hers and was stuffing them in a sack. Étaín quickly turned back to Njáll. She hesitated, and then placed a trembling hand upon his chest as if offering a silent benediction.

Though weak, his heart thudded in its cage of bone.

Étaín drew her hand back as though burned. 'God's teeth,' she muttered, unsure now of what to do. One thing was certain . . . Grimnir would finish him off if he got close enough to realize Njáll yet lived. But would he die regardless if she left his wounds untended? The next agonizing seconds seemed to stretch on for hours as Étaín tried to divine the will of God. But it was through the *skrælingr* that His desires became manifest.

'Get up!' snapped Grimnir. 'You've knelt there long enough. We're wasting daylight.'

And with sudden clarity Étaín knew what course she must follow. She had to commend Njáll to God's keeping and go with Grimnir. To stay meant risking death for the both of them. This way, at least one of them would survive. She nodded. Leaning over him once more, she whispered: 'Come find me, Red Njáll, son of Hjálmarr, slayer of Prince Eothred of Wareham and the Scourge of Exeter. Come find me, if God wills it.' And with a last kiss to his brow, Étaín rose to her feet and turned to face Grimnir. 'I am ready.'

He tossed her the bag with her belongings, caught up his pack, and jerked his head up toward the cave entrance. 'You first.'

With a silent prayer, she pushed past Grimnir and clambered up the stone steps, leaving Njáll to his fate. *And me to mine,* she thought, glancing back down at his prostrate form. *Until God sees fit to weave them together, once more.*

7

From the cave, they headed south along the trail. It snaked to the right as it cut through the low hills, clinging at times to the steep side of the valley formed by the glittering fjord. The trail followed the tree line; on their left hand were the crests of the hills, an expanse of windswept heath where Étaín could see the scorched and jagged footings of an ancient and once-formidable longhouse, stark against the cold blue sky. Soon, their path took a steep plunge into wooded country where gold and brown leaves rattled in the wind.

Here they left the trail, which bore sharply right, and Grimnir led them overland, avoiding settlements and skirting fields left stubbled by the year's last harvest. At times, he maintained a punishing pace, driving her along almost at a jog; other times, they prowled forward like spies infiltrating the camp of the enemy. At these intervals, Grimnir kept his nose low to the ground or snuffled the air. Once, around midday, she caught him having an animated conversation with a gnarled tree – cursing at it in a harsh tongue she took to be the native speech of the *skrælingar*.

'Your Nailed God has infected them,' he said, spitting in disgust.

'Infected who? The trees?'

Grimnir fixed her with a hard-eyed stare. 'The *land-vættir*, little fool! You wretched hymn-singers! You spread your filth like a pox; raising these nithing poles you call crosses that only serve to bleed the land dry of its *seiðr*.'

'*Seiðr* is sorcery, yes?' Étaín felt a measure of her old fire return. 'And sorcery is the domain of the Devil. So a land liberated from the grasp of sorcery – and from all the unclean things that thrive on it, like your *landvættir* – is a land that is pleasing to God. *For the Lord abhorreth all these things, and for these abominations He will destroy them at thy coming.*'

'Then your miserable god is a dolt who would cut off his own nose to spite his face,' Grimnir replied. He shoved her along. 'Move! You're wasting precious time.'

With the waning of the day came shreds of clouds from the west; the chill became more pronounced even though the wind faded to a mere breeze. Étaín was stumbling from exhaustion when they emerged from the trees above a rocky shingle, a sheltered inlet that opened on the root of the fjord: a broad lake whose surface gleamed like molten copper in the late-afternoon sun. Great stands of fir and pine and red-leafed oak ran nearly to the water's edge. Down on the shingle, well above tide level, stood a small cluster of timber buildings – a village, eight houses arranged around a central hall. Firelight twinkled, and smoke drifted up from the hearths. On the edge of the village, she saw half a dozen small fishing boats drawn up for the night.

'Too far south,' she heard Grimnir mutter. He crouched there for a long while, sitting on his haunches in a peculiar fashion, with his knees drawn up under his chin. He stared first at the village and then at the far shore – a purple haze on the western horizon.

Étaín could make no sense of Grimnir's intentions. If

his plans were to sail from Sjælland to England – which was madness this time of the year – they should be making for the west coast to find a ship to take them across the Kattegat to Jutland. From there, if they followed the same route that she and Njáll had taken on their sojourn east, Grimnir would need to secure passage from Ribe on a ship bound for the Frankish coast, and from there cross the British Sea to the shores of East Anglia or Wessex. But, as near as Étaín could tell, the paths he chose were those that led *inland*.

Finally, as the first stars flickered to life among the thickening clouds overhead, Grimnir stirred. He caught her by the arm and dragged her close, his voice soft but full of menace. With his other hand, he tugged a length of plaited leather rope from his pack. 'Listen close and listen good. We're going down to that stinking little shithole of a village and we're taking a boat. That last one, there. The one farthest from their wretched houses. We're going fast and we're going quiet, and if the Sly One's with us these fish-fuckers will be none the wiser till morning.' Quickly, he looped the rope around her right wrist and tied it cruelly tight. She gasped, clawing at it.

'What are you doing?'

'Do I look like a fool? You're thinking, "Ha! Here's my chance to be rid of him! Here's my chance to slip away!" Try it, or try to raise an alarm, and I promise you this: I will not harm one hair on your miserable little head, but I will kill every last man, woman, and child I find down there. Make a sound and I will gut them alive, boil their bones for a stew, and make a cloak from their skins. Do you think I'm lying?'

Étaín shook her head, her eyes wide.

Grimnir grunted. 'Good. You're not as stupid as I thought. Stay close and watch where you step, because if

44

you fall I will drag you across that shingle. Do you understand? Remember what I said.'

Grimnir stood and shouldered his satchel; Étaín followed suit, clutching her meager sack to her chest. And then they were off. Grimnir loped along like a wolf, low and fast; Étaín struggled to keep up. The ground flashed by underfoot. Between them, the rope stretched taut, distending her wrist and twisting it near to breaking. She grabbed on to the rope with her hand to relieve the pressure, and put her trust in God. By some miracle she kept her legs under her. She was breathing hard by the time they reached the rocky shingle and trying not to make a sound as she gulped air. Grimnir wasn't even winded. He stopped, crouching in the lee of a boulder. The boats were twenty yards distant.

Étaín wondered why he had paused; why not make straight for the boats? But she dared not give voice to her question, for fear someone else might hear. *How many children dwell within?* Seconds later, she saw the reason why: a gray-bearded Dane was walking along the line of boats, patting each one as though they were his prize stallions. He wore a pale red tunic, heavy with embroidery around the neck and down the sleeves, and baggy trousers; a woolen cap warmed his balding pate. Grimnir's nostrils flared, lips peeling back from his teeth. He dropped the rope and loosened his seax in its scabbard.

The Dane stopped at the last boat – a nine-foot-long skiff with oarlocks and a high prow. He stood there, hands thrust into his belt, his head tilted up as he studied the clouds filling the starlit bowl of Heaven. His breath steamed in the frosty air. Then, he turned slowly and began to retrace his steps.

Étaín didn't hear Grimnir stir; she didn't miss his presence until she turned to raise a questioning eyebrow. Only then did she notice the low black shadow creeping across the shingle, soundless, the drawn seax glittering like a spike of starlight. Étaín clapped a hand over her mouth; she dared not utter a word. But knowing what was to come, she commended the old Dane's soul to God . . .

'Afi!' a child's voice cried. Suddenly, there came a flurry of movement from the far end of the line of boats as a towheaded boy dashed into view, waving a wooden sword. Grimnir froze; the boy skidded to a halt; and Étaín tasted blood from where she'd bitten her tongue. The old Dane held his arms out to his grandson. The boy, though, had gone as pale as a winding sheet. He dropped his sword, gave an earsplitting scream, and ran crying back to the village. Bemused, the old Dane turned around to see what had spooked the boy so . . .

. . . and saw only the empty shingle behind him.

Étaín exhaled into her hand, silently thanking God, for Grimnir had ducked down alongside the boat, out of sight though still prepared to strike. She saw the old Dane shake his head; he hurried after his grandson lest the boy get the whole village in an uproar.

Grimnir did not move until the old man reached the edge of the village; then, with acrimony to spare, he gestured for Étaín and put his shoulder to the boat's keel. Wood scraped stone as he shoved the boat into the calm waters of the inlet.

Étaín caught up his satchel and hustled over to where Grimnir waited. 'Ymir take that mouthy little rat,' he was muttering to himself. 'Should have gutted the both of them. Hurry up! Get in! Are there oars?'

Étaín clambered over the side of the boat and immediately located a pair of oars; there was also a short mast and a rolled sail beneath the seats, where she stowed his pack. She nodded to Grimnir and almost fell across one of the seats as he gave the keel a tremendous heave and vaulted over the strakes. The boat pitched and bobbed. He took the middle seat, ran out the oars, and fell into a rhythm of long, smooth strokes that set the water hissing against their prow. In no time they were clear of the inlet and heading into the deeper water of the lake itself.

From the village, Étaín saw a line of torches wending their way toward the boats. The old Dane was in the lead, followed by a few other men and women from the village; he held his grandson, intent on showing him there were no monsters lurking on the shingle. Grimnir saw it, too. She heard him curse between oar strokes.

'Will they follow?' she asked, though in her bones she knew they would. These boats were the lifeblood of the village, and they would sail to the edge of the world to repay the insult of its theft. But they had darkness on their side: the men of the village would be hard-pressed to track them across the water.

Grimnir's silence only reinforced her belief.

He bent to the oars, setting an even pace that would have exhausted a man, even such men as Njáll and his kin. Étaín shivered. Grimnir demanded nothing of her, so she sank down in the ribs and clawed at the rope around her wrist until she prized it off. Her shoulders trembled; she tugged a length of sailcloth from beneath the seat. The salt-stiff canvas became a makeshift blanket. She could hear the faint sounds of pursuit, the splash of oars and angry cries. But they were distant, dreamlike. The motion of the boat was hypnotic – surge and rest, surge and rest. Grimnir sniffed the wind and made minor adjustments in their course, taking them on a southwesterly tack across the lake.

As she lay in the bottom of that gently rocking boat, her mind drifted to poor Njáll. She wondered if he had survived the day; she prayed for him, for his succor as well as for her own. *He will find me, if it is the will of God,* she said to herself. But in that quiet moment she wondered what had happened to her. Where was her strength? Where was her famous resolve? Had she not told Njáll, just yesterday, that God helps those who help themselves? And here she was acting like some shy and shrinking Andromeda, chained to a rock and praying her Perseus would arrive in time to save her from the beast. Vividly, she saw herself, axe in hand, striking the *skrælingr*'s head from his shoulders, then carrying that grisly trophy back to Njáll. Étaín smiled. *But you gave him your word,* a small voice whispered in the back of her mind. *You swore to Christ you would go quietly.* She could not deny that.

Exhaustion snared her; she yawned. Sleep tugged at the edges of her consciousness, and her body slowly surrendered to it despite her best efforts. In those final moments of awareness, she realized something . . . an oath made under duress, and to a heathen, was no oath at all. *God will forgive me.*

And the dreams that followed, dreams of her captor's headless corpse flopping at her feet, filled Étaín with a sense of warmth that was far from Christlike . . .

48

8

Grimnir rowed like some mechanical beast forged of gristle and iron. Only dimly did he feel his limbs burning with exertion, and then only if he allowed himself to feel anything at all. He had no time for weakness, no need for rest – he'd learned from his mother's brother, Gífr, what would happen if he succumbed to some half-felt desire of the flesh. *Faugh!* He loved that old bastard, in his own way, but Gífr had ever been too quick to give in to weakness. Rest bred indolence, and from indolence came melancholy and, hard upon its heels, the black sleep of death. That was the curse of his people: no poison could touch him, no disease could lay him low, but the weight of his long years could harrow him like a pox, if he but allowed it.

Instead, Grimnir followed his father's example. Bálegyr the One-Eyed only permitted himself to rest one day out of every ten, and then only grudgingly. He filled the hours and days between with scheming, plotting, and the red froth of slaughter. What was good for the sire was good enough for his son.

As he rowed, Grimnir turned his mind to the problem at hand. Those wretched fish-fuckers were hard on his scent like a pack of dogs. Sharp-eyed beyond the ken of mortal men, he could see the froth beneath the keels of the two largest boats following them. A mile behind, he judged, and twice that distance from the smaller boats that spread like a net behind them. Grimnir counted three oarsmen and one more sitting on the tiller in both lead boats – all men who knew this lake like they knew their wives' thighs.

Miserable bastards! Grimnir did not stop to wonder how they knew what direction he was headed. He doubted any of those ignorant wretches knew the truth of it, either. They followed their 'gut,' or so they told themselves. But Grimnir knew otherwise. He could hear it. With each dip of the oars, the phantom song of the *sjövættir* sent ripples across the water, guiding those wretched Danes to him as sure as if he'd stood up and waved a torch at them. These *sjövættir*, these sea wights, had long memories, and they nursed a deep hatred for his people.

Grimnir hawked and spat into the water. 'Taste it,' he muttered in the harsh speech of his people. 'Taste it and know me as one of Bálegyr's brood. Send these fools to me, and I will salt your water with their blood.'

The song of the *sjövættir* faltered a moment, then renewed in intensity; Grimnir laughed. He slashed the water's breast with his oars. He was more than a match for any three of the white-skinned dolts who followed him. Nor was there any question in his mind that he would reach the far shore first. Once there, he knew how to deal with these cross-kissing little maggots!

Grimnir bared his teeth in a bestial snarl as he redoubled his efforts.

9

'Come find me, Red Njáll, son of Hjálmarr, slayer of
Prince Eothred of Wareham and the Scourge of Exeter.
Come find me, if God wills it.'

The plea held Njáll back from the swaying bridge to
Heaven. He could see the far green country of the afterlife
stretching out before him, across the chasm of Death, ice-
covered mountains glowering in the distance; on the cold
wind, he heard the voices of his kin, his axe brothers, calling out to him, bidding him take his place among them at
the Allfather's table. He could hear them, but he could not
follow. A mortal spark, weak as an ember, held him back.

'Come find me, Red Njáll, son of Hjálmarr. Come find
me.'

He knew that voice. It belonged to a woman – not
his wife, for he was sworn to serve . . . who? A crucified
god, of that he was certain. Odin? It must be, for the
Allfather once hung himself upon Yggðrasil for nine days so
he might learn the secret of the runes. He was Odin's man,
and the voice, the woman who pleaded for his aid . . .

'Come find me.'

'Étaín,' he moaned, remembering the slender, red-haired
girl he had taken from the ruin of Exeter. He felt his body,
then, heavy and leaden, like something hewn from the cold
stone on which he lay. Muscles screamed as he moved them

– his hands, his arms, his shoulders. His throat felt like a mass of bruises and his face burned like fire. *How—?*

Skrælingr. The word was seared into his brain. Rage pushed aside the agony. *Skrælingr!* Odin's Doom was upon them, upon that whole miserable race, and still he had made a compact with one instead of cleaving its head to the teeth! He'd been a fool, and this was the thanks he had for it!

Slowly, Njáll rolled onto his side, teeth clenched as he fought off a wave of nausea. The cloth fell from his face. One eye was swollen shut; he opened the other. Pale gray light filtered down from the fissure in the roof of the cave. By its faint illumination, he saw a scattering of clothes and personal items, sheets of vellum, and two overturned panniers. A bed of cold embers marked the spot of a fire.

He got to his hands and knees. Though every movement drove spikes of pain through his limbs, nothing seemed broken. His head swam. Njáll crawled to the steps, dragging the blanket with him, and pulled himself into a seated position. Shivering, he wrapped the woolen blanket around his shoulders.

He didn't recall what brought him to this cave, or even where it was. He didn't remember why he might have had congress with a blasted *skrælingr*, or how he allowed that miserable wretch – what was his name? Grimnir? – to get the better of him. But he knew in his bones that Étaín was his . . . responsibility, his charge. And he had allowed that bastard to all but kill him and make off with her!

'Come find me.'

Njáll sat a moment with his head in his hands. He was certain she was alive, since the *skrælingr* needed her for something, but what? Where was he bound? *Where?*

Something clicked in Njáll's bruised brain. He raised his head as a name floated from the soup of his memory: *Bjarki*

Half-Dane. 'England,' he said. 'He's bound for England.'

Red Njáll, son of Hjálmarr, slayer of Prince Eothred of Wareham and the Scourge of Exeter, snatched a long splinter of wood off the ground and rose to his feet. The blanket slipped from his shoulders. He knew the bones around his right eye were shattered; he knew he would likely never see right out of it for the rest of his days. And he knew he was Odin's sworn man. It would be a fitting sacrifice.

'Allfather! Great Odin, look here! Grant me vengeance! I offer you my flesh! Odin!' Gritting his teeth, Njáll reached up and dug the splinter of wood into his right eye.

And the roar that echoed from that cave on the road to Roskilde was the roar of a wounded dragon.

10

It was a change in motion that drew Étaín from sleep, a dim awareness that the gentle, hypnotic rocking had ceased and what had replaced it was the sensation of bobbing like a cork. Water slapped against the hull. She opened her eyes.

She lay yet in the ribs of the boat, nestled against the forward thwart, her sailcloth blanket close and warm. It was near dawn; the air around her was still and glacial and smelled of snow. Étaín raised her head, expecting to see the dim outline of Grimnir's back, etched against the lightening sky. Instead, his seat was empty. She looked around and realized with a start that she was alone in the boat. She kicked free of the sailcloth and stood.

The boat scraped against the shore, its painter tied fast to the branch of a tree that grew at an angle from the steep and rocky bank. She saw no sign of her captor on the bank, and a quick search revealed his gear was missing.

Is this some malicious prank or has he truly abandoned me? But, Étaín realized, she didn't need an answer. It was the work of Providence. For whatever reason, Grimnir was gone, and she had no intention of waiting around to discover why. Snatching up the sack holding what few things she had left to her, Étaín jumped from the boat and clambered up the bank, loose stones splashing into the water or thumping against the hull. She would find a way back to

Njáll, and thence to Roskilde, where she would reassume her life as a young monk with none the wiser.

But as Étaín gained the crest of the bank, she heard the blare of a horn. The sound startled her; she whirled, and through the trees, coming hard up on the shore, she caught sight of a Danish boat.

'There!' one of the men in the prow bellowed, drawing an axe from his belt. Three others were arrayed behind him; the last man, on the tiller, was a gray-bearded man clad in a pale red tunic heavy with embroidery – the old Dane from the village.

'Find the bastard's trail and hunt him to ground!' he said.

Though innocent, Étaín did not dare remain here and try her hand at reasoning with them. These men were out for blood, and the blood of a thief, at that. She bolted like a hare. The sudden movement drew the old Dane's eye; his roaring voice stung speed from Étaín's stiff limbs.

'Christ's mercies! There! After him!'

Étaín fled through the trees, following the faint path of a game trail. She could hear the men behind her; the old man's voice lashed them on. She ran in the twilight before dawn, her monk's robe flaring out behind her as she tried without success not to leave a trail that even a blind man could follow.

The path widened into a weed-choked clearing where the charred remains of a steading stood among the brambles. Fallen leaves piled against its crumbling foundations, and from its blackened center post – standing tall like the mast of a sunken ship in shallow seas – hung forgotten reminders of those who once sheltered beneath it: half-melted utensils, stag horns left to cure, and dried bundles of wild garlic left untouched by the flames. Fat flakes of snow drifted from the leaden sky, lending the ruins the forlorn aspect of a life subverted by tragedy.

A stitch burned in Étaín's side. Her stride faltered. She could not outrun the Danes who pursued her; her ignorance of the countryside made it less likely with each passing step that she might stumble over some hidden redoubt. But she was free and she still had her wits about her – perhaps where Étaín had failed, a young and earnest Brother Aidan might be counted upon to pick up the slack.

Étaín circled the ruin, calming herself and breathing deeply. The snow was coming down heavier, now; it stuck to the brown wool of her cassock – cut no differently from the monastic habit of a Benedictine monk. She pulled up the hood, its peak casting her thin face in shadow, and folded her hands into the voluminous sleeves. She walked with a slow and measured pace, as though taking a turn about the grounds of her cloister.

As she passed what must have been the entrance to the steading, she looked up. For an instant, morning sunlight pierced the clouds to illuminate the lintel and center post, creating the silhouette of a mighty crucifix. Étaín stopped. Hope filled her breast. She crossed herself, knelt in the swirling snow, and prayed.

That was how the Danes found her.

They entered the glade from the game trail and fanned out – the old Dane followed by three kinsmen in rough brown and yellow homespun, two with axes and one, the youngest to judge by the wisp of his blond beard, carrying a bow with a broad-headed arrow nocked. They expected the trail of the thief to continue on, or to find him cowering in some bolt-hole. They did not expect to find a monk kneeling in the leaf mold . . .

The younger Danes glanced questioningly at one another, and then looked to their elder. The graybeard drew a sword and laid it flat on his shoulder. He motioned for the others to stay back and slowly approached the praying figure. 'You, there,' he said. 'I saw you running from my boat. Are you a God-cursed thief?'

To her credit, Étaín's voice held the confidence of a man of God – a man who wore his Christian zeal like a suit of finely wrought armor. She glanced up, blinking at the snow that brushed her face. 'I am but a poor son of Christ, brother, lost in the wild and seeking the road to Roskilde.'

'And I say you're a lying thief,' the old Dane replied. 'I know what I saw, and I know I saw you running from the lakeshore. Running from the boat you stole from my village across the way. No one steals from me! Not from Hrolf Asgrimm's son!'

Étaín nodded. 'You did see me, Hrolf Asgrimm's son. But I did not steal your boat. Was it damaged?'

'No.'

Wool rustled as Étaín rose from the ground, smoothing out her cassock. 'Then, rather than seeking vengeance, good Hrolf, why not join me in offering a prayer of thanks to the Almighty for the safe return of your property?'

'I don't believe him,' one of the younger Danes muttered. 'Looks too soft, even for a monk!'

'Be silent, Egil.' The elder chewed his lip. He was on the verge of speaking when an earsplitting scream plunged the glade into chaos. The sound came from the youngest of the Danes, the youth with the bow. His kinsmen swung around in time to see him drop his weapon and claw at a length of steel that blossomed from beneath his sternum like an obscene and gory flower. A torrent of blood belching from his gullet choked off a second scream as the steel slid out of sight; the youth's legs gave way, and rising up behind him Étaín saw the sinister visage of the *skrælingr*.

'Grimnir! No!'

Étaín's cry hung in the snow-flecked air. Each second

57

passed in exquisite lethargy – a lifetime in the single staccato pulse of the human heart. The youth crumpled. Before his cheek touched the cold ground, Grimnir was a blur of motion.

An axe flashed down. It never connected. Wood slapped flesh as Grimnir arrested the blow, catching the haft of the axe and holding the Dane's arm aloft. The man's eyes widened, shock warring with fear as he got his first good look at what had killed his kinsman; an instant later Grimnir's seax ripped across the Dane's belly. A second blow went deep into the man's unprotected armpit. Grimnir stripped the axe from his victim's faltering grip.

Hrolf Asgrimm's son turned toward Étaín; in the lines of his careworn face she saw an echo of Njáll: the same look of recognition, the same moment of shock, and the same glimmer of deep ancestral hatreds. His gray beard bristled as hard and sinewy hands knotted in the fabric of her cassock. 'What deviltry is this? What evil have you brought to my house?'

Her eyes met his. She pleaded with him . . . not for her own life, but for his. 'I beg of you . . . run!'

Over the old man's shoulder, Étaín saw Grimnir fall upon the third Dane, the one called Egil. The man had mastered both shock and disbelief; he called upon the Almighty as he swept in, his axe aimed at Grimnir's skull. Axe haft met axe haft with the sharp *clack* of wood. It was an off-hand parry, clumsy and unbalanced, but still the force of it caught Egil by surprise. And in that instant of hesitation Grimnir's seax darted in, snakelike, and pierced Egil's throat.

The Dane staggered and fell and died gobbling on his own blood.

Snow swirled, flecking the faces of the dead. Grimnir's chest rose and fell; his breath steamed in the frigid morning air. He tossed the axe aside. His clawed hand flexed around the hilt of his seax. Grimnir glared sidelong at Hrolf Asgrimm's son.

'She said run, you wretched kneeler.'

Lips curling in a snarl of hate, Hrolf shoved Étaín away. He reached up and tugged a small cross of hammered silver from beneath his tunic. Hrolf snapped the chain and slung the talisman at Étaín's feet. 'Keep your prayers, witch,' he said, and slowly backed away from her.

Hrolf and Grimnir circled the glade, two wolves squaring off, fighting for territory, for dominance. 'I know what you are, *skrælingr!*'

'And still you stand,' Grimnir hissed. 'You've got stones, old fool.'

'The skein of my life is woven. Why run? So I can die with your steel in my back like a craven?' Hrolf hawked and spat. 'For too long I have been blinded by the false promises of the White Christ. What use do I have for redemption? I want an end to make the *valkyrjar* weep! You will give it to me?'

Étaín saw a grudging respect in Grimnir's feral red eyes. He stopped circling. 'Call them.'

'Odin!' Hrolf Asgrimm's son raised his sword aloft. 'Look here, Allfather! Send out your high-hearted maidens and let them choose which of us will live to fight another day! I offer my life, if you want it!'

A gust of wind rattled the few leaves left on the trees, driving eddies of snow before it; away in the north came the dull rumble of thunder, while in the east the heavens gleamed with golden light. '*The Son of Man shall send his angels,*' Étaín muttered at the sight of it, quoting the Gospel. '*And they shall gather.*'

Grimnir cocked his head, as though hearing something beyond mortal reckoning. 'They come,' he said, teeth bared. 'They come to collect their bounty.'

And suddenly, the wolves surged together. Étaín looked on, transfixed; she expected to see Hrolf's head bouncing over to land at her feet, but the old Dane matched Grimnir stroke for stroke. Sword rasped on seax. Breath *whuffed*. Feet stamped. Whirl and parry, strike and lunge. It was like watching two dancers who were masters of their art.

But Grimnir's iron endurance fixed the ending of the fight. The old Dane knew it, too. He dredged deep and put every last ounce of his flagging strength into a sweeping blow that could have cleft the skull of an ox; Grimnir ducked it by a hair's breadth, and with a cry of triumph he buried his blade up to the hilt in the ribs of Hrolf Asgrimm's son. Thunder reverberated; the light in the east vanished.

The man coughed, a red froth staining his lips. He turned from Grimnir and took a handful of steps in the direction of his slain kinsmen, his sword trailing him. He clutched its hilt in a death grip.

Hrolf raised his face to the lowering sky . . . and laughed.

Étaín wanted to rush to the old man's side, to ease his passing and beg his forgiveness, but Grimnir waved her away. She looked on as he caught Hrolf's swaying body and eased him to the ground.

'I see them,' Hrolf muttered, his beard clotted with gore. 'The Choosers of the Slain. They . . . They drive the c-crossbearers before them. We will meet again, *skrælingr*.'

'Aye, Dane. We will trade blows again, at the breaking of the world,' Grimnir replied. And with a savage twist, he drove the tip of his seax into Hrolf Asgrimm's son's heart and ripped it free.

Grimnir rocked back on his haunches. He cleaned his blade in a fold of Hrolf's tunic and sheathed it as he stood.

Étaín bent to retrieve the cross the Dane had thrown

away. She stared at it; her eyes welled up. She thought of the young boy who ran out to meet his grandfather on the shingle, last night. Were his father and his brothers here among the dead, too? How many widows had this stolen boat made? How many orphans? Étaín closed her eyes and prayed over the tiny silver cross, tears dripping from her lashes.

'They were going to leave in peace,' she muttered.

Her captor merely grunted.

'You murdered them without cause.' She opened her eyes. Grimnir was crouched over the dead. He did not despoil Asgrimm's son, but he gleefully rooted through the possessions of the others he had killed, coming up with a pair of twisted gold and copper arm rings, a small pouch of hacksilver – silver hewn from goblets or decoration and carried like coinage – and a new whetstone. 'Like you murdered poor Njáll.'

'Murder?' Grimnir laughed, pocketing his finds. 'Murder, is it? You filthy hymn-singers are all alike. You call it murder when it doesn't suit your needs. When it does, it's the will of your maggot-riddled corpse god.'

'Whose need did the deaths of these men serve, then?'

'*My* need, foundling. I take what I want and I pay for it with this.' Grimnir slapped the hilt of his seax. 'If any of your kind wants back what's theirs, they need only meet my price. This one' – he indicated the old Dane with a jerk of his head – 'knew it. That's why he came after you with steel instead of words. And you . . . you played your part well.'

'My part?'

Grimnir chuckled as he walked to the edge of the glade and retrieved his satchel, then came back to stand before Étaín. 'You didn't really think I just wandered off and left you alone, did you?'

Her cheeks flushed. 'You used me as bait!'

'Aye, and you did just what I thought you would, once my back was turned – you took to your heels. So much for your oath to come quietly, eh? I scratched two itches, here. Got these swine off my back and put your word to the test.'

'My word does not mean I plan to stand in place like a lamb being led to slaughter,' said Étaín. 'And "to come quietly" means I will neither plot to kill you in your sleep nor sit and hatch incessant schemes of escape. I am here because it is God's will. When His will changes, I will no longer be under your thumb whether you like it or not. And if I am left to my own devices I *will* go my own way.'

'Fair enough.' Grimnir stared at the gray sky. The snow had slacked off; only a few flakes drifted down from the heavens. 'We've wasted enough time. Let's go.' He prodded her, gesturing for her to move off ahead of him. But Étaín shrugged him off and stood her ground.

'Go where? If you hold on to this insane hope of reaching Britain before winter sets in then we must go west, to the coast. There may yet be ships—'

'Oh, aye . . . ships filled with Danes who are convinced my people are devils sent to lead them astray,' Grimnir hissed. 'Maybe once I would have been welcome among the reavers, but no longer. What did your *Christ*-Dane call me? The bane of his people? The truth is *his* people were the bane of *mine*. Your kind covers the earth like vermin, while I am the last of the *kaunar*. The world has changed, foundling. Twilight has come for the Elder Folk, and soon . . . soon will sound the horns of Ragnarok.'

Before she could reply, Grimnir caught her by the arm, twisted her round, and shoved her in the direction he wanted to travel. She stumbled forward, the silver cross still clutched in her fist. Étaín risked a backward glance.

Grimnir, too, was looking back at the glade, back at the blackened ruins and the sprawled corpses. Two ravens had alighted upon the steading's tall center post, huge black birds with glossy beaks and obsidian eyes that gleamed with malicious wisdom; Grimnir sketched a mocking bow to them. 'Go back to your master,' he muttered, barely loud enough for Étaín to hear. 'Go and tell him a son of Bálegyr yet lives, his Doom be damned!'

As if in answer, the two birds took wing, their deep *cr-r-ruck* echoing about the glade.

II

For two days, under skies hewn from the cold heart of winter, Grimnir guided them south and west. They left the settled fjord-lands of northern Sjælland for the wilder country of the south, a land of moors and fens and tangled forests. They ate what food they had left – hard bread and salt pork and the last of her store of apples – and drank from clear running streams. By night, as the temperatures plunged and snow threatened, Grimnir grudgingly built a small fire. Étaín would huddle near it for warmth, but the cold had little effect on the now-taciturn *skrælingr*. He sat away from the fire, muttering to himself in the harsh tongue of his kind or singing some tuneless chant that echoed with the drums, horns, and wrack of war; he was awake when Étaín dropped off to sleep, and awake when she crawled stiff-limbed from beneath her blanket. She wondered if he slept at all.

For the most part, her first impressions were sound. Grimnir was as godless and profane as any heathen Northman. He sneered at her morning prayers and scoffed at her wish to pray at midday, or over her food. He had no time for anything that smacked of Christ. Just the sight of even the small silver cross Hrolf Asgrimm's son had cast aside filled Grimnir with sullen rage. But he made an effort to pause by every moss-covered rune stone, poring over each surface like a priest over the Gospel. What he found there dictated not only the direction they traveled, but also his mood. Stones commemorating those who had fallen in battle left him nigh upon jubilant, while the few they happened across trumpeting some nameless Dane's conversion sent him into a curse-laden tirade.

'Traitors and oathbreakers!' he would mutter. 'May the Wolf gnaw their wretched livers!'

By the afternoon of the third day, as a keening wind whistled down from the north, they descended into a shallow valley thick with some of the most ancient forest Étaín had ever seen. The trees were squat and gnarled, like giants in repose, their spreading boughs half-clad in the finery of autumn. Walking beneath them felt as though she were walking down the nave of a mammoth cathedral; it was silent, and gray light tinged with red and gold filtered down from the clerestory of branches overhead.

With each step, Étaín felt like she came more and more under some fell scrutiny, like something beyond the ken of mortal man was watching her descend into its world, a slice of the pre-Christian past, a twilight world of branch and leaf – something that would judge whether or not to let her live. She glanced at Grimnir; if he felt the same sensation he did not show it. Perhaps he knew what lurked among the trees. That thought caused her to clutch all the more tightly to the tiny silver cross . . .

'There,' Grimnir said, after another hour had passed. The shadows had grown deep and long and Étaín could only just make out what lay ahead of them. The forest hemmed in a lake, its surface as black as a starless night; at the center of this lake was an island that looked overgrown with trees. Hawthorn, birch, oak, ash, and yew grew in such profusion that their trunks twisted and writhed together in a mass as solid as a fortress palisade.

'Christ Almighty, what is this place?' Even as she spoke the words, Étaín felt the hair on the back of her neck stand on end; she turned suddenly, staring into the deepening gloom. The trees around her exuded menace, something hoary and wild and fey that begrudged every breath she took.

'No place where your Nailed God is welcome,' Grimnir said. 'So watch your tongue, little fool.'

Étaín nodded, her eyes wide with fear.

Grimnir led them to the water's edge, to where someone had drawn a slender punt up on shore. Étaín looked dubiously at the flat-bottomed boat. It seemed as old as the forest, its boards black and shiny with use and decay. A pole lay next to it.

'Get in,' Grimnir said.

'We shouldn't be here,' Étaín replied, backing away from the water. 'This place is . . . wrong. It's evil. I can feel it.'

'Evil, eh? What do you know about evil? Get in the boat. We're close, now.'

Étaín shook her head, her trembling hands clasped before her. Something inimical to her lived among these trees, something unnatural whose hatred and malevolence warped the bosom of the earth itself. That island . . .

'Get in the gods-be-damned boat, little fool!' roared Grimnir. The echo of his voice profaned the silence. Boughs rustled on a phantom wind; Étaín imagined she could hear spectral laughter, as though whatever dwelled here took great pleasure in her terror. She backpedaled. She was on the verge of fleeing from this cursed grove when Grimnir sprang.

Étaín screamed. She had the impression of lips skinning back from yellowed fangs and eyes blazing like coals an instant before his fist hammered into the side of her jaw and sent her sprawling into oblivion.

12

Étaín woke by a fire – a great, roaring blaze that filled the glade with warmth and light. She lay with her back against a fallen log, her hands bound behind her. A dull ache radiated from her bruised jaw. Her ears rang, yet. She blinked, looked around, and tried to remember how she'd gotten here – wherever *here* was.

What she'd taken for a glade was actually a bight in the living palisade of trees that girt the small island, a grassy cove dominated by a stone-curbed fire pit. It was fully dark, now, but Étaín could still see the black lake beyond, its surface gleaming like a sheet of dark ice. It was snowing; fat flakes hissed and died in the crackling flames rising from the pit.

She twisted to see what was behind her. Red-orange light sent shadows writhing along the tree-walls; the boughs overhead laced together like a roof, its autumnal thatch sparse, now, with the onset of winter. At the deepest part of the bight an ash tree and a mighty yew stood with their branches and the upper reaches of their trunks woven together; the bases of these two trees did not touch. Indeed, enough space existed between them that they formed an opening in the living palisade – an ominous black gate into the heart of the island. She saw Grimnir a few paces behind her, staring at this dark aperture.

'Why are my hands tied?' she muttered, her words slurred from the swelling in her jaw. The silver cross that had belonged to Hrolf Asgrimm's son was gone; no doubt he had sent it to the bottom of the black lake.

Grimnir did not move. His chest expanded as he took a deep snuffling breath and held it before exhaling. When he finally turned toward her, a frown etched his craggy brow. 'The taint of your kind reaches even here,' he said. He moved to where she sat.

'Loose me,' she said.

With a grunt, Grimnir leaned her forward and checked the knots that bound her hands in place.

'You stay like that for now,' he said.

'What? Why?'

'For your own good.' Grimnir walked around to the other side of the fire and sat on a seat sawn from the trunk of a fallen oak. His eyes gleamed in the light, feverish and bright.

Étaín shifted around, trying to find a more comfortable way of sitting; while not tight, the leather cords kept her arms at an uncomfortable angle. Was this punishment? His way of chastising her for trying to run away?

'Where do the Danes gather in England, eh?'

Étaín looked up. The question caught her off guard. She shook her head. 'It's been a year and more since I've been there,' she replied. 'But, some used to make their camp on the Isle of Wight, just off the coast of Wessex.'

'That's where he'll be, the miserable bastard. That maggot, Half-Dane! He'll hide out among his mother's people and try to convince them he's a gold-giver and a war leader. Ha! Wretched oathbreaker, that's what he is.' Grimnir stood and paced like a caged wolf. 'He's another who plays his part well. A few years back, he had that idiot, King Haakon of the Norse, convinced he was a

68

powerful *goði*. The fool wouldn't move an inch against the rebel sons of Eirik Bloodaxe, who schemed to boot him off the throne, until his pet priest had cast the runes. Well, I got wind of it and tracked the lot of them up-country to a wretched pisshole called Rastarkalv.' Grimnir spat into the fire.

'Haakon was a crafty one. Knew the rebels were coming. He played a ruse to convince Bloodaxe's sons they were outnumbered. Fools fell for it. They took to their heels and Haakon's dogs reaped a bloody harvest among them. I left them to it, circled round, and came at Haakon's camp from the north. That's where I found him, Half-Dane, crouched over the runes like he knew what he was about.' Grimnir laughed at the memory. 'Wasn't expecting me. The swine! My coming was spelled out right there in the runes and still he was blind to it. Well, he had enough sand in his belly to trade a few blows, but when it went ill for him he took off like a March hare. I nearly had him, but we ran full into Haakon and his guard.' Grimnir stopped pacing; his eyes grew stern and deadly as he glared at something beyond the firelight, behind Étaín. 'This time, he won't have a score of Norse rogues to hide behind.'

'Rastarkalv?' Étaín said, after a moment. Her brows knitted. 'That was more than a few years ago. Njáll's grandsire fought alongside Haakon the Good. But . . . if you fought Half-Dane, there, and he also sailed with Njáll and Olaf Tryggve's son, then wouldn't Bjarki Half-Dane be an old man, by now?'

Suddenly, Étaín heard a trio of voices at her back. Harsh and rasping voices, like three different sizes of stones grinding together in a mockery of speech.

'Use your wits, *niðingr* . . .'

'He is only half a Dane . . .'

'Whence comes his father's blood, eh?'

She stiffened as that same feeling of unnatural hatred, of cold menace returned; it crept up her spine, threatening to freeze the heart in her breast. Eyes wide with terror, Étaín turned . . .

Three gaunt figures emerged from the opening in the living palisade of trees. They were naked save for twists of filthy hide knotted about their loins. Their skins were as pale as curdled milk, their hair and beards black, stringy, and matted; they stood as tall as Grimnir though their limbs were heavier and gnarled with age. The eyes staring out from their seamed faces, beneath bushy brows, were dead and black – as lifeless as the eyes of a shark.

They stared at Étaín with an insatiable hunger.

Grimnir moved around the fire. 'Nóri, Nótt, and Náli,' he growled. 'My wretched cousins.'

The three figures stopped. The largest of them, Nóri, stood only a handful of paces from Grimnir; the other two – Nótt and the crookbacked runt, Náli – crouched in their brother's shadow.

'Why have you come here, son of Bálegyr?' said Nóri. 'We have no truck with the one you seek.'

Nótt pointed a dirty, accusing finger at Grimnir. 'When has one of Bálegyr's brood ever come before the sons of Náinn and not asked a boon, eh, my brother?'

'He has brought tribute.' Náli dared to dart in close and sniffed the air above where Étaín was sitting. 'A gift, brothers! One of *his* . . . a woman of the White Christ!'

Grimnir slapped Náli away. 'Back, maggot!'

Náli squeaked and sought refuge in the shadow of his brothers. 'The *kaunr* wants something,' they muttered and hissed to one another. 'What do you want, son of Bálegyr? Does he want gold? What is gold to us, eh? A sword, then? A blade forged in dragon fire by the hands of the mightiest smiths of the *dvergar*? Are we not the sons of Náinn,

70

cousin? What does he want, eh? What does he want?'

'I want to walk the branches of Yggðrasil,' Grimnir said. 'Like my father did of old. I want to take the Ash-Road!'

The *dvergar* – dwarves, for such is what Étaín heard them call themselves – seemed taken aback by Grimnir's request. They huddled together, whispering. Finally, Nótt stepped forth. 'And where would you go, cousin? Not to Ásgarðr, for you are the last of your kind to yet face the Doom of Odin. Would you seek *jarls* and gold-givers among Angrboða's kin in Jotunheimr, or would you wander the mists of Niflheimr, never to plague Miðgarðr again?'

'*Faugh!* I am not fool enough to tempt those whores of Fate, the Norns, by leaving Miðgarðr,' Grimnir replied. 'Yggðrasil's branches pierce this world in countless places. Work your sorcery, cousins, and open a path that leads across the sea to England, to the shores of a place called Wessex.'

Once again, the *dvergar* babbled among themselves. Étaín's eyes flickered from the three horrid brothers to Grimnir and back, again. Yggðrasil? Norns? Ásgarðr? These were stories and fables made up by the heathens to explain the world around them. Myths that could not stand before the truth of Christ the Redeemer. To hear them talk so freely of them, as if they truly existed, filled Étaín with a curious sense of dread.

Finally, the strongest of the brothers, Nóri, silenced the other two. 'It is not as it was in olden times, cousin. The power of the White Christ rises like an unwanted weed in the garden. It chokes the life from the Old Ways and threatens the very roots of Yggðrasil. We can do this thing you ask, but the outcome is not as certain as it was in your sire's day. And there is a price. A blood price.' Nóri leered at Étaín and licked his lips.

Grimnir's eyes narrowed. 'You sell yourselves cheap,

beardling. There's not enough meat on her bones for one of you, much less three. And why would I pay three to do the work of one?' Like a conjurer, Grimnir produced a pair of old dice carved from bone. 'You maggots throw for it. The winner opens the way and gets the prize. Share it or not, that's your own business.'

Avarice brought a gleam of life to the three brothers' eyes; they glanced sidelong at one another. Nóri chuckled. 'We will take your wager, cousin.'

Étaín struggled against her bonds. 'You bastard! I thought . . . I thought you needed my help?'

Grimnir ignored her. He tossed the dice at the feet of the *dvergar*. Like dogs fighting over a scrap of meat, they went at one another in an effort to lay hands on the dice. Amid all the shouting, punching, kicking, and cursing, Grimnir leaned down and grabbed Étaín by the hair, dragging her close.

'Watch, and be silent,' he hissed.

Suddenly, Nóri emerged from the scrum with the dice held high. Crowing like he'd won a great victory, he chivvied his brothers into some semblance of order and quickly sketched out their game: the winner would be whichever one scored the best in three out of five throws.

With a derisive chuckle that even Étaín could barely hear, Grimnir seated himself on the log and watched the three of them go at it. The first three throws took over an hour, with Nóri and Nótt squabbling over even the tiniest nuance, from acceptable stances for throwing to what the phrase 'out of bounds' truly meant; crookbacked Náli accepted their every pronouncement in stoic silence and rolled highest every time he touched the dice. Clearly, he was in the lead . . . until Nóri declared his last two throws invalid because he couldn't stand up straight.

On the fourth throw, Nótt jiggled Náli's elbow, causing

one of the dice to fly off toward the edge of the lake. The two elder brothers went bounding after it, capering like bearded children. 'It plays where it lays, you worm!' Nóri shouted. Demoralized, cheated of his victory, Náli shuffled after them.

But as the crookbacked *dvergr* passed by where Grimnir sat, the latter snagged his arm and drew him close. Étaín saw a flash of iron as something passed between the two; Grimnir gave the runt a knowing wink. Náli blinked; he glanced sidelong from Grimnir to his deceitful brothers and tried without success to hide a gap-toothed smile.

Finally, the dice flew for the fifth and final time. Twisted little Náli was the clear winner, but it was Nóri who stepped forward. Nótt, ever the sycophant, cleaved to his brother's shadow, muttering endearments and licking his cracked lips at the thought of being permitted a taste of flesh, a drop of blood. Sullen Náli stood behind them, his face suffused with black rage.

'I'll take that prize now, cousin,' Nóri said, a gloating smile twisting his features. He started toward Étaín.

And with a strangled cry, Náli struck.

The crookbacked runt shouldered Nótt aside; the knife Grimnir gave him flashed in the firelight as he planted it hilt-deep in his elder brother's neck. Nóri stumbled, his scream of agony turned to a wet gurgle by the rush of black, foul-smelling blood. Étaín saw disbelief written on the *dvergr*'s face. He took a step toward them, and then dropped like a stiffened board, as dead as Judas.

For an instant, no one moved; save for the crackling of logs on the fire, the cove was absolutely silent and still. Suddenly, a peal of tittering laughter ripped from Náli's breast. The runt capered and danced. But, as he whirled in place, crowing and crooning, it was Nótt's turn to strike. Snarling like an animal, the middle brother came

73

up off the ground and wrapped his long fingers around Náli's throat. The runt's crowing turned to screeching as Nótt bore him down; they thrashed and struggled, rolling and twisting and tearing as Grimnir and Étaín looked on. Nótt's clawed fingers tore ribbons of skin from the flesh of Náli's throat; for his part, the crookbacked runt tried to gouge his brother's eyes out.

'Look at the high-and-mighty sons of Náinn, now,' Grimnir said. Náli's bulging eyes implored him for help as Nótt throttled him atop the blood-spattered corpse of Nóri. 'Driven to murder by dice and the promise of flesh.' Grimnir spat. He rose off the log and crossed to the struggling *dvergar*. Before either one could react, he grabbed a handful of Nótt's hair, wrenched his head back near to breaking, and – in one smooth motion – drew his seax and ripped it across the dwarf's throat. A fountain of foul black blood jetted from the ragged wound; it drenched Náli, who coughed and wheezed as he dragged himself free of his dying brother's grasp.

Even still, the *dvergr* wanted his prize. He rolled onto his belly and scuttled toward Étaín, hunger and lust filling his dead black eyes with an unholy light. His brother's stinking lifeblood dripped down his face. Náli licked the gore from his lips; faster he came, like some obscene crab. Étaín recoiled, tried to get her feet under her. She shrank from the thought of Náli's foul touch.

Inches from her, Grimnir caught him. He planted a foot in the *dvergr*'s twisted back, slamming the runt to the ground and driving out what little air he had left in his lungs with an explosive *whuff*.

'Your life is mine, beardling,' Grimnir said. 'Open the way.'

Náli struggled to draw breath. 'Will . . . Will y-you honor our bargain?'

'There is no bargain. Your life is mine. Open the way or I'll carve maggot holes in your belly, you miserable runt!' Reaching down, Grimnir knotted his fingers in Náli's hair and hauled him upright. He gestured to Étaín. On unsteady legs, she clambered to her feet. 'Turn around,' he said, and with one stroke of his seax Grimnir severed her bonds. Trusting she would follow, Grimnir dragged Náli toward the opening in the palisade of trees.

Étaín watched them a moment; then, she caught up Grimnir's pack and hurried after him. 'You . . . You had no intention of bartering me to them, then?'

'Why would I?' Grimnir paused, giving her a chance to catch up. Náli writhed in his grip. 'You need to open your eyes, little fool. Three to one? *Now* the odds are more to my liking.' He shook the crookbacked *dvergr* like a sack. 'Isn't that right, *cousin?*'

'You lied!' Náli screeched. 'Ymir blast your eyes!'

'I never said what your prize would be, did I, beardling?'

'They assumed . . .' said Étaín.

'Aye, the fools assumed.' Grimnir turned Náli loose and shoved him toward the opening in the trees; the twisted dwarf walked slowly ahead of Grimnir, scowling in his beard and fingering his bruised throat. He passed through the wood-wrought doorway.

The woven wall of trunks towered above Étaín's head. It was impossibly ancient, a fortress of gnarled trees and interlaced branches. Slender birches coiled around the boles of mammoth yew trees, while oaks that were young when Christ was a boy erupted in a profusion of tangled shoots and branches that wove in and out among the hawthorn and the beech. Along the edges, like guards tasked with keeping a crowd at bay, stood countless ash trees, from tender saplings to hoary old gray-barks that must have seen the dawn of the world. Étaín hesitated on the threshold of the gate, shivering at the thought of what might lie beyond. Was it truly Yggðrasil, the mythical World Tree? Or was it just some bit of heathen mummery that flourished in the shadows, where the Word of God did not yet reach?

'Go on.' Grimnir's hand thrust her across the threshold. She gasped. But, despite the cold knot of apprehension in her belly, Étaín marveled at the sublime beauty that existed inside the tree-garth. It was a cathedral, of sorts, a heathen shrine made from living wood. Dwarf-wrought lamps, like fantastic beasts hammered from copper and bronze, cast pools of silver or gold or red light. They illuminated an intricate pattern on the floor, a labyrinth of knotted roots that made their footing treacherous. At the heart of the garth grew a primeval ash tree.

'Yggðrasil,' she heard Grimnir mutter.

Étaín coughed. The air here was heavy with the scent of ancient vegetation, of moist earth and leaf mold. From far above, she could hear the rustle of the wind, the flutter of wings, and the faint chittering of a squirrel.

They followed Náli. The *dvergr* approached the tree with a sense of reverence, like a priest attending his god; Grimnir's wolfish face bore an almost childlike look of wonder, though his eyes never lost their cold and calculating gleam – ever did he look like a merchant who marveled at his gold even as he appraised its worth. Étaín herself stepped carefully toward that knotty and twisted goliath with a deep sense of foreboding.

Before the ash tree, and cradled by its living roots, stood a stone basin filled with glowing embers. The great tree's trunk was hollow with age, and set inside it was an arched doorway made from rough-hewn stones, each one carved with a serpentine trail of runes. Beyond the doorway was darkness so utter and complete that Étaín wondered if it was not some trick of the light; harder to explain, though, was the bone-chilling breeze that wafted from the doorway.

Then, something happened that Étaín did not expect: the sullen *dvergr* passed his hand over the basin of embers. Instantly, blue-tinged flames leapt up and curled around his fingers. Étaín recoiled in terror – this was no mere hedge witchery, but an ancient sorcery as old as stone and bough; it was the Devil's bailiwick, and simply witnessing it meant she strayed perilously close to damnation. Out of reflex, she crossed herself . . .

Náli reacted as though she had struck him; the sorcerous flames wavered. 'Ai! Curse you, *niðingr*! Your White Christ has no place here! Lop off her hands and rip out her tongue, cousin, lest she bring the wrath of the Æsir down upon our heads!' Náli trembled and clutched at his temples.

Grimnir seized her by the scruff of the neck. 'Leave off, you blasted hymn-singer,' he growled. 'And none of your miserable air crosses, either.'

Étaín did not reply, though a small voice in the back of her mind wondered what would happen if she flourished a crucifix and sang out the Lord's Prayer. After a moment Náli regained his composure. He shook himself, as though clearing his mind of a foul memory. The flames sprang full to life. The crookbacked *dvergr* stared deep into the heart of the basin, and in a harsh, croaking voice he began to chant.

Étaín could not understand the words; they were guttural and repetitive, but the rhythm of Náli's voice gave the blasphemous suggestion of a heartbeat – as though he tried by savage words to awaken something long dormant. The chill breeze gusted, causing the eerie blue flames to dance and waver. Something deep in the earth shivered, running through root and bole and causing the branches overhead to rustle and shake.

Náli's voice dropped to a low growl:

> *Yggðrasil shivers,*
> *The ash, as it stands.*
> *The old tree groans,*
> *And the giant slips free.*

The *dvergr* nodded to Grimnir. Still holding Étaín by the scruff, he pulled her with him to stand before the stone-bordered doorway, covered now in a rime of frost. The blackness beyond writhed and roiled like a living thing. Sounds came forth, distant and phantasmal: the clash of steel, the roar of voices, music, harsh laughter, the cries of the dying, howling and monstrous grunting and tearing – the din of the Nine Worlds echoing through the roots of Yggðrasil. Étaín clasped her fists together, biting her knuckles to keep from calling out to the Almighty for succor.

Beside her, Étaín felt Grimnir stiffen; Náli had fallen silent and the sudden end of his chanting raised the *skrælingr*'s hackles. Grimnir turned . . .

Suddenly, both of them staggered forward as the *dvergr* rammed Grimnir in the small of the back. Long-fingered hands tried to strip Étaín from his grasp. She had a brief glimpse of Náli's eyes, no longer dead black but alive with lust and vengeance; Étaín screamed. With a bitter oath, Grimnir twisted his body, wrapping her in a protective embrace; with his free hand, he snatched a handful of Náli's beard, dragging the crookbacked *dvergr* off balance. The echo of their struggle ended abruptly as all three tumbled through the doorway, vanishing into the heart of Yggðrasil . . .

13

Étaín fell into darkness, wrapped in soul-searing cold, her ears battered by the clash of iron and the screams of the dying. She opened her eyes and . . .

. . . *winces as an eerie light stabs down from the green-tinted sky. Ferocious clouds boil across the horizon; lightning slashes like drawn steel and thunder rumbles with the roar of kettledrums, calling the ravens to war. Ahead of her, a hillock rises from the windswept plain. Not of stone or earth, this knoll, but of naked bone – a cairn of skulls. Empty eye sockets glare at her; yellowed teeth gnash in the keening wind as tongueless mouths seek to give voice to their scorn. They are the dead of Exeter. Dead because of her.*

Dead because she opened the gate to the Danes.

Godwin slept like an exhausted old fool. He'd spent himself early, rutting in her like a swine in heat despite the fires and the raucous howls of the Danes at the gate. It was nothing to slip from his filthy bed; like a ghost, she drifted from the old fool's house. No one paid her any heed – she was nothing, less than a whore, that silly orphan from Glastonbury old Godwin had bought to scratch a familiar itch – and soon she'd crept through the heart of the city. She avoided the embattled main gate, where a handful of archers kept Red Njáll's reavers at bay, their arrows shattering on shield and corselet. Étaín padded through the shadows along the wall until she came to a small, forgotten postern gate. Its guard, an old soldier named Hereward, slept as soundly as her wretched husband. He snored on as she unbarred the gate; he smacked his lips, dreaming of wine and tits, as she took his lantern and signaled to the invading Danes; old Hereward was still smiling when a reaver's knife slit his throat. She walked down to the dragon ships as the first screams echoed over doomed Exeter . . .

She stumbles to her knees, hands clasped in supplication. She wants to speak but she has no voice; she wants to beg forgiveness but she cannot find the words. The eyes of the dead bore into her. Accusing. Judging. She wants to scream but she has no breath; she wants to crawl away but shame shackles her. She sinks lower, the weight of her crime doubling her over, grinding her brow into the cold earth.

Can the dead understand? Can they understand the burden of being a foundling – motherless and fatherless, unwanted, left by the back gate of a cloister like something unclean? Can the dead understand a childhood bereft of love? Can they understand innocence lost in an abbot's bed, and the shame at being sold for Judas-coin once the first blush of womanhood has faded? Can the dead understand what it is to want to die?

But she does not ask, and the dead do not answer. There is no release in their hollow gaze, no forgiveness. A shadow falls over her. Weeping tears of dust, she raises her eyes to the heavens and beholds a glorious sight: a cross rising from the crest of the hillock, and from that cross hangs the silhouette of a man. A crucified man.

The Christ! He is risen, and He brings with him redemption, for is He not the Redeemer of the World?

Hope fills her breast. If she can only reach Him . . . He is the way and the truth and the life. His blessing is absolution; in His gentle smile she will know eternal peace.

She wills her limbs to move, scuttling forward on her belly like a crab to clamber up the steep-sided cairn. The earth trembles. Bone clatters in an avalanche of skulls. Desperate, she scrabbles higher, pulling herself over leering skeletal faces. Teeth splinter beneath her heels; her knees crush eye sockets and nasal cavities, and the thin sutures knitting together plates of bone pop under her weight. She gropes and claws her way to the crest of the hillock, reaching out, entreating the Christ to absolve her . . .

The earth heaves; the cairn beneath surges and ebbs, and she rides the swell like a leaf on Rán's breast. The skulls of Exeter's dead fall away to reveal ancient bark, gnarled and mossy – the root-knotted base of a monolithic tree. Deep crevices surround her, black and blood-reeking chasms that echo with war chants and ring with the rasp and slither of iron. She looks up, suddenly fearful. The figure of the Christ vanishes, and beneath spreading boughs like great storm clouds she beholds a crucified titan, one-eyed and fey-bearded, with a pair of giant ravens perched on his naked shoulders.

The great birds stare at her; their coal-black eyes glitter with malign intelligence. They ruffle their feathers, shaking their bodies and flexing their enormous wings. In unison, with voices that reverberate like brazen horns, they chant:

From Serpent-girdled Miðgarðr, | by the Ash-Road,
Comes Laufeyjarson's blunder: | filth-born skrælingr,
Against Odin's Doom; | and with him a child
Sworn to the Nailed One, | foe of all.

The titan stirs, tendons in his neck creaking like ship's cordage as his massive head turns. He looks left, then right, gray beard sweeping across his chest. Then, with agonizing slowness, he leans forward – a man seeking the insect that bedevils him. Mastering her fear, she raises her head and meets his gaze. The socket of his left eye is black and empty; the right, however, is the color of a storm-racked sea. It pierces her, flaying her courage, leaving her naked under its cold and terrible scrutiny. In its depths images take form . . . visions . . .

She sees a wood-wreathed ship tossed upon winter's foaming waves. A man stands beneath the dragon prow; his red-bearded visage is familiar to her, though careworn now and scarred by rage, loss, and a thirst for vengeance. 'I will find you,' he mutters, his words lost to the tempest. 'By Odin, I swear it!'

The rain becomes the swirling smoke of a mighty bonfire, its flames curling up into the night sky. Waves crash in the distance, and harsh laughter echoes about the strand. A dozen men sit around the fire – men with plaited beards and amulets carved of bone, cold-eyed and angry, hands caressing sword hilt and axe haft. Their leader, a hunched and spine-twisted giant with a beard like tarry thatch, laughs loudest of all as he jabs an accusing finger at the newcomer. 'I remember you. You were King Olaf's man. Why would you serve me? Why should I trust you, son of Hjálmarr, when last I recall you were panting for my blood on the beach at Scilly?'

The laughter turns to the shouts and screams of dying men on a corpse-strewn moor, a coppery sun sinking into the western mists. The giant is prone in the gore-slimed heather; he claws for the hilt-shard of a broken sword as his foeman, a broad-backed Saxon in chain and wolf fur, plants a foot on his chest and is poised to ram an iron-headed spear into his throat. The red-bearded man – graying, now, and blood-blasted – appears from the mist and catches the Saxon unawares. His axe bites deep into his foeman's spine. He stares down at the fallen giant as twilight descends. 'Stay alive, you bastard,' he says. 'I need you as bait!'

Twilight turns to darkness, and the man to a twisted ash tree limned against the star-flecked sky. Beneath its boughs is a smoking altar, and the air is thick with incense and the reek of blood. Hands drag her forward; those same hands strip her naked and wrestle her spread-eagled onto the altar. A priest hovers into view – gray-bearded and one-eyed, an iron dagger in his upraised fist. He invokes the Allfather, a dozen voices joining his own, and as the chant reaches its crescendo the priest drives the blade into her bare breast. She screams . . .

. . . and recoils from the titan's doom-laden glare. He laughs, then – a sound like the thunder of war drums, loud enough to crack the foundations of Heaven. She scurries back, to the bark-ragged edge of a root chasm; there, with the titan's laughter thudding against her ribs, she stumbles. Her foot catches on a knurl of wood and for a terrifying moment she hangs over the abyss, arms flailing, feet seeking a purchase that is not there. She draws breath to scream anew . . . but before she can utter a sound she plummets into darkness.

And it is sound that catches her. Sound like salt wrack slapping against a hull, like the creak of oarlocks; sound caresses her trembling limbs; horns blare and pipes skirl, their discordant song punctuated by the scrape of iron on bone. Beneath it all, staccato throbs like the beating of an immense heart, matching the rhythm set by the thudding of the distant drum. She listens as the sounds weave into a tale, a ballad of iron . . .

Wild was Grimnir | when he arose,
And when his snake-cunning | foeman he missed;
He shook his head, | his hair was bristling,
As the son of Náinn | about him sought.

The glow in Náli's eyes | was like forge-gledes,
As bloody revenge | for his brothers burned deep;
Under the ash he waited | and gathered his strength,
His teeth he gnashed | and his breath was venom.

Náli spake:

'Give heed, Bálegyr's son, | for here I am
No starveling runt;
False is thy tongue, | and soon shalt thou find
That it sings thee an evil song.'

Grimnir spake:

'Bold in the shadows, | is Náinn's bastard,
Náli, adorner of benches!
Come forth and fight, | if thou would best me,
And I shall teach thee the dirge of the vanquished!'

Swift as a storm | they smote together,
In the murk-wrought tangle | at Miðgarðr's edge;
Born of hate was Grimnir, | Nótt's slayer,
Who set his corpse-wand | against the flesh of Ymir.

In the hilt was hatred, | in the haft was treachery,
In the point was fear, | for the skrælingr's foe;
On the blade were carved | blood-flecked runes,
And a serpent's tail | round the flat was twisted.

Ill went the grappling | for the pale son of Náinn,
Who ran from the fray | on craven's feet;
Dreadful and dark-cheeked | came Bálegyr's get,
Into the maggot-holes | that wounded Yggr's steed.

(Then Grimnir spake, | scorn dripping from the gates of
breath:
'Why dost thou flee, beardling? | Hast thou
No stomach for Odin's weather?')

In the shadows Náli chanted, | weaving potent charms;
He sang a song of darkness | and reddening fires,
And its echo reached | the deeps of Niðafjoll
To rouse from slumber | Hel's draugr-serpent.

Wreathed in corpse-reek, | came the fierce-raging wyrm
And the Ash-Road groaned | 'neath its evil weight;
The skrælingr met it, | war-grim and bitter,
To test night-bringer's edge | against bone-clad coils.

(Then Náli spake, | to match scorn with scorn:
'Where is thy boast, cousin, | now that
The weather has turned against thee?')

With clash of iron, | mighty hammer on anvil,
The strife-bringer | twisted sore in wrath;
Away sprang Grimnir, | though not in fear,
For Fate had spared his foe | till Gjallarhorn's song.

Away sprang Bálegyr's son, | across the Ash-Road
With shoulders cloaked | in the skin of the wolf-father;
The serpent gave chase, | goaded by Náli,
And with him | came the Doom of Odin.

Sound and darkness fade, leaving her awash in green-tinged light — not the eerie glow of storm wrack like before, but rather the gleam of sunlight through a canopy of leaves. She opens her eyes and dares to try and perceive of her surroundings . . .

She is supine upon a branch — the smallest branch of a tree so vast and complex that her mind cannot fully comprehend its enormity; even still, two horse-drawn wagons could traverse this branch abreast and one need never worry the other about slipping over the edge. She stands, her legs unsteady. The branch juts forth from an impossible tangle of limbs, follows a convoluted path, and then plunges back into that leafy mass. Beyond, she discerns an eternal darkness stippled with stars yet brimming with radiance, a universe of contradictions: a windswept emptiness filled with raucous silence; sterile and desiccated but smelling of moist vegetation; dead yet vibrantly alive. Far above, in the mist-wreathed branches at the edge of her vision, three wood-woven spheres catch her eye; from them streams light like that of cold, caged suns — yellow, green, and white, the shades of spring sunlight filtering through leaf and bough. Each a drey that might encompass a world. Each like the one whose edge she stands upon.

Without warning, a violent tremor snatches her feet out from under her. She lands hard, the rough bark stripping the skin from her palms; blood wells from these abrasions, filling the air with a rich coppery scent.

Her blood.

Her scent.

She can see the stench rising before her; it drifts and coils like scarlet vapor, a beacon to whatever nameless hunters might prowl the spaces between worlds. She clenches her fists, tries to make it dissipate. She mutters a prayer.

In answer, there comes an earsplitting howl. She clambers to her feet, suddenly fearful, and heads back the way she came. Barely a half-dozen steps does she take before something explodes from the wall of branches. She skids to a stop.

Through a veil of dust, she spies a wolf loping toward her. It is a dusky beast, thrice the height of a tall man at the shoulders, with hackles bristling and eyes aflame in the shadow of Miðgarðr.

Familiar eyes, the angry red hue of a blacksmith's forge. A skrælingr's eyes.

And on the wolf's heels comes a writhing horror, a bone-scaled serpent drawn from the abyss of nightmare – a son of Níðhoggr, feral-eyed and pale; she reckons by its ravenous gaze that no amount of flesh can slake its hunger. But it will try. And it will start with her. Giving an inarticulate scream, she turns and runs.

The wolf is bestride her in a pace, its rank breath hot against her neck; eyes squeezed shut, a prayer on her lips, she braces for the deathblow – glad, on one hand, to die quickly rather than see her flesh dissolved in the serpent's maw. But it doesn't rend her limb from limb. Instead, the beast snatches her up in midstep, cradling her in its fierce jaws as a mother would its cub. Then, without breaking stride, the wolf veers right and springs out over the abyss. For a frozen instant they hang over nothingness. Even on the threshold of death, curiosity draws her eye to the deeps beneath Miðgarðr, to the shadowy roots of Yggðrasil, where for half the span of a heartbeat she glimpses the stone-curbed Well of Urðar and the three women who gather by its waters. They return her scrutiny with equal parts amusement, indifference, and naked spite.

And then . . . bone-jarring impact. Claws scrabble and tear at the wood as the wolf seeks purchase, pulling itself

87

up onto the dangerously creaking branch. It glances back, allowing her to see the span it had leapt across, leaving the serpent to writhe and hiss in fury. The wolf gives a low growl, almost like gloating laughter – a sound it chokes off as an eerie shadow falls across the branch. A titan's shadow.

With a frenetic burst of speed, the wolf – she a limp rag of flesh in its jaws – launches itself at the point where the branch rejoins the tangled lattice of wood and mud, where an unnatural arch of rune-carved stone lurks beneath a gloomy overhang. The wolf makes a wild lunge for that arch even as the branch shatters and breaks apart under its feet, a victim of the titan's wrath.

She screams. It is too far; they will not make it . . .

Suddenly, perspectives shift. The scale of this reality distorts, as though sure hands weave a new thread into the fabric of this place. In her mind's eye, she sees the three women gathered around the Well of Urðar: a crone, carved of gristle and whalebone; a noblewoman, clad in silk and gold; and a thin-shanked girl, sickly and cancerous. Amused, indifferent, and spiteful. And what should have been a plummet into the endless abyss between worlds becomes instead a fall of a different kind: into the darkness beneath the arch, back into the world of Men.

Wrapped in soul-searing cold, her ears battered by the clash of iron and the screams of the dying, Étaín fell . . .

14

She did not fall from any great height – simply from standing to prone – but Étaín's senses convinced her she had traveled an immeasurable distance. She landed hard, pain flaring up through her arms as she tried to catch herself. Something crunched under her, a sickening sound like bones snapping. Étaín lay there on her belly, wrapped in the stench of wood dust and crumbled cerecloth, gasping for breath like a fish cast upon the shore. Chills and spasms racked her body. A harrowing light stabbed into her eyes, drawing a blinding wash of tears.

'C-Christ . . . Almighty . . .' she managed.

Groaning, Étaín rolled onto her back and struggled to sit, old bones snapping under her hips. For one terrifying instant she remembered: *a cairn of skulls falling away beneath her, a one-eyed titan, a ravenous serpent.* Clutching at the air in panic, she scrabbled back until her shoulders thumped against a rough stone wall. 'Wh-What happened?' Étaín gasped; her eyes widened with shock. 'Where . . . Where are . . . ?'

She heard a chuckle, then. Peering into the gloom, she discerned a shape sitting across from her, a silhouette in a patch of darker shadow. A chill skated down her spine, forming a cold knot in her belly as she recalled again the vile dwarf Náli – with his grasping fingers and lifeless eyes. 'Who's there?' she whispered. 'Grimnir?'

The figure leaned forward; milky light trickling in from above cast Grimnir's wolfish face in sharp relief. He tossed his head back. Fetishes of ivory and silver clicked in his stringy black hair, and his eyes gleamed coal-red from beneath dusky brows. 'Do I look like that wretched beardling?'

'Where is he?' Étaín said. She glanced around, her eyes slowly adjusting to the murk. Gone were the dwarf-made lamps and the stone basin with its peculiar blue flames; instead, they sat in a stone-flagged chamber with a low ceiling. Tree roots pushed down from above and in through the walls, gnarled tendrils that long ago shattered a stone sarcophagus set into the center of the chamber. 'He . . . He was behind me. Tried to grab me.' She looked at Grimnir. 'Where has he gone . . . ?'

'To rot in Helheimr, if the Norns be fair.' Grimnir grunted. '*Nár!* I don't know where the wretch got off to. But he skinned out of there, quick as you please. Should have knifed that maggot right after he opened the way. Filthy night-skulker!'

A chill skated down Étaín's spine, forming a cold knot in her belly. 'He must have drugged us . . . yes, something in the smoke of his fire . . . some poison or other . . . some mountebank's trick to make us think he was a sorcerer, to make us see his visions of blasphemy!'

'No tricks. No smokes or poisons. No wretched visions. We walked the Ash-Road.' Grimnir rocked back on his haunches. When he spoke again there was a note of reverence in his voice, a tone that reminded her of the respect he'd paid to Hrolf Asgrimm's son. 'The Ash-Road! The limbs of mighty Yggðrasil, whose branches twist and weave through all of creation, from Ásgarðr down to the cold roots of Niflheimr, and the rest of the Nine Worlds. Bálegyr walked it; old Gífr, too, after the Æsir drove my people from Jotunheimr. And now I have walked it.'

'No!' Étaín shook her head. *She stands upon a branch – the smallest branch of a vast tree – far above, three wood-woven spheres – from them streams light like that of cold, caged suns – yellow, green, and white – each a drey that might encompass a world . . .* 'Impossible! Your heathen myths are nothing but smoke and mummery – lies whispered by agents of the Devil! I cannot believe – '

'That's twice you've called me a liar, little fool.' Grimnir rose. 'Try it a third time and you'll regret it.' Unable to stand upright, he slouched and shuffled, kicking aside a pelvis and smashing a skeletal rib cage as he searched for a way out of the chamber. He stopped and glanced sidelong at her. 'You can't believe we walked the Ash-Road, but you can believe your Nailed God walked on water, turned it to wine, and came back from the dead?'

'Because it is so written.'

'So-ho! It is written, eh? But you didn't *see* him do it, did you? Did your father see him do it? No? Did your mother's brother see him do it, and then tell the rest of you lot the tale over the council fires? No? But I'm wrong and you – with your miserable books and a paltry score of years to stand on – are right? Even after seeing the Ash-Road with your own blasted eyes?'

'I saw only the Devil's handiwork,' she said stubbornly.

Without warning, Grimnir bent; she watched him snatch something from a pile of debris. As he straightened, he lobbed it at her. Étaín flinched from reflex. The small missile struck her shoulder and bounced into her lap – a heavy, bright bauble, the tongue of a sword belt whose leather had long ago rotted away. Knots woven of gold filigree gleamed as though they were crafted yesterday.

'Give that to your Nailed God,' he muttered, chuckling. 'As payment for the fine wool he's got covering your eyes.'

'I pity you,' she said. Étaín did not try to hide her scorn. She was tired of dancing around as though on eggshells for fear she might offend him. 'I pity you and I will pray for your salvation.'

'Save your breath,' Grimnir replied, matching her scorn with his own. 'That wretch, Half-Dane, has more need of your pity than I do. His day of reckoning is coming!'

'Nevertheless, it is you I pity.' Étaín got her legs under her; using roots and jutting stones in the chamber wall, she pulled herself upright. Her limbs yet shook and her vision swam at the edges, but she could stand. 'I may be narrow-minded in my thinking; there may be things under Heaven and under earth that I do not understand, things that I fear; things whose existence I will deny to my last breath, but it is not my world that is fading away. You've said it yourself: you're the last of your kind. You claim the Old World is ending, but you need not end with it. Njáll was wrong – in the eyes of Christ, even a devil like you can find redemption. Forget this ridiculous errand of yours, this foolish quest for revenge! Peace and salvation can be yours, simply by asking—'

Grimnir rounded on her. 'Ridiculous, is it? Foolish?' Spittle flew from yellowed fangs; he was on her in a heartbeat, knotting one fist in her hair and dragging her close. 'Tell it to the scores of *kaunar* that bastard betrayed in Jutland, when he led the Spear-Danes against them! Tell it to Hrungnir, my brother, who was murdered by Half-Dane's hand! The dead don't clamor for salvation, little fool! They clamor for blood! My brother's shade shrieks for it, and for vengeance! And that's what he'll get, as the gods are my witness!' Grimnir shoved her away. 'Peace? *Faugh!* Keep your Nailed God's empty promises. I want no part of this milk-blooded world you hymn-singers bring with you.'

Étaín stumbled back and fought to keep her balance. 'It doesn't matter that you want no part of it,' she replied. 'The world is what it is, and unless you plan to cut your own throat you *are* a part of it. In your father's world, you might have walked through a tree to cross an ocean, but in our world you needs must have a boat – and the boats we need are to the west. But you tarry about the heart of Sjælland in hopes of what? Finding a magic door to England? *Faugh,* as you say! Lead us west, and perhaps together we can find a way across the ocean, to where your prey waits!'

Grimnir, though, merely grunted and shuffled to the far end of the chamber, where a passage doglegged off – presumably leading to the outside world. He vanished; a moment later she heard the impact of his hobnailed sandal on ancient wood. Once. Twice. With the third blow came a splintering sound as that end of the chamber suddenly suffused with light.

Grimnir laughed. 'Who tarries now, foundling?'

Étaín stifled a sob of frustration. She moved slowly, dragging her feet across the dusty chamber as sharp-toothed hunger gnawed at her belly. She was cold. She was angry. Her heart yet broke for Njáll, her worry for him greater even than her concern for herself. And now this unending nightmare: lost in the wilds of Sjælland and forced to wander until . . . until what? Until that wretch decided to listen to her advice? *I'll sooner see winged swine in the heavens!* But with a prayer poised on her lips, a plea for this nightmare to end, Étaín followed Grimnir out into the light.

Rotten splinters of wood crunched underfoot as she emerged from the heart of an ancient chambered cairn – a tall, green howe made more conspicuous by its position at the crest of a low hill. Gnarled ash trees grew around and on top of the cairn, but beyond its perimeter Étaín could see a forest of thick, moss-girt oaks and spreading chestnuts. It was mild; a breeze out of the west ruffled her coppery hair, and chased lacework clouds across a sky as blue as a field of cornflowers.

'Christ Almighty,' she whispered, crossing herself, for all around her every leaf was green and bright with the advent of spring.

But it was snowing, she thought. *An hour ago it was not yet winter and already it was snowing!* Her legs gave way. She fell to her knees in the weeds bordering the cairn and looked around, unable to believe the truth her own eyes revealed to her: late autumn had given way to early spring in the passage of but a single hour. 'This . . . This is impossible!'

If it was spring, then . . . her mind raced. *What of the Day of Wrath? Did the Ending of the World come with the New Year?* Étaín saw no sign around them of tribulation and distress, nor was there evidence of calamity or misery or darkness or clouds or whirlwinds. There was only sunlight, a breeze that warmed her bones, and the smell of good clean earth. 'Where are we?' she said, her voice rising as a panic gripped her chest with icy talons. 'Where are we, damn you? H-How did that miserable wretch . . . where . . . ?'

'The Ash-Road, just like I said.' Grimnir flared his nostrils, snorting in triumph. 'And that – ' He jabbed a finger at a great mossy stone that stood canted at an angle near the foot of the howe, dappled sunlight picking out deeply incised runes. ' – had better tell us we're in England. Read it. Read it and *you* tell *me* where we are.' Grimnir sat heavily on the exposed roots of one of the ash trees. He looked different in the bright sunlight, darker and more savage; even narrowed to slits his eyes gleamed with a monstrous killing lust. *'Faugh!'* he said suddenly, clawing at the soil of the cairn. 'It must be England. This land is steeped in the poison of your Nailed God. I can feel it. It burns just to touch the earth. And the silence . . .'

But Étaín paid him little heed. She pulled herself to the rune-etched stone and peered at the writing. Familiar patterns in the runes caught her eye, forming names she'd seen before as a child when she'd steal into the library at Glastonbury and read from the Venerable Bede's work on the history of England. She traced them with a trembling finger:

HENGIST THE YOUNGER,
SWORD-*THEGN* OF CENWALH,
SLEW GADEON OF THE DUMNONII
AND TOOK HIS DEATH-WOUND.

'Impossible,' she muttered. Étaín climbed to her feet and stumbled to the edge of the hill. She glanced back . . . and stopped. The same familiarity she'd seen in the runes repeated itself in the lay of the land. She described a slow circle; with each step, that sense of familiarity grew.

'Well?' Grimnir said, breaking her reverie.

'It . . . it can't be!' She took a lurching step and fell forward onto her hands and knees. 'No, it can't be!'

He sprang to his feet; with bounding steps he reached her side. He planted his sandaled heel against her hip and shoved her onto her back. Tears streamed down Étaín's cheeks. 'Tell me?'

'This place,' she sobbed. 'I kn-know this place. It's Heathen's Howe, in the Sallow Wood. When . . . When I was a child this place had an evil reputation as a haunt of goblins and witches.'

'It is England?'

An hour ago I was in Sjælland.

'Is it Wessex?' he bellowed.

Étaín nodded. *An hour ago I was in Sjælland and it was not yet winter; an hour ago I fell across a threshold, and now I am in England, and it is spring!* 'G-Glastonbury is but a half a day to the west,' she whispered as the full measure of her plight crushed down on her. England was a hateful land, so disgusting to her that she had welcomed rape and slavery at the hands of the Danes so she might be free of it. *And now, I am back.*

Grimnir grunted. 'Praise that little maggot's black soul, then. There are villages round about?' Étaín nodded again. 'Good. We will start there. One of these English bastards will have heard the name Bjarki Half-Dane.'

BOOK TWO

THE KINGDOM OF WESSEX, IN THE SOUTH OF ENGLAND

I

Étaín had seen bodies left to rot; she had watched the executions of Danish captives outside the walls of Exeter, their heads left on stakes as a warning to their shipmates; she had seen a man drawn and quartered, one boiled in oil, and another who was flayed alive as her husband, the chief magistrate of the city, hunted for traitors in his midst after the Danes returned in force. But that hateful old prick, Godwin, who had bought her from the abbot of Glastonbury before her fourteenth birthday, never imagined the traitor might be in his own bed. She had seen all manner of death on the night she betrayed Exeter to the Danes. Yet, save for images of the Redeemer on the Cross, Étaín had never seen a crucified body.

It looked like a manikin crafted from aged leather, stretched taut over a frame of bone. Heavy nails flecked with rust and long-dried blood pierced its wrists and went deep into the trunk of an ash tree, where it hung like an offering to the heathen gods – or in mockery of the Christ. The poor fellow had no nose to speak of, and his lips and eyes had long since gone into the belly of a raven. Empty sockets stared down at Étaín; a beard like bleached corn silk framed a collection of broken yellow teeth, his mouth frozen in a perpetual rictus of agony.

'Been dead a year, at least,' said Grimnir, as if it were

nothing unusual to stumble upon a crucified body along a forest path. 'Must be a village close by.' Étaín stared at the corpse for a moment longer before hurrying after him.

The Sallow Wood had an evil reputation. It was like the *myrkvithr* of legend, the great troll-haunted forest that spread halfway across the world. They followed a narrow, weed-choked footpath that meandered between the twisted and moss-furred trunks – one of a dozen such trails they'd come across since leaving Heathen's Howe. Grimnir guided them ever north and west. In that direction, Étaín assured him, stood a number of towns on the forest's eaves.

'Why not south, to the coast? To this Wight's Isle you spoke of?' Grimnir's eyes had narrowed with suspicion.

'Six months ago, yes. But it's the raiding season, now,' she had replied. 'If you want to find empty longhouses and deserted beaches, then the Isle of Wight is our best choice. But, if you want to find a Dane or a Saxon who might know your man, then we needs must find out where they're striking.'

At that, Grimnir had grunted his assent and led the way.

Hour after endless hour they walked, the trees awash in green and alive with birdsong; in that forced monotony, Étaín tried to come to grips with what had happened. 'A test,' she had declared aloud, receiving a glare from Grimnir that spoke louder than any curse. But she did not doubt her epiphany: this ordeal was a test, it was. She was sure of it. For did not God test those who would serve Him? Like Job, she had had her comforts stripped away. The Almighty had cast her adrift on a sea of heathen chaos and made her captive to a monster of legend; the Father of Glory had subjected her to sorceries and visions that could have easily left her faithless and broken. But they had not. She had emerged whole, with her sanity intact and her faith stronger than ever. As a feeling of triumph swelled in her breast, she forced Grimnir to stop by an ivy-draped cross on the edge of a forgotten road through the Sallow Wood; there, she knelt and sang a prayer of thanksgiving.

Now, footsore and hungry, with the sun sliding into the west and dusk coming on faster than she'd like, Étaín wondered what fresh tests lay ahead. When would it end? What did the eerie corpse nailed to a tree portend? Would Njáll—

Grimnir stopped, and so lost was she in her own reverie that she nearly trod upon his heels. His hand dropped to the hilt of his seax, and Étaín heard him mutter a curse. Ahead, she could see the cause of his discomfiture.

They had come suddenly upon a village.

It was small, like most of the forest settlements, a dozen wattle-and-daub buildings arrayed around a crude stone church, the whole surrounded by a ditch and a loose hedge of sharpened stakes. Even at first glance, Étaín could see why they came upon it unawares: no fires burned on the hearths; no dogs barked a warning at their arrival. She could not hear the clangor of the village blacksmith, nor could she hear the chatter of women drawing water at the wells, of children going about their chores, or of men going about theirs. The village was dead.

Grimnir motioned for her to follow. Sunlight slanted through the trees, giving the air beneath an emerald hue that echoed her nightmarish journey under the boughs of Yggðrasil. She shivered and followed him past small fields overgrown with weeds and a pasture with a fence of broken hurdles, now bereft of livestock. Even before they reached the ditch, Étaín could see signs of destruction – burned thatch, charred timber, and blackened stone. The church itself was a shell, roofless and gutted. She wondered if the End of Days *had* taken place, after all.

Grimnir splashed through the shallow water at the bottom of the ditch and pulled himself up through the hedge of stakes, where weeds and sparse grass grew unchecked; Étaín clambered up beside him.

'They make no sound,' Grimnir said, to himself more than to her. He sniffed the air, then crouched and snuffled like an animal. 'Like they've forgotten what they are.'

'Who?'

Grimnir glanced sidelong at her. 'The *landvættir. Bah!* This is your Nailed God's doing.'

'So you've said. What are *landvættir*?'

'Spirits of rock and tree. And in a forest like this, without you lot around to stifle them . . .' Grimnir trailed off.

'And where are "my lot"?' Étaín jerked her chin toward the village.

Grimnir snorted. 'Them? How should I know? This is old work. At least a year, like the bastard nailed to the tree.'

'You're sure?'

Grimnir didn't answer. For some reason, the knowledge that this was the result of human agency and not the work of the Lord eased some of the tension in Étaín's shoulders.

The forest path entered the village and became a street – if she could give such a lofty name to a wide, rutted track lined with huts. It ran to the center of the village, where the church squatted like a stone-browed overlord draped in ivy, before continuing past and out again into the forest. The trees thinned in that direction, which Étaín knew was a good sign they were on the eaves of the wood.

She followed Grimnir in silence as he walked up the road, glancing right and left. His hand never left the pommel of his seax. Midges and lacewings buzzed in the warm air; Étaín's wool habit – meant for a Danish winter – was damp with sweat. She did not pepper him with questions. It did not matter who burned out the village or why; she knew the bodies of the slain would rest in a shallow grave somewhere, and she knew the crucified man was likely the village's elder or its priest. Étaín did not need Grimnir to spell these things out for her.

She stopped and peered into one of the huts. Its thatch was half gone, and nettles had grown up through the packed dirt floor. Whoever destroyed the village had long since ransacked it and looted anything of value. Now, only detritus remained; she saw broken spindles and loom weights, splintered wood from a table, and a scattering of rotted fabric that might have been clothing. Something nearly hidden among the weeds caught her eye. Étaín reached down and pulled it free – it was a delicately carved head belonging to a child's doll, bleached white and faceless. The sight of it, so forlorn and alone, drove a spike of sorrow through her heart. Gently, she put the doll's head back where she'd found it, made the sign of the cross, and said a silent prayer for the villagers who once lived here.

'Foundling,' Grimnir called after her. He had reached the church, a simple construction of local reddish sandstone, poorly cut and mortared into place. It had a rudimentary porch of charred timber and narrow windows, their scorched shutters hanging askew on rusted iron hinges. The door had two holes hacked into it at waist level, a heavy length of chain threaded between and connected by a thick rivet.

Grimnir motioned for her to join him. With a cold ache in the pit of her belly, Étaín mounted the porch and followed his lead. She held the sun-warmed stone and leaned out on the balls of her feet to peer over an ivy-draped windowsill. She knew, then, that she'd been wrong. She would find no shallow grave.

'There's your lot.'

Carpeting the nave and extending back to the church's shadowy chancel were the scorched and broken bones of the villagers. Skulls, rib cages, vertebrae, long bones, finger bones, teeth . . . from the skeleton of an infant tucked in its mother's bony embrace to huddled knots of children to the skulls of men who died from axe blows to the head. Étaín imagined their horrified screams . . .

'This is heathens' work,' she said, looking away. 'No God-fearing man, no matter how desperate or cruel, would dare defile a church like this.'

Grimnir's lips peeled back in a savage grin. 'Good! That gives us a trail. Doubt the bastards came all this way just to sack this little pisshole, so maybe they took a richer prize, eh? Maybe these towns you spoke of? Maybe they're still hanging about . . .'

Étaín shrugged, and then nodded. 'Perhaps,' she said slowly.

'What?'

Étaín looked around. 'Njáll and I . . . we were in Sutton last year, on the border with Cornwall, making ready to sail on a pilgrim boat to the Frankish coast. We heard nothing of any raid, much less one this deep into Wessex. It's just curious, is all.'

'When we find a Dane you can ask him about it,' Grimnir muttered. 'Let's move. We can still go a ways more before nightfall.'

He headed off down the rutted path that would carry them to the forest's eaves. Étaín made to follow, but stopped. Turning back, she surveyed the tiny village. By summer's end it would be little more than a clearing choked with nettle and thorn. Its timbers would rot away in the humid air; its stone foundations would crumble, and the church would fall in on itself to create a cairn over the bones of the dead. What was its name? she wondered. In a way, this place had become like her – an orphan, sundered from its identity, from its history by the cruel knives of Fate.

With a prayer of peace for the restless spirits of the slain, she turned and followed Grimnir.

2

There was no well-defined border to the Sallow Wood; the ancient arboreal giants simply gave way to younger trees that thinned and spread over open hills clad in heather and gorse. Though the land was green and idyllic, Étaín spied the telltale signs of war: groves and hedges hacked and burned, fields left fallow, small villages and halls like the skeletal corpses of the fallen, picked clean by rapacious scavengers. A smear of smoke rose some miles distant, a thin black veil against the ruddy face of the setting sun.

'No, this is wrong,' Étaín said, shading her eyes and staring at the smoke. 'This is more than a raid. This reeks of war, and we would have heard of it in Sutton. Deserters, refugees, someone would have brought word. Christ! We would have heard about something like this in the Danemark!'

The trail leading out of the forest joined a rutted track that came up from the south; it bore upon it the signs of heavy use – not just wagons, but that peculiar churning of the earth that marked the passage of horsemen.

'Aye. Aye, but we're in it now, eh?' said Grimnir, rising from a crouch. 'We're getting off this miserable road until we know the tale of things. Wouldn't do to get skewered by a pack of horseboys, would it?'

Sharp-eyed, Grimnir led the way across the countryside

toward the rising smoke. They skirted hilltops and ridges, keeping instead to the twilit hollows and valleys where already a chill mist was forming; they came across a fast-moving stream with a deep and rocky bed, swollen with springtime runoff, which ran in the same direction they were headed – ever north and west.

Bone weary, Étaín staggered after him. Her mind was numb, her limbs leaden; the sweat-damp wool of her robe left her shivering, and a gnawing ache in her stomach reminded her she'd not eaten since snatching a handful of berries at midday. She ran on pure will. Even that, however, had its limits. Étaín stumbled in the deepening gloom and came up hard against a knotted oak; coughing, she slid to the ground.

How long she sat there, she could not say. It might have been a moment, only; or it might have been an hour. Regardless, the next sound she was aware of was Grimnir's harsh whisper in her ear.

'Up, my tender little fool,' he said. 'This is no place for a nap. I've scouted ahead. A bit further and then you can rest.'

Nodding, Étaín struggled to her feet. Grimnir caught her by the upper arm and loped along beside her – guiding her, prodding her, even dragging her when need be. Soon, she felt the cold shock of water splashing about her calves. Shaking off her stupor, Étaín glanced around and tried to recall how long it had been since night had fallen.

Grimnir half-carried her across the stream, at a shallow ford where the water splashed into a stone-lined channel. On the far bank, lit by an orange glow that seeped over the low hillside, she could see the squat shape of a ruined mill, its wheel long since rotted away; it was an ancient structure whose foundation stones bore the tool marks of dead and forgotten craftsmen. Grimnir helped her onto dry ground, near the mill.

107

The land along the stream was overgrown: tall willows stood sentinel over a riot of thorn and honeysuckle; reeds clogged the mill channel. A footpath led up to the crest of the hill, where the rambling silhouette of a ruined villa stood, limned by distant fire. Sounds came from the far side of the hill: a cacophony of horses and men, brazen horns and pounding drums, shouted orders and screams of rage.

Grimnir motioned for Étaín to follow as he ascended the footpath, taking care in those places where the archaic cobblestones peeked through the weeds, rounded and gleaming with moisture. Oily light pierced the heart of the villa, which was little more than a few crumbling stone walls clad in ivy and broken columns holding up the memory of a roof, several generations gone to rot. In places, Étaín could still make out where a veneer of fine plaster covered the stone, and underfoot – beneath the mud, decayed wood, and leaf mold – she caught glimpses of wondrously colorful pebbled mosaics. In Grimnir's wake, she crept through the heart of the ruined villa to where the front gate must once have stood. An empty archway that opened now on the belly of Hell.

Raging bonfires lit the smoke-clouded night sky as hundreds of men converged on a town sitting on an island in the middle of a shallow river – one that the stream they had crossed was tributary to. Earthworks and a scarred palisade protected the muddy banks of the island, and a second palisade rose beyond that; inside, houses with fresh-thatched roofs and gabled halls clustered around a burned-out church. Men and women alike defended the town's outer palisade.

A volley of flaming arrows lofted skyward, arching over both palisades to strike inside the town, setting thatch to smoldering – that smoke adding to the choking miasma of mud, unwashed bodies, piss, blood, and rotting excrement. A desultory flight of javelins and arrows answered the volley.

'Do you know this place?' Grimnir said, looking sidelong at Étaín.

She shrugged. 'I can't be sure . . .' She racked her brain for the name of this well-fortified island town; only one came to mind. 'This is Nunna's Ford, I think. We're west and a bit south of the forest.'

Grimnir grunted. 'Fight's almost over.'

The besiegers – mailed soldiers fighting under a banner displaying, as far as Étaín could discern, a white willow tree on a black field – concentrated all their efforts on the sagging gates of Nunna's Ford. A troop of brawny men, stripped to the waist, caught up a ram made from logs banded in iron and set off for the gates. Others bearing shields trotted alongside them, offering a measure of protection from the defenders' javelins. Companies of fighters massed behind, ready to surge forward. From the slight height advantage they had on the hilltop, Grimnir and Étaín could see that the defenders, too, were making ready for the final spear-shattering.

A woman's voice rose over the din. The attackers paused in their efforts so they might listen to her song – a song that was familiar to Étaín, in a tongue she spoke fluently:

> Lo, I see here our fathers and mothers.
> Lo, now I see our sisters and our brothers.
> Lo, here is my husband, who is standing at the
>   doors of Valhalla.
> With him stand the Einherjar, who await Ragnarok.
> He calls to me, so let me go to him.
> Lo, do I see the daughters of Odin, the Choosers
>   of the Slain!

The silence held for a moment before the clamor and clangor of the siege resumed.

'They're Danes,' Étaín said, unable to believe what she'd heard. 'The people inside Nunna's Ford are Danes!'

'They came last year,' a voice behind them said. Quick as a snake, Grimnir twisted, drawing his seax in the same motion; for a heartbeat, Étaín saw a starveling Saxon standing there, his young face pale and thin. A few wisps of blond hair struggled to take root on the point of his chin. Then the youth recoiled, as much from the sight of naked steel as from the blazing red eyes and bared fangs of the one holding it. 'Almighty Christ!' was all he had time to say before Grimnir's fingers wrapped around his throat.

Grimnir slammed the young Saxon against the wall; a homemade shank of sharpened deer antler slipped from the lad's grasp and clattered to the ground. He glanced down at it, then fixed the youth with a murderous stare. 'Little fool!'

'Wait!' Étaín said. She hurried to Grimnir's side. 'Who came last year? Let him speak. Who came last year?'

Grimnir loosened his grip on the boy's throat a fraction. 'Answer her!'

'D-Danes,' he gasped. 'Forkbeard's army. They came last year and drove King Æthelred away. This lot took Nunna's Ford, killed my da and shamed my ma. Not seen my sisters since.'

'Svein Forkbeard?' Étaín said. 'The king of the Danes? Impossible! He was quarreling with the king of Norway, last year!'

'Well, he was quarreling with the king of Wessex, too!' the lad said. 'Got his dander up a few years back after Æthelred killed his sister and every other fucking Dane in Wessex on Saint Brice's Day. The lot of them deserved it,

110

I'd say! Evil bastards and Forkbeard's the worst! May God rot his bones!'

Étaín scowled. She started to speak, but Grimnir cut her off.

'Is Half-Dane with him?'

The young Saxon shrugged, looking at a loss.

Grimnir tightened his grip on the Saxon's throat. 'I said, is Half-Dane with him, you milk-blooded maggot?'

The lad's face purpled. 'N-Never . . . never heard of . . . h-him . . .'

Étaín tugged at Grimnir's arm. 'Perhaps King Forkbeard reached an accord with King Olaf; they are both good Christians, and both would not easily forgive Half-Dane's betrayal,' she said. 'He might be an outlaw among his own people.'

With a snarl, Grimnir turned the young Saxon loose. 'Makes sense,' he admitted, but grudgingly.

The lad stared at them, rubbing his throat. His eyes narrowed to slits brimming with suspicion. 'What game are you playing at? King Olaf? He was killed years ago. My ma always said his death was the work of the Devil.'

Étaín and Grimnir exchanged glances. She looked at the lad like he was addled. 'Olaf Tryggve's son is not dead,' she said.

'Go on!' the Saxon replied. 'The heathens killed him at Svolder, the same year my ma said I was born. The Great Year.'

'That . . . That c-can't be,' stammered Étaín. 'The Great Year . . . this . . . *this* is the Great Year . . .' The color leached from her face as surely as if she had taken a knife and opened an artery. By her reckoning, this was the spring of what the abbot of Eynsham had called the Great Year – *anno Domini* 1000, the End of Days, when the Lord was set to return. With a trembling hand she crossed herself. 'Jesus, Mary, and Joseph!'

'What?' Grimnir said.

But Étaín didn't hear him. She paced back and forth, agitated. 'It makes sense. Impossible, God-forsaken sense. The devastation, why nothing he says is familiar . . . God preserve me!' She clasped her hands together, afraid to ask the next question. Afraid the boy's answer would confirm her as either damned or insane. 'What . . . What year *is* it, now?'

The young Saxon almost chuckled, but a look from Grimnir wiped the smile from his lips.

'What year?'

'The priests say it's the year of our Lord one thousand and fourteen.' The Saxon crossed himself, as well.

Étaín expected rage from Grimnir. She expected a black tirade of curses and threats ending in yet another display of violence; with Grimnir's vengeance denied once more, she was certain the young Saxon had breathed his last with those words. But the *skrælingr* simply released him. The youth slid to the floor, rubbing his bruised throat, as Grimnir turned away.

Étaín sank down on her knees. She felt sick. 'Fifteen years? In less than a day? How is that possible? How—?'

Grimnir hissed her to silence. He muttered under his breath in the tongue of his people, a harsh and guttural language, before slipping back into the speech of the Danes. '. . . must be what Gífr meant, that poxy bastard. He never could speak plain. *Time* has no meaning across the branches of Yggðrasil. Time! A day, a week, a month? What of it? Time means nothing between the worlds.'

'We could go back to Heathen's Howe,' Étaín said. 'Go back and reenter the doorway . . . you remember the words the dwarf used to open it, surely? We could return to the Danemark.'

112

Grimnir laughed. 'Oh, aye! And what happens when we find ourselves a hundred years out of sorts, eh? *Nár!* I'll take what we've got and thank the Sly One for it. But if that wretch Half-Dane still dwells in Wessex after fifteen years I'll kneel to your Nailed God.' He walked to the door and stared out at the siege, his eyes blazing as bright as the fires below.

Étaín thought of Njáll – injured and alone. Had he survived? Had he come for her? Had he searched high and low, year after year, and finally given her up for dead? Étaín's heart ached for her Danish friend, so much like the husband and protector she always wanted but never had in her old life. Tears coursed down her cheeks as she bowed her head and prayed. 'Our Father, who art in Heaven, hallowed be Thy name . . .'

3

Forgotten for the moment, the young Saxon gingerly massaged his neck, dabbing at the welling blood drawn by the beast's black-nailed claws. He glared at the pair of them; there was hatred in his eyes, cold and malicious, as he quietly got his feet beneath him. He made only the barest hint of a sound as he backed away, retracing his steps. This was his ground, his element. He was a skulker. And he knew exactly how to make this Dane-loving bitch and her demon pay. Smiling, the lad faded into the shadows.

4

It was the faint crunch of a rotting tile beneath his heel that gave the Saxon away. Grimnir whirled, snarling a curse. Before he could stop him, the whelp hared off into the night.

'Spies!' he bawled at the top of his lungs. 'Spies! Danes in the ruin!'

The Saxon's cry echoed even over the tumult of the siege. It reached the camp of the army attacking Nunna's Ford, well back from the lines and nestled at the foot of the hill, where those not engaged in battering down the walls of the town took their leisure. Wounded soldiers heard the warning and added their own voices to it; it spread to the camp followers, to the sutlers and the whores, the blacksmiths and the fletchers, who added their shouts to the din.

'Danes in the ruin!'

Gimlet-eyed, Grimnir saw soldiers turning. He saw their captain, a hard-looking bastard with a beard like rust, twist in the saddle; the man gestured to a green-cloaked lieutenant, a rawboned man clad in the leather-and-mail of a Welsh prince. Nodding, he cantered over to the few rogues held in reserve – men chafing for some measure of glory. After a bit of jostling, Grimnir watched a score of torch-bearing West Saxons, mounted and on foot, peel off from the reserves and follow their lieutenant up the hill.

Grimnir hawked a mouthful of phlegm and spat. He rasped his seax back and forth in its scabbard and rolled the kinks from his shoulders. 'Off your knees, foundling,' he snarled. 'Time to leg it, and quick!'

5

Étaín did not move. She did not react to the young Saxon's flight, nor to Grimnir's warning; she paid no heed to the jingle of harness and the shouts of the men charging up the hill at them. She remained there on her knees in the flickering orange glow of bonfires – her head bowed, her eyes closed, and her voice a low murmur as she continued with her prayers.

'It'll be close but if we skin out now we can make it back across the stream before that rabble reaches us.' Grimnir hurried past, snatching at the shoulder of her habit.

Étaín shook him off. She didn't look at him, didn't rise and follow; instead, she settled back on her knees and resumed praying.

Grimnir stopped and glared at her. 'No time for games, little fool!' He grabbed her again, this time by the scruff. 'Let's go, I said!'

Étaín came roaring off her knees. She shoved Grimnir away, punching him in his mailed chest. 'Then go, God damn you. Go! Run, you miserable bastard! I'm done with you!'

The vehemence in her voice stunned even Grimnir. He blinked, staring at her through slitted eyes as if truly seeing her for the first time. 'Those whiteskins are out for blood,' he said slowly. 'Looking for a pair of Danes. We—'

'Then what do I have to fear?' Étaín replied. 'I am no Dane. I am West Saxon, you fool. Wipe that snarl off your face! What are you going to do? Kill me? Then have at it!' She bared her throat to him. 'Draw your blade and end this wretched hell you've dragged me into! Everything I've ever known and loved is a thousand miles and fifteen years in the past. Because of you, you miserable bastard! You and your insane quest to kill some other miserable bastard I've never heard of. Well, God damn you and your revenge! Kill me, if that's your answer! Strike me down and have done! No? Then run!' Étaín shoved him, again. 'Run, little goblin! Run and find a hole to hide in! Join your wretched kin in the shadows!'

Wrath blazed in Grimnir's eyes. He took a step toward her, but Étaín didn't flinch; her ice-blue gaze gave back the same measure of heat. His lips curled in a snarl of hate, and slowly he leaned forward and spat at her feet.

'Good riddance, foundling,' he hissed. 'But remember this: when you tell them how much of a West Saxon you are, make sure your Danish accent doesn't betray you, eh?' And Grimnir bared his teeth as the slightest flicker of apprehension creased her forehead.

Outside the ruin, men shouted; mail clashed and hooves thudded, tearing at the earth. The soldiers were close, now. Étaín stiffened, her eyes drawn by a torch, slung by a horseman, arching over the wall of the ruined villa. It struck the mosaicked floor in an explosion of embers. She turned back . . .

Grimnir was gone.

Étaín nodded. *And good riddance to him, too.* She smoothed her filthy habit as she exhaled and conjured forth the spirit of good Brother Aidan – Aidan of Wessex, who vanished fifteen years ago on the road to Roskilde, on a pilgrimage to convert the heathen. She exhaled. Étaín wished for a psalter and a crucifix, some banner to uphold so the good Christians out there would recognize her instantly as one of their own. She had nothing. Not even a cross around her neck.

It will surely be enough if I but put my trust in the Lord. The Almighty will provide a way.

Étaín drew up her hood, squared her shoulders, and walked out the front of the villa with all the confidence of a priest shielded by the armor of faith. Soldiers pounded up the slope – Saxons in corselets of leather and mail, their trousers dull and filthy, with horsemen cantering along their flanks. They shouted at one another, a cacophony of voices she could not precisely understand.

Étaín crossed herself. 'Good men of Wessex!' she shouted, raising her arms to get their attention. 'Hear me!' The green-cloaked lieutenant spurred his mount forward; he cut across the front, thundering straight for her with his sword drawn. She fought down the urge to flee. 'Hear me, I said!'

'Shut your mouth, Danish scum!' the horseman roared. He swung at Étaín, who danced away from the blow.

'Wait!'

The horseman spun his mount and leveled his sword at her. 'Take him alive! Search the ruin! The boy said there were two of them!'

'Listen to me, please!' Étaín held her arms up, imploring the horseman's attention. She didn't see the foot soldiers charging up behind her. She didn't see one of them swinging the butt of his spear like a club. 'Please—'

'Danish bastard!' The haft of one soldier's spear cracked across Étaín's shoulders. She screamed in pain, twisting away from the blow. A second spear butt caught her along the base of the skull. She stumbled forward, her vision awash in blood-tinged spots of light.

'D-don't . . . p-please . . .'

The last blow was the lieutenant's boot. His heel smashed into her forehead, dropping her like a marionette with its strings cut.

6

Grimnir bolted out the back of the villa. With every skidding step down the ancient path to the stream, he cursed under his breath. 'Old fool. Soft in the head, is what you are. Should have just grabbed her up . . . hauled her out of there like a sack of barley!'

Grimnir hesitated on the banks of the ford alongside the mill. He swore and spat. 'Ymir's blood!' This unaccustomed dithering, he told himself, had nothing to do with any great sense of loyalty he felt toward Étaín, nor did it come from any concern for her plight. No, the little wretch could rot in her Nailed God's hell for all he cared. But he still needed someone who knew their way around this godforsaken pisshole of a country, and that meant going back for his wayward hymn-singer. Grimnir swore again. He unconsciously clenched and unclenched his clawed fist as he weighed his options . . .

Suddenly, he glared back at the villa, baring his teeth in a reckless grin. 'I am no old woman, to run and hide from trouble. That little fool is mine! Let those milk-blooded Saxon whoresons try and take her from me.' All hesitation vanished. He spun round and had taken three bounding steps back up the path when the question became moot: a horseman, the green-cloaked lieutenant, barreled around the corner of the ruin.

Quick as a fox, Grimnir dropped to a crouch and scuttled into the undergrowth alongside the path. Even still, the horse caught his scent; the creature shied, ears flattened in fear. Grimnir's slitted eyes gleamed like embers in the darkness as he watched the rider struggle to control his mount.

A dozen or more Saxons boiled out of the ruin and around the far side – hard-looking men eager for a fight, bearing torch and sword or taut-stringed bows. 'He's not inside!' one of them hollered.

'Fan out,' the rider said, gesturing with his torch. He was no Welshman, after all, but a dark-haired Saxon, his unkempt beard threaded with silver. 'Wulfric! Can you track him?'

'Aye, Cynewulf.' A leather-clad archer stepped to the fore, older than the others, his body thin as whipcord and knotted with gristle. He handed off his bow and took a guttering torch from one of the other soldiers. 'The rest of you little bastards stand ready. I'll flush this whoreson out,' he said.

Grimnir watched as this man, Wulfric, read the damp ground; he knew what he would see: churned earth, bent grass, the spoor of Étaín's slender foot alongside his own heavier sandal prints. Grimnir hoped the man was not much use as a tracker, but he recognized patience; saw the Saxon's brow furrow as he let the ground tell the tale. Wulfric was a hunter. Grimnir breathed a foul oath as he drew near.

'He's a big sheep-fucker, this Dane,' Wulfric muttered. A spear's length from Grimnir's hiding place, he crouched and touched a print in the loam with his free hand, studying its outline in the greasy light of his torch. 'Long stride, heavy.'

Unseen, Grimnir tensed, lips peeling back in a snarl. He dropped his hand to the hilt of his seax.

Wulfric stood. He raised his torch, peering into the undergrowth. 'He came this way! If the Almighty be with us—'

Grimnir did not give him a chance to finish. With a blood-chilling howl, he burst out from the foliage; his seax hissed from its scabbard. Driven by muscles of spring steel and twisted iron, the blade crunched through Wulfric's wrist on the upswing. The Saxon screamed as hand and torch spun away. Before he could react, Grimnir stepped in and drove a balled fist into his sternum. Bone shattered. The blow crushed Wulfric's chest like a mace; he hit the ground a corpse, body crumpling into a lanky heap. His fallen torch struck the damp earth and snuffed itself out in an explosion of sparks. Grimnir faded away in the sudden darkness.

Cynewulf bellowed a warning. Bowstrings twanged. Grimnir, whose eyes were better suited to worlds of gloom and shadow, watched their arrows fly wide of the mark. Saxons charged down the path, their torches flaring. He retreated from the circles of light until the waters of the ford lapped at his ankles. He considered creeping into the ruined mill – that edifice squatting like a mossy stone toad to his left – but thought better of it. Too easily could it turn from trap to tomb. No, he needed room to move. Wraithlike, making barely a sound above the splashing water, Grimnir disappeared back across the ford.

7

The darkness exploded with agonizing jags of orange light, each one a hot knife that pierced Étaín's eyes and buried itself in her skull. She felt hands on her, rough and callused; hands that hurled her down upon the churned earth, the cold mud reeking with the fetid stench of rot and human waste. Étaín vomited. She rolled on her back and pried her eyes open; soldiers surrounded her, Saxons whose dull and vicious expressions reflected only the basest desires of the soul. They were angry; they wanted joints of beef, tankards of ale, and some golden-haired Danish whores to service them. They wanted to live, fight, fuck, and loot before going home to toil again under their lord's lash. Étaín saw all this in their faces, in the eyes that glared at her with unvarnished hate.

She screamed as they reached for her; with pitiless laughter, they stripped away her cowl and her habit, leaving her shivering in only a threadbare linen shirt.

'Damn my eyes!' a voice growled, as feral as a dog. 'It's a woman!'

'Lord works in mysterious ways, huh?' More laughter erupted. Someone kicked her in the belly, flipping her onto her back. Hands groped her. 'And a right fetching little Danish minx, at that, for all that she looks like a boy.'

Étaín tried to crawl away, but a man's foot pressed to

her shoulder shoved her back into the circle of soldiers. Despairing of escape, she pulled herself up and onto her knees, clasping her hands together. Her vision blurred. She was unable to focus; the whole of her head felt swollen, bruised, and inflamed. Still, she found her voice.

'O C-Christ the Redeemer,' she said in the tongue of the West Saxons; her throat was so dry that the words crackled like tinder. 'Remember the horror and sadness, th-the spiteful words and harsh torments, which your enemies afflicted upon you. I beseech you, Lord Jesus, to deliver me from all my enemies visible and invisible, and to bring me under your protection to the perfection of eternal salvation. Amen.'

The men around her fell silent. They glanced at one another, suddenly unsure. For most of them it was one thing to despoil a heathen, but to do the same to a sister in Christ smacked of mortal sin. They looked beyond their circle to where another man stood with his back to them, watching the final moments of the siege.

'She ain't no heathen, Captain,' one of the soldiers said.

'Is she not?' The captain turned. He was tall and well-built, broad across his mail-clad shoulders. Gray flecked his rust-colored beard. His fine cloak was war-stained and fringed with ermine; he fingered a heavy silver crucifix that lay upon his breast. 'Perhaps she is but a good liar.' He came closer, looking her over like a merchant sizing up a bale of wares. '*Verbum mendax iustus detestabitur—*'

'*—impius confundit et . . . et c-confundetur,*' Étaín finished for him.

The captain's eyebrows inched up. 'You're familiar with the Proverbs of King Solomon, then? Impressive, especially for a woman.' He gathered his cloak about him and crouched near her. 'What is your name?'

'É-Étaín.'

'We are in a bit of a predicament, Étaín,' the captain said. 'For all that these dogs appear to be Hell's own wastrels, they are actually a pious and God-fearing lot. I've given them leave to have their way with any heathen whore they should happen across, but upon pain of death they're not to despoil good Christian women. Thus, here is our quandary.' The captain gestured over his shoulder, beyond the circle of men, to where a grizzled sergeant held the Saxon lad by the scruff of his neck. 'That boy claims you're a Dane, one of a pair of spies. Worse, he claims you're a witch in league with Satan, himself. But, your manner and your prayers confuse us. Which is it, Étaín? Are you a spy? Are you a witch out to guile us?'

The ring of soldiers drew in, tightening the circle around her. She looked up at the captain and fervently wished she'd kept her head down. His features swam; a nimbus of light surrounded him, a muddy red glow shot through with black. Étaín squeezed her eyes shut. 'I'm . . . I'm n-neither.'

'Ah, then he bears false witness? That is an affront to God.' The captain nodded to the man holding the young Saxon. 'Kill him.'

A knife flashed in the firelight; the boy screamed. Étaín started forward to grasp at the captain's boot. 'No!'

The captain held up a hand, arresting the lad's execution. 'Then he speaks the truth in naming you a witch and a spy for the Danes?'

'He . . . He does not.'

'My dear Étaín,' the captain said, raising his voice over the mutters of disbelief coming from his soldiers. 'The truth may have many sides and many facets, but it cannot be both true *and* false.'

Slowly, Étaín shook her head. 'It . . . It is a c-complex story . . .'

126

'Then explain it to me. Why were you hiding in the ruin? If you are neither spy nor witch, then why did you run from my men?'

'I didn't.' She cradled her bloody face. 'Ask . . . Ask the one who did this if I ran from him.'

Her honesty wrong-footed the captain. He started to speak, but then clamped his mouth shut as a messenger from Nunna's Ford barreled into their midst – a wild-eyed youth clinging to the back of a flyblown nag.

'My lord, the gate's about to give!'

The news galvanized the Saxons; the captain stood. 'Make ready, lads! Time to crush this foreign rabble under heel! Has Cynewulf returned? No? Ah, he must be on the trail of her confederate! May God smile upon Brother Cynewulf and his hunters!' The Saxons cheered their captain.

Étaín felt the world tilting beneath her; her vision clouded, and the buzzing of voices in her mind became a screaming tumult of noise – howls, cries, shrieks, curses. She clutched her skull and toppled onto her side, instinctively curling into a ball.

'What about her?' a Saxon muttered. 'Do we wait for Cynewulf to return with the other one and execute them both at once, or might the lads have a bit of sport, first?'

Étaín heard the captain suck his teeth. 'No,' he said after a moment. 'Put her on a wagon and watch her close. We'll take her back to Badon with us. Lord Hrothmund demands tribute in heathen flesh and he has a special fondness for traitors.'

The captain's boots squelched in the muck as he turned and ordered his men forward. She felt hands lift her, again – this time more gently than before. She felt a sense of pity emanating from them. Pity and fear. 'Lord Hrothmund?'

one man muttered. 'Best kill her now, no matter her crimes.'

After that, the blackness rose up and Étaín knew no more.

8

The sky above glowed brighter as the town of Nunna's Ford burned, throwing the ruins into sharp silhouette; screams filtered over the crown of the hill and down to the stream bank. Grimnir's keen ears picked out faint cries of triumph mingled with pleas for mercy. But the miasma of thatch smoke and roasting flesh filling his nostrils told him there would be none.

Shielded by bulrushes and willow fronds, Grimnir crouched and watched his Saxon enemies. The man called Cynewulf had dismounted and now knelt by the body of Wulfric.

'Find me this God-forsaken Dane!'

He dispatched a trio of soldiers to search the mill while the rest of his men crept carefully through the undergrowth on both sides of the path. Cynewulf himself walked slowly to the water's edge. His eyes raked the far bank.

Aye, he's a smart one, Grimnir thought. *Too smart by far. The swine knows someone's watching him.*

'*Hej!*' Cynewulf called out suddenly in the tongue of the Danes. '*Hey!*' His Saxons started at the sound, but Cynewulf silenced their growing clamor with a sharp word. He returned his gaze to the far bank. 'Can you hear me? I know you're there, Dane. Wulfric, the man you killed . . .

129

he was my cousin. I demand weregild. Show yourself, and let us settle this like men.'

Grimnir gave a low chuckle. He barely raised his voice, so that it reached the soldiers' ears no louder than a silky whisper. '*Nár!* An old ruse, Saxon. Get me out in the open so your lads can stick me full of arrows.'

'It's no ruse.' Cynewulf turned to his men. 'Put your bows down. Put them down!' Nervously, his Saxons complied. 'See? I only wish to talk.'

'Fetch me the girl, then,' Grimnir said. He moved slightly, setting the bulrushes to rustling. Cynewulf turned toward the sound. 'She belongs to me. Fetch her back here and maybe we can parley.'

'The girl? What girl?'

'The one you captured.'

'You mean the other spy? I did not know it was a woman. No, Dane . . . she is beyond both our grasps, now.'

'You killed her?' There was a dangerous edge to Grimnir's voice.

'Not I. I merely seized her and sent her on to my captain, Lord Æthelstan. No doubt he will question her and give her to the men for sport. Once they have had their fill of her, they will add her body to the pyre of heathens, Dane.' Cynewulf indicated the sky behind them, thunderheads of smoke lit from beneath by the light of a burning village. 'The question now is what do we do with you, eh?'

Grimnir snarled and spat. 'Me? I go my way, little fool.'

'Look around and tell me who is the fool, Dane!' Cynewulf said. 'Your people are gone. You have no ships. Your village will be nothing but ash and burned timber by dawn. Where do you think you will go? I know this land like I know my wife's thighs. Hide and I will ferret you out.

Come; surrender yourself to me, Dane. Upon my word, I will make your end quick – as quick as poor Wulfric's.'

'Your word?' Grimnir felt rage build inside him. He drew upon it, tendrils of white-hot fire that crawled through his muscles. He ground his teeth, tasting blood. 'Your word means nothing to me, filthy wretch! I said I go my own way. Stop me, if you've got the balls to try. As for your weregild . . .' Grimnir drew a small leather bag from beneath his armor and slung it across to the far bank. It struck near Cynewulf's foot, the faint tinkle of coins like an unspoken taunt.

Willow fronds rustled as Grimnir backed away from the bank, a silhouette moving through deeper shadow. A few of the Saxons raised their bows. They scanned the darkness, sensing the overhanging trees and thickets of bulrushes, starting at each noise. He did not present them with a target. As he crept away, he heard the echo of Cynewulf's voice:

'Dane! Why make this more difficult than it need be? Dane? DANE?'

9

Cynewulf stood for a long moment, staring out into the darkness at the far bank of the stream. He had been a soldier all his life, first with his father in the wars against the Welsh and later as one of Lord Æthelstan's lieutenants against the invading Danes. He had known pain, deprivation, hunger, fear – not fear of death, for he was right with God; but rather, fear of capture and torture. He knew what that sort of fear tasted like, how it smelled, how it wormed its way into a man's guts and turned his bowels to water. What's more, he knew how to conjure it in other men. He would make this God-cursed Dane's last hours an exercise in terror. *That* would be the blood price for poor Wulfric.

And after he had wrung every exquisite ounce of terror from him, Cynewulf would kill the Dane, slowly . . .

The Saxon chief smoothed his tangled beard. 'Gather round, lads. How many of you have ever hunted a Welsh boar?'

10

Grimnir was near enough to hear those wretched swine cross the ford; near enough that he could see two knots of torches, one heading left and the other right – motes of ruddy light flickering through the leaves, accompanied by the jangle of harness and the snapping of undergrowth. Neither group of Saxons made any effort to muffle their passage. Beaters, Grimnir reckoned, a sneer curling his lips, meant to flush him out into the open.

Grimnir's nostrils flared as he exhaled, creating the faintest snort of derision. A good plan . . . if he were fool enough to run around these unfamiliar woods like the half-witted Dane they thought he was. No, in his long years he had slipped many a noose, laid by far more fearsome hunters than these. With apish strength, he caught the lower limb of a mighty oak near the game trail leading to the stream and hauled himself up into the thick foliage; there, he perched like a raptor, waiting.

Grimnir's slitted eyes raked the darkness between the two knots of men. It was as quiet as a tomb, save for the occasional rustle of leaves that could have marked the passage of some night creature. The limb beneath him vibrated slightly; he felt faint stirrings of revulsion emanating from the *landvættir,* from the spirit of the oak – a sensation that was distant and confused, reminding

Grimnir of an aging lord waking on his deathbed only to discover a rat in his beard.

'*The oathbreaker* . . .' moaned the spirit of the oak.

He patted its trunk in mock sympathy. 'Go back to sleep, little acorn. I will be gone soon enough.'

Movement caught Grimnir's eye. He peered closer, flashing a humorless smile at the four figures he spied creeping through the night. Grudgingly, he admired their stealth. Cynewulf and the three Saxons who followed him had divested themselves of cloaks, belts, and scabbards. No loose metal clashed on their persons; Cynewulf and another carried spears in their hands, the bright steel heads dulled by a layer of mud, while the other two moved with bows ready, arrows on the nock and half drawn.

Making scarcely a sound, they passed Grimnir's hiding place, unaware that he perched not even a spear's length above their heads. He heard their shallow breaths, smelled their rank sweat. They were night-blind and Grimnir knew it, each man dreading the feel of cold fingers about his throat, fearing the bite of iron. They drew strength from the knowledge that they were many while their enemy was alone – in their minds he could not possibly kill them all. Grimnir let them pass, and the four men continued on another fifty yards to a clearing, thick with fern and brambles, where he lost sight of them.

Grimnir gave no thought to simply slipping away, which he could have done with ease; no, Cynewulf had chosen to make this about a kin-slaying, which his own people took seriously. If the tables were turned, Grimnir would hound him until the blood price was paid – even as he now hounded Bjarki Half-Dane. Best to end it here. But how? Grimnir mulled the question over in his mind. If he attacked these four head-on, the other Saxons trampling around the edges could stand off and put arrows in his gullet. What he needed was one of their bows. He needed to blind them, to rid them of their cursed flaming brands. He needed to thin their ranks and make them fear the dark, once more.

A savage gleam kindled behind Grimnir's eyes. He dropped from his roost as lightly as an owl upon its prey and stalked away to the left. He pursued the first knot of torch-bearing Saxons, making no more noise than a breath of wind across the grave.

Cynewulf knelt in the tall grass of the clearing. Overhead, stars gleamed through rips in the smoke and clouds, shining down upon the earth like the lights of Heaven. Torches flickered in the distance, their ruddy glow illuminating leaf and bole as his soldiers beat the brush, looking for the Dane. If all went as planned, their raucous search would hinder the bastard's escape and drive him back toward the stream . . . and onto the steel of Cynewulf and his three companions, men he knew from the border wars with the Welsh. The Saxon chief felt these battle-hardened veterans behind him, arrayed in a loose circle and facing outward; in this way, each man's flanks and back were protected – arrows poised and spears at the ready. All that remained for them to do was wait.

Taking slow, measured breaths, Cynewulf cocked his head to the side and listened to the sounds of the forest: the intermittent *craak* of insects, the faint rustle of leaves high in the trees; he listened for the heavy noise of a body moving through the ferns, for the snap of a twig, or the scuff of a foot on a gnarled root. He strained to hear the rustle of cloth or the thump of a scabbard against a man's hip or the creak of a leather belt. It did him no good to sniff the night air, for the reek of the siege and the miasma of burning thatch yet filled his nostrils. Nor did Cynewulf place much stock in what he could see, for it was as dark as a tomb beneath those trees, and even in the clearing he could barely spot his fingers flapping in front of his face; no, he would hear any Dane long before he could see or smell him.

One of his veterans shifted his weight and touched Cynewulf's left biceps. The Saxon chief turned in that direction in time to see one of the distant torches wink out. There had been four when they crossed the stream; now there were only two. The sounds of a commotion reached his ears, voices raised in alarm. 'He's here!' 'Look out, Eomer! Behind you!' 'Watch—!' A strangled cry as the third torch wavered and blinked out of existence, leaving a single mote of light on the left flank. It burned for but a moment before it, too, was extinguished. A terror-filled scream echoed across the forest, ending in a wet gurgle . . .

The three men around him tensed, eager and ready to move. A hiss from Cynewulf forestalled them. Instead, they watched the half-dozen men stream in from the right flank, their own torches bobbing as they hurried to the aid of their comrades. Cynewulf saw their silhouettes reach the left flankers; he saw a man kneel down as though in prayer. Jags of light flickered from drawn swords as they milled about.

'Cynewulf!' a man called out, a tinge of desperation in his voice. He held a torch on high. 'Cynewulf? Are you there? They're all dead!' The Saxon chief had to bite his lip to keep from bellowing out a reply. 'Cyne – !'

There came a thudding sound, like a cleaver striking a haunch of beef, and the silhouette crumpled; his torch flared before the darkness swallowed it up. Once more, the left flank erupted in a chaos of flickering torchlight, shouts of alarm, and bloodcurdling screams. Steel clashed and rang. Cynewulf could feel his killers straining to be let

137

loose, like hounds scenting blood, but still he held them back. He was wary. Let the Dane exhaust himself, first. He –

Suddenly, Cynewulf heard one voice cry out above the others: 'Almighty G-God! What . . . What are you?'

Laughter answered him – laughter as cold and cruel as a serpent's hiss – punctuated by the drawn-out scream of the soldier. And then, silence.

'What the devil was that?' the veteran to his left whispered. His face was a pallid smear in the night. 'This cannot be the work of one Dane.'

Cynewulf's reply came no louder than an exhalation. 'Steady.' He strained to hear what he could not see. Eleven men had gone silent. Had they stumbled into a trap? Did the Dane have a band of confederates, in truth? A part of him thought about ordering his men to withdraw – Wulfric's weregild be damned – but his veterans would never obey such an order. They were vengeance-minded, now; blood called out for blood. 'Let's move.'

Keeping in a low crouch and moving slowly, Cynewulf led his trio of warriors toward the left flank. Ruddy light flared. Cynewulf stopped, eyes averted from the unexpected glare. A fallen torch must have kindled a bit of dry brush . . . or so he hoped. Surely their enemy could not see them?

Something moved, and by that meager light Cynewulf watched a silhouette rise up and stagger toward them. It was man-high, broad, and it gleamed as though slathered in blood; it clutched a notched sword in one hand and a severed head in the other, and as it came closer it gave forth an eerie moan.

'There!' cried the veteran to Cynewulf's left. In one fluid motion, he stood, drew his nocked arrow to his ear, and loosed. The second archer's shaft was barely a heartbeat behind the first. Both razor-tipped darts flew straight, striking the sinister figure dead center. It pitched back, arms flailing, and for a single heartbeat Cynewulf discerned a Saxon face, eyes gouged out and blood dribbling from a slit tongue . . .

Cynewulf knew it was a trap; he turned, ready to warn his men, even as an answering arrow hissed past his ear and tore through the first archer's throat. He spun and stumbled, blood spraying from his severed jugular. The second archer snatched a fresh shaft from his quiver bag; he no more than touched it to the string when another dart hissed from the darkness. It caught him a hair's breadth above his left eye, the broad iron head slicing through flesh and heavy bone to pierce the soft gray curds of his brain. He dropped like a rag doll.

Cynewulf cursed. He leapt the fallen body and caught the last veteran by the scruff, shoving him back the way they'd come. 'Go! Get back to the stream!'

12

Grimnir slapped his blood-sodden thigh; his sides shook with mirth at the sight of the last two Saxon swine taking to their heels. They'd played right into his hands. For all that they clad themselves in the finery of war and carried the tools of the killers' trade, these piss-blooded scrods were just farmers – spear-fodder good for little more than filling a levy and blunting the edge of an enemy sword.

Fools! Still, enough dogs could bring down a wolf, and Grimnir could ill afford to let these two rouse an army against him. With a last chuckle, he lit off after them with his last three arrows clutched in one taloned fist.

It took no effort to keep pace with the miserable wretches. As they blundered through the night-black wood, Grimnir could have tracked them by the scent of their fear alone. But a sickle moon was rising in the east, and though it filtered through a haze of clouds and smoke and leaves its faint glow was better than torchlight for sharp-eyed Grimnir. He saw the two Saxons break into the clearing, its tall grasses and ferns edged in silver – and he watched, bemused, as the one called Cynewulf suddenly dropped to all fours and scuttled away to the right, ducking down alongside a knot of heavy roots.

The other bastard slowed, panting as he looked for the game trail. If he knew what Cynewulf was about, he gave no sign. Instead, he plunged ahead, sparing not even a backward glance for his chief. Grimnir snarled; he nocked an arrow, drew, and loosed in one smooth motion. The Saxon had gone barely a dozen paces when the shaft pierced his right knee. With a desperate cry, the veteran crashed to the earth. He clawed at the weed-choked ground; gasping, he tried to stand, to get his good leg under him. Grimnir let him. The man struggled. He called upon his Nailed God and spat curses and pulled himself nearly erect. In answer, Grimnir's second arrow – its broad iron head wickedly barbed – slammed into the center of the Saxon's back. This time, the bastard went down hard.

Silence descended on the glade. Grimnir could hear the fallen Saxon weeping in agony; he could smell the blood, the sweat, and the piss; he could hear the subdued panting of Cynewulf, who thought himself clever. Slowly, Grimnir fitted his last arrow to the bowstring. He moved to his left where he could glimpse the Saxon chief. The man's face was pale, his eyes as wide as a cornered stag's; he clutched his spear shaft like a talisman.

The injured Saxon groaned and called out. 'Cyn-Cynewulf? I c-can't feel my . . . my legs. Almighty G-God! H-Help me . . .'

Cynewulf put a finger to his lips, and then gestured for the man to stay down.

'P-Please . . . help me.'

'Yes, help him, little fool,' Grimnir said. Cynewulf flinched at the harsh grating voice. 'I know you're there, swine! By that root ball.' The Saxon chief nearly came out of his skin when Grimnir's final arrow *thocked* into the root, not a handspan from his head. It vibrated like a harp string. Grimnir tossed the bow away; he grasped the hilt of his seax. 'And if you're not going to help your man, I will.' The rasp of steel on leather echoed as he drew the blade.

141

Cynewulf did not reply. Grimnir bared his teeth. A Northman would have taken the challenge – like Hrolf Asgrimm's son, back in the Danemark, who called down the *valkyrjar* and gave a good account of himself. But this Saxon had the air of a Roman about him, milk-livered and arrogant; he trusted he could still win by guile what was lost to him by the sword.

'Have it your way,' Grimnir spat; he stalked out into the open.

'Wait,' Cynewulf said, finally. 'Wait, Dane. Let us parley, you and I.' Carefully, he climbed to his feet and came around the bole of the tree, his spear leveled as though he expected treachery.

'Parley? A parley is for equals. And I am no wretched Dane.'

'What are you, then? A Swede? A Norseman? How –' Cynewulf's words faltered as he got his first clear look at Grimnir, wreathed in pale moonlight. He saw a creature that was saturnine and bloody, his long black hair woven with bits of silver and bone. Eyes smoldered like embers in a wolfish face. The Saxon chief recoiled and nearly fell; his spear clacked against the trunk of the tree, and he made the sign of the cross with his free hand. 'Mother of God! Wh-What . . . ?'

Grimnir reached the stricken Saxon veteran. The man lay in a lake of blood; he thrashed weakly, digging furrows in the slick earth. He fought on even though the skein of his fate was woven. Grimnir stooped, seized a handful of the man's hair, and wrenched his head back. 'I am Serpent-born and Wolf-brother! I am the Hooded One, little manling,' he said, glaring at Cynewulf. 'And if you would have your weregild in blood, then come claim it!'

With sudden vehemence, Grimnir carved his seax through the Saxon's throat. He slashed once. Twice. And

142

on the third blow vertebrae crunched as the dead man's head came free. Grimnir straightened, holding his prize by its long hair.

Cynewulf's face paled. His brow gleamed with fear-sweat. But despite the haze of terror his mind raced; Grimnir could read it in his eyes: even now, he sought a way out, an avenue of escape.

'Run,' Grimnir hissed, 'and I'll make you beg for death. I have a question, little fool. Answer it, and you may yet live.'

Cynewulf nodded. 'Wh-What do you wish to know?'

'Where do the Danes make their camp in this wretched land?'

'They don't,' Cynewulf replied. A measure of confidence returned to him, to judge by his fading pallor. 'They don't. When Forkbeard died, we were able to unite and drive his son, Cnut, back into the sea. If you want to find the Danes now, you needs must travel far to the north, to Mann and the isles off the Scottish coast, or to the Hebrides, or distant Orkney . . . or perhaps across the Irish Sea to Dubhlinn.'

Grimnir loosed a sulfurous tirade of curses. He dealt a savage kick to the headless corpse at his feet and cast about him for something else to kill. From beneath heavy brows, he pierced the Saxon chief with a baleful stare. He grew ominously silent, and then: 'Have you heard the name Bjarki Half-Dane?'

Cynewulf hesitated; he weighed his answer carefully, as though he could sense its import. He tightened his grip on his sweat-slick spear shaft. 'No.'

'Pity.'

Grimnir moved, and his motion was the motion of a striking serpent. Before Cynewulf could react Grimnir slung the severed head at him with sinew-cracking force. That ungainly missile – a grisly twelve pounds of flesh and bone – struck Cynewulf near the juncture of his right shoulder and arm. The impact spun the Saxon chief around. His spear clattered off into the darkness. Cynewulf lost his footing; he fell to one knee. With an oath he reeled up and cast about for his fallen weapon.

Grimnir was on him in two leaping bounds. He clamped Cynewulf's throat in a taloned vise and slammed him against the knotty roots, his spine bent near to breaking. The Saxon kicked, feet thumping in the leaf mold. He clawed at Grimnir's forearm, scratched at his face; he fought to prize those iron fingers away from his windpipe.

To no avail.

Cords of muscle and sinew stood out against his dusky hide as Grimnir slowly squeezed the life from Cynewulf. He didn't release him until he felt neck bones crack beneath his thumbs.

Grimnir shoved the corpse away and sat on the knot of roots. A good night's work, almost a score of men slain and none fit to stand in the shadow of the old Dane, Asgrimm's son; he exhaled, and then coughed from the exertions of the last few hours. Through the canopy of trees, a savage glow yet lit the sky from the burning of Nunna's Ford. Grimnir stared up at it with a jaundiced eye. 'Now you're in it, my wretched little hymn-singer.' He leaned to the side, hawked, and spat. 'And what miserable bastard is going to pull your fat from the fire, eh? What little goblin?' Grimnir scrubbed his nose with the back of his blood-crusted hand. '*Faugh!* I should leave you to it.'

Grimnir knew deep in his marrow he should just put Étaín from his mind and go north, to Mann or the Scottish Isles, where some useless scrap of Danish filth would have heard the name Bjarki Half-Dane. He should follow rumor, half-truth, and even outright legend, if need be, until he had that son of a whore under his knife, ready to pay the price for Hrungnir's murder. He should . . .

But, he wouldn't. By Ymir! He would steal her back from her captors – if only to gloat over how a heathen *skrælingr* saved her from murder at the hands of the Nailed God's followers. Now *that* would be rich, indeed! After, and with her in his debt, they'd head north.

Grimnir cleaned his seax on Cynewulf's soiled trousers, sheathed it, and stood. He set about looting the bodies of the two men he'd killed in the clearing, searching their corpses for food and drink, coin and precious metal. As he worked, a plan formed in his mind. He would scout the burning town ere the sun rose to see if he might spot his wayward little hymn-singer. If she lived, he would shadow their column on its return to whatever pisshole they called home and spirit her out from under their useless noses. If she did not survive . . . well, then by the Sly One's grace he could perhaps reach the lands of the Scots in a fortnight. There, he might find himself a new guide. A new hymn-singer.

Grimnir caught up Cynewulf's spear; he eyed the corpse at his feet, a slow smile twisting his thin lips. First, however, he would send these West Saxon bastards a message.

13

Rain like slivers of ice pattered from the leaden sky. Étaín groaned, averting her bruised face from the stinging droplets. But the cold drizzle helped rouse her from her stupor. Her head throbbed beneath the damp tangle of copper-colored hair. *A heel . . . a heel smashed into her forehead.* Étaín shivered and coughed, tasting blood as she pried her swollen eyes open.

She lay on her side in the bed of an ox-drawn wain, surrounded by half a score of men and women, battered and bedraggled – Danish captives from Nunna's Ford. Close at hand a child sobbed; Étaín turned toward the sound and saw an old woman with a seamed face and lank gray locks cradling a toddler to her chin. The child had scabs and burns over her arms and legs, and the crude bandages about her abdomen were crusted black with old blood. She whimpered with each juddering clack of the wagon's wheels. The old woman tried to soothe her with cord-bound hands. Knotted rope encircled Étaín's own wrists, the fibrous hemp as sodden as the straw beneath them.

'Cruel English,' the old woman muttered in Danish. 'Why do they not give this child a blanket? Clean her wounds?' Her eyes added: *or deliver her from her misery?*

'I d-do not know, old mother,' Étaín replied with effort,

146

her tongue thick against her teeth. She struggled into a sitting position.

Around them, leather creaked and harness jingled as three-score mounted *thegns* on blown horses, weary from long campaigning, escorted the wagon across an ancient bridge spanning a narrow and sluggish river. The Avon, she presumed. The world beyond was sere-gray and lifeless, leached of all color, joy, warmth, and contentment. The twisted branches of trees, the leaves, the decayed stone of the bridge, the wood of the wagon, and even the cloth and leather of the soldiers' gear bore streaks of charcoal and ash, as though the world itself were the victim of a great burning. *No,* she corrected herself, *not devoid of all color.* Étaín blinked. To her mazed vision, every living thing appeared wreathed in a thin nimbus of crystalline vitality. She saw hints of every shade imaginable: emerald and jade, citrine and amethyst, sapphire and lapis, ruby and garnet, diamond and quartz and even onyx, which wormed through the spray of color like a harbinger of death. It was as if the gray veil of reality hid a secret jewel-crusted world.

Étaín blinked again; her limbs shook with fever. She sank down, abrading her elbows as she dragged herself closer to the old woman and the child. The thin cloth of her linen tunic clung to her, providing little protection from the rain or from the chill moaning wind.

'Why waste a good cloak on the dead while the living are in need?' the old woman hissed, jerking her head toward the end of the wagon. Étaín followed her gaze and saw a corpse laid out with reverence, its limbs and foreshortened trunk wrapped in a blood-smirched cloak that had once been green.

Cynewulf. She remembered the name. Brother Cynewulf, who had led his hunters in search of a so-called Danish spy but had instead found death in the woods outside Nunna's Ford. Death and defilement. How long had it been since the captain had his men put the body in the wagon? Two days? Three? She could not recall, as the hours since her capture ran together in a fevered blur.

'What time is it?' she asked.

'Late,' the old woman replied. 'Night comes fast upon us.'

The wagon gave a violent lurch to the right as one wheel bounced into a rain-gnawed crater in the roadbed. The sudden motion drove Étaín's bruised skull against the wagon's wooden slats. The myriad colors flared and died as knives of agony flensed all reason from her; she sobbed, squeezing her eyes tight as a wave of nausea broke over her. Searing bile stung the back of her throat.

'Are you ready to confess, Étaín?' The captain's voice cut through the pain. She drew a rasping breath and trembled; with effort, she opened her eyes. The Saxon waited alongside the road as the wagon plodded over the bridge. As it passed, he clicked his tongue and urged his horse alongside. He did not wear his victory well, looking instead more bedraggled and careworn than he had outside Nunna's Ford; he sat hunched in the saddle, his gaze flickering to the cloak-bundled corpse. Étaín felt a deep sadness emanating from him. 'We used to play together as children, he and I. I remember long summers in the valley of the Severn River where we ran amok, much to my father's chagrin.'

'This child . . . these people, they need—'

'WILL YOU CONFESS?' the captain roared.

Étaín shook her head; when she spoke, again, her voice was barely above a whisper. 'I . . . I h-have told you: I was a c-captive.'

'Cynewulf was a good man. A solid man. He was the sort who would have ridden to the very gates of Hell to save you from these God-forsaken heathens, if he had but known. So why do you protect his killers?'

'I . . . I'm not protecting anyone,' Étaín replied.

'Liar!' The captain smote the side of the wagon with a balled fist, causing the child to wail in terror. The old woman glared at him with undisguised hate. Étaín watched his manner change, rage replacing anger. He leaned over her and hissed like a coiled serpent. 'We found sixteen corpses alongside Cynewulf! Do you think they killed themselves? Do you think he nailed his own head to a tree?'

'No . . .'

'The boy said there were two of you, but that was a lie, wasn't it? How many more lurked in the shadows? Whose war band was it? Give me the name of the bastard who led you here!'

Étaín shook her head; the pain caused her vision to narrow. She wanted to tell him the truth, tell him about being kidnapped by the *skrælingr* on the road to Roskilde; she wanted to tell him about the journey south and the maniacal *dvergar,* whose sorcery let them walk the branches of Yggðrasil, bringing them forth at Heathen's Howe some fifteen years later. She wanted to tell him, but no sane man would believe her. It was too outlandish a tale. She opened her mouth, closed it and scowled.

'The time for games is long past.' The captain leaned back in his saddle. 'Lord Hrothmund is a pious man, a good soldier of Christ, but he has no patience for traitors and heathens. Tell me what I want to know and perhaps I can mitigate your punishment.'

Étaín stirred. 'Punishment for what? I am neither traitor nor heathen. There was only one other with me, and he was my captor. I owe him no allegiance.'

The captain grunted and spat. 'Do you take me for a fool? One man alone does not kill a warrior of Cynewulf's

149

caliber, much less his sixteen companions. He—'

'I never said it was a man.'

The Saxon made no reply; he stared hard at Étaín, his features an inscrutable mask. Finally, he shook his head. 'No matter. Play your games, Étaín – if that truly is your name. Keep your secrets a while longer. Yonder are the gates of Badon. Trust my word on this: Lord Hrothmund *will* pry the truth from you, even if he must do it an ounce of flesh at a time. And as you scream for his mercy, as you beg him for the sweet release of death, just remember I could have helped you.'

'C-Captain! Wait!' But Étaín's weak plea fell on deaf ears as the Saxon lord spurred his horse up the road. Sobbing in desperate exhaustion, she sagged back down into the straw, her limbs growing too weak to bear her. Hopelessness swept over her like a wave. Étaín should have used what time remained to her to pray for strength, for the grace to die well, or for a remission of her sins, but instead she closed her eyes and wept. She wept for her plight, for the curse of having been born a woman – an old bitterness that had haunted her since childhood. She wept, gasping, drowning in her own despair . . .

Beside her, the old woman tsked. 'Stop this foolishness, daughter,' she said, her voice cutting through Étaín's desolation like bright steel. 'Dry your eyes. Hold your head high. If the Norns have decreed this to be the place of your end, then what use are tears? It is better to meet your fate with a curse than with a whimper.'

The crone's reproach was like a slap to the face. Étaín blinked. Shame scalded her damp cheeks; she nodded, forcing a weak smile to her lips as she wiped her tears with the back of her bound hands. She did not look up. After a moment, she said, 'You sound like someone I once knew, many years ago.'

'A good Dane?'

'A good man.'

'Count yourself lucky, then, child. A good man is worth his weight in gold. Most are like this lot: rough slag cast in the shape of a man and cunningly gilded. Pretty to look at, but not worth a tin farthing.' The old woman started to hum, then, for the benefit of the restive girl in her arms. It was a happy tune, and it conjured memories of the long journey she and Njáll had made together.

Étaín studied her clenched fists, her lips quivering as she recalled the happiness she had known, then. In Njáll, she had found the father she never knew, the brother she never had; he was her protector, her confessor, her courage, and her conscience. She had 'shared in his conversion, watching as a bandy-legged priest baptized him in the surf off the coast of Cornwall, and together they had sworn an oath to bring the truth of the Lord to the heathens of the Danemark ere the world's end. It was Njáll who had shorn her copper-colored hair and taught her to carry herself like a man, so she might make that long journey unmolested. And as they enacted the simple routines of the road – rise, pray, walk, eat, pray, and sleep – Étaín had found contentment, that elusive ingredient missing from her life at Glastonbury, and later at Exeter. She could have lived such a life forever, had God not put that wretched devil, Grimnir, in their path. And that gave rise to the question: had the *skrælingr* served Divine Providence by authoring her return to Wessex, where she might atone for her part in the destruction of Exeter? *The Almighty has a long memory,* Njáll would say on those nights when his own crimes weighed heavily on him. Did God require her blood and her tears, as the folk of Exeter bled and wept? Was suffering to be her penance? Perhaps so.

A sense of calm washed away her anguish as from deep

within Étaín found the strength to raise her head, to stare at the hard gray world. The old woman crinkled her eyes, signaling her approval.

The road, stone-paved and arrow-straight, ran from the bridge to the city's gate, a league distant. It cut through a brambled wasteland as dull and monotonous as the sky above; Étaín saw no hint of spring, here. No green shoots grew among the thorn thickets, nor had the stands of oak and beech – the nearest a bowshot from the road – come into bud. Rain dripped from naked branches.

A hundred yards on, a muddy track bisected their path to create a crossroad. Here, a great stone cross stood sentinel, no doubt set in place by Saint Ealdhelm himself, who was a great raiser of crosses. Skeletal crows perched on the arms of the cross. Scores of them, blue-black and grim, iron beaks cracking on the stone like workmen's hammers. They *cr-r-rucked* a warning, sinister eyes glaring as the wagon approached. The old woman shivered. 'Odin's bastard children,' she whispered, gesturing with a sharp jerk of her chin.

Étaín flinched from their baleful gaze. The hatred sloughing off them ran deeper than a mere animal's disdain for Man. It was the hatred of an enemy, of a mortal foe bent upon the destruction of a species. The crows redoubled their attack upon the cross, chipping away at it with chisel-like beaks even as they fouled its surface with their excrement. Étaín almost cheered when, on the captain's orders, a soldier rode up to the base of the cross and impaled one of them on the iron head of his spear. The rest took to wing, but rather than fly away, that somber-hued multitude swarmed *through* the column of Saxons, their harsh voices like fingernails scraped across slate tiles. They passed the wagon en masse, inches from the crown of Étaín's head; she saw the driver – a toothless old soldier with a pox-scarred face and a fringe of gray hair – swat at them as they winged past his ears. He cursed, invoking the name of God. An instant later, one vicious-looking bird, more skeletal and bat-winged than the rest, detached itself from the flock and flew straight at the man. Étaín started, voicing a cry of alarm as the bird punched like an arrow through the driver's chest.

No welter of blood sprayed the Danish captives. The man's flesh appeared inviolate, but to Étaín's horror she saw that vile bird emerge from between the driver's shoulder blades with something clutched in its claws. Something it tore free of the old soldier with a sound like fabric ripping – something made of mist, man-shaped, pale and indistinct. Étaín watched him stiffen; she cried out again as he clutched at his chest and toppled from the wagon. The crow lifted skyward with its prize as another soldier leapt from his horse to the driver's bench and took up the fallen traces.

The captain cantered back along the line of horsemen, sword drawn. 'What goes?'

'It's old Brand, my lord,' replied a soldier who had dismounted and now cradled his aging comrade's corpse. 'His heart must have given out.'

Étaín, though, knew differently. She cast her eyes to the cloud-girt heavens, where the crow – that ethereal burden yet clutched in its talons – had rejoined a great flock that encircled Badon like a besieging army. And amid their deathly clamor, she paled to hear the shrieking of a human soul as sharp beaks and rending claws tore it to shreds.

14

Badon was an ancient city and its stones reeked of blood. Étaín could smell it: a metallic stench like wet copper mixed with the miasma of damp rot and sulfur – a distillate of the decay and violence that diverse hands had worked into the foundations of the city. A thousand years before Alfred the Great forged the West Saxons into a race of conquerors, the legions of Caesar had come into this land and driven out the native tribes, the Britons and the enigmatic Cruithne. Roman axes laid low the tree-garth of Sulis, fierce goddess of the waters, and Roman priests extinguished the eternal flame that had burned since time out of mind in her sanctuary. Cunning in the ways of stone, these Romans had raised walls of ashlar around the sacred spaces; they had carved a forest of marble dedicated to the healing goddess Minerva, and tamed the hot springs by diverting its mineral-rich flow into artificial lakes and fountains.

But as the wagon trundled through the muddy streets, a sulfurous yellow mist pooling in the low places, what Étaín could see of the Romans' stone-cunning was not particularly impressive. The city's walls were as ragged as a crone's smile. Timber baulks shored up crumbling defensive towers, with palisades of rough planking and crude brickwork plugging fissures torn in the walls from the infrequent convulsions of the earth that shook the region. Huts squatted amid the ruins of Roman villas like scavengers, their broken columns supporting roofs of wood and thatch. Underfoot, a slurry of dung, mud, and chaff covered intricate mosaics; their fanciful and half-glimpsed designs bore the heavy tread of Time, defaced by hoof and by wheel and by hobnailed boot, the spaces left by shattered cubes of glass and stone filled in with the filth of countless years. Herds of cattle meandered through the once-opulent arcades of the temple of Minerva to graze in the overgrown ruin of some nobleman's pleasure garden. And on a hillock overlooking the city, Étaín spied a massive fortification, a walled cathedral still partially sheathed in scaffolding. She apprehended this to be their destination, the haunt of the feared Hrothmund, lord of Badon.

Across the wagon's course wafted a jaundiced veil of mist that gave forth the throat-abrading reek of rotten eggs. Étaín shivered, though not from the cold. For, in truth, the chill did not reach deep into the heart of Badon, where the very ground itself seeped a damp warmth. No, she shivered from a creeping sense of menace that stole over her. Shapes moved with the mists, ragged-edged figures of a deeper yellow that seemed to spring forth from the ancient stones. The girl in the old woman's lap, who had dropped into a restless slumber, moaned in the throes of some vile dream. Étaín's first instinct wasn't to proffer comfort, but rather to clap a hand over the poor child's mouth as the shapes in the mist turned toward her.

'Keep her quiet,' Étaín hissed to the old woman. 'Can you not see them?' The crone frowned as Étaín pulled herself to her knees. The girl moaned again, drawing the mist-figures closer. She saw them more clearly, now – like *draugar,* they were, the restless dead; their translucent faces sunken like the visages of plague victims. Trembling, Étaín crossed herself and clasped her bound hands in prayer. '*In nomine Patris, et Filii, et Spiritus Sancti.*' She recited the words she had learned so long ago, at Glastonbury, and with each precise syllable the ghostly shapes recoiled as though some great weapon had been leveled against them; she heard their angered hissing, their sepulchral voices. '*Oathbreaker!*' they said. '*Give us the oathbreaker!*'

Étaín did not know how to answer; instead, she closed her eyes and redoubled her efforts. '*In nomine*—'

The sting of hot saliva on her cheek snapped Étaín from her prayer, the spittle followed by a litany of curses. 'Whore!' the old woman screamed, lashing out with one foot to shove her back. 'Traitor! Crossbearer! Bitch of the White Christ!'

'No, you don't understand, old mother! The words keep them at bay! The words—'

The boards of the wagon shifted as one of the wounded Danes, hands chained rather than bound, lurched up and caught a handful of Étaín's hair. Savagely, he pulled her backward and slammed her down into the wagon bed. An explosion of pain blotted out the morose sky; she screamed, but the Dane's hand, two fingers lost to the siege, wrapped around her throat and choked off her voice. His scarred face floated above her, rotting teeth bared in a thatch-bearded jaw. He muttered something. A woman cried out in alarm . . .

And the last thing Étaín saw before the world faded into blood-tinged darkness was the iron-bright head of a Saxon spear tearing through the Dane's cheek.

15

With the coming of night, Grimnir stirred from his bolt-hole. He stretched his cramped limbs, rolling his shoulders and cracking the tendons in his neck. He glared at the purple sky and cursed the pissing rain. He cursed the dripping canopy of trees that gave him no shelter, the moss-clad stones that offered him no comfort; he cursed this hilltop where once a fortress had stood, now nothing more than a ring of foundation stones. He cast his net wide and cursed every village, field, farmstead, and pasture between this godforsaken place and the siege lines at Nunna's Ford. He cursed Wessex and the lands of the English and all things under Heaven with vitriol to spare.

Grimnir hawked and spat. 'Three days,' he muttered, dragging his kit out from beneath the overhang of an eroded embankment where he'd spent the last few hours hiding from Saxon hunters. For three days he had shadowed the enemy column as it left the burned-out wreck of Nunna's Ford. Three days of belly-crawling through muddy fields and clambering through hedges thick with thorn and bramble, and for what? What did he have to show for it? Nothing! Grimnir ground his teeth as he dug around in his pack, finding a hunk of salt-dried mutton and a flask of ale – part of the spoils taken from the men he'd slain with that bastard Cynewulf.

Oh, he had laid eyes on his wayward little hymn-singer that first day, bundled and tied up in the back of a wagon like a sack of onions. But eyes were all he could lay on her. Rust-beard, the Saxon captain, had taken his mate Cynewulf's death hard; to thwart night-skulkers like himself, he had set a cordon of horse pickets around their camp while also sending out patrols and hunters with dogs in hopes they might stumble across the trail of the raiding party that had ambushed his men. Though it made his task more difficult, that they feared him so brought a fierce twist of glee to Grimnir's lips.

Rust-beard's hunters had driven him far afield; in truth, he let himself be driven. He could have killed them easily enough – as easily as he'd killed Wulfric outside the ruined villa at Nunna's Ford – but he decided the need to remain invisible to the Saxons trumped the need to split their miserable skulls. Now, though, thanks to the tenacity of those blasted hunters, he feared Étaín might have slipped beyond his reach. The Saxons' destination lay just over the low hills, a score of miles distant; a place he'd heard one of them call *Badon*. Even if he could move at speed, Grimnir doubted he could reach the column and spirit her from Rust-beard's grasp before they found refuge behind the cursed walls of this Badon. Grimnir picked a gobbet of gristle out of his teeth and flicked it away in disgust.

And if he needed something more, an added insult to the insolent theft of his hymn-singer, Grimnir's limbs had grown weak and they trembled constantly as from great exertion. He felt . . . *smaller* than he had before. Diminished. His people knew nothing of illness, nor did poison give them cause for concern. That left only one other explanation for this lingering malaise: it was this wretched land! It bore the Nailed God's malignant stink – like iron boiled in brine. It clung to every hill and hollow, this stench of dead veneration. The very air was rank with it. Not like the wild heart of Sjælland, where wind and water, soil and stone yet echoed with the song of the old gods. No, England had suffered too long under the harrow of Christ. It flayed the earth, seeped into its bones, and leached from Grimnir the bitter wrath that kept his black blood flowing, rich and hot. If he stayed too long, he risked becoming like the *dvergar*: a caricature of himself, a goblin in truth, haunter of children's tales who must succumb to apathy, to indolence, and to the cold hand of Death.

Was that the fate of the *landvættir*? He had noticed their absence in the Sallow Wood, and with each passing day that absence grew more pronounced. Most were gone for good, driven into the shadow of oblivion by the misplaced faith of Man, the spaces where they once dwelled as empty and lifeless as a corpse. Others, Grimnir sensed, had quit their accustomed haunts of root and stone of their own volition; anger had unmoored them, the heat of betrayal, and they followed now a longing for vengeance. These things Grimnir knew, for he could taste them on the night air, like the galvanic tingle that ran before a storm. But whatever had drawn the few remaining *landvættir* away, not even the appearance of the last of the hated *orcnéas* could entice them to return. *Not even the last son of Bálegyr . . .*

Cursing his own black thoughts, Grimnir bolted the final bit of mutton, washed the salty flesh down with a last long draught of ale, and tossed the now-empty flask into the undergrowth. He scrubbed his mouth with the back of his hand. He had one last chance to reclaim his foundling, and he meant to take it – Rust-beard, his wretched Saxons, and their Nailed God be damned!

Shouldering his pack, he hitched his seax and set off into the night, still muttering a litany of oaths. Grimnir loped down the hill; at its base, he skidded off the crest of an overgrown dike – part of an old defensive earthwork, abandoned when the bloody-handed Romans brought their heel down on the necks of the Britons. He landed lightly; bent low, he snuffled at the ground like a bloodhound.

Grimnir's lips skinned back. He smelled no Men nearby, which meant the hunters had given up – likely on account of the pissing rain. East, he spied the gleam of ruddy light against the low clouds. Badon, he reckoned. His destination. And though his arms ached and the muscles of his legs burned, his black blood sang out for a fight. *He* would not go quietly into any abyss.

With a pitiless laugh, Grimnir headed east; bone and sinew worked in unison, fueled by the need to kill. He loped like a wolf across heath and moor, setting a pace for himself no mortal could have matched – not even the fabled runners of the Elder Days. Miles flashed by; soon, the wilder lands gave way to partitioned fields. He plunged through hedgerows, leapt wattle fences, and sprang over weed-choked rills. Dogs howled in fear as he ghosted past the steadings of their masters – his passage sending ripples of nightmare into the hearts of the young and the elderly; women gasped in their sleep, and men woke to feel the creeping talons of doom at their throats.

He crested a final hill and beheld the valley of the Avon River, with its ancient bridge spanning the sluggish waters; beyond, the reddish glow of Badon fired the low clouds above. Grimnir cursed at the sight of the town's walls: though mossy with age and poorly maintained, they remained formidable. Grimnir judged them to be thrice his height and more; torches marked the defensive towers and he could see jags of ruddy light reflecting from the mail of soldiers who stood sentry duty above the closed gate. He would need to creep about the circuit of the wall and find its weakest point, that spot where he could – with luck – scale it unseen.

At least fording the river at the bridge would be no problem. He saw no sign of patrols; no eyes other than his own watched the cobbled stone road. Nor did he foresee any difficulty traversing the no-man's-land between the river's banks and Badon's walls; it was overgrown, rife with thickets of beech and oak, thorn and bramble. No, it was the walls themselves, and what lay beyond, that presented the most pressing problem.

Grimnir crouched; a breeze ruffled his lank hair. On it, he could hear the moan of spectral voices. The *landvættir,* shrieking and screeching in anger, but not toward him. There was something else: a sense of vexation – *angr* in the tongue of Grimnir's people – that clung to every ridge and glen, an ancient indignation that kept the early spring at bay. Grimnir tried to make sense of the faint cacophony. They were oblivious to him, of that he was certain. Their wrath was for another . . . a betrayer . . .

An oathbreaker. Grimnir's lip curled in disdain. The old oak wight in the Sallow Wood had mentioned an oathbreaker, but he'd thought it confused. Now, though, Grimnir understood. Somehow, one of their own had turned on them. He could not fathom it, nor could he see how he might use it to his advantage. Could the *landvættir* but crack open the gates—

Suddenly, Grimnir felt a groundswell of otherworldly power, stronger than anything he had felt before in this cursed land. The spectral voices fell silent as a single challenge stirred the breeze to a gust – a pulsing cry that shook the earth like thunder: '*The oathbreaker! The oathbreaker! Bring forth the oathbreaker!*' Grimnir fell backward and scrabbled away from the edge of the ridgeline. '*Bring forth the oathbreaker!*'

In its aftermath, the world fell silent.

Slowly, Grimnir stood. A thrill of fear danced down his spine. Such power belonged to more than a *landvættr,* more than a simple tree spirit or rock wight. Whoever this oathbreaker was, whatever it was, its treachery had awakened something far greater: the Shepherd of the Hills. Grimnir squelched his fear as he apprehended the truth. This oathbreaker – whoever it was – this oathbreaker was *inside* Badon's walls.

And just so, Grimnir saw the answer to his dilemma.

16

Wraiths stalk the shadows of a ruined city. Étaín watches as they emerge from walls of crumbling stone, from colonnades of broken marble, and from the sulfur-blasted earth itself. Saxons and Danes, she recognizes, along with barbarians of every stripe, but with them are phantoms in the antique armor and draped cloth of a long-dead empire; slave-branded Britons in simple garb float among the mass of foreign invaders, their slumped shoulders and defeated air evincing great sadness; skin-clad savages, surely the enigmatic Cruithne, glower from under heavy brows and curse the others in a tongue she cannot comprehend. A wave of cold washes over her. It chills her blood to see the legions of the dead drift toward her, their arms outstretched and imploring. 'The oathbreaker!' they moan. 'The oathbreaker! Bring forth the oathbreaker!'

Étaín cannot run. Her legs have become the bole of a slender tree, her feet like roots running deep beneath the tainted earth – tainted by the oathbreaker's treachery. She feels their pain, and she recognizes it as the denial of everlasting peace, but she cannot help them. She tries to speak but the bones of her jaw are as rigid as those of her bark-clad spine.

The dead swirl and froth around her, breaking like a spume of clawing hands and hissing voices. 'Bring him!

He must be held to account! Bring forth the oathbreaker!'

Trapped, unable to move, Étaín screams in silence as this sea of restless dead rises and engulfs her . . .

Consciousness returned, and with it came awareness. Gasping, Étaín felt cold stone beneath her sweat-slick skin; she heard the dry crackle of straw and a sound like the sizzle of molten pitch dripping from a torch. Her limbs felt weak, drained of life; someone had draped a threadbare blanket over her chest and shoulders. She did not dare move, for with movement would come jagged shards of pain. That she could feel anything at all stood as mute testament to her continued existence. Étaín was not dead, yet, and in that she found scant comfort.

A hand, callused and rough, touched her forehead in gentle benediction. She did not shrink away from it, for the gesture reminded her of Njáll. She lay there for a long moment, hoping beyond hope that she might open her eyes and behold his scarred face; that she might hear the tale of how she had taken sick that night when ferocious storms had stranded them in a cave on the road to Roskilde. She wanted to hear him boast about how he had nursed her back from Death's door. More than anything, Étaín wanted to know that the last few days had been nothing but a fever dream, the phantoms simply an imbalance in her humors.

But when she opened her eyes the face that stared back at her could not have been Njáll's. It was too long, too hard, and too angular. Framed by a matted beard the color of iron ash, scars of wisdom mingled with those of torch and sword on the weathered cheeks. A single fierce blue eye fixed her with curious intensity; the other was gone, nothing but a black-edged socket poorly bound by a crude, blood-spotted bandage.

Étaín tried to sit up, groaning as pain lanced through

her joints, into her spine, and right up into her skull. Her head felt swollen and hot.

'Easy, girl,' the man murmured as a horseman might whisper to his favorite mare. 'Lie still. You're safe, for now.' Étaín sank back down, coughing. The one-eyed man took up a clay cup filled with water and held it to her lips, his free hand supporting her head. 'Drink.' His voice had the hard rasp of a war leader.

Étaín spluttered and choked, but managed to swallow most of the cup's contents. She glanced around, suddenly fearful as she recalled another Dane's spiteful fingers around her throat. 'Wh-Who are you? Where are the others?'

The one-eyed man shrugged. 'I can answer your first question readily enough. I am Óspak. Once I was a gold-giver and *jarl* to the Danes of Mann. Now, I am a dead man, waiting for my body to wither and join my soul in the next world. As for these others you speak of, I have no knowledge. The Saxons brought you here alone.'

'Here?'

'You brim with questions, little sister. Aye, *here.*' The *jarl* gestured, indicating the low-ceilinged room around them. An uneven trickle of light seeped through a grate in the iron-bound door, revealing a space larger than the two of them required – large enough to hold a score of prisoners. 'The cellars beneath the Rock of Badon, where our host, that whoreson dog, Hrothmund, keeps the heathens he means to kill, out of love for his god if you can stomach that.'

'But I'm no heathen,' Étaín said. 'I am a follower of Christ.'

'As am I,' another voice wheezed. Étaín craned her neck. A pale figure lay near; he was younger than Óspak, though there was a resemblance in the jut of his chin, the shape of his nose. Both his hands were gone, leaving only cautery-blackened stumps swathed in filthy bandages. He had swollen, dislocated joints from being bound at wrist and ankle and cruelly stretched to the brink of death. Agony should have been his only portion but he made no complaint. 'Many of us bent our knee to good Lord Christ. My uncle makes no bones about a man's faith, so long as he has fire in his belly and steel in his spine.'

'My sister's son, Skjald,' Óspak said, nodding to his dying kinsman. 'He's right. Half my men were Christian, baptized ere we sailed from Mann. I told this to Hrothmund, tried to reason with him, but the bastard wouldn't hear of it. He tortured and killed them equally, my Christians as well as my heathens. So do not be surprised, little sister, if he chooses not to believe you, either.'

'I . . . My name is Étaín.' She lifted a hand to her forehead, gingerly probed the lacerations left by Cynewulf's booted heel. 'Do you not hear . . . sounds, like distant voices?'

'It's that crack on your head. They didn't break the skull, but not for want of trying. A fever has taken hold. You need rest and a good . . .' He snapped his fingers as he sought for the proper word in the tongue of the Britons. '. . . læknir?'

'A wise-woman?'

The old *jarl* nodded. 'And it's not likely our bastard host will allow you the luxury of either. Perhaps your condition is a gift.' She looked at him quizzically. He continued: 'Aye, a gift in that you'll not long survive whatever tortures he devises for you. Thank your Nailed God, for your suffering will be short.'

Étaín said nothing for a long moment. When she did speak again it was clipped, icy, and directed at Skjald. 'Is your uncle always so forthright?'

166

The maimed Dane managed a wan smile. 'What use are lies and fair speech to dead men?'

'I'm not dead, yet,' she replied. 'Neither are you. So long as we have breath in our lungs, we have hope. And hope is a dangerous weapon in the hands of a man with steel in his spine and fire in his belly.'

'Well put, little sister,' Óspak said. 'Where did these Saxon dogs capture you?'

'Nunna's Ford,' Étaín replied. 'They . . . they thought me a spy because I have traveled with Danes in the past. How many of you are left, *jarl*?'

The one-eyed chieftain sighed. 'I suspect we are the last. They took Thorgil and Herger away a few hours ago. We were ten ships when we sailed from Mann, bound for the land of the Gael to shatter spears and skulls with old Brian mac Cennétig and his Munstermen, against his rebel minion, Maelmorda of Leinster, and his allies, the wastrels of Dubhlinn and my own cursed brother, Bródir. A storm broke our hull and cast us upon this forsaken piece of soil. Twenty-three of us survived the wreck. Of my other ships, I do not know.'

'That was no natural storm,' Skjald put in with a measure of heat, resurrecting what Étaín sensed was an old argument between them. 'It was called, I tell you! Kormlada . . .'

Óspak answered with the same fire. '*Kormlada!*' he hissed. '*Kormlada! Kormlada sang us to our doom!* Aye, so you've said. Perhaps she did, but like as not it was nothing but a run of bad luck.'

'I heard her voice on the wind, Uncle. Kormlada is the herald of woe, but she is just the herald. Forces gather, by Christ; the old gods of the North make ready to strive against the legions of Heaven. We were betrayed!'

Both men lapsed into wary silence. Étaín shifted, suddenly uncomfortable. 'Kormlada?'

'Aye.' Óspak glanced sidelong at her. 'The Witch of Dubhlinn, mother to its king, Sitric Silken-beard, and Half-Dane's whore.'

Étaín nodded, though it took a moment for Óspak's words to register. *Half-Dane's whore. Half-Dane.* Her eyes widened. 'Wait . . . Half-Dane? Bjarki Half-Dane?'

'You've heard his name?'

'More often than I care to stomach,' she replied, grimacing. 'The . . . the wretch I was traveling with was looking for him, to collect on an old debt.'

'Then your wretch need only seek him in Dubhlinn.'

'You're certain he's there?'

'Aye.' Óspak's tone hit a sour note. 'It was his summons that drew us from our harbors. He's offering plunder, slaves, and land to every *jarl* and gold-giver from here to Helheimr who answers his call to arms and puts in to the Bay of Dubhlinn before the day you Christians call Palm Sunday.'

'But his summons drew you in *defense* of the Irish king?'

Óspak massaged the brow above his missing eye. 'Mann stands athwart the Irish shore. As its *jarl*, I must think who would make a better neighbor: some predictable old hymn-singer like King Brian, or that Loki-spawned devil, Half-Dane? That one thinks every Norseman, Swede, and Dane with a grudge will flock to his banner, and in the shield-breaking that follows he will rid himself of Mac Cennétig, once and for all. I have no love for the Gael, but he's a better neighbor and a better king than that starveling dog, Bjarki!'

For a moment Étaín said nothing. She thought of Grimnir; she imagined that fox-faced *skrælingr* skulking and fuming around Wessex in search of the elusive Half-Dane. How long would it take him to discover his foeman was holed up in Dubhlinn, across the Irish Sea? That she knew it and he didn't brought a humorless smile to her lips; that she knew it and would likely carry that knowledge to the grave provoked a paroxysm of laughter that ended in a coughing fit. She clawed her way onto her side and fought for breath. Óspak frowned.

'What ails you?'

'The Almighty moves in mysterious ways, Jarl Óspak,' she said, once her fit subsided. Skjald muttered an 'amen.'

Óspak opened his mouth to reply, but before he could speak the heavy door rattled; they heard a rasping sound as wooden bars were drawn back through iron staples, first the top, then the bottom. Icy apprehension spiked deep into Étaín's heart. The *jarl* clambered to his feet, his back against the wall for support. Weak and sullen-eyed, maimed Skjald could only glare as the door swung open.

A jailer stood on the threshold, flanked by two brutish guards bearing stout clubs. The jailer surveyed the three prisoners; he was scrawny alongside his companions, with a sharp, narrow face that made Étaín think of a rat. His eyes chilled her to the bone – they were as dead and life-less as those of a corpse. He wore a butcher's apron slick with blood and fluids more foul. 'Get up, bitch! Lord Hrothmund wants a word.' He gestured to his men.

'What of Thorgil and Herger?' Óspak said.

A smile twitched at the jailer's thin lips. 'My lord con-verted them, broke them of their damnable pagan ways. They're sitting right with the Almighty, now.'

'Herger was a Christian, you idiot,' Skjald said.

'Not a good Christian. Ain't any good Christians among you lot! Only liars, blasphemers, and thrice-damned Pharisees! So my lord says, and he is fox-wise to your de-ceits, heathen.'

'We were baptized! We took the sacrament!'

'From who? Some sheep-fucking idolater? *Bah!* A dunk in the ocean and a bite of bread don't make you no Christian! Get her up, I said!' the jailer snapped at his guards.

One kept his eye on Óspak while the other guard crossed to where Étaín lay; with little concern for her injuries, he stripped the blanket from her shoulders and dragged her to her feet. Though the fever left her weak as a child, she nevertheless stood trembling under her own power.

'Little sister,' Óspak said. Étaín glanced back at him; lines of sadness and resignation etched the old *jarl's* face. 'Pray to your Nailed God, and thank him for his gift.'

'Where there is life there is hope, brother,' she replied.

The old Dane sighed, and then nodded. 'Hope.'

'That's right touching, that is! Hope, eh? There's none of that left for you, bitch!' The jailer spat and shoved Étaín out the door. She stumbled into the cramped corridor and hit the wall with a sharp cry, abrading her hands against the rough stone as she struggled to keep on her feet. The jailer chuckled. 'Move on, damn you! My lord's waiting!' To Óspak, he said, 'Rest easy, old man. I'll be back for you soon enough.'

As the door slammed shut, Étaín wondered if she'd see the kindly old *jarl* again on this side of the grave.

17

From the cellars beneath the Rock of Badon, Étaín's captors chivvied her up a narrow circular staircase and into a long firelit hall. Four great hearths attracted a variety of soldiers and courtiers to the hall, who stood in quiet conversation and awaited the coming of their lord. Most were West Saxons in bright mail shirts, rich tunics, and black-dyed cloaks bearing the embroidered emblem of Hrothmund – a symbol repeated on woven tapestries and banners and shields hanging from the stone walls. Étaín saw a silver willow tree surmounted by a cross; beneath it, a motto in Latin that read, *In Christo Veritas*. 'In Christ, truth,' she muttered.

'Keep silent!'

Among the faces watching her cross the hall, Étaín spied the captain. The red-bearded lord stood among a knot of *thegns,* goblets in hand as they doubtless toasted the memory of Cynewulf; no small few of them turned and glared at her, sizing her up as an accomplice in the murder of their comrade. Étaín stared back at them, unflinching.

Rain pattered through window slits high on the western wall; a gust of cold wind set the torches to flickering. Étaín shivered involuntarily, for on the wind she could hear the faint, fell voices of restless spirits. She heard the harsh croak of ravens like screams of rage; she heard sobbing cries, peals of maniacal laughter, and curses in tongues she did not recognize. She felt rather than heard a throbbing chant, a single voice pulsing with power and rage, and she knew it from her fever dream: '*The oathbreaker! The oathbreaker! Bring forth the oathbreaker!*'

No one else heard it. Oblivious to the cacophony seeping in from beyond the walls, the collected soldiers and hangers-on merely watched as she ascended a short flight of steps to stand before a door of blackened oak. Her fate lay beyond that iron-studded entry, and likely her death as well. But in that moment she knew no fear. The calm of a Benedictine brother settled over her like a well-worn cassock; the fever quake in her limbs subsided, and even the voices dulled. She was a servant of Christ.

The doors opened on an immense chamber like nothing Étaín had ever seen. Its shape was that of a cruciform cathedral; columns like tree trunks hewn from stone lined the long nave, their spreading boughs of twisted iron with leaves hammered from silver, copper, and bronze. Lamps hung from some branches, colored glass refracting the light into a score of hues. From other, heavier branches Étaín saw iron cages suspended from chains, each holding the tortured corpse of a captive Dane – some freshly dead, others rotting and riddled with maggots. Though braziers of smoldering coals spewed a haze of fragrant smoke into the air, no amount of incense could mask the stench of corruption. Étaín gagged and averted her eyes.

'Look lively, now,' the jailer said, prodding her forward.

At the far end, past the transept, a huge crucifix hung from the vaulted ceiling of the chancel – the carved figure of Christ depicted writhing against the nails that held Him suspended from the cross, His glorious countenance drawn in exquisite agony. A man knelt beneath, his face upturned in a position of adoration, hands clasped in prayer or in supplication. He wore his black hair tonsured like a priest's, but Étaín could see he had the deep chest and corded arms of a warrior. He rose at the sound of their approach and turned.

Étaín tried to look at him, tried to match his self-righteous gaze with one of defiance, but she discovered she could not focus on him. It was as though two individuals occupied the same space, one physical and one ethereal, with the latter moving slightly faster than the other – a man and his ghost, both visible. Vertigo threatened to topple Étaín onto her knees. The young woman bit her lip; the sharp pain and coppery taste of blood grounded her.

The man was clean-shaven and wore the austere garb of an ecclesiastical lord, but the *other* was bearded and fey, clad in robes of rotting willow leaves like some ancient and forgotten pagan priest. Étaín could see that both sets of eyes were aflame with a religious fervor that crossed the line into zealous insanity.

'I am Lord Hrothmund,' he said, two disparate voices speaking in near unison – but where the man spoke West Saxon, the *other* spoke a tongue Étaín could not fathom. He came closer; there was no harmony in his movement, only the unnatural grace of a spirit caged in a prison of flesh. Watching it caused Étaín's world to spin. She screwed her eyes shut. Hrothmund smiled like a cat toying with its prey. 'I see my name precedes me. You've heard, no doubt, of my reputation for breaking the minds and bodies of your brother Danes? I have had occasion to test the mettle of their women, too. An interesting mix of the feminine and the masculine.'

'I'm no Dane,' Étaín replied through gritted teeth. She forced herself to meet his gaze. 'You've made a mistake—'

The jailer drove his fist into her kidneys. Étaín cried out in pain and fell to her knees. 'You will address my lord properly, you heathen bitch!'

Hrothmund held up a hand, forestalling further violence. 'What did you say?'

'I said,' Étaín gasped, 'you made a mistake, *my lord*. I am no Dane.'

'And yet, when you speak your voice carries the accent of the Danemark. If you are no Dane, then you have spent time among them. Time enough to forswear Christ and bend your knee to heathen gods. Fordræd' – he gestured to the rat-faced jailer – 'chain her.'

Grinning, Fordræd seized Étaín by the scruff of the neck and dragged her back into the lamplit transept, where an upright post of knurled iron and wood stood near a table brimming with the implements of torture – the pincers and tongs and gouges and straps designed to inflict equal parts pain and degradation. Each one had the sheen of long use. Futilely, she struggled against Fordræd's wiry strength as the jailer imprisoned her wrists in manacles, the pitted black iron still tacky with the blood of his previous victim. The manacles led to a chain, which in turn ran up through a hasp at the top of the post. Fordræd hauled on the chain; links clacked, and despite her desperate thrashings, Étaín could not stop the jailer from wrenching her arms above her head. Chuckling, Fordræd raised her slowly, her back scraping the post until only the tips of her toes could touch the ground.

'Please,' Étaín said. 'Please, my lord! I am no enemy.'

Hrothmund strolled down the table, his fingers brushing the various implements of torture. He selected a wickedly curved skinning knife. 'Then what are you?'

'A West Saxon, my lord. The monks at Glastonbury found me orphaned. They raised me, and the abbot himself secured for me a suitable husband.' Étaín chose her words with care, since she had a span of fifteen years she could not account for – and she had no wish to delve into her journey with Grimnir across the heathen branches of Yggðrasil. 'The . . . The Danes killed him and took me when they sacked our home. It is true I have spent many years among them, but as a captive. I have only recently escaped and made my way back to this, my homeland.'

'She lies!' Fordræd snapped.

But Hrothmund did not reply. His expression was unreadable, but after a moment, man and spirit shook their heads as though agreeing on some course of action. 'No. No, she speaks the truth. Or part of it. You must have heard something of their plans. With Forkbeard dead, his milk-livered son, Cnut, is king of the Danemark. Will he return to plague Wessex?'

Étaín hesitated. Forkbeard? Cnut? These names meant nothing to her; those who were leaders of the Danes now were children and men of no consequence fifteen years ago. Her pause drew longer, and with each second Hrothmund's smile widened.

'You do know, don't you?' he said. 'You have some inkling, at the very least. If you're no enemy, then why keep this to yourself? Share your thoughts, O child of Glastonbury.'

'I know nothing, my lord. You must believe me.'

Fordræd snorted.

'Must I?' Hrothmund stepped closer. Hanging from the pole – her arms above her head, her body stretched taut – left her midriff exposed. Against her clammy white skin, Étaín's ribs stood out like those of skeletal Famine. 'Perhaps you're not sure of what you know, but know you must. And I'm certain I can tease the truth from you.' The lord of Badon flicked his wrist; the tip of the skinning knife opened a shallow gash along Étaín's flank. She gasped as warm blood welled up along the cut and slowly trickled down her side. 'You see, here is my dilemma: I believe you are, as you say, a West Saxon. But my captain, Æthelstan, says he found you in the company of heathens. Thus, you are either a Danish sympathizer or you are something worse – a spy as well as a traitor.' A second flick of the knife; a second gash. Étaín writhed, hissing in pain.

'If I am a spy,' she snarled, 'then what are you? I see the both of you!'

Fordræd laughed. 'She's lost her mind already, my lord!'

Hrothmund, though, said nothing. He turned away and tossed the knife back on the table. To the jailer, he said, 'Fetch a brazier.' Étaín watched the rat-faced man scurry off to do his lord's bidding even as Hrothmund swung back to face her. 'You can . . . *see* me?'

'I can. What manner of devil are you, spawn of Lucifer?'

The lord of Badon made the sign of the cross. 'I have no congress with the Dark Powers. But you . . . you must have the Sight. A rare gift, indeed, among your people.'

'What are you?' Étaín ignored the physical body of Hrothmund and instead focused only on the leaf-clad spirit.

'I am beyond your understanding.' The spirit threw its arms wide; a heartbeat later, so did Hrothmund. 'This vessel came into my keeping at Ringmere, in East Anglia, where he had gone with his king to crush Forkbeard's invading Danes. He was certain of victory right up until the moment a Danish axe felled him.' The spirit caressed Hrothmund's chest, then thumped his breastbone with a balled fist. 'This vessel was strong. Even mortally wounded, he crawled over the carpet of dead men and horses, through pools of gore and drifts of entrails. He crawled across the blood-blasted heath and into the cool and beckoning shadows beneath a thicket of willows. My willows. The last of my forest.' The lord of Badon's voice dropped to a whisper. 'The days of my kind, the *landvættir,* are numbered in this new world. The coming of the White Christ . . . the growing indifference of Man, these things are like knives. They cut deep, severing us from the land – and the land is the source of our power, the magic of leaf and bole our life's blood.

'But this one . . . this one crawled to me and he prayed. His prayers drew me from the threshold of oblivion. They woke me from a sleep of centuries. His words burned like acid. Out of pity, I . . . I sent my essence into him. I believed my presence would ease his passage into the next world.' Hrothmund turned suddenly. The spirit's eyes blazed with fervor. 'Have you ever experienced faith so beautiful, so perfect, so . . . *alive,* as a man's faith in Christ at the instant of his death? This one's soul departed, but not before it filled me with a new magic, the sorcery of Christ! So profound was it that I forsook my beloved forest, renounced my kind, and went in search of our Lord and Savior.'

Suddenly, the clamoring voices made sense. 'So it's you,' Étaín said. 'You're the oathbreaker.'

'Oathbreaker?' The willow spirit laughed, echoed by Hrothmund. '*In Christos veritas.* What is an oath among heathens worth compared to the truth of Lord Christ? Let them howl, my dying brethren. Let them wail and gnash their teeth in vain. I am protected by the armor of the Lord, and I am eternal!'

'But, if you are a follower of Christ as you claim, then why this?' Étaín rattled the chains that bound her to the post. 'Why do you inflict such suffering? Christ taught us to love our fellow man, and to let God alone be the sole judge of their worth. Why—'

Hrothmund's anger crackled. '*Our fellow man* killed Him! *Our fellow man* tortured the Son of God with scourge and thorn before hanging Him from a wooden cross! *Our fellow man* deserves to burn!'

Hrothmund whirled around as Fordræd returned, his face damp with sweat from the heat rising off the brazier he carried.

'Fordræd, I have changed my mind,' the lord of Badon said. 'This one is neither spy nor traitor. She is a witch. At sunrise, she will burn. But do not look so glum, my savage friend. Bring up some heathens. Let us entertain her before we send her to meet her Dark Master!'

18

Grimnir descended into the valley of the Avon River with the seed of a plan growing in his mind. In his youth, he had traveled far with his mother's brother, Gífr – for he was Bálegyr's second surviving son and his elder brother, Hrungnir, would not stomach any of his kin meddling in the affairs of the wolf ships of the North. At their mother's urging, Gífr had taken Grimnir off to walk the shadowed roads of Miðgarðr, where he might learn the lore of their people and hone his skills by preying upon these starveling dogs called Men.

Gífr recalled the Elder Days before the Æsir had cause to broach the walls of Angrboða's fortress and drive his people from Jotunheimr. He recalled when the Nine Fathers of the *kaunar* were but dwarves, lured into shadow by the Sly One's honeyed words and made to gorge upon the afterbirth of monstrous Fenrir, scaled Jörmungandr, and deathless Hel – a bloody repast that twisted their limbs and turned them from *dvergar* into what they were now. Gífr recalled the Doom of Odin and the harrowing of the *kaunar* and the flight to Miðgarðr on the Ash-Road. He recalled these things and passed his recollections on to Grimnir.

Old Gífr, Grimnir remembered, was as lean as whipcord, his rawboned frame a head taller than Grimnir's

179

own and knotted with gristle and sinew; scars seamed his bald pate, and the fringe of hair that hung about his long ears was the color of storm wrack, woven with countless old bone discs and beads of silver, garnet, and malachite – some from as far away as sand-swept Aegyptus. Sharp eyes burned like forge gledes from beneath a heavy brow as he taught his sister's son the ways of the *goði*, the words of power that could break iron and the battle songs of the ancient skalds.

Or tried, at any rate.

It took no effort on Grimnir's part to conjure his uncle's voice, his hollow, grating laughter that sounded like an iron pot dragged slowly across a shingle. *Skáfi,* Gífr had called him – *little rat* in the tongue of their people: '*You're a precious sort of fool, little rat,*' he would say, every time Grimnir failed to sum up some useless nugget of wisdom he'd been told in passing a century before, '*and dumb as a stump, to boot!*'

And dumb though he may have been, young Grimnir nevertheless picked up the crumbs of Gífr's teachings – especially where it concerned the lands Bálegyr raided, such as the island of the Britons and the green jewel of Ériu in the Western Sea, where the dreams of his people died in the dust at Mag Tuiredh. Long ago, even before the tyrant Odin arose in the North, these lands had been under the sway of the Stone Folk, the Cruithne, who had raised great rings of standing stones. These circles were as temples, and the primordial god they howled to and sacrificed the hearts of their enemies to would, in time, become known as the Shepherd of the Hills. But Grimnir could never pin wily old Gífr down on whether the *landvættir* of these islands were conjured by the Cruithne or if they were the spirits of the Cruithne themselves. It mattered not. For if he could find something of theirs, one of their standing stones, perhaps then he could strike a bargain . . .

Grimnir slunk unseen across the bridge and plunged headlong into the twisted undergrowth on the far bank; he moved slowly, slithering through skeins of briar and thorn, his nose to the ground like a hound seeking some elusive bit of prey. He rooted through drifts of sodden leaves for stones that bore the ancient taint of the Cruithne, whose scratched runes still oozed traces of their old potency. Every promising stone he found he clawed from the damp earth, upending it and muttering over each one. Some he slung aside with a curse; others he replaced with an unexpected sense of reverence.

Dawn was not far off when, mud-spattered and desperate, he found what he sought: the foundations of a ring of eight standing stones. It rested in the shadow of a gnarled oak as old as Miðgarðr itself, on a low rise that preserved it from the infrequent floods that came with the spring thaw. The elements had worn the stones down like a graybeard's teeth; thorn-draped, they barely came to Grimnir's knees. Even still, he felt power massing there, something welling up from deep in the earth. He trod carefully around the perimeter of the stones.

This would do. He glanced at the eastern horizon, already beginning to lighten with the false dawn. Then, with an exhalation of pent-up breath, he stepped into the primeval circle of Cruithne stones and drew his seax. He should have had human blood, or the blood of a sacred ox, but the scraps of wisdom he'd gleaned from Gífr reassured him that any blood would draw in the spirits. Grimnir opened a gash in the heel of his left hand and massaged it until his palm glistened with the black blood of his kind. He began to chant in the guttural language of the *kaunar* as, with this bloodstained hand, he anointed the top of each stone in turn:

Of old was the age | when Ymir lived;
Sea nor cool waves | nor sand there were;
Earth had not been, | nor heaven above,
But a yawning gap, | and grass nowhere.

Soon came hateful Odin | and the sons of Bor,
With spear and sword, | against the frost-king;
They did slay him | on his mighty throne,
And carve his corpse | like a suckling pig.

Out of Ymir's flesh | was fashioned the earth,
And the mountains | made of his bones;
The sky from the frost-cold | giant's skull,
And the ocean | from his blood.

You remember yet | these giants of yore,
Who gave me life | in the days gone by;
Nine worlds I know, | the nine in the tree
With mighty roots | beneath the mold.

Grimnir finished and walked to the center of the circle. He sensed the movement of spirits, like a cold breeze tickling the back of his neck; he heard the creak of tree limbs, the faint clash of stone on stone, and the moaning dirge of the dead. Ravens croaked in the damp dark overhead.

'Hear me, spirits of this wretched place!' Grimnir roared. 'I have lived a thousand mortal lifetimes! I am the Corpse-maker and Life-quencher, the Bringer of Night, the Son of the Wolf and Brother of the Serpent! I am of the flesh of Ymir! I am the last son of Bálegyr One-Eye and I am all that remain of the *kaunar* of the Kjolen Mountains! Taste my blood so that you will know the truth of what I say!'

He felt the spirits recoil from his words even as he watched the smeared blood slowly vanish, soaking into the stones.

182

In answer, they raised a dreadful cacophony; earsplitting howls mingled with humanlike sobs and curses, like a mob that did not know whether to be angry or afraid. A breeze buffeted him; branches clacked and rattled but Grimnir stood his ground, eyes blazing with impatient fury.

Without warning, the disharmony of the spirits died away. Grimnir sensed something impossibly ancient looming over him – something that emerged from the earth itself, a part of it but yet separate from it. A slow, sonorous voice throbbed: 'Synscatha, *I name you. A son of evil, begotten by evil. Why do you trouble this place?*'

Grimnir resisted a primal urge to quail before the power in that voice. He turned. The gnarled oak at the edge of the stone circle had grown larger, its spreading limbs twisting over him in the eerie suggestion of a hand. Grimnir marshaled his nerve. 'I have been wronged, lord of the *landvættir*. Men from Badon have stolen from me. I seek your aid to recover what is mine, and offer payment in return.'

'*Aid? Why would we aid you? Short may be the memories of flesh, but stock and stone never forget. My children remember the wolf ships of Bálegyr and the biting axes of the* kaunar. *As for payment . . . can you give us eternal spring,* synscatha? *Can you heal the rot that turns the hearts of men from us? No. Your kind do not belong here, twisted child of Svartálfheimr.*'

Grimnir gave a short bark of laughter. 'I am the last of my kind, earth wight, but here I stand. Aid me and I will fetch this oathbreaker your spirits blather on about. He dwells beyond your ken, does he not? Inside Badon? Aid me and I will truss him up and bring him out to you, alive and unspoiled.'

'*That traitor!*' The oak shuddered; the force of the Shepherd's anger cracked the stones of the circle and sent

183

Grimnir tumbling to his knees. In spite of himself, he cringed before the display of naked power. *'That defiler! He calls himself* Hrothmund, *now. Lord Hrothmund! He rules the city of stone, under the aegis of the Nailed God of the East. The White Christ's sigils protect him from harm. Would that we could break him, smash him, tear him root and bough! For him we would sacrifice much!'*

'Hrothmund, eh?' Grimnir replied, glancing up at the trembling boughs of the oak. 'Lord of Badon? That is interesting. That is very interesting. We have a common enemy, then. This Hrothmund, his dogs are the very ones who have taken something of mine, something I must get back. We can help one another, eh? You and your cursed wights can't reach your filthy oathbreaker, but I can.'

The Shepherd of the Hills said nothing for a long moment; when it did speak, its voice was subdued. *'What aid do you seek, son of Bálegyr?'*

Grimnir surged to his feet. 'Shake the bones of Ymir! Call up whatever sorcery remains to you and crack open that cursed stone city! Topple its blasted walls and send your spirits to guide me. I will bring Hrothmund to you, and at the same time recover what he stole from me!'

'And the innocents who will die?'

'Innocents? Have they not turned from you and embraced your enemy, the Nailed God? Have they not burned your groves and wrecked your stones? Do they not hunt the last of your followers? Innocents? *Faugh!'*

Silence. Minutes ran free like the sands of an hourglass. Finally, Grimnir heard a great sigh, and then the world grew still. The gnarled oak shrank, its trunk twisted and bereft of the Shepherd's essence. He felt a familiar swell of power, though stronger than before, as though something buried beneath the earth had awakened after a long sleep;

184

it stretched its cramped limbs, tearing root and soil as it came to life.

'*So be it,*' the sonorous voice said from beneath him.

Grimnir turned toward Badon. He heard rather than saw the myriad birds infesting the town's gables and eaves take flight; almost in unison, every cur inside those walls loosed a fearful howl.

Amid screams and cries of alarm, the Shepherd of the Hills reached deep into the earth and stirred the bones of Ymir.

Dolphin's Barn Library
Leabharlann an Charnáin
Tel: 01-4540681

19

The blood dried on Étaín's flanks as she hung from her chains; helpless, she watched while Hrothmund and his rat-faced minion, Fordræd, transformed the eerie cathedral into an abattoir in the name of God. The pair started with the hapless survivors of Nunna's Ford. 'Stop this, for the love of all that is holy!' she pleaded as the two burly jailers dragged the first wounded Dane up from the cellar and to the chancel. 'They've suffered enough! Please!'

No one paid her any heed. As Hrothmund prayed and commanded the Dane to repent, Fordræd bound the man to an upright frame and took up a barbed scourge. He dealt the man thirty-nine lashes – the same number as the Lord received; after the thirty-ninth lash fell the Dane barely clung to life, the white of his spine and ribs gleaming through the gory wreckage of his back. Étaín watched, horrified, as Fordræd then took up a crown of twisted wire with thorns of black iron and hammered it down onto the poor man's skull. The Dane convulsed, a bloody froth spraying from his lips. Étaín heard a faint sigh as an ethereal shape drifted from the man's body only to vanish into the air. She sagged against her chains.

'Another!' Hrothmund said. And one by one, every man, woman, and child captured at Nunna's Ford was brought up into the cathedral and tortured to death. Étaín wept when the guards hauled the old crone past; despite the infirmity of years, she did not quail or quaver. She spat full in Hrothmund's face when he commanded her to repent, tried to kick Fordræd in the groin as he struggled to tie her to the whipping frame, and bit the hand of one guard when he tried to shut her up. The first few lashes brought fresh curses and a promise of doom at the hands of Odin. By the twentieth lash, she no longer spoke; by the twenty-fifth, she hung lifeless from the whipping frame.

'We will array their corpses around your pyre, witch,' Hrothmund said, drunk on the stench of blood. 'Let them watch you burn!'

Skjald came next, already broken and on death's threshold; Étaín prayed for divine mercy and again for thanks when the Almighty granted it: Skjald's soul fled even as Fordræd prepared him for torture.

'No matter,' Hrothmund said. 'Bring the last one, that devil, Óspak!'

The guards hurried to do their lord's bidding even as a terrible clamor arose beyond the walls of the cathedral. The spirits gibbered and howled, as though stung by some supernatural presence.

The willow spirit dominating the body of Hrothmund smiled. 'Can you hear them? The old gods scream for my blood. They claw at the veil between worlds, their talons like nails scraping across shale. I feel them plucking at my soul! Devils, they are! But each drop of heathen blood spilt brings their doom ever closer, even as each heathen I condemn to eternal damnation strengthens Him!' He raised his bloody hands toward Heaven, toward the crucifix. 'Praise Him with me, child!' In a strange and dissonant voice, Hrothmund began to sing:

187

Hail now the holder of Heaven's realm,
That architect's might, his mind's many ways,
Lord forever and father of glory,
Ultimate crafter of all wonders,
Holy Maker who hoisted the heavens
To roof the heads of the human race,
And fashioned land for the legs of man,
Liege of the world-born, Lord Almighty.

Hrothmund's self-righteous zeal sent Étaín into a rage. 'Fool!' She lunged against the chains that bound her to the pole. 'Faithless creature! I adjure you; take yourself back to your grove and leave the world of men in peace! Is this how you keep the word of Christ? Through torture? You would consign the souls of the Danes to eternal damnation, whereas a true man of God would strive to save them! *Go into the world and preach the Gospel to every creature*; that was our Lord's command!'

'*And he that believes not shall be condemned!*' Hrothmund rounded on her. 'Do not adjure me, child, for I am no devil to be cast out! I have read the works of the sainted Apostles. *Brother shall betray his brother unto death, and the father his son; and children shall rise up against their parents and shall work their death. But he that shall endure unto the end, he shall be saved!* I will endure, witch! I will endure to the end and I will be saved! And as Christ Almighty commands, no heathen flesh shall be spared! Their blood shall fill the baptismal font, and with it I shall wash away a thousand years of sin!' Hrothmund roared to goggle-eyed Fordræd: 'Fetch Æthelstan, now!'

'My lord!' Fordræd scurried from the chancel and down the long nave.

There was silence for a dozen heartbeats, and more. Étaín relaxed; a sense of calm settled over her. In Hrothmund's tirade, she apprehended the roots of the willow spirit's apostasy. 'The beauty of Hrothmund's faith is secondary to you, isn't it? You sought the word of God for your own salvation. What did you see when that poor man died in your presence? Did he show you the truth of the love of Christ, or the truth of the Hell that awaits all those who deny Him as their Savior?'

'Both, for are both not true?'

'They are true for the sons of Men.' Étaín shook her head. 'But not even water drawn from the River Jordan by the hand of Saint John the Baptist, himself, can save you. Not the guise you wear – for the soul of Hrothmund has long since gone on to receive the rewards of Heaven – but *you*, willow spirit . . . salvation is for mankind, alone. For your kind there is nothing. No reward for your toils save the long, melancholy twilight before the fall of deepest night.'

'No, witch!' Hrothmund said, spittle flying. 'I have seen my end! Once I have cleansed this land of its heathen blight, I shall go to the king and make my confession; I shall fast and pray, and with the rising of the sun on Midsummer's Day I shall take Holy Communion. Once anointed, I shall cast off this shell and join our Lord in Heaven! Such have been my dreams, and my dreams have ever rung true!'

Hrothmund turned as the great doors of the cathedral opened. The guards hustled down the nave, one-eyed Óspak between them. In their wake came the Saxon captain, Æthelstan, and an unctuous Fordræd, his rat nose twitching. They dragged the Danish chief past Étaín. 'Never give up hope, *jarl*!'

Óspak grinned fiercely, beard bristling as they hauled him toward the bloody whipping frame, surrounded by an orchestra of ripped and discarded corpses.

Æthelstan stopped shy of the chancel. He glared

sidelong at Étaín, but snapped his gaze forward as the lord of Badon approached. The captain stood rigid, fear of his master evident in the way he averted his eyes. 'My lord.'

'I need more heathens, Æthelstan.'

The red-bearded captain hesitated before shaking his head. 'There are no more in Wessex, my lord, save for the war band *she* traveled with. Have you asked after their whereabouts? Who leads them? Or who shelters them, for surely someone has offered them succor?'

Hrothmund turned slowly, transfixing Étaín with a look of otherworldly passion. 'A war band, you say? No, the witch failed to mention that.'

Fear knotted in her belly. 'He's wrong, Lord Hrothmund,' she said. 'I did not travel with a war band. It was only I and another.'

'Lies!' Æthelstan snarled. 'Her confederates killed seventeen of my men, good Cynewulf among them! One man, alone, could not have done that! Lend me pincers and hot irons, my lord. I'll get the truth from her, yet.'

'Interesting,' Hrothmund said. A slow smile spread across his face.

Étaín recoiled, chains rattling. 'I swear to you, my lord, upon my faith in the Almighty, only one other traveled with me, and I was his captive. I—'

Suddenly, a terrible explosion shook the cathedral, followed by the grinding of stone and the dull roar of displaced air. Men screamed. Étaín felt the ground beneath her buckle and shake, as though a coil of the Miðgarðr Serpent tightened mercilessly around the Rock of Badon. The pole tilted, dumping her forward onto her knees as debris showered down around her. Wood splintered nearby and she added her voice to the terrified shouts. Dust choked her; the reek of sulfur filled the air. She heard the tinkle of glass as the colorful lamps shattered down the length of the nave. Tree-columns cracked and fell. Torches guttered and went out. And above it all, she heard the exultant voice of Óspak, roaring the name 'Odin!'

And as the world spun and shook, the spirits answered Óspak's cry with a subdued whisper, a name in myriad languages, a sibilant hiss brimming with hatred and fear. Huddled in the darkness, Étaín knew something ancient and vengeful had come to Badon.

20

The earthquake was terrible to behold. Grimnir could only marvel at the sudden and absolute destruction wrought by the Shepherd of the Hills. He heard a deafening roar as the land bucked and twisted; though their foundations were solid, as solid as anything crafted by the hand of man, Badon's ancient walls could not stand before the Shepherd's onslaught. Stones that had endured since the time of the Caesars ceased to exist, causing the patchwork of brick and timber above them to crack and slough away. Defensive towers now bereft of their legs swayed and crumbled, a cascade of stones toppling inward to crush wood, thatch, plaster, and flesh with equal dispassion. Fissures opened in the ramparts, widening as the ground itself ran like water from a stream.

The bastion that was the city's South Gate disintegrated before Grimnir's eyes, collapsing in on itself. Embers from burning cressets sprayed across the ruins and ignited the rising clouds of pulverized masonry, a deadly brew of dust mixed with residue from centuries' worth of spilled pitch, bitumen, and oil. Grimnir shaded his eyes from the searing light of the sudden firestorm, glad not to be in the middle of it. He spared not an ounce of pity for the men baked to death in that makeshift oven of rubble and less for those burned alive at its edges. They were his enemy, and if the tables were turned they would doubtless dance a jig on his ashes.

Then, as abruptly as it started, the cataclysm came to an end. Grimnir felt the earth settle back onto its bones like cerecloth on a corpse as the Shepherd of the Hills withdrew his power. *'The way is clear,* kaunr.' The now-weary voice issued from the Cruithne stones. *'Go quickly. Follow the spirits, and return with my wayward thrall.'*

Grimnir needed no coaxing. He set off at a run, cutting back through the tangled wasteland to reach the arrow-straight road – its cobbles ruptured, now, with some dangerously tilted. Nimble-footed, he hastened past where the road intersected a cart trail, leaping the shattered remains of a cross as a river of night-black crows winged down from the lightening sky, their brazen cries like the shouts of a victorious army. They led the way; skirting the fiery ruin of the South Gate, Grimnir clawed his way up and over the wall through a rubble-filled cleft. To his left, a knot of mailed Saxons sat huddled atop a portion of the parapet that survived intact. None of them thought to challenge him, nor did they seem to mark his presence, so dumbfounded were they by the unexpected violence the earth itself had visited upon them.

Grimnir descended into utter chaos. Flames licked the night sky; acrid smoke belched from pyres of thatch and timber that had once been hovels, creating a choking curtain drawn by the hand of a god across a thousand little scenes of tragedy. He saw bodies sprawled in the street, pale and bloody, skulls and spines shattered by the rain of debris. Others he saw floating in pools of steaming water, caught when the hot springs beneath the town spewed from their grottoes and sluiced through the narrow lanes, boiling alive all caught in their flow. Still more bodies lay in grotesque contortions, strangled by the noxious clouds of vapor that settled in the hollows created by the rubble.

Survivors tore at toppled stone and wood, frantic in their search for missing loved ones; children tried to rouse fallen parents, mothers cried over slain children. Dogs ·nipped at the heels of their dead masters, or else ran amok among the herds of cattle and goats that were suddenly bereft of their herdsmen.

Beneath the wails of agony and the calls for succor, Grimnir heard the fearful echo of spirits chanting his name in a dozen languages. The sound guided him through Badon's ruined heart, and led him to the sheer-sided Rock, where the burning ruins of a cathedral flared like a beacon in the rising light. Cracked stairs rose to a pair of tall ironbound doors that sagged open on now-ruptured hinges. Wooden scaffolding lay in heaps, and chunks of stone from the façade had wrought horrible slaughter among those who had sought to flee out into the open. Burning oil dripped from broken cressets, pooling into a lake of fire that flickered over the waxen faces of the dead. A handful of survivors streamed out through the doors, servants and courtiers covered in dust and ash and caked blood.

Snarling, Grimnir scattered them like sheep and plunged into the burning heart of the cathedral.

21

Flames lit the transept. Étaín was grateful for their lurid glow as she struggled out from beneath the twisted pole. Wrought from cold iron, it had saved her life when it wedged against the wall of the cathedral. It caught and held the aged oak timbers as they crashed down from the ceiling, which in turn shielded her from the hail of dressed stone and masonry that followed. Repeated impacts had sheared away one link in the chain securing her to the pole; though still manacled, Étaín was able to drag her trembling limbs free of the debris.

Iron rattled and rasped as she crawled toward the center of the transept; she heard other sounds: a gurgling breath, a muttered prayer, the low rhythmic chanting of spirits. Debris shifted and clattered, and the flames consuming the old timbers crackled. The air was heavy with the reek of smoke, stone dust, blood, and charred flesh. Étaín coughed and spat. She spied Fordræd not far away, where the transept met the chancel. He lay on his back, his body crushed from hip to knee by a jagged piece of the ceiling, its faint frescoes splashed with bright blood. A stone flake as sharp as a Dane's axe had lopped off half the rat-faced jailer's skull. Of Æthelstan, she saw no sign.

'Óspak?' Her voice profaned the silence. No reply. She called out again, louder: 'Jarl Óspak?'

This time, she heard a weak answer. 'H-Here, girl.'

Étaín saw a hand move, not far from Fordræd's corpse. She staggered to her feet and, dragging the length of chain behind her, made her way to his side. The one-eyed Dane had taken the brunt of a falling joist; though he had clawed his way out from beneath it, Étaín could see that the skein of his life was nearing its end. She sagged down beside him.

'What . . . What can I do?' she said, grief etching her brow.

Óspak gave her a weak smile. 'I would kiss you, girl, if you'd but fetch me a horn of mead. But, since there's none to be had in this pisshole of a city, let's get those irons off you, instead.' With bloody and broken fingers, he managed to work the catch securing her manacles. The heavy cuffs clanked to the ground. Then, he fixed her with his good eye and shook his head. 'Don't look at me so. It's a small matter, this death. A better end than torture, but still . . . this is not the death I had hoped for. No honor. No glory. The Choosers of the Slain will not be drawn here, and I shall be as a beggar outside the Allfather's hall—' Óspak's voice caught in his throat.

Étaín grasped his hands. 'Christ will welcome you as a brother. You need only ask for His blessing.'

The old *jarl* laughed. 'I would be a poor companion at your White Christ's board, girl. I imagine my songs would not be welcome, there.' A sudden coughing fit racked the Dane's body. Étaín tore a strip of cloth from the hem of her linen undershirt; she dabbed at the scarlet froth staining Óspak's lips, then smoothed his craggy brow. 'Odin has avenged us all,' he muttered.

Étaín nodded. 'He has.'

Before she could say more, Étaín heard the sharp intake of breath behind her, followed by the dissonant voice of

Hrothmund. 'Blasphemy!' The lord of Badon emerged from the smoke; the willow spirit was unscathed, but the vessel he wore was torn and lacerated, the glamour that made him appear alive weakened. No blood oozed from his injuries, and his flesh had a deathly pall to it. He stepped over Fordræd's corpse, his eyes blazing and his face a ghoulish mask of ash-streaked dust. '*Revenge is mine, say the Scriptures,*' he said. '*The day of destruction is at hand, and the time makes haste to come.*' He stooped and scooped up a hardwood club studded with bronze nails.

'Vengeance *has* come, but not for you,' Étaín replied. Summoning up her courage, she clambered to her feet and put herself between Hrothmund and Óspak. 'Do you not hear them? The *landvættir*? The spirits you betrayed? They name your doom.'

Hrothmund cocked his head, listening. 'Cucullo Tectus? Yr un-Chwfl? Grímr? I know what they name, witch! The Hooded One, child of the Plague Folk, spiteful son of Bálegyr. A lonely beast that dwells far to the north – '

'No! *He* was my captor. It was *he* who brought me from Sjælland in the Danemark to Wessex, by way of the dark limbs of Yggðrasil. It was he who killed your men outside Nunna's Ford. He has come for me.'

Hrothmund's snarl could not fully mask his apprehension. 'Then he has come to greet his own death!' He crossed himself and gestured with his club at the image of Christ, still hanging from the shattered timbers of the chancel's vaulted ceiling. 'The grace of God will shield me from the unclean hands of the *orcnéas*, and from the black sorcery of his impotent gods! I wear the armor of Christ!'

'It is stolen armor, and stolen grace,' Étaín said. 'Against him it will avail you nothing. He comes!'

The lord of Badon snatched a handful of Étaín's hair. 'Not soon enough to save you, child of Satan!'

'Let her go!' Óspak bellowed, clawing at Hrothmund's ankles. His cry turned to a gurgle as Hrothmund's club connected with his temple; the bronze studs ripped the skin even as the impact crushed Óspak's skull like an eggshell.

Étaín screamed and twisted in the possessed man's grasp; spitting, she tried to kick him in the groin, plucking at his clenched fingers to no avail. 'You bastard!'

'Where is your "Hooded One," witch? Where is your *Grímr?*' Hrothmund dragged her back toward the center of the transept, where she might have a good look at the crucifix above them. Here, too, the worst of the fires blazed, fed by long-dry ceiling beams and curls of desiccated bitumen meant to seal the now-vanished clerestory from the elements. 'Let him come! He will see me shatter your limbs and hurl you broken on the pyre ere he joins you in Hell! Call to him! Summon your would-be savior! Do it, witch—'

A sudden and absolute silence gave Hrothmund pause. The air around them grew heavy, dense, like the humid warmth that presaged a summer storm. Étaín felt it, too. She stopped struggling. The chanting of spirit voices had ceased, though she could still feel their presence. They watched. They waited.

And then, over the sharp crackle of burning wood, she heard a familiar sound: a low and deadly chuckle.

'Now I see what the Old One meant.'

22

Hrothmund spun around, his back to the chancel, and hauled Étaín to his breast. He looped his left arm around her throat. Beyond the fire, Grimnir crouched atop a pile of rubble near the middle of the ruined nave. His eyes shone like embers through the smoky haze. He gestured with the naked blade of his seax. 'She's not yours, oathbreaker, so take your filthy hands off her!'

Étaín felt Hrothmund stiffen; she felt a small tremor of fear vibrate down his spine. But when he spoke, his dissonant voice dripped scorn. 'Oh, such gallantry from a son of Bálegyr! How touching!'

'Gallantry? *Faugh!* She's mine, you miserable laggard. I stole her, fair and square. And I'll take her back, now!'

'Only if I allow it, *orcnéas*.' Hrothmund seized Étaín by the scruff and kicked her legs out from under her, forcing her onto her knees. He raised his club, holding it poised to strike. 'And I am not feeling magnanimous.'

Grimnir uncoiled like a spring and bounded down the face of the rubble. Daylight as thin and gray as an elder's beard seeped in through ragged holes in the cathedral roof, creating pools of light and shadow. 'So high-and-mighty, willow-man?' A smile curled Grimnir's lips, humorless and mean. 'So cocksure and lofty, eh? We'll see.'

'Kneel, you wretch! Kneel and beg Christ's forgiveness!

Ask the Lord for mercy and you may yet save your black soul from the torments of Hell!'

Grimnir's face darkened. The flames of wrath kindled in those narrowed eyes, and he drew himself up to his full height. Shadows thickened around him as he stalked closer, skirting the fire; Étaín heard the invisible spirits jabber in terror. 'Little fool. I promise you this: before we are quits, you will be on your knees begging *my* mercy.'

Hrothmund backpedaled, dragging Étaín with him. 'Come no closer, wretch! Not if you value her life!'

'I said take your filthy hands—'

It was the crunch of stone that warned Grimnir. Instinctively, he twisted and sprang aside as Æthelstan exploded from the smoky gloom to his left. Wild-eyed, the Saxon captain cleaved the air with a sword blow that would have split a man from crown to crotch, had it connected. But it was no man he fought. With a grace that belied his savage frame, Grimnir slithered away from Æthelstan's blow – presenting his back to Hrothmund as he did so.

The lord of Badon, realizing his foe's mistake, slung the girl from him and leapt into the fray. Catching herself, scuttling to safety on her hands and knees, Étaín watched in horror as Grimnir allowed his enemies to outflank him . . .

Or did he?

Injured in the collapse of the cathedral's roof, Æthelstan was breathing in ragged gasps. His lips set in a grim, pale line, the Saxon captain lunged; Grimnir danced aside. Seizing Æthelstan's wrist, he jerked him off balance and propelled him toward Hrothmund. The two men collided, and Badon's lord missed skewering himself on Æthelstan's blade by a hair's breadth. Hrothmund rocked back on his heels, while the red-bearded captain crashed to the ground, cursing as he clutched at his ribs.

Grimnir gave them no time to recover.

Whirling, he launched himself at Hrothmund. Grimnir came on like a tempest, raining blows with his seax that the lord of Badon was hard-pressed to parry. Chips flew from Hrothmund's club; its bronze studs *spanged* off into the gloom. Grimnir taxed the sorcery that knit his foe's muscle and sinew to the limit; though Hrothmund could not tire, he also could not answer his enemy's relentless onslaught.

The end came with the sharp crack of wood against cold iron. Hrothmund's club snapped. Before he could draw breath, Grimnir's blade hacked through the dead flesh and bone of Hrothmund's wrist, sending the wreckage of his club and the hand that wielded it spinning away.

The willow spirit cursed and recoiled. He staggered back until his spine crashed into a waist-high chunk of debris – a portion of the stone and wood clerestory. Grimnir heard a hiss behind him. Æthelstan had gained his feet. The Saxon captain pushed himself erect; his sword tip scraped stone as he brought the weapon back to the ready. 'Cynewulf!' he cried, taking a staggering step. 'This is for Cynewulf, you son of a—'

Grimnir pivoted at the hip and slung his seax. Point-blank, the weapon flashed through the gloom like a javelin. It took Æthelstan high, in the hollow of the throat. The man's eyes goggled; blood spewed from his lips as the Saxon captain reeled and fell, clutching at the seax hilt. His own sword spun and clattered away, coming to rest among the shards of stone and wood littering the floor between Hrothmund and his foe.

Grimnir glanced down at it, then gazed sidelong at Hrothmund.

The lord of Badon snarled. His eyes judged the distance between the fingers of his good hand and the leather-wrapped hilt; he measured his speed against that of his foe. Hrothmund looked back to Grimnir.

Slowly, the *skrælingr* smiled.

He backed away. One step. Two. On the third step, he inclined his head toward the sword. The message was clear.

I dare you.

The willow spirit shifted and flickered; Hrothmund licked his lips.

I dare you.

In the twinkling of an eye, the lord of Badon was in motion. No human could have matched the grace of that leap, or the speed. He should have snatched Æthelstan's fallen sword from the ground and faced Grimnir bearing a bright length of honed steel. But, for all Hrothmund's alacrity, for all his economy of movement, the son of Bálegyr was faster still.

Grimnir caught him midstride; he rammed his shoulder into Hrothmund's abdomen, lifting him off his feet as he bore him back. They struck the ruin of the collapsed clerestory with a sickening crunch. Hrothmund's vertebrae snapped under the impact. He tried to hold himself up, his legs suddenly useless. Hrothmund scrabbled and clawed at the debris with his uninjured hand but to no avail. He slid to the ground. For good measure, Grimnir caught Hrothmund's head in his hands and, with a savage twist, snapped his neck.

Exhaling, Grimnir took a step back and surveyed his handiwork. A man would be dead, or screaming for death, crippled and in agony, but the willow spirit felt no pain. Simply the dead weight of a useless body. The sorcery animating Hrothmund's frame could repair the damage with time and restore his limbs to usefulness, though the effort would likely tax the willow spirit beyond his ability to function.

'Will you leave me like this?' Hrothmund rasped. 'Or will you finish it?'

'Finish it?' Grimnir spat. 'If I had my way I'd gut you like a fish. No, your master would like a word with you.'

'My . . . My master?' Hrothmund's eyes widened. 'Christ in Heaven! Don't do this! Kill me, if you wish! But do not deliver me to that vile demon! He—'

'*Yesss!*' Grimnir bared his teeth in a snarl of malicious glee. 'Yes! Beg, you filthy maggot! Beg for my mercy!'

Hrothmund's jaws clamped shut and a sullen, stoic heat flared in the willow spirit's eyes. Grimnir laughed at his discomfiture as he straightened and cast about for Étaín. An aftershock rattled the Rock of Badon; chunks of debris crashed down from the cleft ceiling. One, a length of timber embellished with a plaster veneer, struck the heart of the fire and sent a fountain of embers into the air. The Shepherd was growing impatient.

'Foundling!'

'Here,' she replied.

Grimnir clambered over the ruined clerestory and found her not far away, kneeling beside the corpse of a gray-bearded old Dane. She looked a bit worse for wear: blood and dust matted her copper hair, and her face was a raw mass of bruises; she was clad in torn rags, still damp with blood, and her limbs trembled with fever.

'You are ever a thorn in my side,' he said, by way of greeting. 'Let's go. Time to leg it, and none of your lip. We'll be lucky to get out with our whole skins.'

She glanced up at him, her eyes red-rimmed from grief and exhaustion. 'I suppose I should thank you, though I'm sure you had your own reasons for coming back for me.'

Grimnir shrugged. 'I stole you fair and square, like I said.'

'Of course you did.' She stayed a moment longer by

Óspak's side. The old *jarl* was at peace, now; she could see it in his smoothed brow. 'Go with God,' she muttered, touching his cheek. Étaín sighed. This cathedral would be as good a pyre as any for him.

Étaín tried to stand, fell back, and tried once more. Her limbs quaked. Without thinking, she grabbed Grimnir's arm for support, letting him drag her to her feet. He guided her back to where Hrothmund sat; the lord of Badon glared at her, but could do nothing else. Étaín propped herself against the mound of rubble. 'You owe that man a debt,' she said, glancing back to where Óspak lay.

Grimnir went and wrenched his seax from Æthelstan's throat. He cleaned the blade on the dead man's trousers before he sheathed it, and then rifled the body, taking a signet ring and a few coins. 'Do I now?' He looked around; in the rubble, he spotted a fringe of ermine. It was the Saxon's cloak. He tugged it free, shook it out, and tossed it to Étaín. 'And just how am I beholden to a dead wretch I've never seen before?'

'That dead wretch, as you put it, was Jarl Óspak of Mann, and he told me where your cursed Half-Dane is hiding.'

Grimnir felt the cold hands of Fate stroke his spine. He glanced sidelong at Étaín. 'Where?'

Étaín settled the cloak around her shoulders. She spared not even a glance for the corpse of its owner, who might have been a good man except that he would have condemned her to torture. 'I'll tell you once we're away from here.'

Grimnir bristled. He took a step toward her, dropping his feigned goodwill like a mask. 'Oh, you'll do this and you'll not do that, eh? I say you'll tell me *now,* you wretched little hymn-singer!'

Étaín studied him without any hint of fear, her head

cocked to one side. 'Or what? You'll kill me? Stop this game! I think you need me. That's why you came back. And for the moment, I think you need me far more than I need you. You have my word. I'll tell you what you want to know once we're beyond Badon's walls. But my price for this information will be my freedom.'

Rage seized Grimnir in its white-hot talons. He stamped and howled; he kicked Æthelstan's corpse until it lay half in the smoldering embers of the fire. He cursed Étaín in the harsh tongue of his people. And still, she did not quail.

'You're wasting time' was her only reply.

As if to punctuate, another aftershock shook the ruined cathedral. Étaín glanced up through the fissures in the roof. It was fully daylight; thunderclouds of smoke mingled with the ever-present pall of gray that veiled Badon.

'Do we have an understanding?' she said.

Sullen, his eyes like the banked embers of a blacksmith's forge, Grimnir nodded. At this, Hrothmund made a sound between a cough and a chuckle. 'You think this is funny, willow-man?' Grimnir fell on him with unrestrained savagery, putting the hobnailed sandal to him until bones gave way. 'Let's see you laugh, now!'

'Just finish him and have done,' Étaín said.

Grimnir straightened, panting from the exertion. 'Finish him? Oh, no. He comes with us. Another debt.' Muttering under his breath, Grimnir scooped Hrothmund up and tossed him over his shoulder like a sack of offal. He glared at Étaín. 'Follow me, foundling, and keep up.'

23

Étaín remembered little of their flight from Badon. Only flashes, like frozen slices of nightmare: a mud-smeared child, crying beside the body of a young woman; muffled screams from beneath a pile of rubble; rivulets of bright blood running into the gutters. Fires raged unchecked. Survivors struggled and prayed; she heard hoarse and ragged voices calling out for succor – calling upon the Almighty to preserve their lives in this, the hour of their need. She saw a black-cassocked priest kneeling beside a line of corpses, administering the last rites . . .

'Did . . . Did you cause this?' she asked Grimnir as they clambered over the rift in the wall where he had entered Badon only hours before. 'This suffering? Is this your handiwork?'

Grimnir shifted Hrothmund's dead weight from one shoulder to the other, and then glanced back over the devastation. The city lay in ruins. Flames consumed the cathedral at the crest of the Rock of Badon; the low gray sky was thick with smoke and threatening rain. As inured as he was to the horror of war, as much as he reveled in slaughter, even he could barely comprehend the speed and fury of the destruction. He grunted. 'I could do this with an army of my kinsmen and time, perhaps months. But not even my sire, at the height of his power, could have roused the bones of Ymir like this. No, it was *his* kind. Bastard broke an ancient compact, older than stone.'

'And so Men must suffer for whatever crimes the willow spirit committed?'

'They suffer because it's war, foundling.' Grimnir slid down the breach in the wall, pausing at the base of the rubble to wait for Étaín. She came more slowly, and as she drew near, he continued: 'All you hymn-singers prattle on about converting the heathen in the name of this so-called salvation, but what you really want is for followers of the Old Ways to break their oaths and swear a new one to your Nailed God. But do you give half a fig for the *price* of oath-breaking? Look around you. Your kind makes out like the gods of the Elder World are just tales to frighten your brats. Now you know differently, and so do these miserable wretches.'

Étaín could have refuted everything Grimnir claimed, had her mind not been shattered from exhaustion; she could have told him that when the earth shook, every man, woman, and child inside Badon shared the same belief: that it was the hand of God, descended to earth to put paid to some nest of sinners, like Sodom and Gomorrah. No, sin was Badon's downfall, and those whom the Almighty spared would go to their graves hard in the belief that they owed their existence from this day on to divine grace, to piety, and to the love of Christ Jesus. That's what she wanted to say, but Étaín's legs shook, and her skull ached, and a fever burned so bright behind her eyes that it drove all other thoughts away. She stumbled along in Grimnir's wake, barely able to keep pace with him as he led her deeper into the wasteland between the town and the banks of the Avon.

A cavalcade of spirits hounded their steps. She could see them, if she dared glance over her shoulder: a silent throng of misty faces, some ancient and long dead, others who had passed not an hour gone. All of them compelled to follow out of some half-sensed need for justice.

'Grimnir . . .' A note of concern crept into Étaín's voice.

He cut her off with a sharp hiss. 'I see them! Keep up, you laggard!'

Grimnir retraced his steps through thicket and bramble until at last the two of them emerged at the edge of the Cruithne stones. Without preamble, he strode to the center of the circle and flung Hrothmund to the ground. The willow spirit struggled to free itself from the prison of Hrothmund's flesh, its eyes wild with terror.

'Here's your miserable oathbreaker!'

At the edge of the stones, Étaín felt a surge of power; the gnarled oak that grew at the head of the circle swelled, as though something vast and ancient had entered it. Within its outlines, she could see a ghostly form: a figure robed in faded majesty, its gaunt visage stern and bearded, and its head crowned by a spray of oak leaves. The voice that issued forth turned Étaín's knees to water.

'Defiler! O blasphemer! The hour of your doom is at hand! Our dealings are at an end, son of Bálegyr. Go in peace, but do not tarry in this land.'

Grimnir backed away. There came a sound like the tearing of fabric as serpentine root tendrils pushed up through the soil; they crawled through the grass – pale and damp and wriggling – to seize Hrothmund's useless limbs. Immediately, the willow spirit began to writhe; unknown torments racked the ethereal figure as the roots tightened their grip. Pieces of the spirit's essence detached themselves, withering and turning to smoky ash as they drifted up into the morning sky.

The *landvættr* masquerading as Hrothmund loosed an

anguished cry: 'Blessed Christ, why have you forsaken me?'

Grimnir grunted and turned away. Clapping a hand on Étaín's shoulder, he gestured for her to follow him. She resisted a moment, then shrugged free of his grasp and staggered into the circle of the Cruithne stones.

Grimnir hissed. 'Little fool. What—'

'Lord of stone and tree,' she said, ignoring Grimnir's curses, 'this spirit is yours to do with as you will, but the body belongs to the world of Men. He was a man of profound faith, in life, and I ask that you allow me to offer the prayers that were never offered upon his first death.'

Étaín felt the full force of the Shepherd's gaze, then. The spirits rustled beyond the boundary of the Cruithne stones, and she heard the mingled awe and scorn in their subdued voices. She heard Grimnir mutter under his breath. But she could not tear her eyes from the eerie form of the Shepherd of the Hills – more ancient than Golgotha, where her faith was born; the eyes that pierced her soul had seen countless ages of Man, ages undreamed of, from the fall of doom-haunted Atlantis to the rise of the sons of Aryas, and more. She felt the weight of millennia grinding her into the dust she came from, the dust she would return to.

'*The prayers of the White Christ are anathema to me,*' he said, and his voice was like a gentle breeze. '*But such are my thrall's crimes that I will permit you this indulgence, though there can be no peace between the Old Ways and the New.*'

Étaín nodded her thanks and moved carefully to Hrothmund's side. Grimnir spat and turned away, muttering about the 'miserable hymn-singers.' Étaín knelt. Among the collected spirits watching from beyond the boundary stones, those who had been Christian in life also knelt.

Gaunt and hollow-eyed, the willow spirit stared up at

her as the Shepherd's strangling roots siphoned off its life force. 'I cannot absolve you of your sins, spirit,' Étaín said. 'But, if your faith is true, then let these prayers be as a balm to you.' She made the sign of the cross. 'Our Father, who art in Heaven, hallowed be Thy name. Thy kingdom come. Thy will be done on earth as it is in Heaven . . .'

The limbs of the oak shivered and groaned as she spoke the words of the Lord's Prayer. Lesser spirits shrieked and fled, while those dead souls who had pledged their lives to the Son of God took solace from it. With her thumb, Étaín drew a cross on Hrothmund's forehead. Feeling her touch, the willow spirit smiled and closed its eyes.

In a high, clear voice Étaín chanted in Latin:

From the depths, I have cried out to you, O Lord;
Lord, hear my voice. Let your ears be attentive
to the voice of my supplication.
If you, Lord, were to mark iniquities, who, O Lord, shall
    stand?
For with you all is forgiveness; and because of your law, I
stood by you, Lord.
My soul has stood by His word.
My soul has hoped in the Lord.
From the morning watch, even until night, let Israel hope in
    the Lord.
For with the Lord there is mercy, and with Him is plenteous
    redemption.
And He will redeem Israel from all his iniquities.
Amen.

Étaín heard a rattling sigh, like a breeze through the fronds of a weeping willow, as the spirit possessing the body of Hrothmund dissipated; the corpse itself, freed from the animating glamour, decayed before her eyes, blackening into a desiccated husk that reeked of corruption. Étaín fell back on her haunches and scrambled away.

The roots of the ancient oak released Hrothmund's body and tore at the earth beneath him to create a shallow grave. In moments, there was no sign that Hrothmund of Wessex, who died in battle at Ringmere in East Anglia a handful of years before, had ever existed. The gnarled tree became once again a simple oak, old as Miðgarðr and slow to come into bloom.

The Shepherd's voice welled up from the ground itself. *'Our discourse is at an end, daughter of Man. Go.'*

Wordlessly, Étaín rose and staggered from the ring of Cruithne stones without a backward glance. The gathered spirits faded as she passed, their spectral voices growing faint. The weight of the past few days – the grief, the shock, the pain – threatened to topple her into a chasm of despair. Blurry-eyed, she stumbled over root and tussock, managing to keep her feet under her through sheer force of will.

Grimnir crouched not far away, watching. The *skrælingr* – Njáll's would-be murderer, her captor, and yet a creature to whom she owed a debt – looked sullen, the vicious gleam in his eyes undimmed. He could have been a part of this barren landscape, as hard as the stony earth, and as tenacious as thorn and bramble.

He said something she did not catch.

Étaín shivered. She pressed the heel of her hand to her bruised forehead, wincing at the pain. Grimnir spoke again, but she could not focus. The roaring in her ears, unnoticed until now, redoubled. She took a swaying step.

'He's . . . He's in Dubhlinn. Bjarki Half-Dane . . . he's in . . . Dubhlinn.'

Even as the words left her lips, Étaín's world went black.

24

Awareness returned . . .

Cool water passing cracked lips. A rustle of sound. Heat from a fire.

Images and sensations flickered in the darkness, distorted. Dreamlike . . .

Leather and blackened ring mail. The smell of smoke and musky sweat. Intertwined serpents in faded woad curling across swarthy flesh. Damp moss and old linen. Weightless, carried by powerful arms. Thirst. Hunger.

In the netherworld of consciousness time ceased to have meaning. Hours? Days? All were the same. All were nothing . . .

A familiar voice singing, deep but soft; tuneless but filled with melancholy:

> *Where the Wolf?*
> *Where the Serpent?*
> *Where the Giver of Iron?*
> *Where are the ships of the kaunar?*
> *Where are the flames of slaughter?*

Étaín opened her eyes. Blurred shadows resolved into a smoke-stained ceiling made of old timber and thatch. She lay on a cot beneath a woolen blanket that stank of sweat. Above her head, fingers of ruddy orange light leapt, dancing like slender maidens in an endless display of willowy prowess. Étaín heard the crackle of brine-soaked wood; turning her head only slightly, she beheld its source: a stone-ringed pit where a fire blazed, fed by chunks of gnarled driftwood. Her face felt clammy and hot, her fever-ravaged body as hollow as an empty flask.

Beyond the fire pit, framed by the open doorway, she saw Grimnir's broad back. Naked to the waist, he sat cross-legged and worked a whetstone along the edge of his seax. And as he tended the blade, he sang – his song accompanied by the distant crash of surf:

> *Alas for the spear-shatterer!*
> *Alas for the mailed warrior!*
> *Alas for the splendor of the chieftain!*
> *How that time has passed away*
> *dark under the cover of night,*
> *as if it had never been!*

Étaín listened, and the sonorous tune, combined with the soft *slish* of stone on steel and the sighing of the ocean, caused her eyelids to flutter; soon, with measured breath she sank once more into the realm of dreams . . .

It is a cold Danish night; snow swirls over a crackling fire as two sentries laugh and drink mead from a horn. Behind them, the great hall of their lord Hróarr is bright with light and they can hear their kinsmen roaring in song. A dozen stakes line the approach to the hall; on each rests a severed head – black-haired, swarthy and mis-shapen, some bearing tattoos in blue woad. The dreaded skrælingar *of the North, defeated in battle weeks ago by the Spear-Danes of Hróarr. Atop the highest stake are spiked the head and sword arm of a* skrælingr *chieftain, a* word cut by Hróarr's own hand into that broad forehead: Grendel.

'I saw that one rip the heart from Magni's breast and cleave poor Einar from crotch to crown ere Bjarki Half-Dane crossed its path!' one sentry says. His companion hawks and spits at the foot of the stake. 'Half-Dane? Half-skrælingr, more like! Aye, he's one of them, by the Allfather! Should put his head right up beside that ugly brute's!'

The two sentries continue swapping tales of battle and making sport of the trophies. Neither man notices the dark shape loping toward them, eyes like embers, as silent as death. Steel flashes in the firelight; one Dane spins away, blood gushing from his slashed throat. Without pause, the hurtling shape strikes the second Dane full in the chest; both figures crash to the ground. The crunch of steel on bone, a muffled cry, and from this welter of limbs Grimnir emerges, blood-drenched and terrifying. He has come to avenge the death of his brother, the kaunr chieftain Hrungnir.

A dozen more kaunar emerge from the snowy darkness and make their way to the gabled hall of Hróarr; some carry flasks of whale oil and pitch, while others string their bows or heft their spears and take up positions around the hall's entrance. Grimnir silently sends a few around to watch the back. Taking a flask of oil, he begins to douse the planks. The other kaunar follow suit. Soon, pitch and oil drench the boards.

Grimnir takes up a guttering torch and ignites the pitch. The oil crackles and burns slowly, eating into the wood and setting the snow-damp thatch of the roof to smoldering. Greasy orange light illuminates the smoke rising from the hall. Spirits lurk at the edges of the darkness, the Choosers of the Slain, drawn by the promise of

214

violence. Grimnir laughs. Inside, the singing stops and is replaced by shouts of alarm. The tall doors open, and the slaughter begins . . .

The air is thick with spears and arrows, with the shrieks of the dying and the curses of those trying to flee the burning hall. The flames crackle and bite, and the skrælingar howl like the wolves that are their kin. 'Kill them all, brothers!' Grimnir roars. 'But leave that miserable wretch, Hróarr, to me!'

The kaunar do their work well. Those Spear-Danes who make it through the fire and the hail of arrows are cut to pieces by the swords and axes of their ancestral foes. The corpses of men, women, and children litter the frozen ground. Finally, Hróarr himself emerges – an old Dane with a long double-plaited beard that gleams like silver; he is one-eyed, a priest of Odin as well as a warrior chieftain. He leans on a heavy iron-tipped spear, the scalps of kaunar hanging from the haft.

'Villain, I name you! Foul beast that stains the hearth with the blood of good men! The gods curse you, skrælingr!'

'Little fool!' Grimnir snarls. 'Did you think I'd let Hrungnir go unavenged?'

Hróarr spits. 'He earned his death a thousandfold!'

'So have you, old wretch!'

With that, Grimnir and Hróarr crash together. Grimnir is as quick as a serpent; he twists away from Hróarr's spear and hamstrings the old man with a flick of his long seax. The Dane falls to his knees with a bellow of pain and rage. Grimnir's heel snaps the haft of his spear even as he drives his blade into Hróarr's chest.

Grimnir lets go of his blade and holds Hróarr's head in his gory hands. The chief of the Spear-Danes sees his death written in the heavens.

215

'Where is Bjarki Half-Dane, little fool?' Grimnir whispers. *'He is not here. Where has he gone?'*

Hróarr's single eye focuses on Grimnir. A bloody smile splits the old man's lips. *'I ... I s-sent him ... sent h-him away, on the whale-road. S-So much for your vengeance,* skrælingr! *Bjarki will be mine! For all the long years of your cursed life, he will be as a thorn in your side!'*

Grimnir releases Hróarr and kicks the broken spear shaft from his hand. The implication is clear: he will go into the next world weaponless, where the Einherjar will mock him and deny him a place at their table. Grimnir wraps a hand around the hilt of his seax.

'Hear me, Sly One, Father Loki! Bear witness, O Ymir, sire of giants and lord of the frost!' Grimnir saws his blade upward; Hróarr screams his agony as the skrælingr reaches into the open wound and rips forth the Dane's still-beating heart. *'By this blood, I swear! I will not rest until Bjarki Half-Dane is under my blade!'*

The voices of the wolves split the night as the kaunar add their howls to Grimnir's; the world rumbles and thunder cracks. From the mountains of the North, the gods accept Grimnir's oath ...

25

Étaín woke with a cry of terror; wild-eyed, she bolted upright and cast about, half-expecting to find a dozen wolf-like *kaunar* creeping through the gloom, bloody-handed and knife-cunning, as the thunder of the gods reverberated from the icy mountains of the North.

What she saw inside that dank fisherman's hut, by the pale gray light of day, was a single pair of familiar red eyes, glowering at her from the shadows. The echo of thunder rolled on as she sank back down onto her cot, her heart pounding against the walls of her chest. The fire pit was a sullen nest of embers that did nothing to relieve the damp chill. Outside, a tempest howled. Wind-lashed rain pummeled the tumbledown shack; jagged flares of lightning split the heavens, followed swiftly by the titan's tread of thunder.

Grimnir sat near the door, its curtain of poorly cured leather billowing in the storm, and stared at Étaín, his sharp features unreadable. He said nothing as she coughed, then used her fingers to explore the bandage covering her forehead – a poultice of soft sphagnum and peat tar mixed with medicinal herbs and wrapped in old linen. She tried to feel the wound beneath.

'*Nár!* Let it be,' he snapped.

She nodded. 'Water?'

He gestured to the floor beside her. Carefully, Étaín raised herself on one elbow. Beside her cot sat a clay beaker of water and a wooden bowl of stew, a gelid concoction made from fish and dried vegetables that smelled as unappetizing as it looked. She winced and passed over the bowl to take up the beaker; with trembling hands, she drained half its contents. Étaín lay back, once more. 'Where are we? What happened?'

'That crack to the head nearly did you in,' Grimnir said. 'Infection took hold, and that blasted fever . . . treated it best I could.'

'Whatever you did, I'm alive – God be praised – and in your debt a second time.'

'Your god had no part in it, foundling,' Grimnir muttered. He peered out the curtained doorway and spat. 'We're on the coast west and south of that pisshole, Badon. It's been six days since you dropped at my feet, and the only reason you're not waking up alone is this damnable weather. Turned foul two days ago.'

'Six days?' Étaín said nothing for a long while, her brow furrowed in thought. She recalled flashes, washed-out images that could have been phantasm as easily as reality. 'You . . . *carried* me all this way?'

'What of it?'

'I . . . I told you what you wanted to know,' she replied. 'You could have left me to rot outside Badon's walls and been in Ériu, by now. But you didn't.'

'What of it, I said?'

'Thank you.' Étaín lapsed into silence, again; she listened to the rain, to the basso rumble of thunder. This last reminded her of her dream, of the slaughter of Hróarr's folk in the icy wastes. But, was it merely a dream or was it a vision of things past? What did it have to do with her? She stirred, looking over at her companion. 'Grimnir,' she began. 'My dream . . . I . . . I saw you with the last of your people, avenging your brother – his name was Hrungnir, was it not? I saw you slaughtering the Spear-Danes of Hróarr.'

Grimnir glanced sharply at her. 'What do you mean, you *saw*?'

'It was as if I was there, among you,' she replied. 'His head, Hrungnir's head, they took it and put it on a stake . . .'

He grunted. 'Aye,' Grimnir said. 'Aye, but those maggots aren't the ones who took his head. No, that crime sits on the bent spine of another.' He rose and went to the fire pit, stirring the embers to life with a rod of blackened oak.

'Bjarki?'

He gave a sharp nod. 'Hrungnir's bastard,' he said, tossing a chunk of driftwood on the embers and settling back on his haunches.

With that revelation, a great many answers fell into place, from the span of years between Rastarkalv and the raids with Olaf Tryggve's son to the cryptic words of the *dvergar*. 'Your nephew,' she said solemnly. Grimnir gave her a sour look.

'Not mine,' he replied, prodding the fire. 'I don't claim the little wretch as kin. He was Hrungnir's pup, is all.'

'What happened?'

Grimnir was in a foul mood; he looked askance at her, lips curled in a snarl. 'What business is it of yours?'

'Please,' she replied. 'I would hear the reason behind all this.'

Grimnir's nostrils flared. Étaín could sense his impatience, but he could go nowhere until the storm outside abated. Finally, he leaned forward and spat into the fire pit, his saliva sizzling on soot-blackened stone. 'What happened, eh? It's no quick tale, foundling.' Étaín's shrug

219

encompassed the wind-and-rain-lashed coast; Grimnir nodded. 'Hrungnir, my brother – older by nigh upon a century – was a lucky fool who could find silver in pig shit. He was born to raid, and under his hand the wolf ships of our people harrowed the Jutes, the Saxons, and the Angles without pity. They called him *Grendel,* the Bone-Grinder, and through them Hrungnir earned his name as a chieftain and a ring-giver and a slayer of men. After Mag Tuiredh, we thought we were done for. But Hrungnir, he brought us back from the brink.'

'Mag Tuiredh?'

'Aye, the Great Battle,' Grimnir said. 'Where Bálegyr died fighting the *vestálfar* – the cursed west-elves of Ériu – and where some say the Doom of Odin fell at long last on the *kaunar. Faugh!* There were still a few of us left to spite that one-eyed tyrant!'

'You were there?'

At this, Grimnir's face darkened. *'Nár!* I was still lapping milk from my mother's tit. Hrungnir survived that spear-shattering, his first battle, and with Gífr led a single shipload of survivors back to Orkahaugr in the Kjolen Mountains. As eldest, Gífr should have taken the mantle of chieftain, but that old git was ever prowling off in search of wine and silver. No, he passed it on to Hrungnir, who set about rebuilding the wolf ships and making the *kaunar* a folk to fear, once again. Took a few hundred years, but by the time of the Great Plague in Miklagarðr – they call it something else, now.'

'Constantinople?'

'Aye, that's it. Well, by then we were sitting pretty.'

Étaín shifted into a more comfortable position. A flare of lightning cast Grimnir's face in sharp relief, followed by an earthshaking roar of thunder. He said nothing for a long moment. Then: 'But he got lazy, my dolt of a brother,'

Grimnir muttered. 'Lived too high and too soft for too many years. The idiot, he had a weakness for Danes . . . for their women. Took one in a raid on Sjælland, kept her, and got her with child. When her time came, he cut the bastard out of her belly, himself. Should have let mother and child both die. But my precious fool of a brother kept the whelp and raised it, thinking it would serve him as faithfully as a hound serves its master.' Étaín watched a ghost of a smile twist his lips. 'It was the ugliest little maggot I've ever seen. A spindly-legged, hunchbacked wretch the color of piss. For all that, he proved he was no weak-bellied whiteskin. But the little bastard was still only half *kaunr*. His filthy Danish blood made him fork-tongued and oath-treacherous.' A memory bubbled up that drove all sense of mirth from Grimnir's visage. 'Bálegyr would have twisted his head off.'

Grimnir was silent again for several moments, his eyes boring deep into the red heart of the fire. What he saw Étaín could not say; she waited, and soon he roused himself, shaking off the memories like a wolf shaking its coat.

'Anyway,' he said, 'we named the maggot Daufi, "Little Fool," but he called himself Bjarki. Hrungnir taught him the ways of the wolf ships, took him out on raids – let him kill a few Angles and Saxons before testing his mettle against his mother's people, the Spear-Danes of Sjælland. The maggot did well for himself, as I heard it. What's more, he was a smart little bastard. Earned his own ship and crewed it with outcasts when he was just a little older than you. Made Hrungnir proud.'

Étaín's brow creased. 'As you heard it? Where were you?'

'Away in the East with old Gífr, seeking wine and silver and bringing ruin to the plague-ravaged dogs of

Miklagarðr. *Nár!* Hrungnir didn't want me anywhere near him. He was afraid I'd rise up against him.'

'Would you have?'

Grimnir's look spoke volumes; Étaín saw the fires of war glimmering behind his eyes. Civil war or foreign war, it made no difference to him. He was a creature of Strife, and would seek it out in any one of its myriad incarnations. 'I didn't witness the start of the feud between my brother and his bastard. But I heard it was over a joke about his mother that Bjarki chose to take as an insult.' Grimnir bared his teeth in a fierce snarl. 'Little fool! She *was* passed around like a sheepskin on a cold night. Well, the maggot took exception, and soon words came to blows. Even Bjarki's ragtag crew took my brother's side. In the end, things were said that could not be unsaid, deeds were done by firelight, and Hrungnir had to choose whether to kill his bastard or turn him out. Idiot sent the little wretch off when he should have followed our sire's lead, gutted him, and hung him over a roasting fire.'

Outside, darkness crept over the rocky shingle. The wind still howled off the Severn Sea, but the rain had slackened and the lightning had faded in intensity. Inside, the flames crackled and burned blue, the shadows dancing.

'I only found out later what Bjarki did, how he took his revenge. I was still away in the East. It was profitable, this slitting of Byzantine throats. Well, Bjarki's half a Dane and can pass for one of them, so he goes among his mother's people until he catches the eye of Hróarr. There's an ancient hate between my people and his, and the little maggot fed that hate, twisting it back on Hróarr until he was deep in the old chief's counsel. Five seasons came and went. That sixth winter, under Bjarki's banner, the Spear-Danes gathered their numbers and set a trap for Hrungnir.' Grimnir shook his head. 'Lack-witted fool!

Turns out, little maggot knew his sire well.'

'He used women as bait,' Étaín said. 'Danish women.'

Grimnir nodded. 'Wives and daughters of the Spear-Danes, posing as a shipload of slaves. Hrungnir's bastard put the word out that the ship would be braving the waters of the Skagerrak, part of a fleet of fat merchant ships bound for the markets at Borghund. So my brother, who hears it from his spies, trades on his luck and sets out with nine wolf ships to bring the prize home.' Grimnir's narrowed eyes blazed in the half-light. 'The Spear-Danes sprung their trap and drove him ashore on the eastern tip of Jutland, hounded him inland, and caught up with him in a peat bog. My folk lost any hope at a future in that wretched swamp, all because my brother – Ymir take him! – could only think with his prick!'

Grimnir got to his feet; the ivory and silver braided into his long hair rustled as he paced the confines of the small hut. His taloned hands clenched and unclenched.

'Two good lads survived and brought the tale east. A close fight, they said. Hrungnir's blade sang the death song of many a Spear-Dane, that day. He had nearly fought his way clear, but somehow Bjarki got in behind him and took his sword arm off with an axe. Bit clean through it. My brother had some fight left in him, yet. Ha! It was a wild scrum, they said, with black blood spewing from his shoulder . . . he grabbed Bjarki by the throat and was choking the life from him, all the while he crushed another Dane under his heel – broke his skull like an egg. Then, that piss-blooded bastard, Bjarki, got his axe up and hacked it into Hrungnir's neck. Took three blows to see the deed done. For all that, I might have let Hróarr's folk off the hook since it was a fair fight by my reckoning, but they did honor to Daufi and celebrated their victory by putting my brother's bloody head on a spear; this could not be borne.

Gífr and I came back and I took up the mantle of chief. I plotted our revenge, but there were only thirteen of us left. We had to use craft and guile . . . and you say you saw how it played out.'

'But I don't understand *how* I saw it,' Étaín said, after a moment. 'Ever since Nunna's Ford I've been seeing things. Odd things, like auras, spirits, and ghosts. Demons, perhaps. Maybe the blow to the head . . . ?'

'The Ash-Road, more like.'

'But, nothing happened to me on your Ash-Road. If we did walk it, in truth, then I emerged from it unscathed.'

'Did you, now?' Grimnir stopped pacing and snorted. 'Unscathed? Still a little fool, eh, foundling? No mortal can walk the branches of Yggðrasil and emerge "unscathed," as you call it. Its roots drink from the wells of Fate, Wisdom, and Death. Likely the gods have marked you out for some greater purpose. Who can say?'

'There is only one God whose mark I bear, and that is the God of Israel, the blessed Lord God Almighty.' Sleep tugged at the corners of Étaín's mind. She pulled the tattered blanket tight against the chill air streaming through the curtained door. 'What will happen to me, now? Am I still your captive?'

'You have your freedom, like we bargained,' Grimnir replied. 'Go where you will, foundling.'

'Even . . . even if it's with you?'

Grimnir looked askance at her, but said nothing.

'I have no home,' Étaín continued. 'No family. My only friend is fifteen years dead. You . . . you started something when you took me from that cave in Sjælland. If you had told me, before that day, that I would bear witness to such acts of sorcery as I've seen in your company, then I would have doubted your sanity – even as I've doubted my own every day since. I would have quoted to you the work of

224

Saint Augustine, who claimed it was the error of the pagans to believe in some other divine power than that of the One True God. I would have recited the law of the Church that declared sorcery to be a crime against God. And I would have prayed for your everlasting soul. But, I cannot deny what I have seen, nor can I explain it away as the work of the Devil. You've set me upon a road, son of Bálegyr, and I would see its end.'

'Baggage!' Grimnir said. 'What use would you be to me, save as a stone around my neck, eh?'

'Unlike Bjarki, you can't pass for one of us,' she replied. 'And if he hides among Men I can yet be your eyes and ears in places barred to you. Let us start anew, with a clean slate – *tabula rasa*. Without threat or debt.'

Grimnir weighed her offer. 'If you fall behind you're on your own, foundling. I'll not stop to snatch your fat from the fire like I did at Badon.'

'Agreed.'

Grimnir stretched, his joints cracking, and went to the door. Étaín heard him snuffling the damp air. She blinked, her eyelids growing heavy. She heard him muttering: 'That's how you want to play it, eh? So be it! Let the winds roar and the thunder crash! What matter to a son of Wolf and Serpent? There is the promise of blood on the air! Spears will shatter and shields will crack!' He looked back at her, his face alight with savage glee. 'Rest while you can, then, foundling, if you would see this road's end. We sail for Dubhlinn on the tide – and I dare man or god to try and stop me!'

Étaín drifted to sleep as lightning rippled across the storm-bloated sky, but she could not shake the feeling that, much like the memory of his oath of vengeance, the gods had heard.

BOOK THREE

THE GAELIC KINGDOM OF LEINSTER, SOUTH OF
DUBHLINN, THE YEAR OF OUR LORD 1014

I

A terrible storm shatters the Irish night: thunder crashes like a giant's hammer on the anvil of the gods; wrathful lightning forks across the purple sky as the gale drives icy rain before it like flensing knives. For decades after, the Christian Gaels would talk of this night – a night when witches and devils rode the winds, hurling curses and abjuring Christ; a night when the dead walked and children were snatched from their cribs by the servants of Lucifer. A night of myth and superstition.

Off the coast, a wooden currach founders on the boulder-strewn mudflats. Broken-masted and rudderless, it is helpless against the onslaught of wind and wave; each surge of night-black froth sends it careening toward the deadly rocks. Tatters of canvas sail snap like pennons in the gale. The keel rises and falls. Abruptly, there is a grinding of wood on stone; planks crack and splinter as the currach's hull is ripped open. The surf recedes, and a figure emerges from the wreck. It is a creature broad of chest and long of arm, apish in strength, with tattoos of cinder and woad snaking among scars etched into its swarthy hide. A veil of black hair hides its face, but eyes that gleam like the forges of Hell blaze forth. It carries another figure, a woman, pale-skinned and slight and clad in a sodden cloak, fringed in ermine. The figure braces against the ripping waves, the mud sucking at its calves and threatening to drag it down. But inch by inch the creature fights its way ashore, at times driving a long seax into the mud and using the blade as an anchor. Always, it keeps a tight grip on the woman's limp body.

Soon, it is staggering through the windblown dunes to where the soil meets the sand. Lightning crackles; thunder follows with such clamor as to render a man dumb with fear. But, as the shadowy creature's foot touches the good Irish earth, the world suddenly goes silent – save for a keening scream. It echoes across the land, from the fens and hollows of Leinster and Munster to the mountains of Connacht; from the shores of Lough Neagh in fierce Ulster to the sacred hill of Tara in Meath. The scream freezes the blood, stops hearts, and causes even the most hardened warrior to avert his face in fear. It is the lament of the mná sidhe, those harbingers of death; their scream is a warning to the Gaels that one of the Plague Folk has come back to Ériu . . .

2

Kormlada did not wake that night as another woman might, clutching her bedclothes against the frightful echo of the *mná sidhe*. She did not bolt upright with a wild-eyed scream of terror; nor did she stumble onto her knees and with clasped hands beseech Christ Jesus and Saint Pádraic for protection. No, the Witch of Dubhlinn simply woke. As the cry faded she opened her dark, smoky eyes and sat up, a frown creasing her forehead.

A lamp of Byzantine crystal lit her quarters, and by its pale glow her gaze swept over the opulent furnishings as though they did not exist. Amid rugs from the hinterlands of Persia and tapestries from Ghent, behind chests carved from Lebanese cedar and ebon-wood couches covered in Andalusian brocades, Kormlada sought hidden menace; she sniffed the air. Tendrils of aromatic smoke – Arabian frankincense worth twice its weight in gold – coiled up from the perforated copper dome of a censer. Beneath that heady fragrance she could smell only damp stone and ancient dust.

The Witch of Dubhlinn rose from her bed. Silken gown rustling, she crossed to the window and flung open the shutter. A damp gust of wind stirred her raven-black hair as she peered out from the pinnacle of Cuarán's Tower, oblivious to the needles of rain that stung her face. By day, she could see the hills of Leinster, a line of purple away to the south. By night, it was like staring into a stygian maw. A few lights gleamed beneath her, and she knew them to be the shielded lamps her son's Norse mercenaries carried as they walked the circuit of Dubhlinn's walls. But the city itself, which sprouted like some trade-borne fungus on the south bank of the River Liffey, was lost to darkness.

She raised her eyes to the heavens. Chains of lightning stitched the firmament, turning the sky bright as daylight for half a heartbeat; the dull rumble of thunder shook the stones of the tower. In the fierce afterglow of that galvanic blast an image was graven on her mind, a phantasm forged of cloud and storm: a drifting disembodied eye, wreathed in fire. Kormlada's frown deepened as she turned away.

'Something is amiss,' she said. 'Something unnatural.' Kormlada gave a weird whistle, which was answered a heartbeat later by the croak of a raven. A great brute of a bird, coal-black and ancient, came fluttering in from another room. She did not flinch as he came to rest on her shoulder, his talons gripping her flesh with exaggerated care. She scratched the raven under its beak. 'Cruach, my love. Find Nechtan,' she whispered as a woman sighs to her lover. 'Find him. See what he knows.' The raven, Cruach, nodded and took to wing; banking sharply, he plunged through the open window and vanished in the storm wrack. Kormlada stood, watching the play of far-off lightning.

Though not yet fifty, she was well beyond the age when men expected their women to put aside the mirror and take up the spindle, taking that first step down a well-trodden path ending first in the prison of matronage, and thence to a cold, forgotten grave. But the Witch of Dubhlinn was no ordinary woman. The essence of the ageless Tuatha, her mother's people, flowed through her veins, though the blood of her mortal father diluted its potency. She was the daughter of Murchada, the old king of Leinster, and half-sister to Maelmorda, who wore that crown, now; the son of her loins was King Sitric of Dubhlinn, and she had thrice been wed to kings – of Dubhlinn, Meath, and Munster. Her arts rendered her as dark and perilous as fabled Circe, but it was her fey blood that preserved her beauty and lent her the ethereal grace of hard-fought Helen. Yet, despite all her sorceries, Kormlada understood her most powerful enchantment to be both base and artless – it was simple lust, and in that sphere of provocation she was without equal among the Gaels.

The sound of raised voices intruded on Kormlada's reverie. She cocked her head to one side and listened. Her brother's voice, she recognized; her son's, too . . . and another, deeper and more powerful than the other two. Familiar voices, all, rehashing a familiar argument. She left the window, paused to drape a shawl of emerald-hued brocade about her white shoulders, and followed the clamor.

Kormlada glided down a circular flight of stone steps that debouched into a long darkened gallery overlooking a torchlit hall where three men stood around a table. It was a work of art, that table: its edges engraved with elaborate knotwork and its center inlaid with tiles of glass and semi-precious stones in a mosaic map of the kingdoms of Ériu – Ulster in the north, Connacht in the west, Meath and Leinster, and Munster in the south; inlays of bone, rune-etched and yellowed with age, marked the Viking enclaves of Dubhlinn, Veisafjorðr and Veðrafjorðr, Corcaigh and Hlymrekr. Figures of carved wood were scattered about the map like pieces on a game board, each one a token in her brother's bid to oust Brian mac Cennétig from the high kingship of Ériu.

'And I tell *you*,' the man on the left was saying, each word emphasized with a rap of his knuckles on the table's edge. 'Not a man of Ulster will fight for Mac Cennétig! I swear it, by Christ and by Crom!' This was her half-brother, Maelmorda, the rebel king of Leinster – a dark-eyed, ruthless Gael whose prowess did not match his grand delusions: he coveted the high king's throne, but Kormlada wondered whether he had enough steel in his spine to take it.

'And Meath?' asked the youngest of the three, her son, Sitric, king of Dubhlinn. He stood at the right-hand side of the table. Though not as ambitious as her brother, Kormlada knew, her son had the sharp cunning of a Norse pirate – he was like his father, Olaf Cuarán, in that he found it more favorable to rule one city and build his fortune than to beggar himself by trying to rule a nation. 'What of Meath? Whose side do they stand on? Ours or Brian's?'

'The Meathmen play it close to the vest,' Maelmorda said. 'Their king, Malachy, is as changeable as the wind. My guess is he will wait before he announces his allegiance, to see who stands best poised to benefit from the affray.'

But it was the man at the head of the table, in the position of highest honor, who drew Kormlada's eye. The other two, despite being close kin and her own child, were useful only as pawns; like the carved figures, they were resources she could guide into place and expend for her own benefit. The man at the head of the table, though, was no woman's pawn.

'What does Mac Cennétig have?' the man said. His voice never rose above a menacing hiss, but it carried to the corners of the hall. Though a giant in height, he had gnarled limbs and a twisted spine. Long black hair receded from a broad, sallow forehead, and he wore his thick beard knotted in a single plait. 'Good King Brian has Munster and the Dalcassians, his own people, and portions of Connacht – all told, a few thousand bastards in sheep-skins with axes and clubs. But he also has the support of the Christ-Danes of Corcaigh and Hlymrekr. A hardy lot, mail-clad and bearing weapons of good steel. They will be Brian's center. The rest . . .' The man flicked dismissively. 'Chaff for the winnowing.

'Maelmorda, you have Leinster and Dubhlinn, and our Norse brothers of Veisafjorðr and Veðrafjorðr. Even with-out Sitric's embassy to his cousins in Orkney and Mann, you will have a mighty host, armored and thirsty for blood – they are your anvil. And soon you will see your fortunes rise even higher as the reavers of Sigurðr and Bródir arrive. They will be your hammer, and together you will break Brian like brittle iron.'

'God willing,' Maelmorda said. Sitric nodded.

'Thus,' the man continued, 'Ulster stands aloof, and Meath . . . what of Meath, eh? That's the question. There is no love lost between Brian and Malachy. What would it take for Malachy of Meath to throw in with us, or at least to not get involved in the shield-breaking that is to come?' His eyes gleamed cold and grim as he glanced from man to man; Kormlada saw something less-than-human in his features, something predatory, and it filled the Witch of Dubhlinn with consternation, with desire, even with a measure of terror – for here was a man whose power came not from title or blood, but from some elemental source beyond even her reckoning. Bjarki Half-Dane was no king. He was the man who *made* kings. 'Tell me, what would it take?'

Silence met his question. Maelmorda shrugged; Sitric stroked his triple-braided beard – so full and thick that it earned him the nickname Silkiskegg, 'Silken-beard' – and stared at the map, as though he could divine an answer from the arrangement of the pieces.

Bjarki glared at them. He started to speak but Kormlada's voice forestalled him: 'It's simple,' she said. 'Offer him the same thing you offered that Manx bastard, Bródir, and Jarl Sigurðr of Orkney to come and fight under your banner.' The Witch of Dubhlinn descended the stairs that led to the gallery above. She felt their eyes on her, even her son's, as she sauntered around the table to stand opposite Bjarki. 'Offer him gold, land, and the hand of Kormlada.'

'You set great store by your thighs, sister,' Maelmorda said, lips curling in a moue of distaste.

Kormlada graced Leinster's king with a smile that dripped charm even as the gleam in her eyes hinted at flensing knives and scourges. 'I know men, dear brother.'

Bjarki chuckled. 'And Malachy knows you. He put you aside once, already, and if we offer you up again as his prize he's going to know we mean him ill.'

'Perhaps not,' Sitric said, looking askance at his mother. 'Malachy is old, and prone to bemoaning his days of glory. I think he might take her back as a way of seizing on to those bygone years.'

Kormlada caressed her son's shoulder in a gesture of approval.

Bjarki glanced from mother to son. 'Send spies,' he said after a moment's hesitation. 'Find out if what you say is true, if the gift of a well-worn saddle would secure the king of Meath's indifference, if not his loyalty. Leave us.' And Bjarki Half-Dane, a man with no royal blood and no titles, a man who belonged to no storied clan the Gaels would recognize – a man they would kill outright if they but knew his true parentage – dismissed the two kings as if they were naught but rag-clad peasants.

Kormlada stood by as her son and brother withdrew; once they were alone, she whirled. One slender hand shot up and cracked across Bjarki's bearded cheek. 'A well-worn saddle?' she hissed, nostrils flared. 'Is that what you think of me?'

Bjarki took the blow, the sting of it only deepening the cruel smile that drew up one corner of his mouth. He gave a soft snort. 'Witch, I think you've been mounted more often than Odin's favorite mare.'

'Bastard!' Kormlada slapped him again, harder this time. Like flint striking steel, the impact kindled something in Half-Dane's eyes, something hot and murderous that lent his gaze a wolfish gleam. 'I hear no complaints when you're the one doing the mounting!'

'Nor do I complain when I ease my foot into a loose and well-oiled boot,' he replied. 'You've—'

Kormlada cut him off with an inarticulate cry; she drew back to strike him a third time – her fingers hooked into claws that could rip the flesh from his bones or the eyes from his sockets. Her rage came up short, however, when Bjarki reached out and seized her pale throat in one black-nailed fist.

Kormlada let out an involuntary gasp; her eyes widened.

'Odin's balls, woman!' Bjarki said in a fierce whisper. 'You hiss and spit like a wet cat! I've seen two-a-penny bawds with more composure.' Half-Dane gave her a contemptuous shove. Kormlada stumbled and fell back against the table, knocking wooden *thegns* awry. She glared at him as he turned and ascended to the throne of Dubhlinn, rising on its dais beneath the raven banners of the House of Ivar – the Norse dynast who founded the town. With the arrogance of a conqueror, Bjarki seated himself and thrust his legs out before him. 'You've been abroad this night? I heard the cry of the elf hags. Was that your doing?'

With effort, Kormlada mastered her passions. 'No. Something else has roused the *mná sidhe*. I've sent Cruach—'

'But you *have* been abroad? Set your spirit loose to wander?'

The Witch of Dubhlinn nodded. Before the cry of the *mná sidhe* had woken her, her dream self had journeyed far beyond the walls of the city, past the storm-racked height of Carraig Dubh and down into the vale of the River Bhearú, deep in the heart of Leinster.

'And?'

She closed her eyes and *watches a long column of men marching in loose formation, through the rain: Gaels in sodden homespun tunics and ragged woolen mantles; most are naked of armor, though a few sport boiled leather or rusting mail hauberks taken from slain Norsemen. But besides weapons, axe and spear and short sword, the men carry shields – their broad faces daubed white and green, brown, blood-red – of wickerwork covered in leather or hammered from bronze. They march under gilded crosses and limp banners of rich blue depicting an arm holding a sword, or bright yellow with a lion drawn in red.*

She watches as this army of Gaels makes its camp on the banks of a river in spate. They go about their duties mechanically, lacking passion. As night falls and the rain continues unabated, no fires spring up; the Gaels gnaw a cold repast while eyeing the lightning-scorched shadows as if they're unwelcome guests. Watches are set. And with reluctance the great mass of men roll up in their damp cloaks and fall into nightmare-haunted slumber.

She sings to them, then, weaving a sibilant lyric that calls forth the creatures of the night. They creep out from rocks, from trees, from the river itself. They are small, ugly things, sharp-eyed and malicious; she bids them work their evil and they crawl from man to man, whispering revelations of horror, agony, and death. To these warriors, the creatures take delight in describing in gory

*detail how it feels to watch helplessly as a Danish axe lops
off their arm, or to have their manhood ripped away on
the iron-bright point of a Norse spear. Every fear, every
doubt, every misgiving they latch upon and make worse.
They hiss that God has forsaken the Gael, that they will
burn in Hell for each and every sin they've committed.
The tittering creatures conjure images of Lucifer walking
among them. Men wake screaming . . .*

'And?' Bjarki said.

Kormlada's voice was hollow, distant. 'I have seen
Brian's vanguard. I have sat among them and fed their
despair. They will reach Dolcan's Meadow, ten miles west
of where we stand, by midday, tomorrow. Brian's eldest
leads them – Black Murrough of Kincora. He is a harsh
man, but even he senses their misery; he will grant them a
day of rest, there, before setting out for the ruins of Saint
Maighneann's at Kilmainham. Brian has sent his second
son, Donnchad, off with a force of old men and youths to
raid my brother's kingdom.'

Kormlada opened her eyes. 'They have crossed the River
Bhearú and are striking deep into Leinster. A messenger
has come to Dubhlinn, bearing word of the raid to the war
bands of Leinster – the *fianna* – who attend my dear brother.
Already, their resolve is as brittle as old tinder. News of this
raid will be the spark. At dawn, they will seek an embassy
with Maelmorda . . . and try to break their oath.'

'Your art told you this?'

Kormlada's smile was the smile of a cat, toying with its
prey. 'That . . . and my spies among my brother's precious
fianna.'

At the mention of the clannish *fianna*, Bjarki Half-Dane
flicked his chin in dismissal. 'Well, let them try. This embassy they plan will be in vain, regardless of Maelmorda's
wishes,' he said. 'I've come too far to have my plans

thwarted by chance or design. We walk the precipice, now. The pawns line up in their accustomed places, and the lordly puppets dance to my tune. One wrong move, one misstep' – Bjarki caressed the arms of the throne – 'and all this will come to nothing.'

Kormlada's smile faded as she turned her attention to the map table. Furrows creased her brow. She picked up one of the fallen wooden figures, carved to represent a *thegn* bearing spear and shield, and set it upright near Dubhlinn. 'Your plan even I can divine readily enough – lure Brian into laying siege then crush him and his accursed kin beneath the iron-shod heels of the Danes – but to what end? If you seek to propel a weakling like Maelmorda to the throne of high king of all Ériu, to rule through him, then why risk it all by allowing him near the battlefield? You realize he means to lead the men of Leinster in the coming fray?'

Bjarki rose and came back to the table. 'Indeed. I am counting on it,' he said.

'Will you seize Brian's crown, then, and try to rule Ériu under your own auspices?'

'Me? Rule you lot of half-mad Gaels?' Bjarki laughed. 'A fool's errand, that is! No, I trust *you* will rule over whichever would-be kinglet survives the spear-shattering with enough sand in his belly to take up Brian's mantle. My prize is of a different sort.' Slowly, and with exaggerated care, he took the *thegn* she'd just set upright and placed it on the bone inlay inscribed in runes with *Veisafjorðr*; he placed another on *Veðrafjorðr,* and a third on *Hlymrekr.* Kormlada herself moved a fourth *thegn* onto the Viking stronghold marked *Corcaigh.* 'And Mann,' Bjarki continued. 'And Orkney. With their chiefs dead, and with a bit of coercion and the blessings of the Allfather, they will look to one of their own for leadership. To me.'

'You would control the slave markets,' she said, nodding as the last piece of the puzzle suddenly fell into place. 'Gold and silver from abroad. Fleets and crews at your disposal. A kingdom within a kingdom.'

'An empire.'

She picked up a fifth *thegn* and paused with her hand poised above the map. Then, wood *ticked* softly on bone as she placed it on the disc marked *Dubhlinn,* the strongest and richest of the Norse kingdoms of Ériu. Kormlada looked askance at the spine-twisted giant Half-Dane. 'And my son?'

'A trusted ally, of course,' he replied.

'But only if he survives this battle we will force upon the Gael?'

'That is the nature of the game, woman. We roll the dice and hope the Norns weave us a path to Glory. And glory or grave, Sitric Silkiskegg knows this game as well as I.'

The Witch of Dubhlinn listened to his words, but *behind* each syllable she apprehended the naked truth: none of the chiefs of the Danes, nor of the Gaels, would survive. *Not even her son.* Not if Bjarki Half-Dane had his way. They would fight, bleed, and die somewhere beyond Dubhlinn's walls while he stood aloof, a vulture eager to feast off the corpses of the slain. 'An ally?' she echoed.

'The most trusted,' Bjarki assured her, his voice dripping false sincerity as a comb drips honey. 'You understand, now? You comprehend my ultimate purpose?'

'Perfectly.'

They stared at each other for a long moment, each taking the other's measure, before Half-Dane nodded. 'Good.' He stalked past her, toward the door. 'Find me when you learn what disturbed the elf hags.'

Bjarki's footsteps receded. Kormlada's eyes blazed with cold, black fire. She glared across the map table at Bjarki's retreating back, and then shifted her gaze to take in the multitude of wooden *thegns* – pawns like her, all of them dancing for the grave as Half-Dane called the tune.

All but one oblivious to his true intent.

I have abetted him in his schemes for ten years, Kormlada mused as she tried to isolate the source of her anger. *And I, too, would sacrifice my witless brother – and even my son – if it meant bringing peace and unity to the chaos of Ériu.* Why, then, did she rage?

It was the arrogance of it. His conceit. That he, some Northern half-breed steeped in the arts of a bygone world, could play them like a bard plays his lute scraped her raw. *I am the Witch of Dubhlinn! I am no man's pawn!*

I trust you will rule, he had said. And that thought, alone, cooled her anger. *You will rule.* She was Kormlada ingen Murchada, a child of the Tuatha, who was daughter, sister, wife, and mother of kings. Maybe Bjarki Half-Dane was right, though he would have her rule through another, merely as his puppet. Perhaps it *was* high time for the piecemeal kingdoms of Ériu to know the sole and silken hand of a queen.

3

From the long, rocky beach Grimnir carried Étaín inland, scrabbling up through a cut in an eroded escarpment where gray sand met rich green turf. He loped across a rain-lashed heath, thunder shaking the earth and lightning searing the heavens with every step, and sought shelter beneath the eaves of a dense oak grove. 'D-Down,' Étaín muttered. 'Put . . . Put me d-down.' Through thin and sodden clothing, Grimnir felt shivers racking her body. And though her teeth chattered audibly she still managed to add, 'I c-can walk f-from here.'

'Can you, now?' Grimnir set her on her feet with her back to a thick trunk. She stayed upright for a moment before sinking down, her knees hugged to her chest. Overhead, the trees creaked in the fierce wind. Grimnir crouched. He took her chin between his thumb and forefinger and pulled her head up. There was no tenderness in the gesture, but there was the smallest glimmer of concern in his eyes as he studied her drawn and haggard expression. Étaín swatted his hand away. Grimnir rose again, sucking his teeth in disapproval. 'I should have left you back in that wretched shack on the English coast,' he said. 'I knew you'd be nothing but a stone around my neck.'

'I c-can walk, I said!'

'*Faugh!*' She needed shelter, he knew. She needed rest

and food and something to wear besides rags. 'You need a blasted nursemaid!' His nostrils flared as he snuffled the air, picking out the faint scent of woodsmoke beneath the dampness of the rain, the leaf mold, and the rich loam. *A fire*. And where there was a fire he'd likely find her some sort of shelter.

For himself, he needed nothing. This land was like a wellspring of power. He had felt it when he first touched solid earth – when the night hags that haunted fens and moor had raised their voices in warning. This island was hallowed ground. His sire, Bálegyr, had consecrated it with his own blood at Mag Tuiredh, when he fell in battle against the hated *vestálfar,* the west-elves – known to these pathetic Gaels as the Tuatha. And not even the crossbearers from the East, with their miserable hymns and their holy water, could cleanse this land of its heathen taint.

Grimnir felt the essence of his people rising up into his bones, stronger even than in the hinterlands of the Danemark. It surged through muscle and sinew, made him shrug off pain and weariness, sharpened his senses, and quickened his mind; it scourged from him every last vestige of indolence – that stultifying torpor that was deadly to his kind; his black blood sang with the promise of dark deeds and slaughter.

'Up, little fool! Up! This is no place to dawdle!'

Gamely, Étaín struggled to rise; after a moment, Grimnir cursed and scooped her up like a limp doll, bearing her weight as effortlessly as he might an empty sack. He took off at a run. Deeper into the oaks, they ventured, following a trail of smoke so weak no human could have detected it.

A mile flashed past, then another. Though not even winded, Grimnir nevertheless slowed his pace, his long stride becoming the prowl of a hunter as the air grew rich with the scent of prey: woodsmoke and spices, spade-turned earth leavened with dung, human sweat and the acrid stench of a hound's piss. He crept closer until he could see a clearing in the trees. At the center of it stood a stone and timber cottage with a low roof of mossy thatch, rain dripping from its eaves and into a pair of huge barrels. Surrounding the cottage was a patchwork of well-tended seed beds, staked and ready for the spring planting; beyond lay a small grove of fruit trees and a freestanding stone wall pierced by a dozen carved niches, out of which came the muted drone of bees.

Grimnir edged closer; nestled in the crook of his arm, Étaín stirred. He saw a peculiarity about the place: ropes radiated out from the door of the cottage, creating a complex web between the gardens, the orchard, the bee shelter, a stone-curbed well, and a hive-shaped hut that must have been for storage. Firelight seeped out from chinks in the wood-shuttered windows.

Grimnir meant to steal around back and find a dry corner for the foundling while he investigated the main cottage. He wanted to know how many men dwelled within, and how many he'd have to kill in order to secure the place for his own use. That plan, however, collapsed like an earthen dam before a torrent. He had not gone ten paces into the clearing when from inside the cottage he heard the reverberating bellow of a hound.

Grimnir shifted his weight, his free hand dropping to the hilt of his seax; he was poised to draw steel as the door to the cottage thumped open. A spear of firelight pierced the damp night, and it cast into silhouette the figure of a woman, bent and twisted with age, flanked by an immense wolfhound. Only the crone's hand, resting lightly on the beast's neck, kept it from charging.

She called out in Gaelic. She was blind, her head tilted up

slightly and away. After a moment she switched to Danish. 'Who's out there? Gael or Gall? Man or devil, eh?'

Grimnir gave no answer; he took a step back. The movement caused the giant brindled gray wolfhound to bare its fangs with a low growl of menace. He could see its muscles bunching as it tensed and made ready to run him to ground.

'Blind Maeve might not be able to see you, aye, but Conán does not share my infirmity,' the woman said, her accent a thick brogue. 'Come, it is too wretched a night to stand here at loggerheads.'

'Sh-She's right,' Étaín muttered.

Instantly, the crone craned her neck forward, head cocked to one side. 'Is . . . Is there a woman among you? Answer me!'

Grimnir's eyes became slits of gleaming ember. Slowly, he put Étaín down. She gathered her feet beneath her and stood unaided, swaying in the wind-driven rain. Grimnir clapped a hand to her shoulder and motioned to her that she should answer for herself, but leave him out of it. She shot him a defiant look. 'A-Aye. There . . . Th-There are two of us. Our b-boat . . . w-we . . . we n-need . . . m-might we s-seek shelter in one . . . in one of your out-outbuildings?'

The old woman shook her head. 'You think Blind Maeve so poor a host as to offer only a pile of cold straw and no fire? Nay.' She shooed and shoved the hound out of the doorway. 'Move! Aye, get out of the way, you great hairy heathen. Come inside. Quickly, now! This is no weather to be abroad in. Devils stalk the unwary, and only a warm hearth and God's blessings can preserve man or woman's soul on a night such as this.'

Étaín clutched at Grimnir's arm and fairly dragged him after her. He could sense no deceit in the old woman's bearing; she seemed genuinely concerned for the well-being of strangers – a trait wholly alien to his people, who viewed hospitality as a burden and strangers as potential enemies. Warmth drifted from inside the cottage, and in spite of it all Grimnir's mouth watered as he scented day-old bread and herbs and some kind of stew. The hound glared at him as he ducked under the dripping eaves; it growled, ears flattened against its shaggy skull, when his foot touched the threshold. The beast recognized him as an enemy even if its mistress could not. 'Hush, Conán!' she scolded, and the hound fell silent. The crone reached out and touched Étaín's arm, then Grimnir's. 'Don't mind him; aye, he's not one for company. You're soaked to the bone, child. Get yourself by the fire. I'll fetch a blanket so you can skin out of those wet clothes. You, too, warrior. Maeve is my name. Blind Maeve. Be welcome.'

Grimnir slouched and scuttled into the cottage; he edged around the glowering wolfhound, not giving him his back, while Étaín sank on the hearth by the crackling fire. She sighed at the sudden warmth. Maeve retrieved a blanket from an open cupboard and shuffled to Étaín's side.

'Here. Give me those rags. Where you from, child?'

'Britain,' Étaín muttered, peeling off her clothes and wrapping the blanket around her. 'Glastonbury, in the heart of Wessex.'

'Wessex, eh? A long way from home. How are you called?'

Étaín gave a weak smile and sagged against the older woman. 'I am Étaín. My companion, there, is Grimnir. And we have come farther than you could ever imagine.' She shivered despite the warmth of the crackling fire. Maeve's brow furrowed; she laid one gnarled hand against Étaín's cheek, then across her forehead.

'Fever.'

'It struck ere we left Wessex,' Étaín said. 'And then again on the journey across the sea.'

Maeve clucked. 'Don't worry, child. Blind Maeve can fix what ails you. Oh, aye. Root-wise and herb-crafty, she is. Nary a fever's been made by the Almighty that Blind Maeve couldn't quench. Grimnir, is it?' She glanced over her shoulder, her sightless eyes milky. 'There is stew, bread, and mead on the table. Help yourself to it whilst I tend to this poor child.' Maeve rose and fetched more woolen blankets, soft cloths, a copper kettle, and a small chest like the kind carried by Moorish doctors in the streets of Córdoba.

For his part, Grimnir remained silent as he unfastened his ragged wolf-skin cloak. He hung it and his leather satchel from a peg, on the wall by the fire. Next, he drew his seax and eyed the blade, looking for signs of rust. Satisfied, he set it aside and unbuckled his weapon belt, then shrugged out of his iron-ringed hauberk and laid it out by the fire; the padded jerkin he wore beneath it was rust-stained and sodden. He peeled this off, as well, and put it with the rest. Naked but for his kilt and sandals, Grimnir sat at the table, his seax close at hand, and fell upon a bowl of the stew, a savory concoction of winter vegetables and salted pork to which he added chunks of bread torn from a loaf.

'How can you tell he's a warrior?' Étaín asked quietly as the old woman returned to her side.

Maeve tapped the side of her long nose. 'I smell the leather and ironmongery. But—' She paused. '—he is no Gael, neither is he a Northman or a Briton. There is something . . . odd about his scent. Something I cannot place.'

Étaín said nothing. She stared into the crackling flames as, behind her, Grimnir sniffed the mead before drinking it straight from the crockery jug. He watched from the corner of his eye as the old woman examined Étaín with only her hands, feeling out every scar, welt, bruise, laceration, and contusion from the last few weeks.

'You've not had an easy time of it,' Maeve said, feeling the sharp angles of Étaín's cheekbones and caressing her brow. She traced the scabbed wound left behind from Cynewulf's boot heel. 'And this scar, I fear, will never fade.' She palpated the younger woman's neck, probing for swollen glands or signs of imbalanced humors. Muttering under her breath, Maeve turned to the physician's chest and rooted through tinctures, salves, and vials of herbs by feel alone. She ground and mixed, tasted and spat, oblivious to the world around her. The wolfhound lay in the far corner of the cottage, watching his mistress work.

Grimnir finished off a second bowl of stew, then a third, and drained the jug of mead. Warm, sated, he stretched his legs out beneath the table and leaned back, his shoulders against the rough stone of the wall. He closed his eyes and, for the first time since leaving Sjælland, he allowed himself to drift off to sleep.

4

Above the cottage, with its warm thatch steaming in the cold rain, a salt-heavy wind yet lashed the leaves and branches of ancient oaks. There, three shadows met in congress. Three ravens, they were, an unkindness of silent, feathered giants, weird and terrible in their sentience. Cruach was there, and another of his kin, slightly smaller than him in size; the third raven, though, was a monstrous creature, larger even than the other two. Its feathers gleamed like pale moonlight, and it watched the glade below through green and malevolent eyes . . .

'*Fomórach*,' it croaked.

5

The soft touch of a hand to her brow roused Étaín from a light and dreamless slumber. She drowsed by the fire, reclined upon a bolster and wrapped in a blanket of herb-scented wool. Opening her eyes, she saw Maeve beside her.

'I'm sorry,' she said. 'I dozed off.' Outside, the rain had slackened, becoming a soothing patter.

'Nay, child, say nothing of it. Rest only helps the white willow and feverfew to weave its spell. Aye, fever's broken,' the blind Irishwoman said, her voice barely rising above a whisper. Grimnir and her wolfhound, Conán, snored in unison, each seeking to outdo the other with every long, drawn-in breath. 'Feel up to a bite of sup?'

'I think so.'

Maeve rose and bustled about the cottage. The old woman moved with well-rehearsed economy, instinct and long familiarity informing each gesture as she fetched a bit of hard cheese, a loaf of bread, a clay jar of wine, a wooden bowl, and two horn cups and put them in a woven basket.

'When did you lose your sight?' Étaín asked.

'Oh, long before you were born, child,' she said, bringing the basket back to the hearth. Her joints crackled as she crouched. Touch replaced vision; she fished the bowl from the basket and leaned nearer the fire, where an iron pot of bubbling stew hung suspended from a soot-blackened hook. 'It was . . . an injury to the head. A Norseman's axe. A rabble of them came up from Veisafjorðr seeking a bit of loot. I was a girl of ten.' The memory sent a tremble of fear through Maeve; her hand shook as she spooned broth off the stew and into the bowl. 'I had an aunt, my father's sister, who was a wise-woman. Aye, a witch some called her, but she'd studied the physician's art in Moorish Córdoba. Even with all her herbcraft and book lore, it took a year and more to drag me back from Death's door. My sight didn't return with me.'

'I am sorry,' Étaín said, taking the bowl from Maeve's hand.

But the older woman just shook her head as she reached for the wine jar and poured two cups with apparent ease. 'Nay, Blind Maeve don't need none of your pity, child. The Almighty has blessed me plenty. I still got my wits, two legs, two arms, and a spine. I can hear and I can smell . . . better, I'd wager, than that great hairy heathen snoring on yonder floor.'

'I'm . . .' Étaín caught herself before she could apologize again. She sighed and gave a wistful smile. The young woman blew on the surface of the broth before taking a sip. Wind rustled the thatch on the eaves of the cottage. 'This might seem like an odd question,' Étaín said after a moment, 'but where in Ériu are we? We were crossing to Dubhlinn before the storm rose . . .'

'Dubhlinn? So you'll be bound for the Troubles, then? Well, you're not too far off the mark. You're about a mile north of Arnkell's Lag . . . at Lorcan's Wood, in the foot-hills of Cualu.'

'And Dubhlinn?'

'Twelve leagues and a pinch, due north. Will you and

your man stand with good King Brian or against him?'

'Oh, he's not my man,' Étaín said, her face reddening. To hear Grimnir described thus . . . she shuddered at the idea. 'Blessed Christ, no. We merely travel together . . . allies, after a fashion. Though this has not always been so.'

Maeve raised an eyebrow. 'Your *ally*, then. Do you know his mind?'

'*That* I know quite well, for he has never been shy about voicing it. Grimnir is after revenge and I suspect he will stand with the side that makes it easier for him to kill the bastard who crossed him.'

'Some poor *thegn* among the Foreigner?'

Étaín finished the broth, set the bowl aside, and tore off a chunk of bread and some cheese. These she ate slowly as she considered the weight of the name on the tip of her tongue – a name that crouched like a spider at the center of a web of deceits and betrayals, all centered on this emerald-hued land. To speak it might conjure something unwanted. Between bites and swallows Étaín regarded the blind old Irishwoman, her forehead creased and careworn and burnished by firelight. Maeve provoked a deep sense of trust in Étaín, but was that trust misplaced? She glanced over at Grimnir's sleeping form. Grimnir, who trusted no one. *No*, she decided suddenly. *I am not like him.* 'Not a *thegn*,' she replied, 'but one of their *jarls*. Bjarki Half-Dane.'

Maeve shuddered, took a long draught of wine. 'He aims for a lofty target, your ally. God-cursed, that one is! A foul sorcerer of the Danes. Aye, old as Methuselah, men say, and more cunning than the Serpent. And he has a dead man who protects him! Draugen, they call him – an apostate deacon of Christ, slain in the Danemark and given foul life by his master. Ever does Half-Dane lurk behind Dubhlinn's walls with that witch, Kormlada, weaving evil nets that snare the good-hearted and the devout.'

Étaín smiled. 'And as my companion might say if he were awake: *faugh.*'

'You doubt what I say?'

'Not in the least, good Maeve. But, as you said earlier, there is something *odd* about Grimnir. Such things cause him no consternation. He is . . . from a different time.'

'He might be, aye, but his doom is writ in the same blood as any man's,' Maeve said, and after a few minutes of silence she added, 'You need not go with him, you know. To Dubhlinn. Stay with Blind Maeve if you like. The Troubles is no place for the likes of us, child.'

'You would shelter me? A stranger to you, blown upon your doorstep by unnatural winds?'

A shadow crossed the old woman's brow. 'Shelter you from *him*? Is that what you mean? Is he a beast among men? Would he seek to hurt you if you renounced him?' Daggers lurked in Blind Maeve's voice; though sightless, Étaín did not doubt she'd seek to open Grimnir's throat at the slightest provocation.

Étaín touched the old woman's hand in gentle benediction. 'No, dear Maeve. Sheathe your knives. He does not own me. Not anymore. I go where I will, and for now I will go north with him to Dubhlinn. Not to fight, if that's what makes you fearful of my safety.'

'Then to what end?' Maeve sniffed.

Étaín thought a moment, and then replied: 'To bear witness.'

'There is a tale, there, I sense.' Maeve yawned; the hour was late.

'There is.' Étaín finished her bread and cheese, drained her wine cup, and sank back on the bolster. 'Perhaps tomorrow . . .'

Maeve yawned again, putting her back against the

hearth. 'Aye,' she muttered. ''Tis a tale I'll want to be hearing, child. Not now, though. So . . . tired.'

Outside, the rain beat a staccato rhythm; the wind played through chinks in the cottage walls, a soft and gentle whistle that caused Étaín's mind to wander. She relaxed, closed her eyes. A scent tickled her nostrils, then – a cloyingly sweet odor, like flowers left too long on a grave.

The wolfhound growled in his sleep, but then whimpered.

Wood creaked as Grimnir shifted his weight.

Étaín heard Maeve stir. 'No,' she moaned, only half conscious. 'Not them. Why have they come? Why . . . ?'

The younger woman felt a thrill of panic skate down her spine; she tried to no avail to rouse herself, to stir limbs gone heavy with the promise of slumber. And as that dark and unnatural sleep reached out to embrace her, Étaín fancied she heard the door to the cottage *snick* open, followed by the sinister rustle of wings . . .

6

'Up, you laggard!'

The voice was muted, distant. Hearing it, Grimnir came awake with a start. Wood scraped stone as he lurched to his feet. His skull throbbed, as though someone had pried it apart and rifled through its contents. Darkness clung to his vision. Grimnir blinked, cursed; he knuckled his eyes in an effort to dispel the mist that obscured them. Soon, this murk resolved into a silhouette, its outline growing more familiar by the moment.

'Who's there?' he muttered. 'Gífr?'

'Caught you napping, little rat!' That harsh reply lifted the veil from Grimnir's eyes. Gífr was as Grimnir recalled: tall and lean, his hard-gristle frame plaited together with ropes of muscle and sinew, and covered in a sallow hide seamed with scars. Scores of them. Hundreds, layered in a maddening suggestion of feathers. But, as Grimnir blinked, again, Gífr's scars became what he remembered – a tapestry of flesh drawn in iron that told of the fading fortunes of the kaunar.

'What goes?' Grimnir said, glancing about the darksome cottage. The place seemed familiar, though he could not recollect it. Had he been here before? 'Why have you come?'

'To fetch you,' Gífr replied.

Grimnir shook his head, hissing at the jags of pain the gesture provoked. 'Fetch me where, you old git? You're dead!'

'Aren't you a precious sort of fool, little rat?' said Gífr, his laughter echoing about the cottage. Woven into the fringe of hair about his long ears, gray as storm wrack, were countless old bone discs and beads – of copper, silver, garnet, and malachite; they clacked and clicked as he shook his head. 'Do I look dead to you?'

No, Grimnir agreed. He did not look dead. 'Fetch me where, then?'

'To him. He has need of you.'

Grimnir stiffened. A cold lump of dread soured his belly even as jitters of anticipation set his limbs a-tremble. 'Him? He's here?'

'Have you gone daft, little rat?' Gífr scowled. 'Swilled too much mead and took a tumble, I'll warrant! Hit your blasted head! Where else would One-Eye be, fool?'

'Bálegyr . . .' That name had been a talisman for as long as Grimnir could remember, its owner nothing short of the god in whose shadow he had dwelled; he had no memory of his sire save as the echo of a thunderous voice, a menacing shape rough-hewn from half-recalled memories and tales grown wild in the retelling. But more than anything, the name conjured for Grimnir an image of his mother, Skríkja, dark and fell-handed with arms upraised in defiance of the wretched gods of the North: 'Así att-Súlfr Bálegyr skiara tar nekumanza!' she would scream in bitterness, her voice hard as the gnawing ice. 'Bálegyr is the Wolf, come to devour your entrails!' The night of his death, she'd seen in the heavens a single eye, unblinking, wreathed in fire . . .

'Ymir's blood, you miserable shit-bird!' Gífr said, breaking Grimnir's reverie by cuffing his ear with one *horny fist. 'He calls for you and here you stand, mooning like some cow-eyed maiden! And he's not dead, either, if that's what you're thinking.'*

No, Grimnir agreed. Bálegyr wasn't dead, either.

'Grab your kit and leg it, little rat. He's waiting a ways to the north with what's left of the lads, at a place called Carraig Dubh.'

Grimnir nodded. He reached for his seax, but Gífr's laughter brought him up short. 'What?' he snarled. 'What are you cackling about?'

Gífr's smile had all the humor of a grinding ice floe. 'Only a little fool would take a scullery knife to war.'

Grimnir looked again. He cursed under his breath, dug the heel of his hand into one eye then knuckled the other. What he had taken for a seax was, in fact, nothing but a rust-pitted kitchen knife. He slung it aside.

'Your spear is yonder,' Gífr said, with a jerk of his sharp chin. Sure enough, leaning in the corner was a war spear – which at first glance he mistook for an old broom – its iron blade gray and lethal in the dim light. Grimnir snatched it up and made for the cottage door.

'This Carraig Dubh,' he said. 'How will I know it?'

Gífr sat heavily in the chair Grimnir had quit. 'Use your nose, wretch. He's left you a trail of crumbs. Go quick like, little rat. Our precious chief needs you.'

Grimnir gave a nod and took off without a backward glance, running full-out into the perpetual twilight. Gífr smiled and . . .

. . . Shook, shedding the glamour of Grimnir's dreams like a dried husk; it hopped to the table's edge, icy white feathers rustling as it fixed the two sleeping women in its baleful gaze. For a moment it considered ending their lives. But this albino raven – no mere witch's familiar like Cruach, who had gone back to his mistress bearing a message, but a prince of the fading Tuatha – instead took wing and followed in the *fomórach*'s wake, careful never to let him stray too far. With a single, deep *cr-r-ruck*, it wheeled away north even as the rising sun crested the eastern rim of the world.

7

In the oldest quarter of Dubhlinn, on the bluff overlooking the black pool that lent the town its name, the first Norse invaders had discovered a solitary ash tree growing from the stony soil. Beneath its boughs they had erected an altar, and on that altar they had offered nine captives to the Allfather in thanks for safe passage across the storm-racked Irish Sea – nine being the number most sacred to Odin. Their sacrifice found favor and under the Allfather's auspices a city grew from the marshy shores of the pool to be a center for trade in the Viking world. So it was that nineteen times nine years had passed since then, by the reckoning of priests, and the altar of Odin on which was built the foundations of Dubhlinn lay now at the heart of a walled enclosure.

It sat on a platform made of earth and stone: a wooden temple that hearkened back to the harsh land of their ancestors, a land of bleak mountains and wolf-haunted forests. Sharp roof peaks wreathed in sacrificial smoke jutted into the brightening sky, and on every timber stave, every post, and every lintel were intricate carvings made by a generation of master craftsmen – Ragnarok depicted in weathered oak, the Æsir and their *jötunn* adversaries framed by writhing brambles, forever locked in an apocalyptic embrace.

The temple's heavy doors stood ajar, and beyond its scrimshaw threshold lay a world of smoke and shadow, a world that reeked of spilled blood and bowel, ancient wood and incense. Here, cruelly bound upon the altar, a Frankish youth captured in a raid on his homeland drew a final, racking breath; the hands of a Dane no older than he drew tight the silken cord that throttled him. Before his death rattle ceased, a shadow fell over the altar: a one-eyed priest, gray-bearded and fey. Chanting, he plunged the blackened iron blade of a sacrificial dagger into the dying youth's breast and ripped him open. A last violent paroxysm of the lad's heart caused a spray of arterial blood to issue from his lips. And then . . . perfect stillness as his spirit's eyes opened on the grim afterlife.

With fanatical intensity, the priest thrust his arm deep into that butchered torso. Practiced fingers found the liver and tore it free of its mortal housing; he drew it forth and looked at it, peering closely at its lobes and its coloration before tossing it into a broad bowl of hammered copper, where it struck with a wet squelch.

'What say the omens, Ágautr?' A voice issued from the shadows, hollow and heavy with a weariness that transcended flesh. The priest, Ágautr, raised his head and scowled.

'They say much, Draugen. Where is your master?'

A shadow stepped forth, gaunt and corpse-pale, his once-red beard gone to ash. His single eye peered out from beneath the hood of a cloak the color of charred wood. The man called Draugen wore blackened mail, leggings of black leather, and sported arm rings of silver and twisted iron. 'He is about his business, as you should be about yours. What do you see?'

Lip curling in disdain, Ágautr reached in and ripped the heart from the dead Frank's corpse. He brandished it in the thin light. 'Odin's weather! The war reek rises from the land! Monstrous shadows, red-handed and cruel, gather like old men around the corpse fires!'

'I see as much with one eye, priest!' Draugen said.

With both blood-slimed hands, Ágautr drew forth loops of intestine. He leaned over the viscera, frowning; whatever he saw in those glistening ropes drew from him a hiss of fury. 'Your master's enemies grow ever bolder! 'Ware the Gael who hides behind the mask of friendship, for he is the serpent who would strike unawares!'

Draugen nodded. 'And the coming battle, how will it fall?'

Ágautr stepped away from the disemboweled corpse, 'I cannot see. The Norns weave the fate of us all, and they hide the end of things from my sight. Tell him what I have said. 'Ware the Gael—'

'Who hides behind a mask of friendship, you say? You useless old crow, they all wear that mask!' And like a spirit, the man called Draugen faded into the shadows, the echo of his footsteps a sonorous dirge.

8

Morning sunlight slanted through narrow windows high in the walls of Dubhlinn's great hall, casting the warmth of an early spring over a confrontation that had become colder than winter's ice. From the shadows under the jutting gallery, Bjarki Half-Dane observed the lords of Dubhlinn and Leinster meeting with a deputation of Irish chiefs.

Beneath the raven banners of the House of Ivar, Sitric Olaf's son sat upon the edge of his throne, flanked by a dozen Norse giants in heavy mail bearing long, glittering spears and thick shields. On his right, in a place of honor, King Maelmorda of Leinster reclined on a brocaded divan, bleary-eyed and drinking Greek wine from a gold-chased bowl. Kormlada sat beside him, legs drawn up beneath her like a cat. She wore a gown of fine scarlet linen, almost sheer and slit brazenly to midthigh, accented by a torque of woven gold and silver wire, capped by snarling wolves – one holding a pearl in its jaws and the other a bead of carved amber; gold clusters dangled from the lobes of her ears. She sipped wine from a silver goblet and gazed with studied indifference upon the men arrayed before them. Standing in knots of twos and threes were the twelve chiefs of the *fianna* of Leinster – the clannish war bands that formed the spine of Maelmorda's army. They watched their king, to a man stiff-backed and scowling.

Bjarki felt a presence at his back; he turned his head and beheld the somber visage of Draugen. 'Let me guess,' Half-Dane hissed, 'Ágautr sees more blood and thunder?'

Draugen – who had gone by the name Red Njáll son of Hjálmarr before his death some fifteen years ago on the road to Roskilde – nodded. 'And, he says you should beware the Gael.'

Bjarki chuckled. 'He said I should beware you, too, if you recall.' Draugen only grunted at this. And so Ágautr had warned him, fourteen years earlier, when Njáll had sought Bjarki out on the Isle of Wight. *He was King Olaf's man,* the old priest had said, jabbing an accusing finger at Njáll's chest. *Why should he now serve you? And you would trust this treacherous son of Hjálmarr when last I recall he was panting for your blood on the beach at Scilly?*

But the man who called himself Draugen – who claimed he had trod the dank road to Helheimr and returned – had whispered one word into Half-Dane's ear; with that one word all doubt vanished. Bjarki Half-Dane knew that Draugen, alone of all men, would never betray him.

'Which Gael?' Half-Dane asked as the tallest of the Irishmen, a rawboned fellow in a ragged green and yellow cloak, his red-gold hair braided down his back, stepped forward. Bjarki glared at the man's face, sun-darkened and blunt; long bristling mustaches emphasized the fierce jut of his jaw.

'The old charlatan didn't say.'

'Stand ready, then,' Bjarki hissed. 'We may have to kill them all.'

The tall Irishman sketched a perfunctory bow. 'The lads have elected me to speak for them.'

'And who are you?' Sitric replied.

'My king knows me.'

264

'Aye,' Maelmorda said, after a moment. 'Partha, you are, chief of the warriors of Cluain Mhór. A village of shepherds, if I recall, who were ever as rocks in my father's sandal.' There was no disguising the contempt in the king of Leinster's voice. 'What do you want? Why have you roused these others and dragged me from my rest at this unholy hour?'

'We want a king worthy of our respect,' the chief, Partha, replied, answering Maelmorda's truculence with his own. 'But you are what the Almighty has given us. Thus, we've come to parley.'

The king of Leinster's gaze turned to ice. 'Tread carefully, shepherd.'

'Parley?' Kormlada said. 'Are we enemies, Partha of Cluain Mhór? Do you have a grievance? Have my brother or I mistreated you in some manner? Speak plain, man!'

'Aye, I will speak plain, Witch of Dubhlinn!' Partha replied. 'Word came to us last night: the vale of An Bhearú burns! Our homes are destroyed, our women and children murdered, shamed and enslaved, our flocks slaughtered, and for what? So your son can grow richer?' He turned to Maelmorda. 'Lead us away from here, son of Murchada! Be the king we can respect! Let us face the Munstermen on our own terms!'

Maelmorda laughed. Wine sloshed from his bowl as he used it to gesture at the warrior. 'You would have me flee from my own rebellion?'

'We would have you protect what is yours!' Partha answered with heat. The other chiefs muttered assent, nodding. Partha smoothed his mustaches with one scarred knuckle. 'The *fianna* of Leinster serve its king, and none other! Are you that king, Maelmorda mac Murchada, or are you but a silk-clad outlaw sporting a stolen crown?'

Maelmorda staggered to his feet, slinging the bowl

from his hand in fury. The vessel struck the stone flags near Partha with a tremendous *clang,* spattering him with wine lees; to his credit the tall Irishman didn't so much as flinch. 'Your tongue runs roughshod over your good sense, shepherd! I should have you flogged, you insolent wretch! You and your traitorous cronies! Suffering Christ—!'

'Sit down, brother, before you fall down,' Kormlada said.

'Aye.' Bjarki's sibilant voice cut through Maelmorda's tirade like a knife. 'Listen to your sister.' Silence as thick as a death shroud descended on the great hall; the king of Leinster did not even put up a front – he dropped back onto his divan and motioned for a servant to bring more wine. The eyes of the Irish chiefs fastened on Half-Dane, who emerged from the gloom beneath the gallery. Draugen followed him like an iron-shod specter. 'Partha of Cluain Mhór,' Half-Dane said, moving through the knots of Irishmen. 'How often, when your king raised the war banners, have you crossed into Munster to raid for cattle? How often have you driven deep into that miserable wretch Mac Cennétig's lands to plunder villages? How many women have you shamed, stolen, and killed? How many children have you left for the crows, Partha of Cluain Mhór?'

Partha shrugged. The other chiefs muttered among themselves.

'More times than you can count?' Bjarki pressed.

'Aye,' Partha replied. 'What of it?'

Bjarki stopped at the foot of the royal dais and turned to face the assembled chiefs, his voice a bloodcurdling hiss. 'Did Mac Cennétig set aside his well-wrought plans and ride out to avenge those drab-ankled whores and their brats from those burned-out little shitholes no one's heard of, and fewer care about? No? And why is that, Partha of Cluain Mhór?'

Partha's jaw clenched and unclenched. 'He knew – '

'Speak up, damn your eyes!' Bjarki roared.

'He knew what he was about,' Partha said grudgingly. 'We were goading him, and he knew it.'

'*We were goading him,*' Half-Dane mocked. '*And he knew it!* Well, God's teeth, man! It's a stroke of good fortune you were here to school us on strategy! Otherwise, we might have cast aside our plans – plans I've laid for half your miserable life! – and gone off to avenge those whores and brats you left behind, in that shithole you call a village!' Bjarki turned his back on Partha in a gesture of utter contempt.

The Irish chief's face grew black with rage. Steel sang on leather as he whipped a knife from his belt and lunged at Half-Dane. The snarling Partha was but a step away from burying his blade in Bjarki's spine when Draugen's scarred fist tangled in the red-gold braids that swung from the man's scalp. Ever the ghost in Half-Dane's shadow, Draugen hauled Partha back by his hair and slung the Irishman to the ground. His knife clattered away; Partha slid across the rough flagstones and came to rest in a dazed heap at the feet of his comrades. A dozen Irishmen glared murderously at the giant Dane and his master.

Draugen stepped toward them, his cloak fluttering aside, battle madness blazing forth from his one eye; he drew a pair of axes from the small of his back, short and oak-hafted, their bearded blades rune-etched with spells of doom. 'If you want to kill a man,' he growled, 'draw steel and look him in the eye.'

Partha struggled to his feet; the two kings, Sitric and Maelmorda, exchanged looks, apprehension writ upon their brows – they could smell a slaughter on the morning breeze. Kormlada gave a predatory smile as Bjarki Half-Dane mounted the dais to stand between the rulers of

Dubhlinn and Leinster before turning to face the knot of Irishmen.

'So what will it be, Partha of Cluain Mhór? Will you break your oath to your king? Will you lead your rogues out to chase some pack of Munster dogs through the hills and hollows of Leinster just to avenge a village? Or will you cleave to my plan and treble your holdings when we put our enemies to the sword?'

Partha drew himself up to his full height, eyes clouded with rage. 'You piss-colored bastard! You've no clan, no title, and still you think you can give orders to the *fianna* of Ériu? Crawl back under whatever rock spawned you, Half-Dane, and keep your crooked nose out of business that doesn't concern – '

'Draugen,' Bjarki hissed.

Even as the name left Half-Dane's lips, Draugen was in motion, snapping his right arm back and forward in one smooth stroke. The axe in that hand flew from his fingers, flashed through a bar of sunlight, and struck Partha in the juncture of his neck and right shoulder. The blade bit deep; the Irish chief staggered, clawing at the axe haft as bright arterial blood pumped from the wound. Partha dropped to one knee, then toppled onto his side, falling into an ever-expanding pool of crimson.

'Who speaks for you, now?' Bjarki said. 'Will you break your oaths to your king or will you cleave to my plan?'

The other chiefs muttered to one another as Partha gave a wet, rattling sigh and lay still; they shot dark looks at the Danes, and at their king, but after a moment a sullen, black-haired chief stepped forward.

'Othna the Black,' Kormlada said, acknowledging the man with a nod. 'You were ever a voice of reason.'

Othna gave her a cursory bow. 'You're too kind, lady. I will speak for the chiefs of the *fianna* of Leinster. We will honor our oaths to our king, and do what he thinks is best.'

Bjarki turned to Maelmorda. 'And what does he think is best, eh?'

The king of Leinster glanced sidelong at Half-Dane and then stood on unsteady legs. 'My fierce hawks of war!' he said, gesturing broadly – too broadly for a man who was sober. 'We will cleave to our original plan. We will crush our enemies here, before the walls of Dubhlinn, and drive them before us in defeat! And when the time is right, we will descend upon Mac Cennétig's lands and seize it all, from Thomond to the Rock of Cashel!'

The chiefs did not cheer with exuberance at their king's proclamation, but rather met it with a mix of dour acceptance and humorless laughter. Othna the Black knelt and rolled the slain Partha onto his back; he wrenched the axe free of the bloodstained corpse and tossed it at Draugen's feet with a muttered curse. The *clang* of steel on stone was like a death knell, calling the ravens to the banquet.

Nothing more was said as slaves hurried in; some bore a litter, others carried pails of water and sponges to clean the flagstones. In grim silence, the Irish chiefs lifted their slain comrade onto the litter, hoisted him on their shoulders, and bore him from the throne room. The doors groaned shut after they passed the threshold.

Sitric rose from his throne; with a gesture, he sent his Norse guard away. 'These men are supposed to be our *allies*,' he said. 'Will the men of Cluain Mhór seek revenge?'

Draugen tucked one axe into the belt at his back, then bent and retrieved the other. Blood filled the deeply etched runes, which proclaimed the doom of Grimnir son of Bálegyr. He wiped it clean on a slave's trembling back. 'Not if we strike first. We could take them as they sleep . . .'

'Leave them to me,' Kormlada said.

Bjarki glanced sidelong at her. 'To you?'

'To me,' she replied. 'If Othna cannot rein them in, then I will sing the men of Cluain Mhór a song, a soft ballad of madness and despair.'

Half-Dane laughed. Maelmorda, though, glared into the depths of his wine. 'Let Draugen grant them a clean death, if it comes to it. They've earned that, at least.'

Bjarki Half-Dane had a scathing reply ready, but the sudden *cr-r-ruck* of a raven drew his gaze upward, away from the wine-besotted king of Leinster. The raucous cry echoed; through a narrow window came the coal-black form of ancient Cruach. He circled above their heads, through light and shadow, drifting lower and lower; Kormlada swiftly gained her feet and held forth her arm, an eerie whistle escaping her lips.

Cruach ignored her.

Sitric backed away as the great bird alighted on the arm of his throne. He shook his feathers, his unblinking gaze fixed on Bjarki Half-Dane. Red eyes met black; Bjarki straightened, nostrils flaring. 'Speak, old crow! Speak if you have news!'

And Cruach did.

> *Comes from the East, | Bálegyr's issue,*
> *To the halls where dwells | Grendel's bastard,*
> *To the Black Pool | to claim his weregild.*
> *Not gleaming arm rings | nor mountains of gold,*
> *But the blood of Half-Dane | spilled in Odin's*
>   *weather.*

Cruach shook and stretched his wings like a creature coming awake; glancing about, he spotted Kormlada and took to wing, fluttering over to her proffered arm. She stroked the raven's neck, crooning softly. Maelmorda laughed. 'Has your crow learned to spit doggerel, sister, or is this some manner of prophecy?'

'Aye,' Sitric said. 'What does it mean, Mother?'

Kormlada looked askance at Bjarki. 'Only he for whom the prophecy is meant can—'

'It's not a prophecy,' Draugen cut her off. He turned to Bjarki, a grim smile twisting his gaunt features. 'It's the fulfillment of a promise. *He* comes.'

A range of emotions played across Half-Dane's visage in the span of a single breath. His eyebrows rose in disbelief; a glimmer of fear shone from deep within – honest atavistic terror – but then a sheet of anger slammed down like one of Draugen's axes, suffusing his face with rage and narrowing his eyes to glittering embers.

'After all these years.' Draugen nodded, as though trying to convince himself more than anyone else. 'He comes, at last.'

'*Pah!*' Bjarki spat. 'Time to earn your keep, then!'

Draugen's smile widened to a fierce grin. He spun and stalked from the throne room even as Half-Dane whirled and headed for the stairs leading up to the gallery and Cuarán's Tower.

Oblivious, or merely incurious, Maelmorda returned to his drinking. Sitric and Kormlada, however, exchanged puzzled looks. With a soft murmur of love, she sent Cruach aloft and followed in Half-Dane's wake.

9

Kormlada reached the gallery as Bjarki set his foot upon the stairs to Cuarán's Tower. The raven's words made barely any sense to her; that they were Nechtan's doing was beyond doubt, but what was the lord of the Tuatha playing at? What had the warning meant? And, more to the point, what was it that could inspire such a look of fear – however briefly – in a man like Bjarki Half-Dane? What did Nechtan know that she did not?

He comes, Draugen had said. *After all these years, he comes.* Some enemy, to be sure, but who and from what quarter? The Witch of Dubhlinn ground her teeth in frustration.

There must have been a serving woman on the stairs. Kormlada heard a feminine voice, a muffled apology; she heard a curse followed by the sharp crack of Half-Dane's knuckles across flesh. There came a short, terrified cry. The woman must have lost her balance, for what Kormlada heard next was the sound of a falling body and, finally, the sickening crunch of bone as she landed in a heap at the foot of the stairs.

Kormlada stood motionless in a pool of shadow. Bjarki's footsteps came back down – not out of concern for the woman, of that she was certain. She watched as he stepped out into the gallery, his back to her. Like a vulture he crouched over the serving woman, a fair-haired Briton who tended to her bath and toilet; Kormlada saw her, as well: her neck at an unnatural angle and her golden hair floating in a pool of blood, spreading out from her lacerated scalp. She gave a final wheezing moan and was still, sightless eyes staring at the smoke-darkened ceiling.

Bjarki pondered the arrangement of her limbs. He studied the patterns of spilled and spattered blood as though trying to divine the future in the viscous fluid; after a moment, he spat a litany of words in a tongue Kormlada didn't recognize, rose, and resumed his ascent.

Kormlada emerged from the darkness and stared down at the woman's body. The fall had rucked her coarse saffron dress up around her thighs, and one soft leather shoe was gone. Close to her heart she'd worn a silver chain, and from it hung a pendant made from a rough garnet captured by a cage of silver wire – a gift from some Norse admirer, no doubt. The fall had crushed the wire cage. The pendant lay in the woman's blood, where it had taken on the appearance of a red, gore-streaked eye. *Like the eye in the clouds, last night.*

'He fears whatever it was that roused the *mná sidhe*,' she whispered, frowning. She heard a flutter of wings; turning, she found that Cruach had alighted in one of the openings of the gallery. The ancient raven cocked his head, stared unblinking at the corpse. 'What was it, Cruach, my love? You know, don't you? You know what roused the night hags . . . you know what *he* fears, for they are one and the same.'

Cruach shifted his gaze to her, a primordial light kindled in his eyes. There was hatred, yes, and something deeper. Something Kormlada had never seen in the raven before now.

'You . . . You fear it, too? Does this terror have a name?'

When Cruach spoke again, she heard the echo of a darker age in his croaking reply. He uttered a single word:

'*Fomórach.*'

And with a chill running up her spine, the Witch of Dubhlinn suddenly understood the warning cry of the *mná sidhe*.

10

Run, little rat, *Gífr's voice commanded.*

And he did.

Though bandy-legged, Grimnir set a steady pace, his long, loping strides like the gait of a hunting wolf. He kept the sea on his right hand as he crossed deep glens on the flanks of a thickly forested range of hills; he skirted settlements and kept to the tree line, breaking only to scoop handfuls of water from streams in spate.

Run, *Gífr's voice prodded.* Run till your lungs burst! Run! Run till your blood boils and your bones crack!

And he would, though he needed no urging.

Despite the constant haranguing, Grimnir drew up near the edge of a rocky shelf overlooking a shallow, wooded valley. He wrung sweat from his eyes; bending low to the ground, he ferreted out the trail Bálegyr had laid down for him – the stench of the vestálfar, *like corpse rot and ancient cerecloth, mixed with the heady iron scent of* kaunar *blood. It led away from the coastal glens and high into the mountains, where ancient oak and rowan gave way to pine, and thence to stony moors and sedge-girdled mires. Grimnir's nostrils flared; hatred for their west-elves rose up in him, ancestral and as old as root and bole. He bellowed a challenge; it echoed over hills, into hollows; it faded, and only silence came in answer. No birdsong,* no creak *and* craak *of insects, no barking of dogs; the red squirrel kept to its drey, the owl to its hollow, the fox to its den; the land itself felt like it had drawn in the breath of wind and was holding it in expectation of violence. Grimnir's laughter echoed across the lonely moors.*

Run, damn your eyes, *Gífr* roared. Run, to Carraig Dubh or to Helheimr! The stinking whiteskins have your sire at bay and you stand here laughing? Run!

Grimnir cursed and blew froth from yellowed fangs. He set forth again at a redoubled pace. He was the son of Bálegyr, a black-hearted knot of vengeance, a weapon honed to a thin, cruel edge. He was tireless, sleepless, deathless, and pitiless; his enemies would get no mercy, for mercy was the dominion of weaklings and fools! He understood strength. He understood fear. And he understood violence. But he was not without craft – no son of Bálegyr could claim to be. His guile was the guile of the serpent. And like the serpent, he would strike at Bálegyr's enemies –

Not if you're too late, little rat, *Gífr* said.

'*I won't be, you old git! You're the lazy swine, not me!*' *And so Grimnir ran on, ducking branches and leaping fallen trunks, his endurance beyond anything mortal. Deeper he went into the heart of Ériu, to find the survivors of Mag Tuiredh while there was still time . . .*

Lost amid the glamour of the Tuatha, Grimnir failed to mark a wind-scoured face that stared out from a thicket of rowan and hazel. The man, whose fierce silver beard bristled, lurked in the lee of a great boulder – like a giant's head, split and weather-scarred, its chin bearded in flowering moss. The man watched him pass, felt his eyes rake over him without comprehension; then, crossing himself, he withdrew and went to find help.

II

Morning faded and afternoon was in full bloom by the time Étaín finally stirred. She thrust herself up from the bolster, knuckled sleep from her eyes, and squinted at the warm sunlight slanting through chinks in the cottage's shuttered windows. 'What happened? Grimnir?' Her voice was raspy and dry. No one answered her. A springtime breeze spiced with the scents of damp earth, grass, and budding fruit trees drifted through the open door; birds warbled in the distance. And like the faint thrum of a heartbeat, Étaín could just barely hear the murmur of surf on the rocky coast. 'Grimnir?'

'He's gone,' Blind Maeve said. Étaín craned her neck and saw the old Irishwoman sitting in the same position she'd been in since the night before, with her brittle spine against the unyielding stone of the hearth. Pain thinned Maeve's lips, making deeper the lines etched around her mouth. She tried to move and winced from the effort.

Though she wore not a stitch of clothing beneath her blanket, Étaín nevertheless clambered to her feet and tottered to Maeve's side. She helped the old woman rise; with exaggerated care, the pair of them shuffled over to a padded chair where Maeve could sit. By the light of day, she seemed more careworn to Étaín. More fragile. A thatch of unkempt gray hair half-obscured the gnarled scar of the

277

wound that had robbed Maeve of her sight. It reminded Étaín of her own scabbed-over wound. But Maeve was not merely blind – the physical organs of her vision had atrophied, as well, becoming shrunken and unfocused, vestigial reminders of a gift lost to violence. At the sound of movement, the wolfhound Conán trotted in from outside the cabin. The great beast whined; he nuzzled Maeve's trembling hand. 'Aye, I'm alive, you great hairy heathen,' she said.

'Grimnir's gone, you say? Gone where? What happened to us? That was no natural sleep.' Étaín found a knitted shawl the color of autumn leaves and wrapped it around Maeve's shoulders before snatching her blanket off the hearth and covering herself.

'Aye.' The old woman pulled the shawl tighter, shivering despite the sunlit warmth of the cottage. 'Aye, that was a rare bit of deviltry, indeed.' Maeve reached for Étaín's hand. 'I am sorry, child. Whatever trouble your Grimnir has caused you in the past, whatever you were hinting at last night . . . well, he'll trouble you no longer.'

'Why?' Étaín said, crouching by Maeve's side; a knot tightened in her belly, a knot of . . . *was it fear?* She was alone, now. Alone and . . . free. *Free.* For the first time since she could remember. The knot of fear sharpened to a pain. 'What happened? Where has he gone?'

'To a place you cannot follow.'

'Please, Maeve! Tell me.'

'They have claimed him.'

Exasperation brought a flush of color to Étaín's cheeks. She clenched her fist, hard enough that her nails bit into her palm, and then exhaled. 'Who are *they*, Maeve? Not the Norse, surely? Was it some faction of the Irish, allied with . . . Half-Dane, perhaps?' Étaín grasped at shadows. Grimnir's gear – his shirt of rings and his jerkin, his cloak and his old Roman satchel – still hung by the hearth where he'd left it the night before; she spotted his seax under the table, cast aside like it meant nothing. She saw no blood, no evidence of strife – both things she fully expected to find even if someone came upon him unawares – nothing. 'You mentioned deviltry. Was it . . . *something* else?'

'You'll think Blind Maeve mad, child.'

'No, I assure you. What was it that took him?'

Maeve sighed. 'The Fair Folk. The Tuatha, who were the masters of Ériu before the coming of good Saint Pádraic. This was their doing. They sang us a right lullaby and lured him away, all in the same breath.'

The fear knotting Étaín's guts suddenly turned to dread. She recalled something Grimnir had said back on the coast of Britain, about Mag Tuiredh and the doom of his people. 'These Tuatha . . . do they have a name among the Danes?'

'Elves,' Maeve answered.

'*Vestálfar.*' Étaín shook her head. 'Merciful Christ! Where would they have taken him?'

'Likely to the Black Stone atop the spike of Carraig Dubh, where they dwell. And if you be wondering why, well, Blind Maeve can't answer that . . .'

'Oh, I know why: the sins of the father visited upon the son, and his father was – by all accounts – well-steeped in sin.' Étaín rocked back on her heels and stood. She nodded, to herself rather than to Maeve. 'I have to go after him.'

Maeve tilted her head. 'Aye, are ye daft, child? The only help you can give your Grimnir is to pray, and pray hard, for he is beyond your reckoning. No mortal can resist the Fair Folk, but if he is a good Christian then perhaps the Almighty will intercede.'

At this, Étaín laughed. The sound of it brought a frown to Maeve's seamed brow. Étaín saw and hastened to add, 'I would do as you say if there was any hope under Heaven it would help, but Grimnir is none of the things you mention.'

'What do you mean, child?'

'He is neither mortal nor a good Christian.'

The old Irishwoman's sightless eyes widened, and then narrowed. 'Aye, your tale, is it? Best tell it from the beginning.'

Étaín looked around for her clothes – mere rags, now, but better than running about in her skin. 'Have you anything I could wear besides this blanket?'

'Whatever you can find that Blind Maeve has is yours, child. So long as you explain yourself.'

And so, as she hunted around the cottage for clothing, Étaín began to tell her tale: 'I met him in a cave, on the road to Roskilde in the Danemark, in the autumn of *anno Domini* nine hundred and ninety-nine. That was fifteen years ago, by the reckoning of any sane person, but to me it was scarcely a fortnight past . . .'

Étaín chose her words with care, and painted for Maeve an image of the cave and the creature that lurked there; she did not stint when she told of Grimnir's attempt to murder Njáll or her own terrible descent into the fringes of the Elder World. Blind Maeve shivered and crossed herself at Étaín's description of the *dvergar* and their shrine to Yggðrasil, and of her nightmarish journey along the Ash-Road.

Étaín spoke quietly of her capture, of the destruction of Badon, and of her encounter with the Shepherd of the Hills. And she talked of those lost on the way: of Njáll and Hrolf Asgrimm's son, both victims in their own way of Grimnir's fury; Jarl Óspak of Mann, who had shown her extraordinary kindness; and she spoke of Grimnir himself, who was, for all his profane ways, possessed of a rudimentary sense of honor. 'He carried me. For six days he carried me and I still do not understand why; all he had to do was leave me where I fell. Do you think *me* mad?' Étaín asked suddenly, as she put the bundle of clothing she'd found on the table and let the blanket slip to the floor. 'I would, if I heard this tale from another.' She drew on a long linen tunic the color of old charcoal that fell above her knees, girdled at the waist with a broad belt of rough leather and green brocade. Among Maeve's things she also found a pair of soft leather shoes with hardy oxhide soles, and a patched cloak of russet wool – which she settled over her shoulders and gathered under a ring-pin brooch of gilded bronze. Étaín ran a hand through her short copper hair. 'I would think the teller either mad or a liar.'

It was Maeve's turn to laugh. 'Not among the Gael, child. We of Ériu have long believed in the power of the Otherworld. Aye, it ebbs and flows around us like the tides; wild and fey with no rhyme or reason to it – and sometimes our only protection from it is in the salvation of Christ Jesus. There is magic, there, too.'

'Salvation,' Étaín said, barely above a whisper. There was a sense of heaviness in her voice, the echo of a pain borne too close for too long. She crouched, fishing under the table to retrieve Grimnir's fallen seax; as she straightened, she added, 'When I was a child at Glastonbury, there was a novice from Ériu, a Gael called Aidan, who would gather us foundlings together and take us out beyond the walls of the monastery to harvest herbs for the kitchen. We expected a sermon, something from the Gospels, but instead Aidan told us stories – tales of orphans who did battle with sinister witches or caught talking fishes; girls who rode the shoulders of giants or boys who ran with the skin-changers of the North.

'Well, we clamored for more; all hours of the day and

281

night, and young Aidan would oblige us. He had more passion for those tales than he had for the Word of God, I think. One evening near midsummer, in my twelfth year, Aidan should have been at Compline. But, God bless him, we'd lost one of our own to the bloody flux that day, so he came to see us, instead. Crept into our sleeping hall and raised our spirits with the tale of Cúchulainn.' Étaín smiled at the memory; but as quickly as it appeared, her smile faded. 'The abbot found us out, of course. That man knew nothing of kindness, nothing of restraint, not even for one of his own. He packed Aidan off, back to Ériu I presume. Our punishment – for the crime of leading his novice astray – was dealt right to where it would hurt a cast-off child the most . . . our bellies.'

Étaín went to where Grimnir's weapon belt hung and carefully slid the seax into its wood-and-leather scabbard. The weapon belt, and the rest of his gear, she brought back over to the table. 'For a fortnight,' she continued, 'we ate only stale bread and bitter herbs. At each meal, as we gagged down this meager ration, the good abbot would reiterate how foolish we were to believe such stories, and that there was no magic left in the world – and if by chance some *did* exist, then it was the province of the Enemy and we would be damned for all time if we so much as looked upon it. "There is only Christ," he told us. "Christ and the Church, and the only concern you should have is that your soul is pure enough come Judgment Day to earn entrance to the Kingdom of Heaven!" '

Étaín turned from the table. Tears glistened in her eyes, the bounty of long frustration; she swiped at them with the heel of her hand. 'What happened to that promised Kingdom, Maeve?' Étaín's voice cracked. 'What happened to it? It never came to pass, did it? And the world as I knew it has upended! Salvation? I have looked upon the sorceries of an elder age, walked a shadowed road that has never known the light of Christ, and held forth with creatures both deathless and profane! But day and night marches on, as it has since the Almighty spoke light into being, and I begin to wonder if this long-promised salvation is a myth! Am I . . . Am I already in Hell . . . ?'

'Oh, child.' Maeve held out her hands; Étaín came and took them in her own. Maeve drew the younger woman down, kissing the crown of her head as she knelt. That gesture, one of infinite tenderness, wrenched a sob from deep within Étaín's breast. Her shoulders trembled with pent-up grief. 'Listen to me.' Maeve stroked her hair. 'You are no more in Hell than is old Blind Maeve, here. The Almighty's given you a precious gift, child. Aye, a gift and a burden, as well . . . for He has chosen you to walk the boundary between the worlds. You are the beacon of Christ, and if the fey folk reject His offer of salvation, then His word will be your blade.'

'But . . .' Étaín gasped between sobs. 'But the . . . the Ending of . . . of the World?'

Maeve answered with a derisive snort. 'And who says it will end, child? This abbot of yours? Or some other learned fool who thinks they can divine the will of the Almighty from scratchings in a book? Nay, God himself will choose the time and place, if an ending is to happen, and He'll not seek the counsel of these cross-kissing charlatans. All we must do, child, is live well, help where we can, and take the good times with as much grace as the bad.'

Étaín blew out her cheeks and nodded. 'Live well?' she said.

'Aye, live well.' Maeve's callused thumbs smoothed tears from beneath the young woman's eyes. Étaín caught Maeve's hand, kissed it, and stood. She dried her face on the sleeve of her tunic. 'You'll be going after him, then?'

'If it is my gift to walk the boundary,' Étaín said, 'then I don't see how I can not follow my instinct. Grimnir's going to need me, I know it.' She returned to the table and started making a bundle of Grimnir's belongings – rolling his cloak and shirt of iron rings together and strapping them to the Roman satchel; she settled his weapon belt over her neck and shoulder, where it hung like a baldric, the sheathed seax heavy against her hip.

'You know the way to Carraig Dubh, do you?'

Étaín paused. 'If you could point me in the right direction . . .'

'North toward Dubhlinn, then into the hills. Do you have food?' Maeve stood and went to her pantry. By feel, she put a loaf of hard bread into a linen sack, along with a cloth-wrapped cheese, a crockery jar of wine, two onions, a sausage, and a slab of smoked mutton. She came to the table and pressed the sack into Étaín's hands despite her protestations. 'You have to eat, child, and Blind Maeve's got plenty.'

'Thank you, again.' Étaín stowed the food and caught the satchel up by its strap. Its fetishes and finger bones clacked together. The leather itself smelled like Grimnir – the animal reek of sweat mixed with smoke and old blood. 'North, you say?'

Maeve chuckled. 'Nay, I've a better idea: Conán can show you the way.' She gave forth a low whistle; in answer, the giant wolfhound trotted in from outside the cottage. He sat in front of her, tongue lolling. His head was even with Étaín's shoulder. Maeve put out her hand; Conán gave it a nuzzle, licked it. 'Aye, you great hairy heathen! Show her the way to Carraig Dubh. Do as Blind Maeve says, now. You understand?'

Conán tilted his head. He looked quizzically between the two women, and then growled. Étaín started to speak but Maeve cut her off, her voice sharp. 'Nay, you great lump! Maeve will be fine. Show her the way to Carraig Dubh, now, and none of your sass! You make sure you keep her safe, you hear me? And don't you lose her on the road!'

Conán hung his head a moment before lumbering to his feet, turning, and trotting back out the cottage door. Maeve patted Étaín's arm. 'You best hurry, child,' she said. 'That old heathen will get you there, but he's going to be antsy about getting back. Use my name if you meet anyone on the road, you hear me? Blind Maeve has a reputation in these parts, and won't nary a Leinster lad or a whiskered Gall dare to lay a finger on you if they know you're one of mine. Go on, now.'

'I don't know how to thank you,' Étaín said, clasping the older woman's hand. Maeve smiled.

'When all is said and done, child, come back here and tell Blind Maeve everything. It's a rare thing for me to curse the loss of my sight, but this day I curse it heartily. Oh, to see what you're about to see . . .'

Conán loosed a thunderous bark, impatient to be away.

'I promise you,' Étaín said. And then, with a last fleeting kiss to the old woman's cheek, she was gone.

12

Grimnir, as mud-slimed and filthy as one of the bog skrælingar *that once haunted the fens of Skaane*, scrabbled up a crumbling scarp, passed through a tangle of gnarled yew trees, and staggered to the summit of Carraig Dubh – with its single standing stone rising from the windswept precipice. Framed by the setting sun, he saw nothing else: no cursed whiteskins, no kaunar – and no sign they'd been there, either.

'I am here!' he bellowed, his voice small against the red-streaked sky. 'Where are they, you lying sack of piss?'

They come, *Gífr said.*

Yes, *Grimnir agreed.* They were coming. *He could hear them: the spectral clash of arms echoing from the valleys to the west; the roaring war cry of Bálegyr as he drove his people back to the wolf ships, laden with plunder; the screams of west-elves as they died under the blades of the* kaunar *– and who died as fools, thinking they could stand between the dark tide of reavers and their ships.*

Grimnir slowly circled the standing stone, its weathered surface black with age; he imagined he could see the faint outlines of a man in its carved form. He came to the edge of the precipice and peered over. It was a murderous drop of a thousand feet and more to the stony talus; from there, the land sloped away through leaf and bole to a cultivated *plain where he spied a walled town, perching like a vulture over the mouth of a river, its waters – and the water of the bay beyond – burnished to a coppery sheen by the westering sun.*

'What town is that?' he said, the idea something was amiss tugging at the edges of his consciousness.

There is no town, little fool, *Gífr replied.*

No, Grimnir agreed. *There was no town on the plain below.*

He turned as Gífr stepped from the lee of the stone, a silhouette darker than the gathering gloom around him. Eyes blazed, green like those of a cat. 'Ymir's blood, you miserable wretch! Will you stand out in the open for all to see? Get under cover, fool, ere you betray our position!'

Cursing, Grimnir scurried over and crouched at the base of the stone. He sat on his haunches, spear across his knees, and glanced up at Gífr. 'How soon?'

'Soon. Let our people pass, then take those stinking whiteskins in the flank as they hurry after.'

'Alone?' Grimnir frowned. 'I am but one – '

Gífr chuckled and spat. 'Aye, you can count, you little shit-bird. Are you not his son?'

'One against . . .'

'It does not matter,' Gífr said.

No, Grimnir agreed. *It did not matter. He would roll up the flank of those wretched west-elves; he would spatter their pale blood over this miserable rock, as the Sly One was his witness. He would break them.*

'Let them come,' he said, lips peeling back in a snarl of hate. 'Let them come, and stand aside, you old git! I'd hate to put you down by accident!'

'Look out for yourself, little rat!'

And Grimnir would. Knuckles cracking, he tightened his grip on his spear. Oh, he would . . .

13

Long shadows streaked the sides of Carraig Dubh; as the sun dipped into the west, shrouding in gloom the forest a thousand feet beneath that mighty precipice, Bran of the Uí Garrchon gave no thought to making a camp for the night. He had *seen* something earlier in the day, a figure that had loped past him in the valley below – something with blood-hued eyes and yellowed fangs, its dusky hide etched with the stigmata of the heathen. Despite that, he knew it was no Dane, nor was it a Norseman or a Swede or a Gael. These he knew; these Bran of the Uí Garrchon had crossed spears with and lived to tell it. No, whatever it was had given him enough of a fright to send him scurrying off in the other direction. Now, hours later, Bran cursed his own moment of weakness, so unlike a kern of the Uí Garrchon; he cursed the now-cold trail, which he worried at like an old hound with a bone in the deepening twilight. Mostly, though, he cursed the pair of blundering fools who carped at his back.

Like himself, both were Leinstermen, outsiders, sons of the Fortuatha who dwelled in the hills around Arnkell's Lag. They were father and son, the pair: Ruadh Mór of the Ua Feghaile, and crop-eared Dunlaing, who had once been a thrall of Thorwald Raven, chief of the Gall of Veisafjorðr. And like Bran, they had had their fill of Maelmorda's rebellion against the white-haired and kindly old king, Mac Cennétig. They meant to cross the mountainous heart of Cualu and join the high king's army.

Nor would they come empty-handed. Though they had no war gear apart from axe, sword, and spear, they nevertheless led a string of three ponies, each laden with joints of smoked venison, sacks of barley, winter vegetables, and early cabbages nicked from under the king of Dubhlinn's nose.

'You spied one of the feckin' Gall, I tell you,' Ruadh Mór said after Bran had stopped once more, this time to examine a few strands of hair snagged on a low branch. 'Some black-haired son o' a Danish whore, out looking for the likes of us, I'll warrant!' Ruadh Mór leaned on his spear. He was a swag-bellied man in a tunic of patchwork brocades, whose long weather-beaten face bore the scars of a childhood pox. 'Bleedin' Christ, man! You're chasing shadows! Let's kindle a fire and have a bite o' sup ere it gets too dark to see.'

'Aye,' Dunlaing agreed.

But Bran merely grunted. He was a hard knot, bald and sporting a fierce silver beard – a manikin of fire-blackened oak carved and twisted by the hand of God; he wore trousers of supple doeskin and a broad woven belt beneath a cloak of faded green linen, which he wrapped about his torso like a tunic. 'Weren't no Gall,' he said. 'Nor a Gael, neither.' He held the strands of hair under his nostrils and snuffled at them. Even among the Uí Garrchon, a folk noted for their ability to track a lizard across a rock, Bran was a huntsman of uncommon skill. 'This ain't the hair of no man I ever saw. More like wolf fur, like as not. An' I can smell something else . . . leather, an' sweat. Aye, the thing I saw ran on two legs, but it weren't no man. Glared at me with the Devil's own eyes!' Bran straightened and

289

pointed up and away, through a hole torn in the forest canopy by a fallen oak. 'Recognize it?'

Dunlaing spoke up. Ruadh Mór's crop-eared son sported the tattered finery of a Norse lord – no doubt looted from the same corpse that gave him the longsword he wore at his hip. 'Aye, Carraig Dubh. Means we're still too feckin' close to Dubhlinn, is all!'

'An' that's where it's headed,' Bran said. 'Ain't nothing up yonder for God-fearin' folk, so you got to be wonderin' what deviltry is afoot.'

'I ain't got to be wondering no such thing,' Dunlaing replied.

Ruadh Mór moved over to stand next to Bran. He, too, made a show of crouching, of surveying the ground; he brushed aside a patch of leaf mold and scraped a fingernail through the rich black loam, still damp from the storm night before last. 'You might be right, Bran-me-lad. Aye, you might be right. Look here. Can you smell it?' He sniffed at the black earth, held his hand up so Bran might follow suit. The older man inhaled, but shook his head. 'You don't smell that? Why, smells like horse shit to me.'

Ruadh winked at his son. They held their sniggers as long as they could, and then broke out into raucous laughter.

'Idiots, the both of you! I know what I saw!'

'You saw one o' them Dubhlinn Norse in a wolf-fur cloak, you daft bastard! Bleedin' Christ! What, you think it was some *faoladh*? One of those feckin' heathens from up by Osraige? Aye, cursed by Saint Pádraic, himself, to take the form of a wolf-man for seven years? You start thinking like that, we might start thinking you're not right in the head!' Ruadh Mór shouldered past the older man, tsking under his breath. 'It'll be dark, soon, lad. Might as well bed down in yonder clearing, tonight. You fetch some wood. I'll see to the ponies.'

290

'An' him?' Dunlaing nodded at Bran. A shrug was Ruadh Mór's only reply.

Working in unison, father and son soon had their ponies unloaded, hobbled, and fed, a fire kindled, and an iron pot of venison and cabbage bubbling over the coals. Wrapped in his cloak, Dunlaing drew his sword and tended to its edge with a stone and a flask of oil.

Bran, however, did not move. He stood in the same place, staring up at the heights of Carraig Dubh through eyes grown to slits from suspicion. The ponies fidgeted. Last year's leaves and undergrowth crunched beneath their hooves; a breeze rustled the canopy above. In the distance, he could hear the mocking call of a raven. Overhead, the flame-colored evening sky gave way to the silver sheen of night.

Concern for the older man etched Ruadh Mór's brow. He came up, a bowl of stew steaming in the cool evening air. 'Just having a bit o' fun, Bran,' Ruadh Mór said, quietly. 'Don't take it to heart. Me and the lad, we're tired, is all. We could all do with a bit o' rest. This Gall o' yours—'

'You think me daft, Ruadh Mór? Softheaded, aye?' Bran glanced sidelong at his distant kinsman. 'Listen. What do you hear?'

'Nothin',' Ruadh Mór replied after a moment.

'An' that's the problem. I'm thinkin' whatever I saw has circled about and gotten in behind us.'

'Bollocks!'

'Bollocks, is it?' Bran clapped a hard-knuckled hand to Ruadh Mór's shoulder. 'You might be right. Might be nothin'. Might be naught but some shit-handed Dane who got his dander up when your boy, there, went an' stole his cabbages. But if it is some bit of deviltry whistled up from the belly o' Hell by the feckin' Witch of Dubhlinn, then your fire and your bit o' sup is going to draw the bastards right to us.'

And Ruadh Mór, who was a better poet than he was a soldier – and no great shakes at either – turned pale as curdled milk. 'Bleedin' Christ!' He turned to where his son sat by the fire, rasping stone on steel. 'Put it out, boy! Put that fire out!'

'Not feckin' likely,' Dunlaing said. He looked up, scowling. 'What's gotten into you, Da?'

'I said put that damned fire out!' Ruadh Mór hissed.

'Wait,' Bran said. His silver beard jutted defiantly as he glanced over his shoulder, peering hard into the thick underbrush. His hand dropped to the iron-strapped haft of a bearded axe sheathed at his waist. 'Too late, lads.'

Ruadh Mór followed Bran's gaze. There, amid the thickets of hazel and ivy, fern and honeysuckle, he saw the gleam of eyes . . .

14

From her hiding place well back from the uneven circle of firelight, Étaín watched the three Irishmen and wondered what gave her away. How did that sly, silver-bearded old man know someone was out in the darkness? The trio had made their camp near the forest path – the same sort of little-used game trail that Maeve's wolfhound, Conán, had sped along for most of the day, trusting that she'd follow. And follow she did, as best she could. Their road took them over hillocks crowned with ancient stones and into leaf-girt hollows that had not known the tread of a human foot since the days of the Cruithne. The hound was a matchless guide – smarter than most men she'd known and silent save for his expressive growls. Conán had brought her through the Cualann Mountains and to the foot of Carraig Dubh in half the time. And only now did her path cross that of another living soul.

The three might have been foragers, if the provender stacked near their hobbled ponies was any indicator. But whose foragers were they? Étaín could not tell a man of Leinster from one of Munster; nor could she make sense of their speech, though some of the words sounded familiar to her ear. That they did not make straight for Dubhlinn gave credence to her notion that their allegiance might lie with King Brian. Or, perhaps they were simply bandits, human jackals content to exploit the bedlam caused by Leinster's insurrection for their own gain. Whatever they were, Étaín reckoned they shared a common destination: Carraig Dubh.

If I go around them, I risk having them at my back. She chewed her thumb in indecision. *But if I let them go ahead of me, they likely ruin any chance I might have to come upon the* vestálfar *without being seen – and if they are skittish or easily alarmed, I might never find them, again.*

Of course, Grimnir would simply kill the lot of them. Murder them without even an ounce of regret and leave their bodies to rot in the forest. She could hear his voice even now, flint-hard and dripping scorn. *Faugh! There can be no peace between the Wolf and its supper,* he would say. And, to her dismay, Étaín could see his point. Even still, she could not countenance murder. She was no fell-handed *kaunr,* out for blood and glory, but a child of the White Christ . . . and like that, it dawned on her. *These Irish foragers, whether they're men of Munster or of Leinster . . . are they not my brothers in Christ?*

Close at hand, Conán gave a low growl. She could feel an undercurrent of impatience running beneath the wolf-hound's placid exterior; the hour grew late, and he was eager to return to his mistress.

'Bide with me a bit longer,' Étaín whispered, reaching out to tangle her fingers in his brindled coat. Her brow creased as she considered her problem: she could not kill them, nor could she ignore the Irishmen. So, what to do? Incongruously, she thought of Glastonbury. The abbot had had a saying he was fond of in times like these, though that impious bastard employed it as a means of shirking hard labor: 'Many backs make light the load.' No doubt, Étaín thought. The weight of confronting Grimnir's *vestálfar* captors might lessen if shared among many . . . but how?

294

The answer was plain: she would have to convert them, make allies from potential enemies. *Convert them like I converted Red Njáll son of Hjálmarr.*

Étaín exhaled. She had no cross to kiss, so instead she muttered a prayer in Latin and worked Grimnir's seax loose in its scabbard. And though the blade might not do her any good if things went awry, its proximity brought her a measure of comfort.

'Don't let them get me, you great hairy heathen,' Étaín said. She leaned in and hugged the giant wolfhound around the neck. Conán whined. 'And if they do, don't let them keep me.'

Then, with three sharp exhalations that dredged up a reserve of courage she was certain wasn't her own, Étaín called out to them. She did not waste her breath with West Saxon or Latin; rather, she let the example of Blind Maeve guide her and sang out in the tongue of the Danemark. 'I mean you no harm, good sons of Ériu! I am but a poor child of Christ!' And from their sudden bristling manner Étaín knew all of them had understood. To their credit, the three men did not easily startle. They knew something was out there, and the sound of her voice – a human voice – seemed to give them a measure of relief.

Still, they snarled at one another in Gaelic. Finally, the silver-bearded one silenced the others with a sharp gesture. He answered her in Danish: 'Child of Christ, eh? Show yourself, an' then we'll know you mean us no harm.'

'Swear by the bones of Saint Pádraic that you will not harm me, in return.'

'You've my word,' the eldest said.

'And yet, your companions yet hold their weapons ready.'

Beard bristling, the old Irishman growled something in Gaelic over his shoulder even as he took his hand away from the haft of his axe. The second man, a pox-scarred fellow perhaps a handful of years his junior, reversed his spear and drove it blade-first into the earth. The third man, the youngest of the three, was a crop-eared Gael as tall and broad as any Dane; at first, he made no move to sheathe the sword he clutched in his scarred fist. Only after both the older men rounded on him did he grudgingly comply – though his hand never strayed far from the worn leather-and-wire-wrapped hilt. The eldest turned back to face her. 'See? Aye, I give you my word! Now show yourself!'

Étaín crossed herself . . . and stood. She emerged from the undergrowth and edged forward into the light, the bone fetishes on Grimnir's satchel clacking with each step. The men stared, disbelieving. She could see in their eyes that they expected something rough and fearsome to step forth from the night. But this thin wisp of a thing? She was no different from their daughters back home – save for a worn-hilted seax that hung at her hip. Étaín kept her hand clear of the blade as she moved to closer to their fire.

'Bleedin' Christ!' This from the pox-scarred man. 'She ain't your feckin' wolf-man, is she, Bran?'

'Nay,' muttered the one called Bran, the silver-bearded elder. He scowled, shook his head, and looked past Étaín as though the true threat yet lurked in the red-streaked shadows.

The pox-scarred man stared at her, sizing her up. 'What are you doing out here all alone, girl? Lost your way?'

'I'm not lost,' Étaín replied; she looked to Bran. 'Are you King Brian's men?'

'Not yet,' he said.

She noticed, then, that the Irishman with the mutilated ears – who bore more than a passing similarity to the scarred man – had crept nearer. Étaín shivered. He had the same look of base lust in his eyes that she'd seen on the face of the crooked-back *dvergr*, Náli. He licked his lips, muttered something in Gaelic that brought a snarl of anger to Bran's lips.

'Enough!'

'Enough, yourself, old man!' he spat. 'Your balls might be shriveled up and useless, but mine ain't! All's fair, eh, Da?'

Étaín drew herself up; though fear gibbered through her brain, filling her mind with scenes of brutality and rape, she nevertheless stood her ground and made herself meet each man's gaze. Her eyes were the cold blue of a winter sky. When she spoke, she heard the scrape of flint in her voice. 'I am no man's property, and if you think to take me . . . well, you'd best make your peace with the Almighty.' She let her hand rest lightly on the hilt of Grimnir's seax. The blade drew their attention – as did the rolled-up shirt of iron rings, the yellowed finger bones, and the long-haired scalps decorating the battered satchel she carried. She saw uncertainty stamped on Bran's face, saw it mirrored in the gray eyes of the pox-scarred man. But that third Gael, with the cropped ears, responded by holding his hands apart in mock surrender.

'A good speech, girl,' he said. 'But you'd best give me that pigsticker. Wouldn't want you to hurt yourself with it.'

He took a step toward Étaín, then another. With the third step, a malicious smile twisted his lips . . .

And became a rictus of fear as a deep and thunderous howl reverberated beneath the canopy of trees. He had time enough to grasp the hilt of his sword before the wolf-hound, Conán, sprang from the darkness and dragged him down. Man and hound skidded across the weed-choked clearing in one snarling, screaming knot. And with an echoing cry of alarm, the pox-scarred man lunged for his spear . . . but never completed the movement.

The ash shaft slipped from fingers suddenly bereft of will and clattered on the ground; he stared, eyes wide and goggling, at the rune-etched length of cold iron which Étaín pressed expertly to his throat – though she did not recall drawing it. The one called Bran held himself aloof, watching.

'Conán,' she said, her voice betraying none of the emotion coursing through her body. Even her hand held itself steady. Where was the whimpering woman who had pleaded for God's intervention barely a fortnight before, in a cave on the road to Roskilde? Gone, she hoped. 'Don't kill him, you great hairy heathen.'

Conán backed off the fallen man, who spat curses and clawed for his sword hilt, tangled now in his cloak. It mattered nothing to him that he was largely unharmed; his pride bled, and only blood spilled in return could stanch such a wound.

'Bleedin' Christ! Filthy whore! Someone kill that feckin' beast! Bran! Hold her! I—'

Before he could finish, before he could so much as free his hilt from the offending folds of linen, Bran stepped in and delivered a vicious kick to the side of the young Irishman's head; not enough to hurt him but more than enough to leave him senseless. And the murderous look in the old man's eyes warned Étaín, as well, not to do something foolish.

'He is your son?' Étaín said. The pox-scarred man nodded, careful not to slice his own throat. 'I told you I mean you no harm. And I mean that still. But if he tries to touch me again, I swear he will not live long enough to regret it. Do you understand?'

'I . . . I h-hear you, girl,' the pox-scarred man replied.

'Aye, none here will touch you,' Bran said. 'An' you have my word on it.'

Étaín backed away; carefully, she sheathed Grimnir's seax. Conán came and sat at her side, tongue lolling. Though she ran her fingers through the wolfhound's scruff, her eyes never left those of the silver-bearded elder. 'Your name is Bran?'

He nodded. 'Bran of the Uí Garrchon,' he said. 'Aye. Once an oath-man of Maelmorda, but no longer. That's Ruadh Mór of the Ua Feghaile, there, and the sorry bastard with the axe-trimmed ears, yonder, is Dunlaing mac Ruadh.'

'I am Étaín,' she replied. 'And I need your help, Bran of the Uí Garrchon.'

15

Incense spewed from copper censers; through the coiling smoke, Kormlada watched Bjarki from her vantage in the shadowed gallery. Unaware of her scrutiny, Half-Dane sat hunched over a scrying table, as still as a cenotaph carved from whalebone and gristle. He had sat there since sunset, murmuring ritual phrases over and again in a guttural tongue, while he focused the whole of his ferocious intellect on a rune-etched dish brimming with black water drawn from the Liffey. She watched as the hours crept by; watched as the costly smoke wove a tracery of hypnotic shapes above his bowed head – a phantom landscape of serrated peaks dominated by a single windswept precipice . . .

And with a start, she realized she could put a name to it: *Carraig Dubh.*

'Nothing!' Bjarki rose suddenly and flung the scrying table aside. The bowl – ancient fire-blackened alabaster – struck the floor and shattered like glass. The sound drew Draugen from hiding, fell-eyed and axe in hand.

'I cannot find him!' Bjarki roared. 'Something hides him from my art! The runes, the entrails, the *seiðhjallr* . . . all useless!'

Draugen only shrugged. 'And so? Why waste yourself with this witchery?'

Half-Dane looked askance at his grim *thegn,* as though the man had gone softheaded. 'Why? Because he is a thorn that festers beneath my skin, that's why!' Bjarki kicked the ruin of the scrying table; cursing, he ground the fragments of the dish beneath his heel as he paced back and forth like a caged lion. After a moment, he regained a measure of calm. 'The Romans told a tale about a fearsome warrior whose hide was made proof against blade or blow when his mother dipped him into the river of the underworld – all save for a single spot on his heel, no bigger than the bitch's thumb. The warrior's name came to rival Death, itself. And he would have risen higher still had some jealous godling not revealed his weakness to his enemies. A poisoned arrow ended the warrior's ambitions.' Bjarki stopped and made a savage gesture. 'That bastard, out there – that wretched, conniving little *niðingr* who has snuffled at my shadow since the days of Hróarr – he is a poisoned arrow shot by the Sly One, himself! But, you are right. When art fails, let craft take its turn at the oar. His kind cleaves to the wild places. Send riders up into the moors of Cualu. Have them search as far as the deep hollows of Ranelagh – '

'No,' Draugen said – and Kormlada reckoned him the only man alive who could gainsay Half-Dane. 'Do nothing. Weave your plots and lay your snares for the day when the spear-shattering brings Mac Cennétig's crown into your reach.'

'*Wait* for the arrow to strike? Wait to feel the bite of its venom?'

'No, sharpen your steel and bide. The *skrælingr* will come to you. And unlike this warrior your Romans boast of, you will have a shield ready to take the arrow before it can strike.'

Half-Dane gave a derisive snort. 'Be your bait, you mean! That goes down ill with me, Draugen. Besides, what if the men of Munster have him? He could be a potent ally . . .'

Kormlada had heard enough. She withdrew from the gallery, ascending the stairs to the pinnacle of Cuarán's Tower. The hem of her brocaded nightdress whispered on the cold stone.

Carraig Dubh. Her brows furrowed. She hadn't been to that place since she was a girl – since that bloody night when her mother had initiated her into the cult of the Mórrígan, the goddess all the women of her line had given their oaths to – but she recalled it down to the last detail. Bjarki could not see that wind-scoured spike of rock, so plainly drawn in the drifting smoke; for all his art, he was blind to it. *Carraig Dubh, where Nechtan makes his lair. The Tuatha must have him, that's why the* fomórach *was beyond Bjarki's sight* . . .

The Witch of Dubhlinn stopped at the center of her opulent chambers, one arm outstretched. From the sill of the open window, the raven Cruach gave a *crake* of greeting. The bird flexed his wings; talons scraped stone as he lifted into the air to settle lightly upon her proffered arm. He cocked his head. In their black depths, the raven's eyes glittered with an ancient and inscrutable light.

'Cruach, my love, take me to Nechtan,' she said. 'Take me to Carraig Dubh. I must speak with him in person. I must see this creature with my own eyes.'

The giant raven stared at her for a moment; in that gaze, Kormlada felt a curious sense of judgment, like that of a gatekeeper pondering whether or not to let some shoeless vagabond into his demesne. Then, in answer, Cruach gave forth a weird and lilting sound, like a flute tuned by no human hand. It drifted out the window. Before the echo of it died, a dozen smaller black shapes darted through the casement. Lesser ravens mixed with rooks, carrion crows, and magpies; dozens became hundreds, and the croak and caw of their harsh voices created a cacophony of discordant sound. Cruach took flight, the breeze from his heavy wings ruffling her hair.

The birds circled her – a black wall of feathers, swirling darkness; closer they came, until her chambers vanished behind a veil shorn from the fabric of night. The Witch of Dubhlinn closed her eyes . . .

. . . And felt her perceptions shift. Gone were the familiar scents of precious incense and tallow, warm wood and beeswax, damp stone and dust; in their place she could smell bracken and heather, rotting sedge grass and peat . . . and something else, something rank and musky like the stench of a cornered beast. Gone were the carpets underfoot and the sense of being enclosed. Kormlada opened her eyes as the veil of darkness around her dissipated, and found herself at the edge of the precipice of Carraig Dubh. Stars wheeled overhead; stretching out beneath her, through serried ranks of pine and oak soughing in the faint breeze, she could see the plain of Dubhlinn as far as the peninsula of Howth. But even as she made to turn, to look upon that ancient standing stone known as the Rock of Brule, a pale hand snaked from the darkness and seized her by the neck. It exerted no pressure but simply held her there, where the slightest nudge might propel her over the edge and to her doom.

Such was the steel in Kormlada's spine that she did not flinch.

'Daughter of Murchada,' a solemn voice whispered in her ear. 'Why do you intrude? Did I summon you? Speak not too loudly.'

'No, Nechtan,' she whispered in reply. 'I come of my own free will.' The hand that grasped her by the neck spun her about so she might see her captor.

Nechtan stood a head taller than she but was thin to

the point of emaciation; he wore a hauberk of overlapping silver scales, each one masterfully wrought in the shape of a raven's feather. Beneath it he sported frayed silken brocades in every shade of moonlight. In Nechtan's translucent skin, in his pale hair and hollowed cheeks, Kormlada could see the kinship with her mother, for they were born of the same womb. But where her mother's eyes were as dark as the space between the stars, Nechtan's were a deep and ancient green – veined like the leaf of an oak, and shining with the alien light of the Otherworld.

Those eyes transfixed her. In their emerald depths she saw her own death writ plain, should she answer with anything less than the unvarnished truth. 'And why have you come?'

'The *fomórach*,' she said.

'What of it?'

'I wish to see it for myself.'

Nechtan chuckled, a sound as soft as a knife's edge on stone. 'Do you, daughter of Murchada? Then, by all means.' With exaggerated care, Nechtan moved aside; his long fingers remained curled around the nape of her neck – which, Kormlada realized, made her part of a glamour he had woven.

'He will see us as nothing,' Nechtan said in answer to her unspoken question. 'A patch of deeper night. Our voices, nothing more than the rustle of insects. Look there, in the shadow of the Brule Stone.'

Kormlada saw a figure crouched there, murky and indistinct. 'Can we move closer?'

Nechtan obliged her. Slowly, they approached the stone.

'Where did it come from, this beast?'

'Who can say? When the world was young, their kind came from the north in black-prowed wolf ships. Some

304

said the Northern gods drove them out, but I believe they came simply to loot and burn. They cannot create, you see, only destroy, and they are not content save when they breathe the fume and wrack of war.'

'But our people defeated them, did they not?'

Nechtan stopped; Kormlada felt his mind wander back through the centuries. When he spoke again, his voice was distant and tinged with deep melancholy. 'Not at first. Peace had made us complacent. The *fomóraig* came upon us at unawares, protected by a fog called forth by their vile chieftain, Balor of the Eye. Only after he and his wretched followers had laid waste to the green vales beneath the Hill of Slane did we of the Tuatha gird our loins for war. Lugh of the Long Arms, my kinsman, led the chase – the *fomóraig* were laden with booty and slaves and eager to get back to their ships. But we caught up with them on the plain of Mag Tuiredh, and slew them by the thousands. Lugh himself killed their accursed chieftain and cast his head into the sea.'

'So, this one has returned for . . . ?'

'My amusement,' Nechtan said. 'Behold, daughter of Murchada . . . the enemy of our people.'

Kormlada saw the crouching figure more clearly, now – a figure as hard and savage as Nechtan was ethereal. Naked to the waist and clad in a grimy kilt, it cradled a broom in its knotted arms, no doubt ensorcelled to look like a spear; eyes like sullen embers glared out through a curtain of stringy black hair, rife with fetishes of bone and silver. Some dark thought crossed its mind, causing the hard line of its lips to skin back in a serrated snarl. *Like a wolf,* she thought, *baring its fangs at an enemy.* It muttered something in a tongue she did not understand.

'It looks . . . familiar,' Kormlada said, her disquiet at its appearance growing.

A flicker of amusement crossed Nechtan's pale brow. 'I doubt it not. It is in the structure of his cheekbones, you see? In the sharpness of his nose. Give this wretch a beard like a thatch of tarry weeds and the familial resemblance would only increase.'

Kormlada took an involuntary step back, nearly breaking Nechtan's glamour. She gasped as though the creature had raised its hand against her. 'Bjarki! It looks like Bjarki! But . . . h-how? How is that possible?'

'I imagine a Danish whore spread her thighs for silver, not caring if the thing that left its seed in her was man or *fomórach*. Your Half-Dane's blood is so diluted not even the *mná sidhe* take note of him. But this . . . this is a hate of the Elder World, a spawn of Balor, himself . . . not some half-thing who plays games with Ériu's mortal thrones.'

Kormlada stirred, sloughing off the shock of recognition. 'What will you do with it?'

'What does the cat do with the mouse?'

'Must you kill it?' Kormlada held up a hand to forestall the suspicions brewing in the Tuatha's eerie gaze. 'Long have I sought some bit of leverage over Bjarki, and ever have I come up empty-handed. Until now. He fears this one, though I do not know precisely *why*. The war with that old fool Mac Cennétig will soon end and Bjarki will triumph. After that, he will be impossible to dislodge. My son and my idiot brother will be his puppets and he will rule Ériu.'

'And if Mac Cennétig wins this war of yours?'

She gave Nechtan a hard look. 'Fall fair or fall foul, his naked rabble of Gaels will break themselves on the iron spears of the Norse. No, it is only a question of who will rule in the aftermath, Bjarki Half-Dane or—'

'Or Kormlada,' Nechtan finished for her.

She acknowledged his recognition of her ambitions with

a slight bow. 'Here is the weapon I have long desired. I understand your need to slay it, but could you not put an enchantment on it, instead? Something more than a simple glamour. A *geis,* perhaps?'

'The last of the *fomóraig,* enslaved for eternity,' Nechtan said, brows drawing together in thought. 'The notion has some appeal, I admit. But such an enchantment . . . it will not be easy.'

'But can it be done?'

Nechtan's otherworldly eyes narrowed; a malicious smile spread across his bone-gaunt face as he gathered the shadows about him. 'Oh, it can be done . . . especially if the *fomórach* is dead.'

16

As the night waned and the stars overhead paled with the coming dawn, the three Irishmen left their camp – with Étaín in tow – and ascended the south flank of Carraig Dubh. They left their ponies hobbled and tied, their fire banked, their goods protected by the snoring bulk of the wolfhound, Conán. He would be gone ere they returned, or so Étaín had said; for Dunlaing, who yet nursed ribs and ego equally bruised, it was good riddance. The dour young Irishman walked point, picking his way carefully through the thinning forest, the stony ground underfoot becoming steeper and more treacherous as they neared the summit. None of the Irishmen had proper war gear – neither hauberks nor helms nor the round wood-and-leather shields favored by the Gael – but they moved in silence, and stealth was likely their greatest asset.

Étaín came next, her satchel muffled by the loose folds of her cloak. She did not fully trust crop-eared Dunlaing, whose eyes still burned for her, but she trusted the two older men who followed her – insofar as she could bring herself to trust a stranger. They weren't the sort who took their oaths lightly, not to God or to man. And though her muscles ached and her eyes were hot and gritty from exhaustion, she trudged on without complaint.

Bran and Ruadh Mór brought up the rear of the cortege.

The pair were a study in contrasts: Ruadh Mór lumbered, joints creaking, his weight on the spear he used as a walking stick; Bran, however, moved with a nimbleness that belied the silver in his beard. He had taken a hunting bow from their gear – as fine an example of the bowyer's art as any, with rune-etched bone inlays decorating the leather-wrapped grip – and went forward with an arrow on the nock, its broad iron head gleaming in the moonlight.

Ruadh Mór glanced sidelong at Bran as the older man paused to scan their backtrail. 'What's gotten in to you, Bran-me-lad?' he whispered in Gaelic.

'Just keepin' an eye out, is all.'

'Don't go playin' the daft old man with me,' Ruadh Mór snapped. 'An' you feckin' know what I mean! With this! With her!' He jerked his chin at Étaín's back. 'You said it yourself: ain't nothin' up yonder for God-fearin' folk, but up yonder we go, anyway! Like three fools gulled by a bit o' the split-tail, you ask me!'

'You could have stayed with the ponies,' Bran replied.

Ruadh Mór's face flushed. 'Bollocks, you feckin' arseling!' He pushed ahead, but Bran caught up with him easily enough. They walked side by side for a dozen paces and more. Finally, Bran broke the silence.

'I ain't no great thinker. You've known me long enough to know that. An' we ain't got no skin in whatever her fight might be, but when a slip of a thing like her has guts enough to come upon a scraggle o' salty knots like us and ask for help, well, that ain't somethin' you take lightly. An' it ain't like we're puttin' ourselves out. We were takin' this road anyway. Might as well see if anyone's lurkin' about, up yonder.'

'An' how do you know she ain't leading us right into a trap?'

'My gut,' said Bran. 'You an' me, we ain't lived this long

'cause we ignore what nags at the pit o' our bellies. She's holdin' back, I'll warrant, but she don't strike me as the sort to lead men astray.'

Ruadh Mór exhaled; he scrubbed his nose with the back of his hand. 'I hope you're right, Bran-me-lad. Bleedin' Christ, I hope you're right.'

Étaín faded back. 'Is everything all right?' she said in the tongue of the Danes.

In Gaelic, Ruadh Mór snarled, 'Oh, aye. Right as the feckin' rain.'

She looked quizzically at the pox-scarred Gael, and then at Bran, who added, 'He says he's glad we're nearly there. Aye, an' his fat arse could use a rest.'

Étaín nodded, smiling. But in her eyes the old hunter saw the funereal glow of a woman who had witnessed too much. She knew the score, this one, and she knew sooner or later there would be a reckoning. Men did nothing – undertook no good deed, performed no kindness – without first attaching a price to it. Bran knew it, and so did she. So with every glance, Étaín tried not only to discern their price, but also the manner of when and how it would come due.

A birdcall warbled in the night; Bran frowned. Ahead, he could barely make out the silhouette of Dunlaing. The younger man crouched near a bramble-choked cut in the last crumbling scarp before the summit – its aspect too uniform to be natural, like an earthen rampart fashioned by long-dead hands and allowed to fall fallow. Dunlaing waved for them to hurry, but gestured for them to be silent. Bran, Étaín, and Ruadh Mór padded quickly to his side.

'Someone's up there,' Dunlaing hissed. 'Seen a light.'

'A fire?'

Dunlaing shook his head, his face a pale smear in the gloom. 'Not feckin' likely. Looked . . . green.'

Étaín's lips set in a resolute line; she dropped one hand to the hilt of her seax. Iron grated softly as she worked the blade free of its scabbard mouth. 'I'll go first,' she said. 'The ones who took my companion, they might be skittish, or so I've heard. Might bolt if they see us coming.'

'Danes? Skittish?'

'Never said they were Danes.' And without a backward glance, Étaín shouldered past the three Irishmen; she scrambled up the cut, heedless of nettles or snagging thorns, and pulled herself onto the damp grass at the top of the scarp. Some thirty paces ahead of her lay a tangled copse of yew trees through which she could see the glimmer of green fire. Étaín waited there, crouched, as Bran joined her, followed by Dunlaing. But while those two helped Ruadh Mór pull his swag-bellied bulk to the top of the ridge, Étaín left them and scuttled to the edge of the trees.

Eerie lights danced within; above the moaning wind, she heard two voices, both faint – Grimnir's harsh and grating tongue and another that was grim and solemn and heavy with portent. She knew, in that moment, that she was not too late to intervene in the life-and-death drama unfolding just beyond the thicket. And while her heart thudded against her sternum like a terrified beast, battering the walls of its cage in an effort to fly, she nevertheless drew from its scabbard Grimnir's cold iron seax.

Suddenly, she was not alone. Bran came up alongside her, silver beard bristling and an arrow half drawn. Dunlaing was a half a step behind; he drew his sword and kissed the steel in silent benediction. Finally, Ruadh Mór shambled up, his breathing ragged and shallow. He cuffed sweat from his eyes. But the hand that gripped the shaft of his spear did not waver, nor did he tremble as he made the sign of the cross.

And with a nod of thanks to each man, Étaín led them into the wood, following the unnatural lights and the spectral sounds until the stone-crowned summit of Carraig Dubh came into view . . .

17

Grimnir crouched in the lee of the standing stone and listened to the creek and craak of insects. They were near him, and their incessant clamor wore on nerves already frayed by anticipation.

'Where are they, you old git? Damn your eyes! Are you sure this is even the right place?'

Look yonder, my tender little fool, Gífr's voice commanded.

And Grimnir did. Downslope, beyond the line of trees, hundreds of orbs shimmered into view – fool's lamps, wisps of greenish faery light that danced over the grass and under the leaves. Grimnir could see shapes moving at the heart of the lights; he heard the faint rustle of wings.

'Nár, parái vestálfar!' Grimnir hawked and spat, not disguising his raw hatred for these dogs who snapped at his sire's heel. 'Say the word, you old git! Gífr?' Grimnir stood; he glanced about, suddenly suspicious. 'Gífr?'

Then, without warning, hundreds of fool's lamps pulsed to life above him, at the pinnacle of the stone – a stark green glow that was as blinding as the light of an otherworldly sun. Snarling, Grimnir turned away and shaded his eyes.

That gesture saved his life.

At his back, Grimnir spied four shapes creeping through the misty light, each a head taller than he and thin to the point of emaciation. There was a resemblance to them that made it impossible for him to tell them apart; the uniformity of their translucent skin, pallid hair, and hollowed cheeks carried over in their choice of garb: hauberks of silver-green scale over trousers of pale brocade. Slender hands wrapped around the hilts of leaf-bladed swords or gripped the hafts of short, heavy spears. They fanned out, edging toward him in a semicircle. Of Gífr he saw no sign.

'Sneak-thieving swine!' Grimnir whirled; he pushed away from the stone. 'Think I wouldn't notice you lot skulking about, trying to knife me in the back? Which one of you drew the short straw, eh? Was it you?' He gestured at one of the figures on his left. 'Or you, longshanks? Ha! No matter! You've thrown the dice and come up wanting . . .'

And quick as a striking serpent, Grimnir lunged to his left. The two who came at him from that side gave ground, while their brothers on his right surged forward. Grimnir, though, was ready for them. In a display unmatched by any human, he sprang off his lead foot and launched himself to the right, turning his lunge into a feint; his spear blade sang in the unnatural light, a long, leaf-shaped bar of killing steel. Grimnir twisted, putting his weight behind the blow. The spear blade took the first vestálfr high, bisecting his skull at an angle from his left temple to the right side hinge of his jaw.

But there was no shock of impact. No flesh caught the force of that perfectly executed leap. Grimnir spun through the blow and tumbled to the ground. He rolled on his shoulder, came up into a crouch, and whirled back to face his enemy, panting. He should have been staring at a corpse flopping at his feet; instead, he watched a shadow dissipate like bog mist.

'Sorcery,' he hissed.

A somber voice answered him, pitched low and resonating like an echo from the grave. It came equally from the throats of the remaining three enemies: *Aye, fomórach. The glamour of the Tuatha. But which blade is the illusion and which has your doom writ upon it?*

To illustrate, an enemy spear thrust for Grimnir's throat. He could not say for certain whether he looked upon a dream blade or one anvil-born. It had weight; its razored edge glittered like ice in the faery light. Behind it, slender sinews creaked with effort, and breath whistled between his foeman's clenched teeth.

At the last moment, Grimnir swayed aside; the spear passed him by a hair's breadth, and his riposte would have gutted any living enemy. But again he struck cold nothingness, wasting the power contained in his broad shoulders and long arms to turn an illusory enemy into a drifting cloud of vapor. He recovered his balance and cursed as the last two charged in tandem – the one with a sword stabbing at Grimnir's face while his mate swept in low with a spear.

Grimnir ducked and parried the incoming spear with his own. He aborted a return blow when his weapon's shaft met nothing but spectral mist. His sword foe's attempted thrust carried him past Grimnir; the latter whirled and was on him before he could recover. With a bellow of rage, he sprang for the west-elf's back . . .

. . . and passed through him.

Ever nimble and quick-footed, Grimnir turned what could have been a graceless fall into a tuck-and-roll. When he came up, he flung his arms wide and roared a deafening challenge at the impassive stone with its crown of faery light, at the shifting figures beyond.

'Bálegyr!'

Wretched fool, the somber voice replied. Balor is dead,

slaughtered with the rest of your miserable kind at Mag Tuiredh! That pitiful one-eyed vagabond you call a king – we hacked off his thrice-cursed head and threw it into the sea!

'Balor, eh? Is that what you call him?' Grimnir said. 'You maggots can't even say his name! He is Bálegyr of the Eye, son of Ymir, champion of the Sly One and master of the wolf ships of the kaunar. He is my father.'

He was a worm and he died as the worm dies, caught in the beak of the raven!

Grimnir panted, his tongue lolling from his mouth. 'Faugh!' he spat. 'Lies and mummery!'

The voice gave a derisive laugh. Perhaps. But is a death-blow couched in so-called mummery any less grievous?

But Grimnir had no breath for a reply. As the somber voice spoke, a horde of vestálfar boiled up the slope at him, singly and in twos or threes – each alike in every way and indistinguishable from a living thing until it encountered the blade of his spear. He whirled and parried, dodged and struck; in the pit of his stomach he was certain he faced nothing but an army of ghosts, but how could he ignore his most basic instinct for self-preservation? To stand idly by while his enemy took potshots at him? That went against his grain, and to willingly lower his guard was to tempt the humor of the Norns. He might block ninety-nine phantom blades but that hundredth spearhead, the one he mistook for a dream, would doubtless prove real as it tore into his guts.

So he fought back, and fought hard, with every ounce of craft and guile his long life afforded. He fought until sweat stung his eyes, until the muscles of his arms and back burned like fire; he fought until even the legendary endurance of his people began to flag. Only then did the stream of foes cease.

We know you, *fomórach, the voice said*. Does that surprise you? We have heard your legend on the wind: the Corpse-maker, they call you; the Hooded One, Bringer of Night. Some claim you are born of Fenrir; others that you are brother to the Serpent who encircles the World. Regardless, you are the sad and pitiful remnant of a cursed race.

Grimnir stood in a circle of drifting shadows, chest rising and falling, the light atop the stone searing into his brain. Froth dripped from his bared fangs; his hair hung in lank strands about his eyes, which blazed with defiance. He coughed and spat. 'Then you know,' *he panted.* 'If what you say about my sire is true, I will have the blood price from you, you white-skinned whore's son!'

I had forgotten, *the somber voice laughed*, how much sport your kind can give. Perhaps I shall keep you alive . . .

Grimnir flexed his shoulders, sloughing off his weariness. 'Come take me, then, if you dare!'

'Oh, I will,' *the* vestálfr *said*.

'I will,' *a second west-elf echoed. Then another. And another. More and more responded, until the precipice itself seemed to vibrate with the force of their collective voices.* 'I will. I will! I WILL!'

Grimnir turned, describing a slow circle. His narrowed eyes searched for any threat of attack; his black-nailed fist clenched and unclenched, and he adjusted his grip on the sweat-slick haft of his spear.

'I will,' *a voice at his back whispered.*

Grimnir spun round, and as he did he had a split-second glimpse of the same tall and funereal form he had killed time and again – the same long, pale hair and dark-hollowed cheeks. But where the others had had eyes like milky opals, the eyes that bored now into his were a deep and ancient green.

Grimnir opened his mouth to loose a roar of triumph, his spear in motion for the killing blow; as he did, one of the vestálfr's *long-fingered hands came up and uncurled like a pale orchid. He pursed his fleshless lips and blew a palmful of silvery ash full into Grimnir's sallow face.*

Light exploded across his vision. He stumbled, his spear falling from fingers gone suddenly nerveless. His roar turned to a bellow of agony as he tried to blink the light away, each movement causing grit to scrape over his eyes like ground glass. He staggered, tripped; grunting, he came up hard against the standing stone. Grimnir writhed. The light wormed deep into his brain, hard and white and unflinching. He could taste it on his tongue, as salty and cold as frozen sea spume. And it burned. It burned down his gullet, into his lungs; it made every breath torture.

Grimnir could not see. His limbs would not move; he sagged down alongside the stone – its form suggestive of a once-living being. And the final sound he heard before his world turned to fiery white oblivion was a voice echoing across the limitless chasm between the living and the dead: He is not for you, elf! *It was a familiar voice. A woman's voice.* Loose him from your spell and get thee back to the shadows!

Grimnir dragged a last deep breath into his smoldering lungs, where it rasped and rattled only to emerge once more as croaking laughter. 'Hymn-singer.'

18

Étaín watched Grimnir from the thicket of yew trees. She did not rush out to greet him, for she knew instinctively that something was amiss. He was naked to the waist, his black hair stringy and matted, his hide made ashen by the eerie light streaming from the pinnacle of the Black Stone. In that wicked green radiance, he seemed to dance. His partner was an old broom, and with it he lunged and sprang, rolled and thrust. Grimnir ducked shadows and sidestepped wraiths only he could see. Nor was he silent. His grating voice provided the music – a lyric of roared curses, howls, and the inarticulate cries of rage denied. He paused only to gulp great lungfuls of air, or to wring sweat from his eyes. It might have been a comical sight – cathartic after all the grief he'd put her through – if Étaín wasn't convinced Grimnir was fighting for his life.

'Bleedin' Christ,' she heard Bran mutter. Making no more noise than the wind itself, the three Gaels came up and crouched alongside her. Wide-eyed, they watched the strange figure capering at the crest of Carraig Dubh. Thankfully, shadows and distance masked the damning details of his appearance. 'Your mate?'

Étaín nodded.

'What's gotten in to him?' Dunlaing hissed, loud enough to disturb a bird roosting overhead.

Étaín silenced him with a sharp gesture; she pointed past Grimnir, singling out a well of shadow near the base of the stone that defied even the otherworldly light coming from above. In that patch of night lurked the suggestion of eyes – eyes alight with the same cruel joy shared by cats, which also toy with their prey to the point of exhaustion.

And as they looked on, that patch of darkness shredded; tendrils of it coiled and spun away, dissipating like lamp smoke in a breeze. In its absence stood a man and a woman: she was dark-haired and perilous; he was tall and pale, regal in the manner of dead kings. His scaled hauberk rustled like ravens' wings as he came up behind Grimnir and spoke.

'I will,' he said, his voice as somber as the grave.

Grimnir whirled. And with sinuous grace, the figure raised his hand, fingers unfolding, and blew a fine white powder full into Grimnir's fanged face. His reaction was instantaneous. He stumbled and writhed as though the tall figure had set him ablaze.

At this, Étaín started forward. She had seen enough. Though Bran tried to haul her back, she shrugged free of his grasp and strode out from the relative safety of the yew trees. What had Maeve called her? The beacon of Christ? Well, she would let that beacon shine, even in defense of a heretic like Grimnir. The strength of her faith filled her heart; she drew on it, and let the glory of the Almighty speak through her: 'He is not for you, elf! Loose him from your spell and get thee back to the shadows!'

The pale prince of the Tuatha half-turned, brow wrinkling, and fixed his emerald gaze on her. There was a flash of recognition. 'You,' he said. 'Go back to sleep, child. This is no concern of yours.' He flicked his hand at her, a negligent gesture. But Étaín suddenly felt her limbs grow heavy with the chains of weariness. She could barely move, so deep was her exhaustion. She craved sleep . . . just a few hours . . .

You are the beacon of Christ!

The echo of Blind Maeve's voice galvanized Étaín. She shook herself, sloughing off the Tuatha's enchantment as if it were but a handful of sand he'd tossed at her.

'Dog of Satan!' Étaín crossed herself. 'I adjure you, elf, through the might of the living and the true God, that you are put to flight from this place!'

The Tuatha hissed and flinched from her words, as though the very syllables stung like embers flung from a fire. He drew himself up and started to speak, but the black-haired woman forestalled him. She spoke a sibilant word to him in a language older than humankind; then, she began to sing. It was a soft and rhythmic chant, a threnody that evoked a woman's tragic end. In her mind, Étaín saw the tall cliffs of the Irish shore, green and chalky; she saw a copper-haired woman at the precipice, the wind snapping at her cloak. Red-eyed from weeping, she mourned for her lost love, taken by the gods of the sea, and called upon the Mórrígan to bring her succor. And as the song reached its crescendo, Étaín felt the burden of that woman's grief. It was her own – a weight so heavy it threatened to suffocate her in its melancholy folds. Tears sprang unbidden to her eyes; seeking solace, she took a step toward the edge of the precipice of Carraig Dubh . . . and then stopped. She felt the burden lifted.

'For the Lord is my shepherd,' she said to the dark-haired witch. 'My mercy and my refuge; my support, and my deliverer – He who teaches my hands to fight, and my fingers to war!' Étaín leveled the seax at the pair. 'I warn you for the last time: the son of Bálegyr is not for you! Go, elf, and take your whore! Trouble the world of Men no longer!'

The Tuatha's pale face screwed up in a rictus of hate. He stalked past the woman, his hand falling to the hilt of his leaf-bladed sword. 'You presumptuous little ape! You want that wretched *fomórach*? Then let us see how well your hands have taken to your Nailed God's teachings!' Metal rasped on metal as he slid the elf blade from its scabbard. 'Fight or run,' he said. 'It will make no difference.'

Étaín stood her ground.

His word will be your blade!

'Our Father, who art in Heaven, hallowed be Thy name . . .'

Suddenly, the Tuatha recoiled; as he staggered back a step, Étaín heard the clash of scales followed by the sharp *crack* of an arrow splintering on the breast of his hauberk. Behind her, Bran of the Uí Garrchon roared:

'. . . Thy kingdom come. Thy will be done on earth as it is in Heaven!' By stanza's end, the silver-bearded Gael had drawn, nocked, and loosed a second arrow. It struck less than a finger's width from the first, and had the same effect: the willow-wood shaft with its broad hunting head shattered against the scales of the Tuatha's corselet. 'Get to your mate, girl!' Bran said, fishing a third arrow from his bag. 'An' we'll send off this sorry lot, eh, lads?'

'Oh, aye! And get feckin' rich to boot!' Dunlaing bellowed. 'That one yonder, she's a right prize! The Witch of Dubhlinn, she is! An' I'd wager good King Brian will fill our laps with silver if we bring him her pretty head!'

Étaín nodded; quick-footed, she darted wide and to the left. The elf prince made to follow, but a third arrow – which passed so close to his face that the fletching nearly tangled in his silver hair – brought his attention back to Bran.

'Aye, to me, you devil!'

And, lips writhing in a snarl of contempt, the Tuatha

322

crossed the interval between them with murderous purpose, eerie green eyes burning in the half-light. Bran cursed; a fourth arrow went wide. Bristling in defiance, the old Irishman slung his bow down and clawed for his axe even as the Tuatha's sword sang a death note in the chill air above him.

And Bran of the Uí Garrchon would have died beneath the Tuatha's sword if not for his kinsman, Ruadh Mór. Though more a poet than a warrior – and no great shakes at either – that swag-bellied son of the Ua Feghaile nevertheless managed to catch the Tuatha's mighty blow on the iron-banded shaft of his spear. The blade rebounded.

Ruadh Mór yelped and backpedaled as the Tuatha's riposte nearly took his head off.

Nor did Dunlaing stand idle, though it was the dark-haired woman who had the younger Gael's attention. He stalked toward her, malice smiling in his eyes. The Witch of Dubhlinn smiled back. Her lips pursed, she whistled an eerie tune . . .

. . . And called forth the darkness. It flowed down from the heavens like a mist, a stygian blanket that covered the summit of Carraig Dubh and snuffed out the faery light at the crown of the Black Stone. And this darkness – so terrifying and absolute – came on with a sound Étaín had heard before . . . a sound like the rustling of a thousand pairs of wings. 'The ravens,' she gasped. 'Outside Badon!'

Étaín stumbled; she fell to her hands and knees as *something* passed over her. Crabwise, she scuttled on by feel, making for the last spot where she'd seen Grimnir's prostrate form.

Out in the darkness, Dunlaing screamed as though unseen knives flayed him alive. There came a sound, then, like water pattering on the dew-slick grass. Like a stricken ox, Ruadh Mór bellowed his son's name; she heard Bran curse after him. Closer at hand, the low, unearthly chuckle of the Tuatha sent a chill down her spine.

'Grimnir!' she hissed. She clutched his seax like a talisman. Her free hand brushed the stone; she flailed around, growing more desperate by the moment, until her fingers met warm flesh. For a brief and terrifying instant, she thought she'd grasped the foot of the elf prince, his sword poised above her head like Damocles' own. Then, she felt a hobnailed sandal; though she curled her nose at the rank stench of sweat, her hand nevertheless raked up his body. 'Get up, you *skrælingr* bastard!' Étaín punched him in the ribs; she pummeled his chest with her balled fist and slapped him across the fanged mouth. 'Get up!'

Moonlight trickled through the veil of darkness. Étaín's sight returned by increments. She glanced up, wild-eyed, and saw a twisting cloud of birds. Something pale glimmered at the heart of the maelstrom – a jerking manikin of blood-slick meat that she recognized as Dunlaing. He fell to the ground and lay there, quivering. Ruadh Mór ran toward him, waving his spear over his head like a farmer trying to scare off a flock of crows. One giant bird – a coal-black brute who could likely count the span of its life in centuries – wove in between Ruadh Mór's mad flailing and, in a gesture that reeked of contempt, casually raked the swag-bellied Irishman's eyes out. Ruadh Mór screamed and reeled, hands clutching the bloody ruin of his face. Other birds dove in, plucking at his scalp, tearing at his patchwork tunic with their talons.

Étaín cried his name as he ran from the hideous flock. She cried for him to stop as he stumbled past the smiling witch . . . and over the deadly precipice of Carraig Dubh.

Bran alone remained; as he scrambled for his fallen bow, he looked plaintively at Étaín. There was no rancor in his gaze, no condemnation, only sadness – she realized he wanted to look up to discover she had fled. He snatched up his bow, clawed for an arrow . . .

The pale prince of the Tuatha bent and picked up the shattered head of an arrow, a handspan of shaft still attached. With inhuman grace, he straightened and slung it at Bran with a snap of his wrist. It struck the silver-bearded Gael in the crook of his right elbow, the broad iron head slicing muscle and tendon. Bran grunted; he loosed prematurely, his arrow wobbling in weak flight.

The elf snatched it from the air, twirled it about, and launched it back at the archer like a dart, its flight steeled by a whispered word. Bran spun away, thinking he was protecting his head and his vitals from some trickery. But that arrow struck with enough force to drive the air from his lungs. It took him low, piercing muscle and the bones of his spine to lodge deep in his vitals. Gasping, he stumbled on legs gone suddenly useless and went down hard, writhing as he tried to grab at the fletching of the arrow protruding from his back.

Laughing, the Tuatha turned away.

At her wits' end, Étaín stabbed the seax deep into the stony earth, twisted it, and drew it out. Bits of damp soil clung to the blade. Then, clenching her jaw, she drew the edge along the meat of Grimnir's thigh. Black blood welled, and she smelled a strong scent of wet iron. 'Your people died on this land,' she whispered, smearing the dirt on the blade into the cut. Her eyes never left the long and sinister face of the Tuatha, his green eyes a-sparkle with malice. 'Their blood soaked deep into it; their bones rotted beneath it. Their voices are on the wind. They bid you rise. Rise and take your vengeance, son of Bálegyr.'

'What did you say to him?' The Tuatha sheathed his sword; his green eyes shimmered in the moonlight, holding in their depths the promise of long torment.

325

With her allies dead or nearly so, Étaín felt her will to fight ebb. She rose to her feet and backed away from the pair, leaving Grimnir's seax where it lay – across his belly.

'What did you say to him? Do you think that carrion will rise up and save you, like your Nailed God?'

'Make a sacrifice of her, Nechtan,' the Witch of Dubhlinn said. 'The night wanes. Give her to the Mórrígan, so that our plans might bear the Great Queen's blessing.' Nechtan, though, gave no indication he heard her.

'Do not touch me,' Étaín said, one hand braced against the rough stone monument. She risked a glance off to her left, at the crumbling edge of Carraig Dubh. 'I'll not go to your heathen altars, witch! I will give myself to the true and living God, first!'

'Foolish child,' Kormlada replied. 'So naïve to think you have a choice.'

Nechtan stepped over Grimnir's prostrate form. He loomed over Étaín like the pale shadow of Death. 'Where is your redeemer now, little ape?'

19

'Where do the dead go?' Grimnir stirs the fire, his eyes as bright as the sullen embers that crackle up and swirl into the overcast Danish night. The threat of snow hangs heavy in the air. 'Our dead, not theirs.'

Old Gífr, who is his mother's brother, looks up from his work – tending the edges of a score of iron broadheads with a yellow-gray whetstone – and spits; in the dancing light, his face looks as cold and immobile as a bust of fire-blackened ivory. 'Nár! Where do you think, eh?'

'Helheimr,' Grimnir says. He stabs at the fire's heart. 'To the great hall of Éljúðnir, to await the horns that will call us to Ragnarok and the breaking of the world.'

Gífr chuckles. Beneath a heavy brow, ancient eyes smolder like molten iron as he rasps the stone along the damascened arrowhead, forged from metal that had fallen from the sky when the world was young. 'You're a precious sort of fool, little rat . . . and an idiot to boot if you think Helheimr is our portion!'

'Then where?' Grimnir replies, a defiant jut to his narrow jaw. His face is sharp, wolfish; though his swarthy hide bears the scars of a warrior in his prime, something in his manner betokens a juvenile – sparse are the bone fetishes in his stringy black locks as he tosses his head and glares at his elder. 'You're so high-and-mighty! You tell me where the dead go!'

Gífr raises the arrow and squints down the shaft, then looks askance at his younger companion. 'Not to some piss-damp hall in Helheimr, where there is no mead and no fires. We are the sons of the Wolf and the Serpent!'

'Where, then?' Grimnir's lips skin back in a snarl of contempt. 'Faugh! You don't even know, do you? Some goði you are! Useless old wretch!'

Gífr lays the stone aside and takes up an oiled cloth, using it to wipe the freshly honed arrowhead clean. That done, he eyes Grimnir across the fire. When he speaks again, his voice is an eerie chant:

> I know a hall standing | far from the sun,
> In Nástrond, under the | shadows of Niðafjoll;
> War-reek rages | and reddening fire:
> The high heat licks | against Heaven itself.
>
> Here are the kaunar, | sons of Wolf and Serpent;
> Plundered of life on | Miðgarðr's hateful shores.
> Here they abide | in strife without end;
> Until the death-note blows | on Gjallarhorn.

'Nástrond!' Sparks crackle skyward as Grimnir stabs the fire's heart again and again. His eyes gleam no less brightly. 'Until the death-note blows!'

'But not you,' Gífr says. Grimnir glances up. 'Not now.'

'What are you yammering on about?'

'Not you, little rat.'

'Why?'

Gífr takes up a new arrow; he raises his stone, spits on it, and strops it along the broadhead's edge. 'Nástrond's *for fighters, not some dull-witted bog* skrælingr *like you, done in by a bit of elf witchery. You are dumb as a stump, aren't you? You recall nothing of what I taught you? The death songs of the* jötunn, *the metallurgy of the* dvergar ... *these things are real, and their power comes from stock and stone, blood and bone; the glamour of the* alfár? Nár! *That comes from a weak mind. If you die in their wretched snares it's because you don't have the will to get yourself out!'*

'Ha! What do you know, then? I'm not dead, you miserable old git!'

'Prove it,' Gífr says.

Grimnir starts to protest, but a sharp pain in his thigh brings a hiss of rage to his lips. Then, as heavy flakes of snow start to fall and the dark lowering sky promises an icy squall, another voice echoes from the heart of the crackling fire: 'Your people died on this land. Their blood soaked deep into it; their bones rotted beneath it. Their voices are on the wind. They bid you rise. Rise and take your vengeance, son of Bálegyr.'

Grimnir woke.

His body did not jerk with the shock of consciousness; rather, he was just suddenly aware – aware of his dreams fading and the waking world pressing in on him. The sensations of smell and sound were the first to come back to him. And pain. Dull wires of barbed agony threaded through his muscles; his joints and bones ached as from long exertion, and there was a taste of brackish iron on his tongue. He felt a familiar weight resting across the corded muscles of his belly. It was the cold iron blade of his seax.

For an instant, Grimnir feared he might have slept too long and given his black blood a chance to stagnate in his veins. But no. While his body felt as heavy as a corpse, he had not gone to slag. His heart yet beat; his lungs expanded, taking in the myriad scents around him – the salt decay of the sea and rich dampness of the soil; corpse rot and ancient cerecloth; fresh blood and fear-sweat . . . and beneath it all, the faint musky stench of his own kind.

That wretched foundling was right. Grimnir's lips twitched and curled, peeling back in a sneer of triumph. *Half-Dane was near.* But . . . where? And where was he? Not in that blind hag's precious cottage. No, not anymore. And not in Dubhlinn, either – the place around him felt remote, far from the haunts of Men. Wind whistled through chinks in stone, and the insects . . .

No, not insects. Grimnir's eyes opened to slits. What he took for the trilling of crickets resolved into voices. Something passed over him, then: a pale shadow whose sinuous gait raised the hackles on his neck. What's more, he knew it for what it was – and just so, the glamour that had cloaked his dreams faded and the truth took shape: *vestálfar.* Miserable whiteskins! They'd taken him in his sleep.

'Where is your redeemer now, little ape?' the wretch said.

Grimnir heard a familiar voice answer him. 'I am the wheat of God,' Étaín replied, and her strength of conviction caused even him to flinch. 'Even as I am ground by the teeth of the wild beasts! I long after the Lord, the Son of the true God and Father, Jesus Christ! I am eager to die for the sake of Christ!'

The *vestálfr* hissed in anger.

'Take her, Nechtan!' a third voice added – a woman's voice. 'The Dark Queen demands tribute!'

'Be silent, daughter of Murchada!' this Nechtan said. 'I would make a slave of her, as I will make of this one!' And Grimnir knew the whiteskin wretch meant to bend him to his will by filthy magicks, to keep him alive even after indolence had hardened his black blood and robbed him of his long life. The very idea of it kindled an elemental fury in his guts; rage surged through his veins.

Étaín's voice cracked like a whip. 'My only master is Christ Jesus!'

'No, little ape. You will soon call me master, same as he! You begged me for a weapon, Kormlada? I will oblige you . . . from this pair I shall breed you an army! Imagine a horde of such empty vessels, bereft of purpose until you fill them with your dark will! We—'

Grimnir did not give him a chance to finish. With a snarl of contempt – as much for the agony that sought to rob him of movement as for his enemy – Grimnir seized the hilt of his seax and rolled up into a fighting crouch, his weight on the balls of his feet.

'Nechtan!' screamed the woman, Kormlada. Her warning hung on the night air as Grimnir struck. His blow came low and fast. Even as Nechtan turned toward the sudden motion, his hand reaching for the hilt of his sword, the first three finger lengths of Grimnir's blade caught him below the hem of his hauberk, behind the right knee. Cloth, muscle, and sinew parted equally beneath that honed iron edge, forged in the flames of an elder age.

Nechtan cursed; he staggered sideways. Instinct caused him to claw at the wound with his sword hand. But as his right leg buckled and he went down on one knee, the pale prince of the Tuatha realized his error: his scabbard had twisted so that the hilt of his blade pointed away from him, out of reach. He went for it with his left hand, but Grimnir's next blow split the Tuatha's flesh between wrist and index finger. Nechtan groaned; he glared up at his ancestral enemy, emerald eyes wide with disbelief.

'*Master,* is it?' Grimnir hissed. He cast about, bent,

331

and retrieved the old broom he'd pinched from he blind hag's cottage. He struck the broom's head off with a single angled blow of his seax, which left him with two and a half feet of sharpened oak. 'Great prince of the *vestálfar*? *Faugh!* You whiteskin rats are naught but pale wights who play like you still mean something to the world!'

'We are the victors!' Nechtan gasped. Pale blood spurted between his fingers; with each pulse of his heart, his glamour ebbed. '*We* slaughtered your kind at Mag Tuiredh! *We* harrowed the moors with the blood of your miserable people! *We* slew Balor – that pitiful one-eyed vagabond you called a king – and cast his thrice-cursed head into the sea! Wh-What . . . What have your wretched k-kind done?'

'What have we done?' Grimnir's voice dropped to a bone-chilling hiss. 'Little fool, we made you lot fear us.'

Driven by the power in his knotted shoulders – and fortified by the bestial rage of his people – Grimnir stabbed that oak handle down into the hollow of Nechtan's throat. He hawked a wad of phlegm and spat it full in the dying elf's face before shoving him away with the hobnailed heel of his sandal.

For a moment, he towered over his fallen foe, grim and vulpine; from beneath a swarthy brow, red eyes gleamed like coals plucked from a fire. He swiped a hand through his tangled hair, fetishes of bone and silver rattling,

'Foundling,' he said to Étaín, who still had a hand braced against the Black Stone; she nodded back. Grimnir's smoldering gaze then shifted to Kormlada; he leveled the tip of the seax at her. 'And who are you, eh? You smell like one of Half-Dane's whores,' he said, with a sidelong glance at Étaín. 'My brother's bastard has his sire's pathetic taste in women.'

'She's a witch,' Étaín said.

Grimnir's raised an eyebrow. 'So-ho? Is she, now? A witch? Well, let's have a bit of fun ere I send this ragged lickspittle back to my wretched kinsman!' He stropped the flat of his blade across his forearm, leaving a trail of pale blood in its wake. 'Answer me this, witch: can you warm Bjarki's bed without hands or a tongue?'

'Cruach!' the Witch of Dubhlinn screamed.

Grimnir heard an eerie whistle; he fell into a fighting stance, ready to kill whatever man or beast might step from the night. A multitude of rustlings followed the whistle. Grimnir tensed, eyes narrowed; he gauged the distance between himself and the witch, in half a mind to simply carve her head from her shoulders and have done.

'*Cruach!*'

'*Bah!* Call your lads!' He took a step toward her . . .

Étaín called out a warning. 'Grimnir! Wait—'

Suddenly, ravens exploded over the precipice of Carraig Dubh – a swirling wall of darkness that hit Grimnir like a physical blow. He staggered, throwing an arm up to protect his eyes as hundreds of nail-like claws raked his callused hide. The sound was deafening; Grimnir roared and lashed out in a rage, felt hot blood spatter his knuckles as his seax sliced through feather, beak, and talon.

And then, silence. Grimnir lowered his arm and straightened.

Nechtan, the witch . . . both were gone, snatched up by that cursed flock of crows.

The witch's sorcery had saved her, and in the same stroke she had robbed him of his final expression of contempt for the *vestálfar*. She had stolen Nechtan's body before he could defile it. Before he could repay the desecration of his father's corpse. White-hot rage coursed through Grimnir's veins.

'Run!' he bellowed. 'Hide behind your filthy walls! Tell

333

that wretched oathbreaker a reckoning is coming! Blood for blood! Hear me, Sly One, Father Loki! Bear witness, O Ymir, sire of giants and lord of the frost! Hear me! Blood for blood!' Grimnir screamed at the cloud-laced sky, lightening now into the twilight that preceded the dawn; he loosed a titanic howl, as deep and merciless as that of a hunting wolf.

It echoed down the slopes, through cleft and hollow, until it reached the palisades and earthworks of Dubhlinn. The sound froze the blood of the Danes and Norsemen standing the night's final watch atop the city's ramparts; they stared up in dread at the tree-clad mountains, muttering prayers or clutching at the hammer-shaped amulets worn around their necks. The eldest among them shivered and hid their eyes, for they knew the sound. They knew it from their childhood in the frozen North.

It was the voice of Fenrir, god of wolves, and to hear it meant the chains that kept the beast from the world were close to breaking.

20

Kormlada held Nechtan close as the raven-veil parted, revealing the familiar walls of her chamber atop Cuarán's Tower. Dawn's light seeped through the open casement as Cruach resumed his accustomed place there. The huge black bird ruffled his feathers; he stared down at them with the flat, expressionless gaze of his kind as Nechtan sagged against her, and then sank down onto both knees. The Tuatha groaned, wheezing, threads of blood oozing from his slack lips.

In the rising light, she could see the extent of the damage. The stake had pierced him high in the chest, entering through the hollow of his throat above his sternum. A mortal would be cold and dead, already, but the Tuatha were wrought from sterner stuff. Still, Kormlada wanted to help him. She wanted to ease his agony somehow, but Nechtan shook his head. 'L-Leave ... me ... b-be.'

'Have ... Have you magicks that can mend your flesh?'

Nechtan smiled, then: a ghastly death's-head grimace. 'N-Not against ... this. N-Not ... anymore. Unless ... Unless you c-can fetch a ... a healer f-from the Otherworld ...'

Kormlada tried to stanch the bleeding; she watched,

335

helpless, as the glamour of the Tuatha faded, as his *anima* bled out along with what little vital fluid remained in his veins. The emerald fires in his eyes dimmed, and his skin drew taut over his fragile skull to give him the appearance of a long-desiccated corpse.

'There must be something—'

'*As I was walking all alone,*' came a singsong voice behind her, '*I heard two crows making a moan.* Isn't this a touching bit of theater.' Bjarki stepped from the shadowed doorway. He stroked the long plait of his beard, lips twisted into a malicious grin. 'Nearly moved to tears, I am!'

'Send for a leech, my lord!'

'A leech?' he replied, crouching beside Nechtan. Bjarki eyed the broom handle, its placement, the blood; he shook his head. 'There's not a leech alive that can help this poor sod. I see you've run afoul of the little snuffler who haunts my steps, eh?'

'Please,' Kormlada implored, clutching at the embroidered sleeve of Bjarki's tunic. 'Can you not help him? Your art—'

Twisting, Bjarki struck her across the mouth with the back of one scarred fist. She sprawled back in a daze, blood from a split lip drooling down her chin. 'Be silent, you treacherous hag!' He turned back to Nechtan. 'You should have come to me, elf. What were you thinking? That you could best him alone?' Bjarki tsked. He leaned closer, his voice barely above a hiss. 'The glory days of your kind are gone. Nothing but dust and memory. Against the likes of *him,* only another *kaunr* has the sand to come out on top.'

A gleam of defiance returned to Nechtan's eyes. He chuckled around a mouthful of blood. 'Th-Then why . . . w-why would I . . . c-come to you?'

Bjarki took hold of the stake and slowly twisted it.

Nechtan stiffened, but did not scream. 'Where is he?'

'S-Soon . . . he w-will come . . . f-find you. S-Soon . . .'

From his perch, Cruach cried out in the harsh voice of his kind:

> To *the halls where dwells* | *Grendel's bastard,*
> To *the Black Pool* | *to claim his weregild.*

Bjarki glanced up at the giant raven, eyes smoldering with sullen hate, and then back to Nechtan. The Tuatha's bloody grin widened. 'B-Blood of . . . Half-Dane s-spilled . . . spilled in Odin's w-weather.'

Slowly, Bjarki rose from his crouch, nostrils flaring as he exhaled. 'Where is he?'

'S-Soon . . .'

Bjarki's lips skinned back in a snarl of contempt. With both hands, he gripped the oak handle; he thrust a hob-nailed boot against Nechtan's thigh for leverage, and hauled the thick shaft out through his body, foot by gory foot. Nechtan gave a gurgling cry, then slumped forward, dead before his forehead touched the floor.

'And you,' Bjarki said, turning to Kormlada. The Witch of Dubhlinn struggled into a sitting position, her vision still doubled by the savage blow Bjarki had dealt her. He used the gory tip of the broom handle to push her back down. 'Going behind my back, are you? How did you find him when I could not? How?'

'Not me.' She nodded at Nechtan's corpse.

'Where was he?'

Kormlada daubed at her lip; she glared up at Half-Dane, weathering the fury in his eyes and meeting it with a hatred of her own. 'Carraig Dubh,' she said. 'Nechtan cornered it at the Rock of Brule.'

Bjarki nudged the oak stake at her. She flinched away

from it, at first, braced for a fresh beating; instead, he gestured with it again. Kormlada grasped the handle and allowed Bjarki to pull her to her feet. Her head swam, her ears still ringing from the blow.

'Was he wounded, my little snuffler?'

Kormlada shook her head.

Bjarki grunted. He turned away and began to pace; with each step, he rapped the point of the broom handle on the stone tiles. 'Of course not. I am not so lucky. Why now? Why did he choose this moment to interfere?'

'It . . . He seeks revenge.'

'Of course he does.' After a moment Bjarki turned back to her; he dragged the weathered oak handle up and used it to gesture out the casement. 'The snuffler seeks revenge.' Next, he lowered the handle to indicate Nechtan's corpse. 'This one sought . . . what? To end an old blood feud?' Finally, he leveled the stake at her. 'But, why were you there, eh? What were you seeking? An end to Bjarki Half-Dane, perhaps?'

Kormlada felt the precipice beneath her feet. Her breath caught in her throat. A wrong word, an insincere tone, and the makeshift spear that ended Nechtan's life would author her own doom. The moment stretched for a lifetime as she weighed every conceivable response.

'Why were you there?' Bjarki repeated.

'It was not of my own volition,' she said at length, her voice steady. Kormlada looked past the angled tip of the broom handle – with its veneer of Tuatha blood – and met Bjarki's serpentine gaze. 'He summoned me.'

'Why?'

She conjured the answer from nothing; it was a bald-faced lie, but like the best deceptions, it was simple and spoke more to her understanding of Half-Dane than of Nechtan. She delivered it with perfect inflection – a woman's disdain

338

for the business of men. With a slight and contemptuous toss of her head, Kormlada said, 'To boast.'

And slowly, Bjarki Half-Dane lowered the stake. Chuckling to himself, he tossed the oak handle atop her bedclothes, heedless of smeared blood. He added to the insult by wiping his hands on a brocaded tapestry. 'Draugen would have me bide my time,' he said. 'Do nothing while the snuffler prowls and prods at my gate.'

Kormlada sagged, suddenly exhausted. 'If it is revenge he's after, then that makes sense. He will come to you—'

'On his terms!' Bjarki's spine stiffened; when he spun back around his eyes were slits of cold fire. 'That dunghill rat has called the tune since this dance began! I'm done following his lead!'

'What will you do, my lord?' Kormlada studied Half-Dane anew; she could see the same lines in his face, the same arrangement of bones and distribution of features that she saw in the face of the *fomórach* atop Carraig Dubh. But in Bjarki there remained something . . . *human*. She realized, then, that for all his art, his ambition, his arrogance, and his presumption of power, Bjarki Half-Dane could never be the gold-giver he imagined himself to be. He was a pariah, hated by his own people as much as by the Men around him.

'Not me,' he said suddenly. 'You. You will betray me. You will go to *him*, parley with *him*, and gain his blasted confidence. That done, you will lead him by secret paths here, into Dubhlinn's heart – tell him you know a foolproof way to plant a knife in my gullet. Lure the wretched snuffler in, and I will be waiting to spring my own trap!'

'That beast will never trust me,' Kormlada said.

'Make him!'

'My lord, I—'

In two long steps, Bjarki seized her; long, black-nailed

339

fingers wrapped around her throat as he dragged her face to within inches of his own. His breath stank of wine and old meat. 'Make him, or – by Odin! – I swear you will join your precious Nechtan in the Halls of Hel!'

Kormlada tried to twist out of his grasp, but Half-Dane did not relent. His thumb ground into her windpipe, cutting off her air. He watched her face darken; her struggles ignited a light in his bloodshot eyes – a base and terrible lust. While she fought to breathe, Bjarki's free hand pawed the juncture of her thighs, feeling for her sex through the fabric of her nightdress. Kormlada tried to knee him, clawing at his face with one hand while plucking ineffectually at his iron fingers with the other. Bjarki's smile widened. He hauled her about and steered her back toward the divan, its bedclothes foul with Tuatha blood.

From above them came an eerie laugh. It was Cruach, and he mimicked Grimnir's voice down to the most minor inflection: '*My brother's bastard has his sire's pathetic taste in women.*'

Bjarki stopped as though whip-stung. He shoved Kormlada back against the divan and whirled around to face the giant raven. The Witch of Dubhlinn coughed; she glared at Bjarki's twisted back. 'What did you say?' she heard him growl. 'What did you say, you miserable squab?'

Kormlada's hand brushed the end of the broom handle. In her mind's eye, she saw herself taking up the oak stake, spinning it around, and ramming it through Half-Dane's groin till he screamed for death. In her mind's eye, she was fast and agile enough to kill him before he could get on with raping her. But the Witch of Dubhlinn had wisdom as well as imagination – she was no warrior, but she had an instinct for vengeance and a serpent's cunning. Half-Dane would pay; she would see to it. *I will make certain of it!*

She coughed again, rubbed her bruised throat.

Cruach repeated the *fomórach*'s laugh; his flat black eyes gleamed with inscrutable hate. '*My brother's bastard . . . pathetic.*'

'*Pah!*' Bjarki spat. 'Come in arm's reach of me and I'll twist your wretched head off!'

But even as he turned back to Kormlada, the brazen call of a distant horn reached her ears. Then another. They came from the seaward battlements, accompanied by a flurry of voices, indistinct but jubilant. She knew its meaning as well as he: the dragon ships had come. That Manx pirate, Bródir; Sigurðr of the Raven Banner, *jarl* of Orkney, and their ilk. Beneath striped sails, their black hulls slowly filled the broad Bay of Dubhlinn – thousands of mail-clad reavers and the sons of sea kings called by the ravens of war, whose axes thirsted for the blood of the Gael. These, the horns welcomed.

Bjarki Half-Dane, nostrils flaring with the scent of victory, gave forth a bellow of triumph. 'Ériu is between the hammer and the anvil, now!' He leered at Kormlada. 'We'll finish this later, after you've brought the snuffler to me.' Whirling, he stalked out of the room. She could hear him on the stairs, roaring for his slaves to fetch Sitric and Maelmorda.

Kormlada pushed herself upright; with trembling hands, she smoothed her disheveled hair, adjusted her nightdress. Cruach fluttered down and perched beside her, on the back of the divan. Gently, almost lovingly, that monstrous bird caressed her cheek with his coal-black beak. There was concern in his eyes. In answer, she stroked the feathers of his breast in silent benediction.

'Between the hammer and the anvil,' she whispered, 'that's where steel is forged. Find him, my love. Find the monster that killed our kinsman.'

And Cruach, head cocked as he fixed her in his unblinking stare, nodded and took wing . . .

21

As immobile as the great Black Stone, Grimnir sat at the edge of the precipice of Carraig Dubh and stared out over the valley of the River Liffey. He watched a great host of dragon ships nose into the waters of Dubhlinn's harbor, where brazen horns and shouts of fellowship greeted them. And away to the west, through the trees, he watched a yellowish haze come rolling down the valley toward Dubhlinn – thunderheads of dust raised by the tramping feet of an army.

When Étaín came to him and brought his gear, Grimnir merely grunted. Nor did he seem to pay her any heed as she sketched out what had happened since Blind Maeve's cottage. He did not offer to help retrieve the ponies the Irishmen had left at their camp, nor did he help see to the body of poor Dunlaing; he could have found the corpse of Ruadh Mór easily enough but made no offer, and when injured Bran called out for water and succor, Grimnir did not lift so much as a finger.

Étaín did. Though harrowed by the cruel scourge of exhaustion, she nevertheless made Bran comfortable, laid poor Dunlaing under a cairn of stones, fetched the ponies, and tried to no avail to find Ruadh Mór's body. Returning, she brought water from a trickling spring in the yew thicket, kindled a small fire, and made a stew of venison and cabbage. All the while, Grimnir crouched on his haunches, with his long arms folded around his knees and his eyes fixed on the valley below.

Weary and disheveled, Étaín brought a bowl of stew to him and unceremoniously dropped it by his side. Grimnir looked askance at the concoction and sniffed in disdain. 'Bring me meat, foundling. Red and raw. Not this slop.'

'Piss off,' she replied. She made to turn away, but stopped. 'No, you know what? You owe me! You run your mouth about blood prices and oaths, but what about life debt, eh? I could have left you to the elves, but I didn't! I came after you! And this is my thanks? Bollocks!'

Grimnir spat. 'So-ho! Here it comes, then! What's your price? A fistful of gold? The head of an enemy? A pound of flesh? What's my life worth to you, you wretched hymn-singer?'

But Étaín was too tired to fight. And she recognized in it a losing proposition. She'd sooner hold a storm to blame for its thunder than change a *skrælingr*'s ways. Coming after him had been more about repaying a debt of her own: regardless of his motives, Grimnir had followed her to Badon, plucked her from Hrothmund's grasp, and carried her for six days when he could just as easily have left her to die. Her slate, now, was well and truly clean.

'Not a tin farthing,' Étaín said quietly. Shaking her head, she turned away.

Around clenched teeth, Grimnir's jaw champed and writhed as though he chewed a foul-tasting word. Finally, he spat it out. 'Wait,' he said. He moved the bowl aside and gestured for her to sit.

Étaín sighed. She made no move toward him. 'I have no stomach for bickering.'

'*Nár.*' He wore a painful grimace. 'No bickering. Sit.'

And so, mindful of the crumbling edge, Étaín joined

him. Grimnir fished a chunk of venison from the bowl, and then offered the bowl to her. She looked at him as if he'd gone mad, but then shrugged and plucked out a piece of her own. They ate in odd, uncomfortable silence. Finally, Grimnir spat out a bit of gristle he'd been worrying and scrubbed his mouth with the back of his hand. He glanced sidelong at Étaín.

'Old Gífr, he's the one who taught me about oaths and debts,' Grimnir said. 'Never swear the one lightly, and never forget the other. He was right on that score, the useless git!' Grimnir gave a bark of gallows laughter. 'Miserable wretch had as many debts owed him as he had debts he owed others. Me, I never got a taste for owing anybody for anything – not for food, not for shelter, and not for blood. But' – his lip curled in a moue of distaste – 'you pulled my fat out of the fire, fair and square. I owe you. And on my oath, I will make this debt right.' Grimnir reached for the hilt of his seax, but Étaín's hand on his arm brought him up short.

'What say we call it even?'

'Even?'

Étaín nodded. 'For what you did at Badon.'

Grimnir sucked his teeth for a moment before slowly nodding. 'It's even, then.' He gave her a sly look. 'Though . . .'

'What?'

'If you're such a stickler for fairness, then I'm still owed for saving your wretched hide on the Ash-Road.' Grimnir bared his teeth in a malicious grin.

Étaín's expression hardened. 'Well, if we're splitting hairs . . . I'm still owed weregild for my dead friend, Njáll.'

At this, Grimnir's mouth clamped shut; his brow lowered in a scowl. He looked away, muttering under his breath something about their accounts perhaps being even, after all. Étaín snorted, and then laughed aloud.

'God bless you! You look like you just ate a turd! A ripe, stinking floater!' she said, and added, 'Can I confess something to you? When we left him in that cave back in Sjælland, Njáll wasn't dead.'

Grimnir looked askance at her. 'The Christ-Dane? *Nár!* My hands were around his throat! I know I choked the life out of him!'

'No.' Étaín shook her head. 'You hurt him, but he was very much alive when we left.'

Grimnir cursed and spat, though Étaín sensed a measure of admiration in him. 'You miserable kneelers! Can't even trust you to die right!' He lapsed into silence.

The sun reached its zenith and began its decline into the cloud-wreathed west; the shadows beneath Carraig Dubh lengthened and the river below turned to a ribbon of fire. 'He knows I'm here,' Grimnir said at length. 'Bastard knows I could put right a five-hundred-year debt with a single thrust to his black heart. So he hides behind those wretched walls and draws more flies to his stink, thinking they'll save him from the reckoning.' Grimnir nodded away to the west, where a column of smoke marked the approach of the other army. 'But who are these swine? More of Half-Dane's cursed allies? Out for a lark and burning the countryside?'

Étaín realized, then, that Grimnir wasn't aware of Ériu's current strife. There'd been no time to tell him what she knew before they left Wessex, and even less time since washing up on these shores. 'No,' she said. 'That's the army of Ériu's high king, Brian mac Cennétig. He makes for Dubhlinn with the intent to crush an uprising led by that witch's brother, King Maelmorda of Leinster. Half-Dane is his ally – well, more like the instigator of the whole thing – and in Óspak's words he's 'offering plunder, slaves, and land to every *jarl* and gold-giver from here to Helheimr who answers his call to arms.' I'd wager those ships bear Manx reavers and freebooters from Orkney.'

Grimnir's eyes blazed with interest as he studied the landscape anew. 'Just like Rastarkalv,' he said, half to himself. 'Back then, Bjarki goaded the sons of Bloodaxe into rising up against that idiot, King Haakon.'

'Why?'

Grimnir slowly rose from his crouch, his limbs creaking and cracking as he stretched his muscles. 'Reputation, mostly. He wanted the Norse to see him as a powerful *goði*, so he spooled off some lies about prophecies and omens and then manipulated the situation to fit his needs. What's his play, this time?'

'A throne, perhaps,' Étaín said. She, too, clambered to her feet.

'Could be. I need to get closer.' Grimnir's gaze shifted to the approaching army. 'This high king of theirs, what do you know of him?'

Étaín shrugged. 'Not much. He is an old man, I've heard. A good king and a devout man of God. Jarl Óspak thought enough of him to sail from Mann in his defense, even against his own brother.'

'That one.' Grimnir jabbed a thumb over his shoulder; down the slope from the precipice, their makeshift camp lay hard by the yew thicket. Bran of the Uí Garrchon rested there, beneath an awning of branches and blankets. She could hear him moaning in feverish agony. 'Is he one of the high king's men?'

'He was going to join up, he and his mates.'

The fetishes in Grimnir's hair *ticked* together softly as he drew on his jerkin and laced it up, bending his back, twisting at the waist, and rolling his shoulders to work the stiffness from the leather. His shirt of rust-flecked iron rings came next, followed by the belt supporting his seax in its scabbard. His cloak of tattered wolf fur he left rolled on his satchel. 'Take that wretch on to their camp,' Grimnir said. 'I'll rig up a drag and you can use one of those flea-bitten ponies.'

Étaín shook her head. 'He'll not survive. That arrow . . .'

'He won't survive either way, but if he dies down amongst the Gael we can at least use it to get you into the old king's good graces.' Grimnir shoved his satchel into her hands. 'Take this and leg it, foundling.'

'I don't understand what you're asking of me,' Étaín said.

Grimnir leaned in closer; she was reminded of something, then. Something close proximity had caused her to forget: here was a creature wrought from ten centuries of strife, twenty mortal lifetimes bound into a monstrous form most men would kill if they had half a chance. And she was colluding with it. 'We're between rock and ruin, foundling. Two starveling wolves, we are, outcast and alone. But we have a chance to change that. So I need you to be yourself. Be a good cross-kisser and all, brimming with the milk of human kindness. I need you down there amongst the Gael and spinning your yarn. And spin it loud, for any who will listen.'

'If I do,' Étaín finished his thought for him, 'then, perhaps, the wolves won't be quite so alone.'

22

Grimnir crept down from the heights of Carraig Dubh as the day waned. His path brought him through the forest of pine and oak blanketing the mountain's flanks, along logging trails used by the town's woodcutters, and past empty camps where Danish shipwrights once gathered to dicker and trade over the best wood for keels, spars, masts, and oars. Logging trails became horse and cart paths as forest gave way to fallow fields. These Grimnir crossed at speed, pausing only to examine the weed-choked walls of a burned-out farmstead. 'Old work,' he muttered.

Étaín he had sent in the other direction, down the gentler path that would bring her and that cursed Irishman out in the rear of the approaching army. *'Keep clear of the vanguard,' he told her as he cut four yew branches and lashed them together to make a drag. 'The young ones, eager to blood themselves and make a name . . . they'll lead the army. Look for the rabble that will be following the main body, and ask for one of your cursed priests. By the looks of him, this one's going to be needing your death-rites.'*

'His name is Bran,' she said, her voice hard. 'Bran of the Uí Garrchon.'

'Whatever this wretch's name is, make sure you sing out your story – and sing it loud. You want their miserable king to hear it.'

'Why does it matter if it reaches King Brian's ear?'

Grimnir paused in his efforts to truss the drag to one of the ponies, its ears flattened to its skull in terror. 'It matters. Something happens to me, a king is a good ally to have, foundling.'

Grimnir chuckled at himself. Listen to him! He sounded like some soft-bellied matron. All this hand-wringing over Étaín's safety? *Faugh!* He didn't care. All that mattered was weregild – the weighing of the blood price and the slow, terrible extraction of that price from Bjarki's worthless hide. When the blade met the bone, Grimnir reckoned all bets, all allegiances, would be off.

Farmland gave way to creek-laced meadows, rich in tall grasses and orchards; rain-swollen, these watercourses drained into a pair of rivers – the smaller was sluggish and black; the larger, fast-moving and tidal. At their confluence Grimnir spied a deep black pool that opened on the sea, and on a promontory above it sat the fortress-city of Dubhlinn.

Grimnir crept closer, through an apple grove gone to seed and into the thin shelter offered by the stone foundations of a long-ruined church. From there, he surveyed the town's defenses and found them formidable. The walls were stronger than Badon's, constructed of stone, earth, and timber, well-kept and well-manned, to boot. The black pool served as a harbor, and even from Grimnir's vantage he could see it was packed with ships – dragon-prowed and shield-hung, keels beached in the soft loam; a second palisade protected the landward bank of the pool. Doing a quick tally of the masts, taking into account others he could yet see in the glass-blue waters of the bay, beyond, gave him a rough estimate of sixty ships – well over two thousand fighting men.

Grimnir hawked and spat; he scrubbed his chin with the

back of one hand. 'Bastard's as snug as a maggot in a dead man's arse.'

Undeterred, he slunk out of his hiding place and retraced his steps through the apple grove before setting off on a track parallel to Dubhlinn. Grimnir reached the overgrown banks of the more sluggish of the two rivers – its waters black with silt and peat; it ran deep, but he was able to ford it with the help of low-hanging branches and a fallen log. The ground rose on the far bank, giving him ample vantage to study the main landward gate into Dubhlinn.

Like the walls, the gate was strongly built of iron-bound wood and flanked by earthen ramparts topped with a timber palisade. It stood open to let in a flood of refugees from the hinterland – Norse settlers driven from their homes by the advancing Gaels; long-faced men bearing axes and spears stumped behind trundling oxcarts laden with the dross of their miserable lives, wives and squalling brats raising a clamor that set his teeth on edge.

Grimnir considered slipping in with the refugees. *Creep in like some peaching sneakthief . . . but then what? Knife Bjarki in the dark, in his bed? Or fight him in the open and hope to kill him before his lads carve me up and feed me to the crows?* No, as formidable and well-ordered as the defenses surrounding Dubhlinn were, Grimnir knew he could find a way in. His problem would be getting close to that snake Bjarki – and thornier still would be getting out again with his head unbroken once he had done the deed.

For the better part of an hour Grimnir crouched there in the tall grass, watching the gate. *Bastard knows I'm here,* he thought. *How could he not? The witch would have told him, even if he missed the shrieking of the night hags when I set foot on this cursed isle. He knows . . . but he won't run. Not this time. Little fool has too much invested in this bit of treachery – armies marching at his command, kings bowing and scraping, the cursed gods looking on. What, then? How can I get close—?* Grimnir suddenly rapped the side of his head with the heel of his hand three times in quick succession. Nár! *You're a stupid git! That's what he wants! He wants me hemmed inside those blasted walls! Then, no matter where I turn he'll have his swine ready to nail me to the ground, damn his yellow liver!*

Suddenly, Grimnir's eyes narrowed to slits; flaring nostrils caught the acrid scent of smoke, underscored by the savory stench of roasted flesh. He knew what that reek portended, better than most. Shading his eyes with one grimy palm, Grimnir looked off to the west. Beyond a low range of hills two columns of smoke stained the sky; closer to hand, he heard a horn blare from atop the battlements, followed by the creak and pop of hinges as the gates of Dubhlinn slowly trundled shut. The refugees left on the road raised a clamor, screaming and cursing and scrambling to get inside.

Using the sudden cacophony as cover, Grimnir scuttled to a new position just below the brow of the hill; the grass was thinner, here, but it afforded him a clear view of the heavily rutted road. As he looked on, the men among the retreating Norse chivvied their families away from the ponderous oxen and bid them run. Older children scooped up their younger siblings amid cries and terrified bawls, and those closest to the gate exhorted the stragglers to hurry before it closed. Only a handful slipped inside before the gate's iron-banded bar fell into place with the cold finality of a death sentence. The rest who remained on the road scattered like hares. A quarter of a mile from the walls of Dubhlinn, the men turned about and stood shoulder-to-shoulder with their grim-faced women, spears and axes ready, as the Irish vanguard thundered into view.

352

They were outriders, and there were scores of them – howling, half-wild Gaels mounted on shaggy ponies, armed with spears and bearing small round shields but not a hauberk or helm among them; theirs was the discipline of a pack of feral dogs. As a mob, they bore down on the ragged line of refugees. Knowing they faced death, those stalwart men and women nevertheless gave a good accounting of themselves. Their spears brought down a handful of ponies; their axes soaked the hard-packed earth with good Irish blood. But the refugees could not stand long. Grimnir hissed a silent warning as riders swung out and got in behind the Northerners. Half of them turned to fend off this new threat and got a spear in the back for their troubles.

In the blink of an eye, the uneven skirmish became a slaughter. Grimnir saw a red-bearded Dane, wounded unto death, drive a knife into the throat of the woman who stood alongside him; they sank down together, husband and wife, as the Irish storm broke over them. Riders threaded in among the oxcarts, spearing stragglers as they ran, snatching up children and dashing their brains out, and dragging what women they could find out into the open and stripping them naked. Butchery gave way to rape.

Grimnir expected some response from those hard-eyed Norse who peered over the walls of Dubhlinn. A strong sally to retrieve the dead, a flight of arrows to serve as an iron-tipped rebuke, something. But he did not expect silence. Grimnir's lip curled in a snarl of disdain. It reeked of Bjarki's handiwork – *the sniveling yellow bastard!* He would hide behind his walls; he would hide behind the spears of these Norse curs who thought he was something that he wasn't. *Just like Rastarkalv.*

'So be it!' He could play that game again. But Grimnir wouldn't just skulk around the edges of the fray the way he did in those days, when he was content to let the sons of Bloodaxe call the strokes. No, this time he meant to guide the spear. That meant forging an alliance with the cross-kissing Irish king, Brian mac Cennétig. That meant using Étaín to get in his good graces . . .

That meant patience. Grimnir ground his teeth in frustration. *Patience!* The wretched maggot was *right there,* closer than he'd been in half a century, and it galled him to sit on his hands and do nothing. Still, the idiot was snake-cunning; it wouldn't do to come so far only to end up with his hide hung on a bramble because he was too reckless to think things through.

Near at hand, a horse snorted and shied as it caught Grimnir's scent. He cursed under his breath; he knew he'd tempted the Norns, those fickle bitches who wove the fates of all, by creeping too close to the fray. Grimnir watched as the horse's rider, a fiercely mustachioed Irishman with triple-plaited red-gold hair and a pox-scarred face, stroked the beast's neck and cooed in its flattened ears. Eyes the color of hoarfrost flickered across the crest of the low hillock. He saw something that didn't sit well with him, his blood-spattered brow furrowing. The Irishman straightened abruptly; as he turned at the waist and whistled for the others to give heed, Grimnir slipped back over the crest of the hillock – his movements hidden by the gentle sough and sigh of the grass as the wind rustled through it.

23

Cormac O'Ruairc whistled up a few lads. These men of the vanguard, like himself, were Connacht-born, the bloody-handed Uí Ruairc from the hills and deep valleys around Lough Gill. And like him, they had pledged their oaths not to that doddering old fool King Brian, but to his savage-minded son, Murrough – a prince of the Dalcassians whose temperament closely matched their own. But while the father preached against rapine and slaughter, the son had given him explicit instructions to harrow the ground with the blood of these filthy Northron invaders. Make them rue the day they ever set foot on Ériu's blessed soil. And that was what he did. That was what his lads were best at . . .

Only a handful of riders paid any heed to O'Ruairc's summons, so intent were they on despoiling the dead. The few who cantered up were older men, for the most part, who had no use for lusts that fired the blood of their younger kinsmen. 'Saw one slinking off, yonder,' O'Ruairc said, jerking his chin toward the low hill and beyond. 'And he didn't look like a farmer, either. A spy or I'm a feckin' priest! A few of you lads go and track him down. We'll finish up this lot before the Northrons get their dander up and try to drive us off.'

Cormac O'Ruairc turned away as five of his lads

vanished over the crest of the hill; a distant gleam caught the Connacht chief's eye: sunlight on mail links. He espied a delegation watching them from the battlements of Dubhlinn Castle. O'Ruairc grinned, his mustaches bristling. 'Look lively, lads!' he called out. 'Their ruddy king's come out to take a gander! Little Silky-beard has crawled out from under his bitch-mother's skirts!'

A chorus of curses and taunts rose from the throats of the Irish vanguard; a few rode nearer to the gates, leapt off their ponies, and flashed their lily-white backsides. Another tried twice to lob a child's body over the palisade. On his third attempt, as he leaned from the saddle to snatch the bloody, towheaded corpse off the ground, a Norse arrow punched through his face from the back of his skull. He toppled into the dirt; his pony shied and pranced, then bolted as a second arrow gashed its dust-streaked flank.

Still laughing, O'Ruairc led the outriders away from Dubhlinn's walls.

24

King Sitric paced the battlements of Dubhlinn Castle, his mailed shoulders wrapped in a voluminous green cloak pinned at the breast with a brooch of Byzantine gold, and watched as the Irish vanguard retreated from the gates. He scowled at the bodies left in their wake: farmers and settlers who had lived to the west of Dubhlinn, mixed with refugees from the now-burning village of Kilmainham, three miles distant – men, women, and children abandoned by their king, left to rape and slaughter under his very nose. His honor, his pride, sacrificed for the ambitions of that wretch Half-Dane. Dubhlinn's king unclenched his jaw.

'Again,' he growled to his lieutenant, who turned and motioned to the dozen or so archers among the Norse. These men, as lean and sinewy as hunting dogs, drew back their yew bows and sent a second flight of arrows aloft. The king saw one saddle emptied, but the balance of the volley fell short. He cursed.

'That's women's work, Silkiskegg,' said a voice at Sitric's back. He stiffened and turned, glowering at the men who joined him on the battlements. His uncle was there ... soft, languid Maelmorda, accompanied by the chiefs of the newly come dragon ships: Sigurðr, *jarl* of Orkney, a thick-bearded bear of a man who fought under the raven banner of Odin; at his side, in stark antithesis, stood Bródir of

Mann – as lean and feral as a rabid wolf. If the skalds sang true, Bródir was as rune-wise and battle-cunning. Of dwarf make was the axe cradled in his arms, and from that blighted folk came the spells of protection that were woven with silver wire through the links of his mail hauberk. 'Women's work,' he repeated. 'Why do we tarry? Send forth our reavers and we'll slay these Irish dogs that scratch at your door!'

'Aye.' Sigurðr's voice was a basso rumble. 'I didn't come all the way from Orkney to rub beards with the likes of you lot. Give the word and we will crush them ere the moon rises and bring that cross-kisser, Mac Cennétig, back to you in chains.'

Maelmorda scoffed. 'If it were that easy, why would we need you louts?'

'Lout, is it?' Sigurðr started forward, hands knotting into fists; he took two steps toward the pale king of Leinster before his companion's hand on his shoulder stilled him instantly. Neither of them saw the twisted shadow of Bjarki Half-Dane lurking behind them, watching.

'Because you have no men, Hollow King,' Bródir said, making no effort to mask his scorn. 'No men, no land, no crown save for that useless bauble you wear.'

'The men of Leinster fight for me!' Maelmorda drew himself up, seeking to regain some standing among this gathering of chiefs.

Sigurðr's booming laughter echoed off the battlements. 'Men?' he said after a moment, wiping the tears of mirth from his eyes. 'Those yapping dogs? They don't fight for you, idiot! They fight because those curs' – he jerked his shaggy head toward the fires at Kilmainham – 'pissed on their doorstep!'

Bródir cracked a rare smile, mirthless and cruel.

'Enough!' Sitric roared. 'Gold, land, honor . . . what

difference does it make? We're all here for the same reason, and we dance to the same tune!' The king of Dubhlinn glared at the silent figure of Half-Dane.

'True,' Bródir said. 'And the war note plays on, Silkiskegg! The Choosers of the Slain ride in the twilight of the North, and the web of fate is spun! Sound your trumpets, add to the din, and let us bring doom upon the Gael!'

Sorcery lurked in Bródir's words and its effect was not lost on Sitric. Dubhlinn's king felt his blood sing; he very nearly loosed his war cry and called on his Norse mercenaries to join him on the red-stained road to Glory and Death. Bjarki's silky voice, though, snuffed Bródir's enchantment the way a man snuffs a candle's flame.

'You have seen them?' Bjarki said. When he moved to join the chiefs, the king of Dubhlinn noticed an emphasis to his limp, to his sense of twisted infirmity. He was playing a role – the misshapen *goði*, his health sacrificed in the acquisition of wisdom. Sitric would have laughed had he not seen a look of fear pass between Sigurðr and Bródir when Half-Dane stepped from the shadows. 'You have seen them, mighty Bródir? You have beheld the *valkyrjar* with your mortal sight? No?' Bjarki grimaced; even under the afternoon sun, a gloom seemed to cling to Half-Dane. His eyes burned like embers as he fixed his gaze on first the *jarl* of Orkney, then the chief of the Manx reavers. 'I have! I have seen the twelve daughters of Odin, terrible and fair, with eyes like corpse light and hearts as cold as a whetstone's hollow. You say the web of fate is spun? I tell you, Bródir of Mann, the Norns yet weave the cloth of this spear-shattering upon the loom of slaughter! I have glimpsed it: severed heads they used as weights, sinews for the weft and entrails for the warp; a notched sword was their beater, and the shuttle was a barbed arrow! The omens are plain: the swords of the North will remain in their sheaths, this day, their spears grounded and axes un-whetted! Ignore these signs at your own peril!'

'How long, then?' Sigurðr said. 'How long do we wait?'

Sitric glanced sidelong at Bjarki, who had lapsed into silence. 'The priests will take the omens, again, with the dawn,' said the king of Dubhlinn. 'We will know the gods—'

'Two days hence,' Bjarki said suddenly. 'Mac Cennétig must die on the day those wretched hymn-singers celebrate the nailing of their god to the cross. That is the will of Odin.'

Bródir's vicious smile returned. 'Long Friday,' he said with a curt nod. 'Fitting.'

'Aye.' Sigurðr grunted; he scratched at one bearded cheek. 'But, will the bastard meet us on his holy day?'

'Never.' This from forgotten Maelmorda. 'It is a sin to spill blood that day. The old fool will refuse battle.'

'Then we make him meet us,' Sitric replied, drawing himself up to his full height; the chiefs of the dragon ships nodded their approval. Even Bjarki held himself silent, watching. 'Mac Cennétig's choice to draw steel or not, that is between him and his god. But we *will* draw steel, my brothers. We will harrow the ground with that red piss these Gaels call blood, whether they choose to fight us or not!'

'Then you'd best pray, Silkiskegg,' Sigurðr replied, a twinkle in his eye. 'You'd best pray the mead holds out! My lads are a thirsty lot, and those Manx bastards drink ale like fish drink water!'

Sitric laughed with them. 'My uncle will show you where I keep the barrels and bottles, for he is well-acquainted with that part of my castle.' Braying with laughter, Sigurðr crooked an arm around Maelmorda's neck before the latter could object and dragged him off like a boon companion;

Bjarki and Bródir fell in behind them, side by side. After a moment, the king of Dubhlinn was once again alone on the battlements of his castle, looking down on the ravages of an enemy.

Soon, he felt his mother's presence beside him. Kormlada was cloaked and hooded, as dark as the ravens that were her familiars.

'You heard?' the king said.

Kormlada nodded.

'He has gone too far,' Sitric said quietly. 'My own men look to *him* for their orders, as though I am my wretched uncle made over – an empty tunic with a borrowed crown.' He exhaled. 'These deaths are on my head. They came to me for safety and this is how I repay their loyalty? I should have ridden out and engaged their vanguard, but he ordered me to stand down and closed the gates. *He* ordered *me*!' Sitric hissed between clenched teeth, penning his emotions behind the walls of breath. 'I am the son of Olaf Cuarán, not some monster's plaything!'

'Persevere, my son,' she replied. 'Temper your anger and play your part. It is I who conjured this demon into our midst, and it is I who must banish him back to whatever hell spawned him.'

Sitric turned away. 'Whatever you're planning, Mother, do it quickly. We are running out of time.' Dubhlinn's king withdrew from the castle walls, leaving Kormlada alone. A shape caught her eye; she glanced up to see a dark fleck riding the updrafts over the long sloping plains. It was Cruach, rising ever higher into the blue and gold sky, searching, hunting, bearing her message to the monster she had met atop Carraig Dubh. There was her answer, beautiful in its simplicity, for the problem of Half-Dane's continued existence.

It takes a monster to kill a monster.

361

25

Grimnir eluded the hunters that the Irish chief sent after him with hardly any effort. Indeed, a *kaunr* whelp, his mother's milk yet damp on his lips, could have run circles around the louts, so lazy and spoor-blind were they. He considered having a bit of sport with them, hounding them to the edge of exhaustion and then picking them off one by one, but he thought the better of it. He meant to strike an accord with the Irish king, and that meant earning his trust. What fool would trust him, then, if it got around that a swarthy, fanged demon had ambushed a few of the lads in the forest?

So, Grimnir let them slip away ere temptation got the better of him. He retraced his steps, reaching the crumbling foundations of the burned-out farmstead near sunset. The sky above shone a deep blue through the ragged drifts of cloud, turning to ruddy fire on the western horizon. It was the same hue as the banked heart of a blacksmith's forge.

'Red sky,' Grimnir muttered, trying to recall some bit of doggerel Gífr had been fond of. He considered hunkering down there, amid the brambles and the fallen rocks, when the doom-laden *cr-r-ruck* of a raven raised the hackles on his neck. He heard the rustle of giant wings. Recalling the witch's minions, Grimnir dropped to a crouch; he whirled toward the sound, drawing his seax as an ancient raven alighted on the pile of moss-rotten stone that had once been the farmstead's chimney.

For a long moment the two stared at each other – the raven's coal-black eyes glossy and unblinking, while Grimnir's eyes narrowed to slits and smoldered like the westering sun. Slowly, he straightened.

'What of it, old crow? Has that one-eyed whoreson of a god sent you to bedevil me?' And it did not startle Grimnir in the least when that giant bird answered him, its voice the harsh croak of his kind:

> Wise is the wary | when speech is sought
> So let the death-dealing | be stayed.
> From high-stone hall | above the Black Pool,
> The daughter of kings | seeks counsel.

Grimnir grunted. 'Daughter of kings, eh? You mean Half-Dane's whore?'

> The daughter of kings | seeks counsel.

'Does she, now?' He looked askance at the bird; he did not flutter and twitch in the manner of his younger kin, but rather kept still – a certain quiet majesty draping from him like a fine cloak. The creature was a familiar, a soul-servant, and he reeked of a primeval sorcery, now long forgotten. 'Why?'

> Entwined is the lady | in the plots of the foe,
> Though bale and hatred | be his portion;
> Wisdom she would share | with wolf-born Grimnir,
> Against thy kinsman, | Grendel's slayer.

Grimnir smelled a trap. She had wanted him as a pet, and that whiteskin he'd killed had meant something to her, of this he was certain; why meet with his killer unless she had vengeance on her mind? Perhaps, though, he could twist this into an opportunity. He needed to know the mind of Half-Dane, to find out what that blasted little fool had planned. He needed something he could translate into leverage. And who better to put the irons to than his wretched bedmate? 'Tell her midnight. The Black Stone. Tell her to come alone.'

> *Thence she will come | by her own devices,*
> *But what oath do you give | that she will leave?*

'I give her no oath!' Grimnir laughed. 'What oath does she give me, you buzzard? That's right . . . none! If she can't look after her own skin what use is she to anyone? Tell your so-called daughter of kings that if she wants to parley, come to the stone by midnight!'

And without another word, the raven lofted into the twilight sky on powerful wings, leaving Grimnir alone once more. He looked back at the walls of Dubhlinn, its palisades and earthworks tinged with fire, its roofs the color of blood; he chuckled. The bitch had spleen, he gave her that. To call for a parley? That took more sand in her belly than most men could claim. But was she honest? That, Grimnir would not give her. Was she not Half-Dane's whore?

Grimnir withdrew through the darkling wood and ascended to the heights of Carraig Dubh. There, in the shadow of the Black Stone, he would bait a trap for the Witch of Dubhlinn . . .

26

The Irish host made its camp at Kilmainham, where the thatch yet smoldered and the stones still radiated the heat of a hundred pillaging fires. And like the mythical phoenix rising from the ashes, a new village sprang from the war-ravaged bones of the old, at once larger and far more diverse. Tents lined its crooked streets; some were no more than a cloak stretched between three poles, while others were sprawling pavilions made from colorful linen and embroidered in the Saracen script, looted from the mysterious East and brought to market in Hlymrekr or Dubhlinn itself.

Neighborhoods sorted themselves out by kin and clan even though the soldiers gathered under common banner; in their makeshift squares cook fires blazed. By that diffuse light the chiefs and captains of the army ate a quick bite with their men and gave orders for the rotation of the watch before trudging up the long slope to the ruined monastery claimed by Brian mac Cennétig, to attend the high king of Ériu.

Cressets burned in the courtyard of the monastery. For three centuries it had stood watch from a ridge overlooking the turbulent waters of the River Liffey, and those centuries had not been easy. Stones blackened by ancient burnings now bore a veneer of moss; roofless and open to the elements, the monastery – dedicated to Saint Maighneann – had been spared the indignity of being used as a roost for flocks of birds or as pasture for cattle, since its cracked paving stones allowed only ragged weeds to take root. Instead, heathen hands had turned its walls into a mosaic of scratched runes, pictograms, and obscene etchings.

Outside the nave, under an awning of plain linen, King Brian held court. Though past seventy, his hair and beard both gone to silver, Brian nevertheless remained formidable in manner – the dangerous light in his eyes undimmed and the steel in his voice unbroken by the shadow of his advancing years. He surveyed this gathering of his captains, drawn from the clans of Munster and Connacht and reinforced by war bands of fearsome Galloglas fighters from Alba across the Irish Sea and mailed Danes from Hlymrekr, newly baptized to the Christian cause. Leading the convocation was his eldest son and heir, Murrough mac Brian. The son, like the father, cut a redoubtable figure – rangy and muscular, his black hair shot through with silver and his scowling visage etched by the stylus of war. He wore a tunic of iron rings beneath his cloak-wrapped shoulders, woven in the manner of the Dalcassians.

'I gave an order, Murrough,' Brian said. 'Who defied me? On whose shoulders did you place the responsibility for leading the vanguard?'

The prince turned and nodded to Cormac O'Ruairc, who stood among the captains of Connacht.

'I had that honor, sire.' Cormac stepped to the fore. To his credit he did not fidget, nor did his face betray any hint of emotion. 'I led the Uí Ruairc of Lough Gill in advance of the main army. It is by our hand that the invaders were driven from this place.'

'Did my son fail to make my wishes clear?'

O'Ruairc glanced sidelong at Murrough, whose face darkened in anger. 'Answer him, by God!'

'No, sire.'

'Then tell me this, kern: by what right did you feel you could ignore the wishes of your king?' Brian growled. By using the label for a common warrior, 'kern,' he denied O'Ruairc the dignity of his title before his peers; the insult brought a flush of color to the man's cheeks. 'I gave leave to plunder, for anything these foreigners possess is hardwon from our people, but I forbade the slaughter—'

'Blame the feckin' Danes!' O'Ruairc snapped. 'Aye, blame them for not giving up the road! Blame them for not letting go of their paltry belongings! And if you must find fault, sire, then put it where it belongs: square on the heads of those miserable swine that fought tooth and nail for land that wasn't theirs, and died to the last man and woman!'

The silence that followed was gravid with the threat of violence. Murrough flexed his scarred fingers, eager to throttle the life from his oath-man. But he didn't move. No one did, save the king. Slowly, Brian mac Cennétig leaned forward, his throne creaking as he nailed O'Ruairc with a look that could melt iron.

'And what of the children?' he said quietly. 'Did the children fight you as hard as their parents? Mark me on this, Cormac son of Airt of the Uí Ruairc, when the spears have shattered and the ravens have fed, you will stand before me in judgment for these crimes – and if you and I fall beneath the axes of the Danes, then we will both face the judgment of the Son of Man, himself! Now get out of my sight!'

Jaw clenched and fuming, O'Ruairc sketched a perfunctory bow to the king, glared hard at Murrough, and stalked from the convocation. Muttering followed in his wake.

'Heed me well, all of you.' Silence returned as Brian rose to his feet. 'This is my army. It trades upon my name, and its authority comes from me. And my authority' – the king's voice rose to a thunderous pitch – 'my authority comes from the Almighty himself! So when Dubhlinn falls – and it *will* fall! – I'll not have it bandied about that King Brian is only Christian when it suits him! Kinsmen or not, you will control yourselves and your men or you will become my enemy! Go, now. Rest and prepare for the morrow.'

The chiefs and captains bowed in turn and filed from the courtyard of the monastery until only Murrough and the king remained. The son waved off a servant who hurried to his father's side; instead, he offered Brian his own arm to lean on. The king was weary. His years had more than caught up with him over the last weeks, and with each passing day it became harder and harder to hide his infirmity from their enemies.

Brian smiled at the frown etching his son's scarred brow; with one liver-spotted hand he patted the strong forearm that helped support him. 'Why so glum, boy? I'm not dead, yet. Though I expect this will be my last spear-gathering.'

'And then what? You'll hand me your crown and go off to sit in the sun at Kincora?' Murrough chuckled at the thought of his father idle. 'Nay, you've got fight left in you, old man.'

Arm in arm, father and son shuffled across the moonlit courtyard to where Brian's own tent stood. It was a simple pavilion, its austerity befitting the old man's personality; before it rested a four-wheeled cart bearing the Cross of Kincora, carved from the stone of Golgotha by the apostle Peter and brought from Rome by Saint Flannán as a gift to the faithful of Ériu. Four young monks tended it, praying day and night for the Almighty's blessing, while the sons of Thomond sat round, whetting their terrible Dalcassian axes.

With Murrough's help, the king knelt and kissed the base of the Cross before he entered the royal pavilion. Inside, the younger man winced at the stifling warmth, at the musty stench of age barely masked by drifting tendrils of incense. A night lamp flickered from the center pole of the pavilion, and a brazier smoldered beneath it. The king released Murrough's arm and shuffled to his divan, where he sat with an audible groan.

The prince glanced about. Besides the divan, the pavilion contained a tree for the king's cloak and crown, for his axe from his days with the war bands, for his brightly painted shield, and for the sword that was his symbol of power; the white bearskin on the back of the divan Murrough recognized as a gift from the chief of the Hlymrekr Danes, while the open Gospel on its stand near the head of the divan came from the monastery at Iona – its leather-and-gilt covers the only touch of ostentation to his father's spartan quarters.

'Where was Malachy, this eve?' Brian said. 'The men of Meath did not answer my summons.'

'He's camped to the west of us, near Dolcan's Meadow. That old snake claims not to trust you, though I'd wager he's treating with the Norse on his own and planning to betray us.'

'He feels ill-used,' Brian replied. He reclined against the arm of the divan, where an old rolled cloak served as a pillow. 'And with good reason. I ousted him from his throne and took Kormlada from him to be my wife, even if *that* proved ill-thought. I would not trust him, either, were our situations reversed. Give him the benefit of the doubt, my son. Tomorrow, invite Malachy to cross the Liffey and scour the lands north of Dubhlinn. Go with him. With luck, it will draw that pup Sitric and his faithless uncle out from behind their walls if they see the rich estates of Howth in flames. But' – Brian looked at his son with a stern expression that brooked no dissent – 'that blood-thirsty villain O'Ruairc stays in the camp. Let him watch the Dubhlinn road.'

Murrough pursed his lips. 'Do not judge him too harshly, Father. He may have flouted your wishes, but he followed mine to the letter.'

The old king sighed, a sound that pierced Murrough to the core; though a man in the prime of his power, wise to the ways of axe and sword, the prince ever despaired of disappointing his sire. 'I guessed as much. I saw the look that passed between you.' Brian invited his son to sit. 'Why would you do this, boy? Why would you condemn our people to hellfire and damnation? We're not beasts.'

'Last season,' Murrough said quietly, 'I met a man in single combat – I say man, but he was only a handful of years older than young Turlough, your grandson. This was on the banks of the River Sláine, in Leinster, where a Danish war band sought to thwart our raid into their territory. He knew my name, this lad. Thrice, he called it. I could not ignore the challenge.' Murrough rubbed his face, suddenly weary in the stuffy warmth of the king's pavilion. 'He said I had killed his own father, years before, and that he had grown up with a thirst to slay me. So, he tried.' The prince looked down at his scarred hands. 'My axe felled him like a sapling. But, I wondered, in the days and weeks after, if this pup might not have a pup of his own, back in some stinking longhouse. A pup whose bitch-whore of a mother might wean it on tales of vengeance against Black Murrough of Kincora.

'We reap what we sow, Father. And I have sown a field of Danish bastards hot for my blood – or for the blood of my son. I don't want that for Turlough. I'd rather him grow old reading the Good Book, tilling his fields, and finally dying in his bed when he has a score of years on you. That is my dream. To make that dream come to pass means reaping the harvest I've sown, aye, but it also means harrowing that field with salt. For this to end, every Dane must die . . . and every Dane's son, wife, or daughter.'

Far from angry, the king looked upon Murrough with great pity. 'The Almighty preserve us, my son, but I once thought the same as you. I reckoned that with the sword I could buy peace and long life for all my sons. But, alas, such is not the way of the world. Blood begets blood; slaughter begets slaughter. Only in forgiveness can we find peace.'

'If we need only forgive our enemies, why do we sit with an army three miles from Dubhlinn's gates? Why threaten battle at all, Father, if a mere apology from Maelmorda is all that prevents us from retiring to enjoy the first fruits of spring?'

Brian's gray eyes flashed in the faint light. 'Don't be daft, boy. I didn't raise you to play the fool. You know as well as I the difference between a just and an unjust war. *Order* is what we keep with the sword, not peace. And Order demands punishment for those who would flout it. I would forgive Maelmorda his treason, if he but asked. But Order still requires that I punish him for it.

'Slaughter is an offense against Order, my son. And the slaughter of innocents is an offense against God. That is why O'Ruairc must face judgment.'

Murrough stood; he pulled the bearskin over the king's shoulders. 'Then judge me alongside him. And forgive me, Father.'

Brian grasped his son's hand and kissed it. 'Ask the

371

Almighty for forgiveness, my son, and remember this day when you wear the crown.'

Murrough nodded and withdrew. Brian watched him; the weariness that crushed his body weighed his soul down like an anchor.

27

When Étaín finally emerged from the trees south and west of the Irish encampment, she breathed a sigh of relief. Exhaustion cut her to the bone; she was thorn-scratched and footsore. Sweat matted her copper hair to her skull. Cramped fingers knotted in the halter of the pony, which plodded along with its head down despite its lightened burden. Bran lay on his belly on the drag, unmoving; when last she checked, the silver-bearded Irishman still clung to life, his pale forehead damp and feverish.

Stragglers yet streamed after the Irish host – a polyglot of sutlers and whores, scavengers and merchants. Wagons plodded along, some clanking with wares and others empty in anticipation of spoils gleaned from the killing fields; a profusion of carts carried whole families, human carrion-crows and rootless vagabonds drawn by the promise of war. The whole converged on a second camp that lay in the shadow of King Brian's, like a fungus growing in the stubbled fields once claimed by the Norse settlers of Kilmainham. Étaín joined the flow of this human river without a single challenge, as though they knew she belonged among them.

Étaín paused at the edge of a makeshift market to let a barrel-laden wain trundle past. Around her, though the hour grew late, this crude city of camp followers yet seethed and jostled. She heard snatches of song, of music; hawkers extolled their meager goods, their cries shrill with desperation; merchants hounded after the likes of her, plucking at the hem of her tattered cloak in an effort to get her attention, to draw her eye to woven baskets filled with bits of cast-off rubbish, to hard-baked biscuits and wilted greens scavenged on the march, or to a back-bent slave offered by the hour. Étaín brushed aside their importuning hands and ignored their palaver. 'A physician,' she said, over and again as she traversed the edges of the torchlit market. 'I seek a physician!'

Before she reached her wits' end, however, the figure of a man stepped from the throng and blocked her way – a Dane, by the look of him, sinewy and gray with age, a spade-shaped beard brushing his chest; he wore a plain white tunic and cross-gaitered trousers beneath a charcoal-colored cloak and bore no weapon that she could see. He looked her up and down with eyes a pale shade of blue. 'This lot, little sister,' he said, his voice deep but soft. 'This lot has never seen a physician.'

'Have you someone who can treat wounds, then? A wise-woman perhaps?' Étaín said.

'Let me look.' The Dane came and crouched alongside the drag. Bran mewled as hard-callused fingers gently probed the wound. Frowning, the man leaned closer and sniffed it. His face grew solemn; he straightened and stood. 'He needs a priest, little sister. And soon. Come.' He gestured a short distance away, to where a fly-rigged pavilion stood. A trio of Danes, all equal in the simplicity of their dress, handed out bread, cups of watered wine, and wooden bowls of thin broth to the latecomers. 'I will send someone to fetch a priest.'

'Who are you?'

The Dane smiled without showing his teeth. 'Ragnall of Corcaigh. Here, take some wine.'

Étaín gratefully accepted a cup, drained it, and returned it to the taciturn Dane. To her surprise, he refilled it and handed it back.

'How are you called, little sister?'

'Forgive me.' She passed a grimy hand over her brow. 'I am Étaín, once of Wessex. My poor friend, here, is Bran of the Uí Garrchon, who was crossing the mountains with his mates to join good King Brian's army.'

Ragnall motioned for his companions. 'Étaín of Wessex, these men will see your friend is made comfortable. I bid you, sit and rest. A priest will come soon.'

'Are you . . . monks?'

Ragnall laughed. 'No, little sister. We were slaves, once, till King Brian freed us. We swore an oath to the White Christ that we'd offer an equal measure of succor to the Gaels that the king offered to us.'

'But I am no Gael.'

'All the same.' Ragnall shrugged. 'Are you not in need?'

Étaín nodded. 'I thank you.'

Ragnall sat beside her on a bench of salt-scoured wood. 'What happened to your friend? I've never seen an arrow lodged so deep. You said he traveled with his mates?'

Étaín looked up from her cup of wine; shivering, she felt a Divine hand on her, propelling her into the role of witness. She exhaled. *I am the beacon of Christ.* 'The tale is long in the telling, good Ragnall, and by its end you might think me a madwoman . . .'

28

At the stroke of midnight, a maelstrom of birds converged on the moonlit spike of Carraig Dubh with a deafening cacophony of voices – shrill *tweets* and *croaks, caws* and staccato *crakes*. Silver glittered from beak and claw as they swirled over naked stone; then, as suddenly as they appeared, they dispersed ... leaving in their wake the cloaked and hooded figure of Kormlada.

The Witch of Dubhlinn stood motionless near the edge of the precipice, one wrong step away from its deadly thousand-foot drop. Before her was the Rock of Brule. Black and rune-etched, the Rock could have been a giant turned to stone, with its suggestion of human form and the eerie impression of eyes where the face should have been. It had kept silent sentinel over the shores of Ériu for time out of mind, as the name *Brule* slowly faded from the Gaelic memory and attained a gloss of myth – it was the cenotaph of a god, some said, from a time before a great cataclysm had ended the Elder Days; others called it the cairn for a great king of the Cruithne, the Stone Folk. In truth, however, not even the Tuatha knew the Rock's origins.

Beneath the hood, her eyes raked the line of twisted yews down the slope from the precipice. If her enemy was here, she could not see him. Slowly, she picked her way down closer to the Rock. The glamour of the Tuatha no longer clung to this place. Nechtan's death had stripped it away; within a generation, she was certain the looming height of Carraig Dubh would crack and crumble down the mountainside.

Kormlada prowled the fringes of the Rock, searching, pausing now and again to listen to the breath of the night. Nothing. She felt no scrutiny, heard nothing that led her to believe the *fomórach* lurked nearby. Was this some ruse? Some game of dominance? As she came full circle, she wondered if the beast had not found some way into the barrow beneath the great stone – though the other-worldly stairs that led to his lair should have vanished with Nechtan's demise. Kormlada turned, her lips poised to emit the whistle that would summon Cruach . . .

. . . and stopped. There, in the well of moon shadow at the base of the Rock, she saw him – squatting on his haunches, apish arms resting on wide-flung knees; red eyes smoldered like forge-gledes through a veil of coarse hair.

'Half-Dane's whore,' the creature said, chuckling. The sound came out low and mean, and it touched that place of atavistic fear in the pit of her belly like nothing and no one she had ever known. 'I've had my eye on you since those wretched birds shit you out upon the rocks. You must have seen me? No? Ah, pity.' His nostrils widened as he snuffled the air. 'You have his stink on you.'

'Bjarki's why I've come,' she said, recovering her composure. 'You and I, we have a common goal: we both want that bastard dead. That makes us allies, after a fashion.'

Grimnir raised an eyebrow. 'So-ho! Not wanting to lift your skirts for him anymore, are you? You'd rather see him swing at the end of the rope he's knotted for himself?'

'I want that sallow son of a Danish whore dead, even if I have to wield the knife myself!'

Grimnir uncoiled like a spring; before she could move

– before she could so much as flinch away from him – the beast was on his feet and within arm's reach of her. Black-nailed fingers seized her by the chin. Grimnir's other hand stripped her hood back as he tilted her head into a bar of silver moonlight. That pale glow revealed discolored bruises on her cheek, the swelling of her bottom lip. His eyes bored into hers; she took his savagery and blood madness in full measure and did not look away. He grunted. 'And you'd do it, too. If you could.'

Kormlada wrenched free of his grasp. 'His art is too formidable. That's why I need you—'

'His *art*?' The *fomórach*'s laughter was harsh and stony, tinged with malice. 'You tender little fool! Art? The only art that idiot can claim is the art of the trickster; the honeyed word and the sleighty hand, that's his *seiðr*. And he's lived long enough to have seen everything your miserable kind can devise, which puts him two steps ahead of your precious little schemes. *That's* why you need me.' Grimnir's humor vanished without warning; it fell away like a mask he no longer needed. Red eyes flared in the darkness. 'What I don't know, witchling, is why I need you.'

Kormlada blinked. Her mind spun and whirled with the revelation that the man she had feared as a sorcerer, whose mastery of the arcane she had time and again deferred to, was nothing more than a charlatan – a fraud. It was almost too much to comprehend. 'I can . . . I can get you inside the walls . . . past the axes of his Norsemen.' Even as the words left her lips, Kormlada realized her error. She had stepped into his trap.

Iron fingers knotted in her midnight hair; she heard a soft, quick rasp as, with his free hand, Grimnir drew the cold iron of his seax. 'Do you take me for a fool?' the beast hissed, his rank breath hot against her cheek. 'I should gut you like a fish. Open your belly and pitch you over the edge of this filthy *elf* rock!' Kormlada made to reply but Grimnir scraped the blade along her throat, creasing the skin at the side of her neck. Blood welled around the shallow gash. 'You so much as open that maggot-hole in your face and I'll carve you a new smile! He sent you, didn't he? That ugly little rat's spent too much time among men. He's forgotten that a true son of Bálegyr suckles deceit at his mother's teat. Let me guess: I step into your little cloud of birds and when I come out at the other end there's a spear waiting to bury itself in my gullet?'

Kormlada nodded.

Grimnir snarled and shoved her away. 'The dolt can't even plan treachery right. *This* is the art you so fear? *Bah!*'

'I . . . I could bring us to a different part of the castle,' the witch replied, daubing at the runnel of blood trickling down her neck.

'I'd be a bigger idiot than him if I trusted you, now.' Grimnir paced in a tight pattern, deftly twirling his seax in one clawed hand. 'No,' he muttered. 'No, we're at loggerheads: you want him dead and I have sworn to end him, but I'll not enter Dubhlinn knowing he's waiting to spring some ill-thought trap, nor will I suffer some other hand to strike the killing blow. *Faugh!* Old Hróarr spoke true when he said Bjarki would ever be a thorn in my side.' Grimnir stopped and shook his head. 'Enough of these games! I will take that wretch on the battlefield, as the Sly One intended!'

'The battlefield?' Kormlada echoed. A slow smile twisted her dark lips as she finally found a measure of her old equilibrium. 'Now who's the tender fool? Bjarki has no plans to step foot on the battlefield, not when there are others more willing than he to raise the spear. My brother,

Maelmorda; my son, Sitric; Sigurðr of the Orkneys and Bródir of Mann – these men will lead Dubhlinn's host against the Gaels. And Bjarki need only bide his time' – she gestured to the town, slumbering on the silver ribbon of the Liffey – 'snug behind those ramparts, until the death birds reap their gory reward.'

Grimnir turned to her; from under the tangle of his locks, slitted eyes gleamed with blood-mad fury. He clenched his jaw, muscles writhing as his teeth ground together. Whitening knuckles cracked around the haft of his seax. 'Then I will gut this Bródir, carve the head off Sigurðr, split your brother from crown to crotch, and tear your wretched son's spine out if it gets me a step closer to my brother's bastard! By Ymir, I will rip those walls down with my bare hands and kill every soft-bellied fool I find!'

'Harm my son,' Kormlada replied, her voice deadly quiet, 'and I will sing the song of your doom, *fomórach*.'

Grimnir tsked. 'My doom was written by one far greater than you, witchling. But, if you would save your brat, make sure Bjarki leads that rabble.'

'Impossible! His mind is like iron, once it's set to a task. How—?'

'Iron? Don't be daft! That idiot's mind is as weak as any other. Are you not the Witch of Dubhlinn? *Sing* his doom, little bird, as you would sing mine. Use your precious art to lure him onto the field. I will do the rest. Or would you rather me face your son?'

And like a bolt from the heavens, the realization struck Kormlada that her whole world had changed with the *fomórach*'s simple revelation. She was no longer one of Half-Dane's pawns, constrained from fear to play her part. She was the queen; the board was hers to command.

Grimnir chuckled as a predatory gleam kindled in her dark eyes. 'Yes,' he hissed. 'Now you understand.'

'He claims to know the will of Odin,' she said. 'The omens say the battle needs must take place two days hence, on the morning of the day the Christians celebrate their god's crucifixion. But Brian is devout. He will not take the field. He means to lay siege to us, as he's done in the past.'

'That day will be as good as any. You'll make sure that wretch leads Dubhlinn's forces?'

'I will,' Kormlada replied, with conviction.

'Then the hymn-singers' king will be there to face him. I will make sure of that.' Grimnir raised a hand; with the tip of his seax, he gouged a shallow furrow in the ball of his callused thumb. Black blood welled and ran. Kormlada grimaced. The thought of mingling her blood with that of a monster disgusted her, but nevertheless she extended her own hand to receive a similar cut.

Quick as a snake, Grimnir snatched the witch up by the throat, his blood joining with the blood oozing from the thin slice on the side of her neck. 'Look here, Sly One, Father Loki! Bear witness, O Ymir, sire of giants and lord of the frost! Let this blood seal our pact!'

In answer, a howling gale blew down from the north. Trees creaked below Carraig Dubh; on that naked height, there was no shelter. It struck the pair of them like a fist, threatening to rip them off their feet. Its chill was like the chill of a glacier, and it stank of burning pitch and spilled blood. On it Kormlada heard the clash of steel and the berserk laughter of the *úlfhéðnar*; as the sound drifted away into the night, the wind receded until its fierce bluster was once again the freshening breeze off the sea. 'It is witnessed,' Grimnir said, releasing her. 'Betray me, little bird, and there will be no branch high enough for you to hide.'

'See you hold to your end of this pact, *fomórach*,' she

replied. And without another word, the Witch of Dubhlinn turned and walked away. She held out an arm, and down from the darkness fluttered the giant raven, Cruach. Alighting upon her proffered limb, the bird gave forth an eerie whistle; by the time she reached the crumbling edge of the precipice, a whirlwind of shrieking birds descended like a cloud of darkness and carried Kormlada off into the night.

29

Grimnir stalked to the edge of Carraig Dubh, where the breeze stirred his lank hair; he expanded his chest, nostrils flaring as he drank in the tang of salt spume that drove in off the sea. It tasted of blood. Nights such as these were the parchment on which the gods wrote their prophecies of doom. The stars wheeling overhead were the ink, and in their gleaming and chaotic patterns the wise could read harbingers of the days to come, warnings against the fickle nature of the Fates.

Even as men drew round for the coming strife, Grimnir could sense a gathering of another sort at the edges of mortal perception. The Great Wolf strained at his fetters, drawn by his oath; the Serpent twisted and writhed. War drums throbbed like a beating heart, calling the restless spirits of the *kaunar* to the fences of Miðgarðr to bear witness. Ghostly eyes gleamed from the shadows as Grimnir felt the scrutiny of his people. Among them, he recognized the presence of Gífr, who had fostered him like a son; of Hrungnir, called Grendel by his foes, whose foolish vanity had set this game in motion; of their mother, Skríkja, who was as fell-handed as any warrior. And, looming from the darkness, the savage one-eyed figure of Bálegyr, mightiest of the Nine Fathers of the *kaunar*.

'I want nothing from you,' he said, peering over the

rim of Carraig Dubh. '*Faugh!* What could you give me that I couldn't earn half again as well with the edge of a blade?' Far below, the ruddy lights of Dubhlinn glimmered through the canopy of trees; beneath the sough and sigh of the sea wind, he heard faint snatches of ale song. 'I am the last of our people. After me, the blood of our kind is at an end.' Grimnir looked up at the spectral shapes, their fanged grins matching his own. 'But if this clamor and shield-breaking sets me among you – if the Doom of Odin falls at long last – then I swear to you, my kinsmen, I will make of it a death that will echo through the ages!'

30

The woman who emerged from the raven-borne tempest and onto the flat, dark roof of Cuarán's Tower was not the cold and composed Witch of Dubhlinn, but rather a shrieking wretch. Disheveled, naked from the waist up with her gown half torn from her, Kormlada appeared on her knees, rocking in terror. She bled from nose and mouth; long scratches scored her cheeks, her arms, and her pale bosom. The silent Norsemen who waited with leveled spears knew all too well that they looked upon the victim of a savage rape. A pair of them stepped back, allowing Bjarki Half-Dane to enter their circle, with Draugen ever in his shadow.

Bjarki clicked his teeth. 'I didn't expect that.'

Hearing his voice, Kormlada launched herself at him; she screamed mindless imprecations, invoking gods best left unnamed on a night when blood stirred upon the wind. Draugen caught her before she could lay hands upon him; he seized her by the flailing wrists and whispered to her, his deep voice calm and soothing. Slowly, Kormlada stopped struggling until finally she hung like a limp doll from the arm that encircled her.

Bjarki stepped closer and took her chin between thumb and forefinger, raising her eyes to meet his. 'Your errand failed, I gather.'

'Bring down the mountain,' she hissed, bloody froth flying from her bruised lips. 'Marshal your art and unleash it on that bastard's head! Rip the bones from the earth and grind Carraig Dubh to dust!'

Bjarki laughed. 'Use an axe to kill a fly? I think not. No, I'll find another way to catch the snuffler. This' – he waved at the spears – 'this was simply a throw of the dice.' He made to turn, stopped, and looked askance at her. 'A word of warning: scour your womb clean, for if anything he put in there takes root, I will kill it and you, as well. Daughter of kings be damned! I'll not have some half-breed maggot underfoot!'

Kormlada said nothing, for the scathing look she gave him spoke all that was necessary. 'Loose me,' she muttered to Draugen. He hesitated, concern furrowing his brow. She pushed him away. 'Get your filthy hands off me! Damn you! Damn all of you!'

Draugen let go of her; Kormlada stumbled and collapsed back to her knees, spasms and sobs racking her thin shoulders. Draugen gestured for the others to leave, and then backed away from her. 'Your concern is touching,' Bjarki said with a derisive snort. To Kormlada, he added, 'Pull yourself together. We have guests, and they're going to want to see the prize they mean to fight for.'

Half-Dane whirled and left the rooftop; Draugen lingered a moment, and then he, too, was gone. After a few minutes, Kormlada stood, whole and unscathed, as cold and composed as when she left Carraig Dubh; the glamour she had worn remained on the stones, sobbing and cursing in pale imitation of her. Disdain for it curled her lips; with an arcane gesture, the broken, disheveled figure dissolved into a mist that the breeze snatched into tattered shreds. Kormlada's eyes narrowed to slits of baleful black ice. 'Artless fool. Gulled by the simplest enchantment.'

Cruach joined her, and together they descended into the heart of Cuarán's Tower.

Raucous laughter echoed up from below, from the great room where the kings held court. Like a wraith, Kormlada padded down the steps and across her chambers to the gallery; darkness afforded her the opportunity to observe the drunken scene playing out below. It was certainly a notable gathering of rogues: Bródir and Sigurðr and those men of rank among their crews roared and drank alongside the Dubhlinn Norse, led by her son, Sitric – Olaf Cuarán's son was no slouch among the cups. At another broad board, she spotted her brother, Maelmorda, plowing one of her serving women while Othna the Black and the noble captains of Leinster sat by and hollered encouragement. A surreptitious cheer went up as Bjarki joined the throng, with Draugen ever close at hand. Sigurðr filled their fists with horns of foaming ale and exhorted the pair to catch up with their hosts. Among the Manx, a fight erupted, but not even drawn steel and spurting blood could put a damper on their debauchery.

Confident she would not be disturbed, Kormlada withdrew from the gallery. She barred the door to her chambers. Cruach watched her from his accustomed perch, head cocked, eyes glittering in the wan light. Kormlada steepled her fingers. A question hung in the incense-laden air: how? 'How do I make him change his plan and take charge of the battle?'

Cruach ruffled his feathers.

> Strong is the hauberk | of contempt
> But it is not | without flaw.
> A crease there is | in his foul breast,
> Cousin to conceit, | arrogant pride.

'His greatest weakness.' Kormlada nodded. She could see the wisdom in that. From a chest against the wall, near her brocaded divan, she drew forth a triangular *cláirseach*, the small harp favored by her people. Of willow and oak was its sound box, and its graceful neck was carved and inlaid with bone; it bore twenty-nine strings of spun silver wire, with a thirtieth string wrought of black iron that had fallen from the sky. Kormlada sat in a straight-backed chair and teased out an eerie melody with her fingertips. 'His pride,' she said. 'And he is a proud creature. Proud of his deceit, proud of his lies, proud to claim what is not his portion to claim.' Her eyes crinkled as a subtle theme emerged from the melody; the soft sounds snared the incense smoke, weaving it into disembodied figures that danced and writhed . . .

And, with a smile of unrivaled malice, the Witch of Dubhlinn began to sing.

31

Dawn broke over Irish encampment, and beneath a blood-red sky the Gaels and their allies shook themselves and came awake. A haze hung low over the valley of the River Liffey, the mingled reek of campfires and burned-out huts and the smoldering pyres of the enemy dead; kicked from their beds, still-yawning boys staggered out to fetch water upriver while older warriors prepared to break their fast on oatcakes and gruel and pork left from the night before. Their chiefs went among them with word that Prince Murrough meant to lead a war band across the Liffey.

'Aye,' a captain of the Galloglas said as he gnawed on a scrap of boiled bacon, 'Finegall and Howth, that's where we're headed, lads. Give the bloody Danes a taste of their own vinegar, eh?' The men who overheard nodded with grim purpose. Whetstones came out, and the sound they made as the warriors tended the edges of axe, spear, and sword was like the susurration of a predator.

The rasp of stone on steel drifted among the tents, as distinct as a war cry. It echoed among the mossy stones of the hilltop monastery, sending shivers down the spines of the young monks who prayed at the Cross of Kincora. The sound intruded even into the king's pavilion, where Brian mac Cennétig knelt on a prayer bench in silent contemplation. He stirred at the sound of men preparing for war; glancing up, his eyes found his graceful Dalcassian axe where his steward had left it – hanging by its leather wrist thong from his cloak tree. Seeing that axe, hearing the *slish* of the whetstone, smelling the smoke . . . all of it reminded the king of his long-ago youth. He pined for the days when it was he, and not Murrough or his second son, Donnchad, who led raids into enemy lands; it reminded him of a time when his wine cup was full and sweet, before age and infirmity had left him with nothing but the bitter lees.

Brian shook his head. 'A maudlin old fool,' he muttered. His limbs creaked as he rose up off the prayer bench and called for his steward. It was Ragnall of Corcaigh who answered the king's summons, clad still in the tunic and trousers he'd worn the night before. Brian raised an eyebrow.

'Still serving your penance among the poor who follow us, eh?'

'I have much to atone for, sire,' Ragnall said. 'And no one has ever gone astray by following the Lord's example.'

Ten years Brian's junior, Ragnall had lived more lives than most men could count – by turns a reaver, a mystic, a merchant, a thief, and a slave. A score of years earlier, in an act of charity, Brian had purchased Ragnall's freedom from a *jarl* of Corcaigh and in return had earned a ferocious partisan.

The king sat on his divan. Stiff fingers massaged the muscle of his thigh where a spear had pierced him to the bone. Though nobly won, this and a dozen other old wounds left him feeling more like a cripple than a king. Brian stirred. 'Who has Murrough left on watch?'

'The Uí Ruairc, sire, as you commanded. They watch the river and the road to Dubhlinn,' Ragnall replied. 'Old

Domnall mac Eimen and a few of his Scots watch the western road from Dolcan's Meadow.'

The king raised an eyebrow. 'On guard against betrayal from Malachy?'

'Your son has a devious mind, sire.' Ragnall shrugged. 'And in that the acorn is true to the tree. Murrough fears for your safety, since Malachy refused his offer to lead the raid on Howth.'

'Age has made the old trees of Ériu overly suspicious and sleepy,' Brian said. 'A dozen years ago I'd have Malachy's head on a spike for the insult he pays me. Now . . .' The king sighed. 'Well, no matter. Ready my horse. I'll go speak with that cantankerous old bastard myself.'

'It will be done, sire.' Ragnall bowed and turned to leave; he relayed the king's orders, and then paused at the threshold of the pavilion. Outside, a haze of gold-tinged smoke hung over the Irish encampment, and dew made the grass of Saint Maighneann's monastery look like a jewel-strewn carpet. 'I heard something, last night, sire. A tale told to me by a young woman I found out among the camp followers. An extraordinary story, really.'

Brian rose and hobbled to Ragnall's side, where he availed himself of his steward's knotty arm. Together, they stepped out into the bright morning. ' "Extraordinary," eh? You don't use such a word lightly, my old friend.'

'No, sire,' Ragnall said. 'Nor is it my habit to beg a favor . . .'

'You want me to hear this woman's story?'

'I . . . I think you must, sire.'

Down the slope, where the muster for Howth had taken place an hour earlier, a knot of Gaels stood round: mailed Dalcassians who served as his guard, courtiers from kith and clan, and cassocked priests, all drawn by the king's appearance – they worried for his health, and were troubled by his growing infirmity. A young page brought the king's magnificent white stallion; Ragnall helped him into the saddle.

'There is eerie music on the wind, sire,' the old Norseman murmured. 'A song of doom that calls down the grim daughters of Odin from the North.'

Brian frowned. 'For whom do they ride?'

But Ragnall could not say.

The high king of Ériu leaned down. 'Bring this woman to me upon my return. Any tale that causes you to recall your heathen ways, old friend, is an extraordinary tale, indeed.'

Harness rattled and rustled as the Gaels dispersed after their king, who rode west to Dolcan's Meadow. Soon, only Ragnall remained. And the taciturn Northman, who was once a reaver, a mystic, a merchant, a thief, and a slave, scowled at the sky . . .

32

Sunlight cast a cheerful glow over the wreckage of Dubhlinn's throne room. To Draugen, roused from his drunken stupor by the importuning of a servant, the room looked like a debauched battlefield; bodies in various stages of undress sprawled amid a rubble of splintered tables and overturned benches, with Gael and Gall twisted together in a nigh unbroken carpet of sweat-stinking flesh. Draugen coughed. He leaned forward and spat into a puddle of spilled ale mixed with vomit and blood. Shards of broken crockery crunched underfoot. Before him stood a young man with a wispy chestnut beard and tattooed cheeks, fresh blood soaking the front of his long white tunic. He glanced about nervously.

Draugen tried to focus on him with his one good eye. He recognized the lad as the priest Ágautr's son. 'What did you say?'

'Lord Bjarki?' the youth stuttered. 'The omens . . . they . . . he must come! Quick!'

Draugen groaned as he clambered to his feet; though he had been blind stinking drunk, somehow the sullen Dane had had the presence of mind to drag a divan from an adjacent room and defend it from this lot. One of his axes lay on the damp flagstones; the other was wedged blade-deep in the skull of a dead Norseman. 'Boy,' he muttered, 'there's nothing quick about this morning. Wait here.'

Clutching at his back, Draugen none-too-carefully
picked his way across the room to the royal dais where
Bjarki lay draped across Silken-beard's throne, a bent
copper candelabra perched on his brow like a crown.
Snores ripped from hairy bellies; men groaned and cursed,
coughed and retched. A woman squealed, reminding
Draugen that Maelmorda had proven his worth beyond
reckoning – though as a pimp rather than a king – when
he summoned all the drab-wives, harlots, and two-copper
strumpets he knew from the stews of Dubhlinn. And that
was only after the reavers had finished plowing every last
slave under Sitric's roof.

'Bjarki,' Draugen said as he limped up the steps of the
low dais. One of the raven banners of the House of Ivar
had been torn from its mountings to serve as a blanket; the
other hung askew, scorch marks along its lower edge where
someone had tried to burn it. 'Bjarki, the gods damn you!'
Half-Dane snarled and groused under his breath. Draugen
kicked the throne. 'Wake up, you piss-colored bastard!'

'Pester someone else, you one-eyed stormcrow,' Bjarki
rasped.

'You've been summoned.'

Bjarki raised his head slightly, the makeshift crown
slipping off to clatter across the dais. Wincing, he peeled
back one jaundiced eyelid. 'Who would dare?'

Draugen gestured back at the blood-spattered youth.
'Your pet priest.'

Both eyes opened, now, and the ale-fogged gleam in
Half-Dane's gaze could yet scorch iron. 'Is this some kind
of jest, boy?'

The youth trembled, shook his head. 'My father, lord.
He bid me fetch you. The omens . . . you must come.'

'Oh, must I?'

'Please, lord!'

Bjarki looked at Draugen, who gave a halfhearted shrug. 'You're the one who claims to give a fig about the omens. Here's your chance to prove it.'

'*Pah!* Bugger you and your wretched omens!' Nevertheless, Half-Dane heaved himself from the throne. He stretched and looked around, tendon and sinew cracking in his shoulders and down his twisted spine. 'Too bad Mac Cennétig isn't here. Look at this sorry lot! One fucking Irishman and a knife is all it would take to rule an empire.'

'Lucky for us.'

'Please, lord! Hurry!' the priest's son repeated.

'Go on, you rat! I'm coming.' Bjarki staggered down the dais and across the room to follow in the boy's wake. Draugen came after, pausing only to retrieve his axes. Neither man saw Kormlada's drawn and haggard face in the shadows of the gallery overhead, watching with a thin smile curving her pale lips.

To reach the precincts of the temple from the throne room at the heart of Dubhlinn Castle was a journey of a thousand steps – across arcaded courts and up narrow stairs, past the stables and through the kitchens – and most of it blissfully shadowed. Only at the end was Bjarki forced out into the harsh morning light. Squinting, he shouldered open the temple's heavy doors. As his eyes adjusted once more to the gloom, he took in the details of a slaughter.

Eight sacrificial victims lay naked on the blood-smeared floor – a mix of Irish prisoners and slaves plucked from the market – all of them strangled and gutted, their viscera slopped across the stones like streamers of flesh; a ninth was stretched supine on the altar, his belly ripped open. The silken cord that killed him was still looped around his neck. Above him, ghoulish in the dim light, stood blood-spattered Ágautr – his gory arms up to his elbows in the dead man's guts. He tore an organ free, looked at it, and then slung it at Bjarki's feet. It struck with a wet splatter.

'The Allfather has spoken!'

'What goes, Ágautr?' Bjarki said.

Ágautr raised his hands and implored the incense-wreathed heavens. A madness was upon him, Bjarki could see it. 'Nine times, has the Hanged One's will been made manifest! Nine times have the livers been heavy with yellow fluid, the lobes of war engorged with blood! Nine times have the entrails spelled out the doom of our people! The signs are clear! The omens do not lie!'

'What are you yammering about? Speak plain, man!'

'Battle will be joined upon the morrow,' Ágautr replied.

'Aye, and so?'

'It is Odin's will that you lead the armies out from behind the walls of Dubhlinn! The Allfather has chosen you, Bjarki Half-Dane! And if you shirk from this honor the Hanged One has paid you, then our people will suffer defeat at the hands of those sworn to the White Christ! So it is written in the flesh of the dead!'

Bjarki sobered instantly; his eyes narrowed. 'You're certain?'

'Nine times have I read the same omens. This is the will of Odin.'

'Do it again.'

'You are chosen, Half-Dane!' Ágautr said. 'Do you doubt it? Nine is the sacred number. Nine is all the gods allow—'

'The gods will allow a tenth!' Bjarki snarled.

Bjarki whirled and seized Ágautr's son by the throat. The father started forward, then stopped; with a look of grim purpose, he shoved the ninth victim off onto the temple floor, where it splashed in the broth of blood and fluids that pooled at the base of the altar.

'Do not be afraid, my son. The Allfather waits in the shadows, and he will greet you with open arms.'

But far from being calmed by his father's sentiment, the boy struggled in Bjarki's grasp, plucking at the long fingers that encircled his neck like bands of iron. Half-Dane hauled him to the altar, through puddles of blood and drifts of ripped intestines, lifted him bodily as though he weighed nothing, and slammed him down upon the place of sacrifice. Ágautr took hold of his son's thrashing limbs while Draugen rushed forward and ripped the lad's tunic open, revealing the pale and hairless flesh of his torso.

'Hear me, Odin!' Bjarki cried. 'Allfather, ever-wise, I give you the gift of this life!' Slowly, he squeezed the boy's throat till cartilage popped, choking off his air and killing him by inexorable degrees. While his legs yet trembled in the death throes, Half-Dane took the sacrificial dagger from Ágautr's hand and split the still-moving body open from sternum to navel, like a butcher jointing a haunch of beef. Hot blood sprayed; steam rose from the pierced bowels, and a stench of overwhelming despair. Undaunted, Bjarki plunged his hands into the reeking heart of the boy's corpse. He looked. He felt the slippery blood, the vital fluids, the sacks of flesh that gave the body its *anima*. He searched for the omens . . . and they were there. In the coloration of the viscera; in the weight of the spleen and the way the twisted guts mirrored the carvings on the temple's staves; in the engorged liver, yellow and angry; in the way the heart wanted to escape its cage of bone . . .

After a long moment, with Ágautr peering over his shoulder and Draugen waiting in breathless anticipation, Bjarki Half-Dane had no choice but to concede. 'It's true.'

'It is the will of Odin,' Ágautr muttered. 'I told you.'

Bjarki nodded. It *was* the will of Odin. Unless he personally led the Norse against the Gaels, the battle would end in a slaughter. Dubhlinn would vanish in an orgy of flame and the vengeful Christians would crucify him the way the Romans had crucified their Nailed God. Ten sacrificial victims told the same tale. Odin had selected him, Bjarki Half-Dane, to strike a blow for the Old Ways, to lead the Northmen to victory.

The Allfather had chosen *him*.

Bjarki reeled back, chest swelling with pride. He raised the bloody knife to the smoke-laced heavens. 'Odin!' he roared. 'Odin! Look here! I accept your mantle! I will not fail you!'

And in the distance, as if an answer, came the mocking cry of a raven . . .

33

Cormac O'Ruairc shaded his eyes against the bright sun and watched as thunderheads of smoke drifted inland. Finegall and the rich peninsula of Howth burned. Farms, villages, the estates of those Norse and Irish bastards allied with King Sitric . . . all of it an open pocket ripe for the picking. Names and fortunes were being made, yonder, yet here he sat on the south bank of the Liffey, miles from what looked to be a fine spear-whetting, watching a road only a fool would use. All because Brian mac Cennétig had become squeamish in his dotage.

'Damn him,' O'Ruairc muttered for the hundredth time. 'Damn him to the pits of Hell!'

The Connacht chief turned away. He couldn't bear to look any longer; the thought of his enemies growing fat and happy on the spoils of a generation of reavers-turned-landsmen made his blood boil. His men, who had the honor of leading the vanguard yesterday, now ranged about a low hill between the river and the road from Dubhlinn to the Irish camp at Kilmainham. They groused and bitched about the idle nature of their task, and O'Ruairc had no call to disagree. One man or two could have easily watched the road; instead Murrough – at his father's insistence, no doubt – had dispatched the whole of the Uí Ruairc of Lough Gill? Cormac fumed; despite his transgressions, belittling his clan was an insult that screamed for redress. *But how?*

The land hereabout was marshy and flat, save for a few rises like this one, and but for a tree here and there and the remains of an old stone wall – wrecked by floods in the past – it offered nothing in the way of cover. On his right hand, looming in the distance, Carraig Dubh rose from the forested foothills and joined the peaks of the Cualann Mountains.

A sharp whistle brought Cormac around.

One of his Connachtmen, a bowshot from him, gestured up the Dubhlinn Road; frowning, O'Ruairc looked in that direction and saw movement. A dark-clad figure emerged from the tall grass at the edge of the road, its arms outstretched in a gesture of submission. It had an eerie gait to it as it moved forward, as though someone had taught a wolf to walk upright. But at this distance, O'Ruairc could tell precious little about the figure, save that a swatch of patchwork cloth muffled its visage.

O'Ruairc's lads vaulted from their saddles and leveled spears at the newcomer, as though daring it to take one step closer. Man or beast, the figure was smart enough to understand. It stopped and kept its hands away from the blade it wore strapped to its waist. It must have said something, for he watched his boys exchange perplexed looks. More of his riders drew near, and O'Ruairc himself swung up into the saddle and touched his heels to his horse's flanks.

And as he trotted closer, Cormac O'Ruairc of Lough Gill heard the figure speak; in that moment, he knew that while he was hearing a male voice it was not necessarily the voice of a Man.

'Your king,' it said. *'Faugh!* Which one of you dunghill rats can get me to your king, eh? I got a message for him.'

Its strangely accented tongue mingled the speech of the Danes with that of the Norse, with strange words drawn from another language, as well.

O'Ruairc's horse balked. Even so, the stubborn brute refused to give ground. Its ears flattened; it snorted in anger at the newcomer. Cormac patted its neck. 'Are you Dane or Norse, friend?'

'Neither,' answered the stranger.

He was clad in odd war gear: a shirt of iron rings, a horsehide kilt, sandals like those Cormac had seen plucked from the graves of long-dead Romans, and a long seax in a worn leather scabbard. Still, something about him set O'Ruairc's teeth on edge – the swarthy skin, the faint suggestion of red eyes deep within the makeshift hood, the way no horse would come near him; all of it triggered a primal need to gut the stranger ere another moment passed. But O'Ruairc stayed his hand.

'I need to see the old king.'

'King Brian? And why do you need to see good King Brian?'

'That's my business, wretch!'

Cormac's eyes narrowed. He swung a leg over his horse's neck and dropped to the ground; his men, all feeling the same instinctual desire to drive their spears into the stranger until he was nothing but a red ruin at their feet, opened their leaguer so he might come face-to-face with the stranger. 'You'd best keep a civil tongue in your feckin' head, then! I am the chief of the Uí Ruairc. This is my road. You want to see the king? Convince me why.'

Cormac felt the stranger bristle. An odd snuffling sound came from the depths of the hood. One of the stranger's sinewy hands, long-nailed like a beast's talons, hovered near the hilt of the long seax at his belt, its bone and silver haft worn from use.

O'Ruairc braced for an explosion of violence; that was the sense he got from this devil who wore the guise of a man, that bloodshed was its dominion. Instead, however, the stranger gave a harsh and humorless chuckle, a sound like the creak of the gallows. '*Faugh!* You hymn-singers are all alike! I try to do a right turn by your king and this is how you repay me? By hoisting me like a hog to slaughter? Who's off in the grass, there,' he said, inclining his head to the left. 'More of your cursed kneelers with their arrows on the string?'

'Slingers,' O'Ruairc replied.

'So-ho! Going to take me alive, then, are you? And what? Torture me? Ungrateful wretch!' The stranger ducked his head and spat, and then held his arms up and away from his sides. 'I promise you this, maggot: if that's your plan you'd better put me in the fucking ground, because when I'm done saving your miserable hides from the trickery of the Danes, I will find you! I will crack your spine and suck the marrow from your bones, hymn-singer! By Ymir, I swear it!'

For a long moment, Cormac O'Ruairc studied the savage figure of the stranger. He weighed his words, and though his gut told him to kill the beast, Cormac could not gainsay anything he had said. 'What's this about the Danes?'

The stranger shook his head. '*Nár!* That's not a tidbit for the likes of you. Take me to your king.'

O'Ruairc exhaled. 'Will you surrender your blade and submit to having your hands bound? You have a foul appearance, friend, and that makes me wonder what manner of mischief you might be part of, to be cursed so by God.'

'Bugger your god.' With exaggerated care, the stranger drew his long seax and flicked it point-first into the ground between them. 'Come, we're wasting time.'

O'Ruairc bent and scooped up the rune-scored blade

before motioning for his men. 'How are you called?'

'Many things, but what's it to you, swine?' The stranger drew back his hood; O'Ruairc's lads recoiled from his monstrous face, sharp and feral. There was no fear in the thing's unsettling red eyes, and even a trace of mockery in the curl of his lips – as if he knew some deadly secret they didn't.

And as the creature allowed one of the Uí Ruairc to bind his hands with ropes of braided leather, Cormac wondered what sort of devil's bargain he had just brokered.

34

At the mouth of the River Liffey, on the long strand beneath Dubhlinn's walls, Bjarki Half-Dane crouched on the damp sand and watched as crews of reavers floated their dragon ships on the outgoing tide. The sun was setting, and for all intents and purposes his allies from the Isle of Man and the Orkneys were fleeing in droves – taking to the water like rats from a burning scow.

At least, that's how Bjarki hoped it looked.

'You think they're watching?' Maelmorda asked. The rebel king of Leinster stood off to one side from where Half-Dane crouched, his cloak-wrapped figure lean and irresolute.

'They're watching. They will think we've had a falling-out; an argument over spoils, perhaps. I'd wager my eye-teeth that, once he hears of it, this so-called turn of events will cause that idiot, Murrough, to rest a little easier, this night. We'll catch that cross-kissing wretch on his knees, tomorrow.'

Bjarki glanced down the strand to where Bródir's black-prowed ship pulled out into the bay. The Manx lord stood beneath the carved figurehead and screamed obscenities at them, calling upon his ancestors to make the balance right. In the opposite direction, Sigurðr's thunderous voice matched Bródir curse for curse.

'Seems like a useless bit of theater.'

Bjarki came up off the sand and whirled to face Mael-morda. His eyes gleamed in the fading light. 'You have a better plan, son of Murchada?'

A bit of steel found its way into the king of Leinster's spine. He squared his shoulders and met Bjarki's gaze. 'You foreigners.' He sniffed in disdain. 'You've never understood the Irish. You want Murrough to come to fight? You need only tell him when and where and he'll be there. He's no great thinker, Brian's son.'

'Aye, true, but neither are you. This way, we can catch him at unawares. He'll be expecting space to breathe and time to worship his useless god. What about you, eh? Any qualms about drawing steel tomorrow?'

'The cost of any rebellion is blood, and the butcher's bill has come due. But, what I don't want is to be served up like a fatted calf. Who is to say our allies will return?'

Bjarki chuckled. 'Those greedy bastards? They'll be back, for they love the song of battle, the chance for glory, and the lure of spoils more than they love life. Come the dawn, you and I will lead the companies from Dubhlinn and Leinster out and over the old bridge, into the fields of Chluain Tarbh between the River Tolka and Tomar's Wood. Bródir and Sigurðr will land their fleet at our backs. We'll march forward from there.' Bjarki sobered. 'It is Odin's will, this battle. It is Odin's will that we meet the Gael tomorrow, in defiance of their Nailed God. And the chosen of Odin will stand in the vanguard. How can we lose?'

'Because Odin hates a liar!' a voice roared at Bjarki's back. Half-Dane turned to face the furious king of Dubhlinn. Clad in a hauberk of iron and silver mail, a heavy broadsword at his hip, Sitric stalked across the damp sand to confront his rival. Draugen came warily in the young king's

405

wake, followed by the pale figure of his mother, Kormlada. 'That's how you will lose – by profaning the omens to suit your own ends! Odin's will, my arse!'

'Guard your tongue, boy!'

'*Boy?* You impertinent wretch! How did you do it, eh? Did you buy off the priest with my gold, or is this more of your cursed mummery?'

'I did nothing, little fool!' Bjarki snarled. He and Sitric circled one another like sharks, waiting for the scent of blood to trigger a frenzy of violence. 'One omen is easy enough to conjure . . . but *ten*? Not even my art is that potent! No, the Allfather has spoken! This—'

'Drop this charade,' Sitric said. 'You have no audience but us, now, and we know what you're about, fool! You steal my men, you steal my wealth, you steal my city, and now you would steal my chance at glory? You forget yourself, Half-Dane!'

Bjarki exploded. Though unarmored and unarmed, he crossed the interval between himself and Sitric and thrust his bristle-bearded face nearly nose-to-nose with that of Dubhlinn's king. 'I stole nothing, you miserable pup! It was my plans and plots that gave you a name, beyond the spineless son of a thrice-wedded whore! Who sent you abroad to gather the likes of Bródir and Sigurðr? Who strengthened your walls with good stone and trained your men to fight like the heroes of old? What have you done, little Silky-beard, besides whine and clutch at your mother's skirts?'

Sitric bellowed in fury, a lust for blood kindling in his eyes; he shoved Bjarki back and clawed for the hilt of his longsword. Half-Dane staggered and nearly fell, his footing uneven on the damp sand. But, before the king of Dubhlinn managed to bare more than a handspan of steel, Draugen caught him from behind in a rib-splintering hug. Sitric tried to break the grapple; he tried to ram the back of his head into Draugen's face, but the old Dane was a wily fighter. He held the king close, his encircling arms like iron bands.

Bjarki's twisted form seemed to grow in the thickening gloom until he towered over Sitric. A horny fist smashed into the king's jaw, splintering teeth and drawing a bloody froth. Draugen held the younger man upright. Kormlada started forward, stopped. Maelmorda simply watched. A second thundering blow and Sitric sagged, his hand relinquishing the hilt of his sword. Bjarki caught a fistful of the king's famed beard and wrenched his head up, heedless of the blood and snot. With his other hand, he drew Sitric's longsword. Half-Dane held the damascened blade to the king's throat.

Kormlada hissed a warning; Bjarki glared at her but said nothing. His eyes returned to those of Sitric. The king displayed no fear; indeed, he matched contempt with contempt.

'I should end you, here and now!' Bjarki snarled. 'But you still have use to me. Tomorrow's glory will be mine, boy. That is Odin's will. The gods have decreed that your place is upon the walls, with your mother.' At a nod from Bjarki, Draugen turned the king loose and shoved him to the sand. Half-Dane drove Sitric's sword into the earth by his head and knelt. 'By day's end, if I let you call yourself king of Dubhlinn, much less allow you to live, it will be because mercy suits my mood!'

Bjarki rose and swaggered off the long strand, Draugen in tow. Maelmorda lingered a moment. Though related by blood, the king of Leinster felt no great loyalty for his nephew; he knew whose hands held the reins of power, and until things changed he would follow Bjarki's lead. Without a word, he turned and trotted after him like an obedient hound.

That left Kormlada, who went to her son's side. Sitric spat blood and shoved her away. Through broken teeth he rasped, 'It's done! I've allowed him to humiliate me like you asked . . . now, tell me why! To what cause have I bartered my pride, and the pride of the House of Ivar?'

'The cause of vengeance,' Kormlada replied.

Dubhlinn's king blinked. This time, he accepted his mother's help. With her support, he hauled himself upright. His ears yet rang from the blows, and lights danced before his eyes. He wiped the froth from his beard with the back of his hand and tried to focus on his mother's pale face. 'What do you mean?'

'I came to you and asked you to provoke him, to suffer humiliation and perhaps risk death, as a way of driving home the final nail in our enemy's coffin,' she said, her voice all but lost to the keening wind. 'If all goes well, my son, by sunset tomorrow Dubhlinn will again be yours.'

35

In the second hour after sunset, the Irish who had raided deep into Finegall and Howth returned to their camp wreathed in triumph. They bore the spoils from half a dozen razed estates: herds of cattle and goats; ox drays overloaded with sacks, bales, and barrels of loot; strings of fine ponies; coffles of hollow-eyed women and trembling children bound for the slave markets at Corcaigh and Hlymrekr. The whole camp turned out to celebrate and among those who looked on was Cormac O'Ruairc, who was in no mood for merriment. The chief of the Uí Ruairc of Lough Gill elbowed his way through the mass of soot-stained fighters until he found Prince Murrough.

The prince stood with a knot of Dalcassians, his son Turlough among them. Father and son were cut from the same cloth; of a similar height, both had the raw and muscular build of Brian in his youth. Though only fifteen, dark-haired Turlough already had a grim reputation with an axe.

'I don't trust the bastard,' Murrough was saying; he hawked up road dust and smoke and spat it out to one side. 'Known Malachy since I was a lad, but I wouldn't let that old snake stand at my back with a spear even if Christ himself commanded it.'

'You think he'll betray us?' Turlough nodded to O'Ruairc, as much for his father's benefit as to acknowledge the Connacht chief. Murrough clapped his son's broad shoulder and leaned in, his voice a conspiratorial hiss.

'I think he already has.' The prince turned to greet his oath-man. 'What's the word, O'Ruairc?'

'It comes from Dubhlinn, my lord,' Cormac replied. 'Sitric's so-called allies – the Manx and Orkneymen – have put back to sea. One of my lads got close enough to hear them screaming threats at each other.'

'Is it a ruse, you think?' Murrough's heavy brows beetled. 'What does my father say about it?'

'That's the feckin' question isn't it, my lord.'

'Did you not report it to the king?'

'I am now,' Cormac replied.

Murrough cuffed him hard, across the mouth. The Connachtman took the blow; he grimaced and spat blood. 'You have a seditious tongue, O'Ruairc,' Murrough snarled.

'Aye, but it's honest.' O'Ruairc followed the prince to where a barrel of water stood. Murrough plunged his head into the barrel and came out spluttering, the water sluicing away a day's worth of grime, sweat, and blood. The prince swiped hair from his eyes and fixed O'Ruairc with a fierce glare.

'Even an honest tongue can be torn out.'

'There's something else. My lads and I, we came in with . . . with *something* we captured on the Dubhlinn Road. A devil, if you ask me. We've kept it out of sight.'

'A devil?' Murrough's eyes narrowed. Though his belly griped with hunger and his limbs ached, to hear the tone of uncertainty – of awe – in O'Ruairc's voice bothered him more than he cared to admit. 'What do you mean, a devil? It's either a man or it's not . . .'

'Once you see it, you'll understand.'

Murrough whistled for his son. 'Let's go, boy.' To O'Ruairc, the prince added, 'Bring your so-called devil up to the monastery. We'll sort all this out together, for good and all. And if it is one of Lucifer's own you snared, at least we'll be on holy ground.'

Cormac O'Ruairc chuckled; he gave a cursory bow and retreated back through the throng of clansmen and camp followers. Murrough, flanked by his son and the chiefs of the Dalcassians, turned his steps toward the hilltop ruin of Saint Maighneann's.

Light filled the courtyard of the monastery. Saint Flannán's gift, the Cross of Kincora, stood ringed about with cressets and lanterns; candles burned, along with torches and braziers whose smoldering coals gave forth the sweet smell of precious incense.

Murrough saw his father sitting on his throne beneath the linen awning, old Ragnall behind him; at his feet, perched on a low settee, the prince beheld a slender woman in a long faded tunic, its gray linen stained, torn, and hastily mended. She wore a broad belt of rough leather and green brocade, and her copper hair was short as a youth's.

'Father,' Murrough said warily.

Brian mac Cennétig looked up and gave his son a smile both peaceful and sad. 'It is the eve of the Lord's crucifixion, and yet I fear you bring news that will gather the ravens to war.'

'There is much news,' Murrough replied, walking across the monastery courtyard to the awning where his father's throne rested. Other chiefs filed in after Murrough, along with the captains of the allied Danes and the petty kings of Connacht and South Munster. 'But is it for every ear?'

'She is a friend of Ragnall's . . . and of mine. Étaín of Wessex, my son.'

411

'Prince Murrough,' she said, in the tongue of the Danes.

Murrough nodded to her, but looked sidelong at the king. 'Are we to count the camp rabble in our councils of war, now?'

'Do we count them among the dead? Among the spoils of victory?' Brian replied. 'I am not so arrogant that I would ignore wisdom from any quarter, my son. Especially not from those whose lives our swords defend. Speak. Tell me your news.'

After a moment, Murrough shrugged. 'Finegall burns and they will sing laments to this day in Howth for many years to come. What's more, the raid seems to have provoked dissension among our foe: Dubhlinn's allies from over the sea have pulled up stakes and fled, sire. It might be a ruse, or it might be bad blood among their captains – especially if they were promised estates in those districts we put to the sword.'

'The pagans do our work for us, you think?'

'It is worth considering,' Murrough said.

In a momentary lull, a harsh growl echoed from the rear of the monastery: 'It's a trick, little fool.'

'Be silent!' That was the voice of Cormac O'Ruairc. Men shifted from foot to foot, nervously looking at one another. Prince Murrough turned, a scowl drawing his black brows together.

'*Faugh!* I came to speak with the old king, not his lackey!' There was the sound of a fist striking flesh, followed by a soft spitting sound and a low chuckle that froze the blood. 'I'll remember that, swine!'

'Bring your devil closer, O'Ruairc,' Murrough said.

A rustling arose from the gathering of chiefs and captains. Men long inured to the perils of strife, grim and unforgiving in matters of war, hastily crossed themselves,

412

averting their eyes from the thing the lord of Lough Gill brought forward at the end of a rope.

It had a broad chest and long arms knotted with muscle; bandy-legged, it had a slouch to its shoulders when it walked that nevertheless lent it an aspect of gnarled strength. Tattoos in cinder and woad snaked across its swarthy hide. It glared at the weapon-men through a stringy veil of black hair, its locks woven with beads of silver and gold and carved bone. Slitted eyes blazed with unquenchable hate.

Even Black Murrough of Kincora took a step back. 'You did not lie when you called it a devil, O'Ruairc.'

'Aye, we caught it on the Dubhlinn Road, sire. It—'

The thing snarled at Cormac, lips skinning back from yellowed fangs. 'Caught? *Bah!* You didn't catch me, runt!'

Étaín stood. 'He is a friend, sire.'

King Brian raised his hand for silence; he glanced at Étaín. 'Is this the . . . the *creature* you spoke of? The *fomórach* from your tale?'

'He is called Grimnir, sire,' she said. 'And he is the last of his kind, one of the *kaunar* – known to your people as *fomóraig,* to mine as *orcnéas,* and to the Northmen as *skrælingar.* In the time I've known him, he has been ever a fomenter of trouble, a murderer, and as cruel a bastard as any I've met.'

'Hanging me out to dry, eh, foundling?' Grimnir's confidence faltered; he glanced about, suddenly all too aware of his predicament. He licked his lips with a pallid tongue.

But Étaín continued unperturbed. 'I can vouch neither for his honesty nor his morals, as he is bereft of both. And while he did kidnap me, threaten me with death, mock my faith, and expose me to the hates of a forgotten world, he also saved my life . . . twice.' She winked at him, then.

413

Grimnir blinked, caught off balance, and then roared with laughter. 'Finally learned to be crafty, you blasted little hymn-singer!'

'You trust him?' said the king, unsure of what to make of the creature.

'God help me, but I do. Prince Murrough, may I borrow your knife?' The prince looked to his father, who nodded. Steel rasped as he drew his heavy war dagger and handed it over to her. Étaín went to Grimnir's side; she took his wrists and slashed the cords that bound them. 'Don't make me regret this,' she muttered.

'So, you're a spy?' Murrough said, taking his knife back and sheathing it.

Grimnir flexed his fingers, massaging his wrists where the cords bit into him. 'I am many things, princeling. Most of all, I am no ally of Dubhlinn's, not while Bjarki Half-Dane shelters behind those walls.' Grimnir glanced from son to father, from prince to king. 'He knows you mean to lay siege. So they will come at you tomorrow. This launching of ships? A ruse! They mean to gull you, catch you making merry on some holy day you hymn-singers hold dear, and slaughter you.'

'Good Friday,' Étaín said.

Murrough stared hard at Grimnir. 'But who's to say you're not part of their plot, too? Some foul-looking rumormonger sent to sow discord?'

'What does your gut tell you, my son?' Brian asked.

The prince snorted and glanced back at his assembled captains; he saw his son, Turlough, standing among the sons of Thomond, the princes of Dal Cais. Murrough's eyes crinkled. 'Aye, damn them! If I were a heathen I'd do the same thing. If we believed Dubhlinn's allies have deserted them, then we might take the day to observe the crucifixion of our Lord.'

'Bjarki's wagering on your religion winning out over your good sense.'

'What will you do?' Étaín, like the others, looked to the king.

King Brian exhaled. 'I am loath to fight on Good Friday. To spill blood on such an auspicious day . . .'

'Aye, but what choice do we have?' Murrough shrugged. 'I say we steal across the Liffey tonight and get a leg up on those heathen bastards. Unless they want to stray far afield, there are only a few places near Dubhlinn where they can land their ships and mass in formation.'

Turlough stepped forward. 'The mouth of the Tolka, Father?'

'Aye, that's my guess. There's a fishing weir there by the plain of Chluain Tarbh, not far from Black-Hair's old bridge. If we can catch them there, maybe we can push them back into the sea.'

After a moment, the old king nodded. 'Make your preparations, then. Ragnall, send word to Malachy. If he would lift a finger in defense of his land, now is the time.' He looked to Grimnir. 'Will you fight for me?'

'I will fight,' Grimnir replied. 'But I will swear no oaths. I fight for myself, and when I've done what I need to do – when that murdering wretch Half-Dane is dead – you'll not see me again.'

'Fair enough.'

'Rouse your men,' Murrough said, turning to his assembled captains. 'Bid them take only food, water, and their war gear. Leave everything else! And leave the fires burning . . . let those God-cursed rebels and their heathen allies think they've gotten one over on us!'

And as the warriors of Ériu mustered and made ready, Étaín walked out into the torchlit night. Stars wheeled in the heavens; in the darkness between lurked the gods that were, cruel and fair and eager for blood. She heard their doom-laden song, heavy with the clangor of war, with the echo of the grave.

Étaín did not flinch away; she was the beacon of Christ, and in a clear voice, she replied with a song of her own:

> Hail now the holder of Heaven's realm,
> That architect's might, His mind's many ways,
> Lord forever and father of glory,
> Ultimate crafter of all wonders,
> Holy Maker who hoisted the heavens
> To roof the heads of the human race,
> And fashioned land for the legs of man,
> Liege of the world-born, Lord almighty.

And the darkness between the stars trembled . . .

BOOK FOUR

THE PLAIN OF CHLUAIN TARBH, NORTH OF DUBHLINN

GOOD FRIDAY, APRIL TWENTY-THIRD

THE YEAR OF OUR LORD 1014

I

The ravens gathered under a lightening sky, driving the birds of morning deep into hiding. From a rocky perch at the edge of Tomar's Wood, north of Dubhlinn, Grimnir watched the flocks of wheeling black shapes staining the firmament, drawn by the promise of blood and slaughter. As he watched, he sang – his voice like iron scraped across flint:

> Brothers shall strive and slaughter,
> Sisters shall sin together;
> Ill days among men:
> An axe-age, a sword-age,
> Shields shall be cloven;
> A wind-age, a wolf-age,
> Ere the world totters.

Grimnir squatted on his haunches; his shirt of antiquated iron rings gleamed with a fresh coat of grease. He wore trousers of leather, now, and heavy Danish boots taken from the spoils of Finegall. He carried his long seax sheathed at his waist, along with a bearded axe fitted with a curved haft a few spans longer than his knotty forearm. The helmet that rested on the rock beside him once belonged to a Norse chief; the iron had chasings of bronze, with a thick ridge that came down to a heavy nasal carved with a wolf's head. A crest of black horsehair hung from a socket at the peak of the helm. A spear he had, too, and a limewood shield, banded and bossed in cold wrought iron, that bore on its blackened face the fresh-painted sigil of the chiefs of Orkahaugr in the Kjolen Mountains: the red Eye of Bálegyr.

Grimnir sang on:

> *The sun shall be darkened,*
> *Earth sinks in the sea,*
> *Glide from the heavens*
> *The glittering stars;*
> *Smoke-reek rages*
> *And reddening fire:*
> *The high heat licks*
> *Against Heaven itself.*

As the harsh echo faded across the mist-wreathed plain of Chluain Tarbh, Grimnir heard the soft tread of a woman coming up beside him. He glanced sidelong at Étaín, her slight form cloak-wrapped and trembling with exhaustion. The Irish army had marched through the night – great divisions of men moving ever north and east, curving through the silent groves and fallow fields between Finegall and the Howth Peninsula, until they reached the thick forest called Tomar's Wood. Here, Murrough, the grim prince of the Dalcassians, had called a halt.

'I remember that song,' she said, leaning on the great boulder that was his perch. 'You sang it once before, so many years ago it seems, on the road to Roskilde. It does not speak to hope, does it?'

'Hope for what, foundling?'

'Tomorrow,' Étaín said. 'The day after. Next week. Next

year. Hope for the future; hope that there is more to our time on this earth than war and loss and heartache.'

'We are all born, and we all die – be it from age and illness, like your people, or from battle, like mine. Everything between is what you make of it,' Grimnir said. 'Do you know what hope is to a *kaunr*? That we die wreathed in glory; that songs are made of our deeds, and that our enemies remember who we were and tremble around their fires at the mention of our names.'

From beneath her cloak, Étaín drew out Grimnir's satchel. 'I almost forgot.'

Grimnir looked at it, its leather yet supple despite being older than any ten men around them, combined. 'Old Gífr got that off a dead Roman,' he said. '*Nár*, keep it, foundling. I might come back for it.'

Étaín nodded; she hugged the satchel to her and studied the plain before them, with its low ridge that sloped down to the sandy beach and the rolling surf of the Irish Sea. From just over the ridge he heard the faint sounds of men mustering. After a moment, she said, 'Who will make your death song?'

'My enemies,' Grimnir replied with unaccustomed gravitas. 'I stand hard up against the long night of my people. The Nine Fathers are no more, and even half-breeds like Bjarki would rather embrace the world of Men. When I go to the great hall of my people at Nástrond to await the call of Gjallarhorn and the breaking of the world, my name and the tale of my deeds will go with me.'

'Your name will not die, not so long as I draw breath,' Étaín said.

Grimnir turned and looked at her, his swarthy brow creased with furrows. 'Why? I have done you ill, foundling. Why would you do this?'

'Those ills you've done me have also strengthened my

faith. I have no veil of ignorance to hide behind, now, because of you. And I know my own destiny is bound to this wondrous island. I thank you for the ills you have caused me even as I mourn the dead you left in your wake. I meant what I said last night: you're a fomenter of trouble, a murderer, and crueler than you need be, but you're also devout, honest, and you scrupulously keep your word. It is not my place to judge you, but it is my place to remember you, be it for good or ill.' Tears sparkled on Étaín's lashes; she looked down, her gaze fixed on the painted face of his shield. 'May your gods and mine watch over you, son of Bálegyr.' And with that, she was gone, leaving Grimnir alone.

'*Faugh.*' He picked up the helm off the rocks beside him. 'And you, foundling,' he whispered. 'And you.'

Grimnir glanced up as a lone horn sounded. He arose and leapt to the ground. Around the great boulder, the sudden clamor of thousands of men making ready for the coming battle shattered the stillness of Tomar's Wood. Battalions of grim-faced Gaels rose up from the dense undergrowth and girded their loins; rangy Scots and mail-clad Danes drew steel and made their peace with God. The horn called the ravens to war . . .

2

From the northern end of the plain of Chluain Tarbh, the three divisions of the high king's army moved into position. The sun rose on their left hand, its golden light casting long shadows across the folds of the earth; it was a brilliant morning, with streamers of cloud drifting across a cornflower-blue sky, in sharp contrast to the fresh green of the plain. The stench of yesterday's burning still hung in the air, but a freshening breeze off the sea helped drive the stink of it inland. Across this idyllic landscape, the war march of eight thousand men shook the foundations of the earth.

The Dalcassians anchored the Irish left against the gray-green sea, those dark-eyed sons of Thomond whose axeplay was unrivaled, even among the Danes. They followed Turlough mac Murrough into battle; though he had only fifteen summers, already his reputation was such that his father and grandfather were confident of his ability to lead the ferocious war bands of Dal Cais.

Murrough himself commanded the center division, the clansmen of Connacht and of Munster – half-wild fighters in wolf skins and rough homespun who relished the coming spear-grab the way other men relished a country dance; among them strode the Uí Ruairc of Lough Gill and their chief, Cormac, who howled and clashed sword on shield with reckless abandon.

On the far Irish right, inland from the sea, came companies of Norsemen from Corcaigh and Hlymrekr – mail-clad sons of the North who sported crosses rather than pagan symbols; alongside them marched shock-headed Galloglas mercenaries from Alba, who wore quilted jerkins and steel caps and carried long Danish axes. Domnall mac Eimen was their chief and he strode forward in grim silence. But of the Meathmen and their treacherous king, Malachy, there was no sign.

Grimnir walked alone. Around him, men shouted and cursed, bolstering their courage. Brazen horns howled; drums pounded like the pulse of some great war beast, stretching and making ready to rip its victim to shreds. As he came on, Grimnir glared at the mustering enemy across the plain in search of a sign as to where his foeman might be. Had the witch's ruse worked?

Thousands of mailed reavers poured from ships drawn up on the north bank of the Liffey and on the beaches of Dubhlinn Bay, near the fishing weir at the mouth of the Tolka; they formed two divisions that spread across the plain to the old wooden bridge, whose timbers groaned beneath the weight of the division that hurried across from Dubhlinn.

There. Grimnir's visage twisted with a grin of savage delight as he spied the ancient sigil of the Spear-Danes of Hróarr amid the banners of Dubhlinn: a dirty white scrap of cloth sporting a crude black hand. Under it marched the hunched and twisted giant Bjarki Half-Dane, a long, broad-bladed sword naked on his shoulder. A red rage washed over Grimnir; he loosed a frenzied howl that pierced even the din of the assembling hosts.

The Norse of Dubhlinn and the rebel Gaels of Leinster formed their battle array on the right, their serried ranks ready to face the iron axes of Corcaigh and Hlymrekr;

Maelmorda stood among the *fianna* of Leinster, bellowing threats and shaking his great spear at the high king's army, his courage nailed to his spine with a mead horn.

The enemy center was the demesne of Sigurðr of the Raven Banner, whose Orkneymen stood shoulder-to-mail-clad-shoulder with their cousins from the Hebrides and champions drawn from all the lands of the North: Hrafn the Red, Prince Olaf of Norway, Thorsteinn of the Danemark, Ámundi the White, Thorwald Raven, and many more besides. Sigurðr gleamed in a gold-scaled corselet as he took his place at the point of a broad fighting wedge.

Hard against the sea that was their life's blood gathered the Manx reavers of Bródir, eager to pit their axes against those of the Dalcassians. Their fell-handed chief stood forth in his dwarf-forged mail and called on his men to drag a Gaelic prisoner forward; there, in sight of the Irish host, Bródir drew his knife and sacrificed the man to the glory of Odin. Howls of rage washed over the sunlit plain of Chluain Tarbh.

When only two bowshots separated the Gael from their hated foe, Brian mac Cennétig called a halt. There would be no parley between the two armies, no last chance to come to terms. Iron would decide the day. Grimnir saw the old king, now, mounted on his white stallion. He rode across the Irish front, his sheathed sword held up and inverted like a crucifix. He drew rein near the center of his army.

'Men of Ériu!' The voice that came from the old king's chest rolled like thunder, drowning even the clangor of the enemy, eager to come to grips. 'Friends and allies! On your valor rest the hopes of your country today; and what surer grounds can they rest upon? Oppression attempts to bend you down to servility; will you burst its chains and rise as free men? Your cause is one approved by Heaven!' A roar erupted from eight thousand Irish throats. 'You do not seek the oppression of others; you fight for your country and sacred altars. It is a cause that claims heavenly protection. Let every heart, then, be the throne of confidence and courage. You know that the Danes are strangers to religion and humanity; they are inflamed with the desire to violate the fairest daughters of this land of beauty, and to enrich themselves with the spoils of sacrilege and plunder. Witness!' The king spun his horse and leveled the cruciform hilt of his sword at the enemy. 'The barbarians have impiously chosen the very day on which the Redeemer of the world died on the cross! Victory they shall not have! From such brave soldiers as you they can never wrest it; for you fight in defense of honor, liberty and religion – in defense of the sacred temples of the true God, and of your sisters, wives and daughters! Such a holy cause must be the cause of God, who will deliver your enemies this day into your hands!' Brian mac Cennétig reversed his sword and drew it from its sheath, thrusting it aloft. 'Onward, then, for your country and your sacred altars!'

And so, to the music of brazen horns and hide drums, of skirling pipes and raw voices, the Battle on the Plain of Chluain Tarbh began . . .

3

Grimnir marched in the forefront on the Irish right, his red and gleaming eyes fixed on the thatch-bearded figure of Half-Dane. He came for blood; his jaws champed spasmodically, and slaver dripped from his yellowed fangs in anticipation. He fought the urge to dart forward and end this five-hundred-year dance of vengeance with a single spear cast. No, he wanted to savor it. He wanted to taste Daufi's fear in these final moments of cursed life that remained to him.

Grimnir laughed.

A hundred yards separated the two fronts, now, and Grimnir was close enough to see the tremblers among the ranks of the enemy – piss-legged farmers who only played at war; pale merchants who thought dandling a brat on their knee was better than seeking a storied death; townsmen who only owned a hauberk because it made the whores wet. *Bah!* Grimnir spat. The iron-shod dogs at his back deserved a better enemy!

At fifty yards, Grimnir drew breath. He meant to bellow a challenge, to call Bjarki out, when suddenly a one-eyed figure in black mail stepped out from the enemy ranks, blocking his view of Half-Dane. The man carried a bearded axe, and his shield was quartered red and black. His gray beard bristled as he threw back his head and loosed a challenge of his own.

'Grimnir! Wretched *skrælingr*! Come forth!'

The challenge elicited roars of approval from both sides. Nor did Grimnir shirk from it; he stalked out into the no-man's-land between the two armies and answered: 'Go back to your hearth, old man! Leave the fighting to your betters!'

'We have old business, you and I! Or have you forgotten?' The mailed fighter made a savage gesture with his axe. 'You killed me once before—'

'I've killed many men, little fool! And those I send to Hel's gates stay dead!'

'We met on the road to Roskilde. We had words, and you left my corpse in a cave, or so you thought!'

It took a moment, but roots of recognition finally found purchase in Grimnir's brain. 'So-ho!' he said, laughing. 'Christ-Dane!'

'Aye, I was a hymn-singer, then. Men knew me as Njáll, Hjálmarr's son,' he replied, hefting his shield. 'But no longer! Draugen, I am called, and the only hymn I will sing this day will be your death dirge, fiend!'

Men chanted and clashed swords on shields; they howled for blood. Grimnir stalked forward, his spear low and ready as Draugen edged toward him. His eye caught the telltale signs of the blow the Dane intended to make – the tensing of muscles, the widening of his eyes, and the flaring of his nostrils prior to the explosion of pent-up fury.

'*Faugh!* I will tell your precious foundling how you died a second time,' Grimnir hissed. 'That will amuse her.'

Draugen's one good eye blinked. He flinched as though Grimnir had dealt him a physical blow. 'Étaín?' He hesitated a moment; his shield dipped. 'She . . . She lives? Where—'

And in that moment, Grimnir struck.

Powerful muscles propelled him forward, a pantherish leap that spanned the short distance between them; with a thunderous roar, Grimnir twisted his torso and slammed the iron-banded edge of his shield into the blind side of Draugen's head. The blow rang on his helmet, bursting the straps that held it and ripping it from his head, along with part of his scalp. Sheeting blood, one-eyed Draugen toppled senseless to the ground.

Grimnir straddled Draugen's body. 'Little Half-Dane!' he screamed above the warring shouts of approbation and censure. 'Have you no greeting for your kinsman, Daufi?'

Bjarki drew himself up to his full height, overtopping Grimnir by a head. 'The day has come at last, snuffler,' he replied. 'The Doom of Odin has caught up with you! The skein of fate is woven, and the Norns have decreed your end! The Allfather has chosen me—'

'To die!' Grimnir slung his spear across the interval. It wobbled, iron head flashing, and caromed off Bjarki's hastily raised shield to bury itself in the neck of the yellow-bearded Norseman at his side. The man staggered, pulled by the weight of the shaft. He spewed blood as he fell, and the red droplets hung like a handful of rubies cast up into air gone bright and still.

Up and down the Irish front, Grimnir's casting of his spear was like an axe cutting the yoke off a mighty beast – a beast that pawed the earth with iron claws as its great muscles hurled it forward, into the face of its prey. A deafening shout went up – the *barrán-glaed,* the warrior's cry – and it rocked the foundations of Heaven. From the first kern of the Dal Cais on the left to the last *thegn* of Hlymrekr on the right, the divisions of the high king of Ériu surged forward like a storm-driven tide to crash into a bulwark of steel.

Trumpets howled and shrieked over the din, but not to

relay orders. This was no game of thrones where generals sacrificed and maneuvered on the backs of their soldiers; this was the most primal sort of conflict – Odin's weather, the red chaos of slaughter – where men stood breast-to-breast and shield-to-shield, and dealt the same blows they took in kind.

Spears cracked and shivered. Shields split. Links of woven mail parted beneath the edge of an axe. Swords flashed in the rising dust, and blood dampened the earth. Thunderous cries mixed with piteous howls. Men struck and reeled; the dying clasped the knees of the living like a lover refusing to be put aside for another. The air – so bright and clear only moments before – reeked now of iron scraping iron; it was redolent with the coppery stench of spilled gore, with the hot stink of vomit, and with the fetor of riven bellies.

Grimnir was in his element. Laughing, he came at Bjarki low and fast; his axe sang clear of its moorings, lashed out, and rebounded from the face of Half-Dane's shield. There was little room to swing a broad-bladed sword, so Bjarki tried thrusting it at Grimnir's face . . . only to nearly lose it, and his hand, to his kinsman's riposte.

Breath whistled between clenched teeth. There was no time for speech, no time even for taunts. Grimnir let the blade of his axe speak for him. Again and again he smote Bjarki's shield, hammering at the black sigil of Hróarr like a smith working a stubborn lump of ore. Splinters flew from its face until Grimnir was certain the arm beneath must be broken – and if not, he would break it soon enough. The spine-twisted Half-Dane tried to fall back, but the press of men pushing forward from the rear gave him nowhere to turn and Grimnir, a snarling knot of hate, gave him no respite. The axe blade flashed and thudded; Bjarki's rim-warped shield cracked like an eggshell, and the bastard son of Hrungnir bellowed in agony.

'Odin!'

But it was not the Allfather who leapt to Half-Dane's defense. A trio of Norse mercenaries from Dubhlinn, their heavy mail standing them in good stead against the spears of the blood-maddened Gaels, came at Grimnir from his unshielded right.

As much as Grimnir wanted to deal one last, fatal blow to his hateful kinsman, his sense of self-preservation proved stronger than his thirst for vengeance. Screaming in rage, he shifted and brought his shield to bear in time to deflect an axe blow; a spear licked out, ripping through the leather and iron rings at the top of his shoulder to crease the swarthy flesh beneath.

'Swine!' Grimnir spat. His short-hafted axe struck the lead Norseman across the eyes; he clutched his face and reeled away, gagging on bloody froth. A dying Scotsman lunged forward and snarled the legs of the second man, giving Grimnir an opening to stave in the Norseman's skull. Grimnir wrenched the blade free of the ruin of bone and brain even as the third of Half-Dane's defenders drew back to strike . . . and died choking on the head of a Hlymrekr spear. Grimnir whirled back around and cast about for his foe, but to no avail.

In the scrum, Bjarki Half-Dane had managed to slip away.

Grimnir howled like a stung wolf; he stamped and slashed and swore in the harsh tongue of his kind. He slung his shield to the ground, ripped his seax from its sheath, and let go of the last vestiges of his sanity.

Flanked by Scots and allied Danes, he led a murderous spike into the heart of the Dubhlinn Norse . . .

4

Anxious faces lined the northern walls of Dubhlinn, watching in earnest as the Battle of Chluain Tarbh unfolded. The broad parapet, part stone and part timber, echoed with the distant shouts, the brazen horns. Wives suckled babes at their breasts and fretted if the end of the day would see them widowed, their children made fatherless; gray-haired matrons went about their spinning as though this were just another day, their stoic silence tempered by experience – fall fair or fall foul, the sun would rise tomorrow. Old men crouched in the lee of the walls and swapped war stories, revisiting old glories that were as fresh in their minds as if they happened yesterday. Men of the garrison leaned on their spears and listened; occasionally, their eyes wandered to the higher parapet of the castle, where King Sitric stood apart from his remaining nobles, his mother at his side.

Kormlada and her son did not speak for the better part of the morning, preferring to watch in silence as events unfolded on the distant plain. The king remained pride-stung. Generations to come would remember this day, when the cream of Ériu spent itself on the field of Chluain Tarbh, when the iron heel of the North crushed the neck of the high king, once and for all; songs would commemorate the deeds of valor, the glory of the fallen. Heroes would spring from the tongues of skalds. But who would honor the king who watched from afar?

'How did he know?' Sitric said, breaking the long silence between them. 'How did Mac Cennétig know we would launch our attack this morning? How did he see through Bjarki's ruse?'

'The *how* of it matters little,' the Witch of Dubhlinn replied. 'The outcome is all that is important. The son of Olaf Cuarán is king in Dubhlinn, once more. The balance is righted. The rest . . .' Kormlada turned away.

Sitric glanced at her. 'The battle isn't over. Will you not see it to the end?'

'I have seen its end.'

'Who triumphs?'

Kormlada stopped. A breeze from the sea lifted her long raven tresses; in its salt tang she could smell the changing weather. The Old World was ending, teetering on the edge of the Long Night; a New World was poised to arise in its place, and that world would have no need of her. The Witch of Dubhlinn would diminish, and Kormlada ingen Murchada would become nothing but a name etched on a stone and perched above a cold and forgotten grave.

'Mother?' Sitric repeated. 'Who triumphs?'

Kormlada smiled a melancholy smile. 'The living, my son. It is always the living who will recall the deeds, who will write the histories. It is the living who will triumph.'

The Witch of Dubhlinn turned away and disappeared into the shadows of Cuarán's Tower . . .

5

As the day peaked and waned, Étaín watched the battle rage away across the plain of Chluain Tarbh. She watched from the high king's pavilion near the eaves of Tomar's Wood, unable to make sense of the roars and the screams and the flashes of steel winking through a low veil of dust. All she knew for certain was that men died, yonder, and the fate of the high kingship hung on the balance of a blade.

The king had dismissed all but six of his guards – Dalcassian elders, their mustaches gray and faces seamed from the long years of fighting – and had given leave for his servants to join the fray. Ragnall had gone forward, seeking news. Brian himself knelt inside the shadow of the pavilion, his hands clasped in prayer. Étaín paced. An hour. Two. Thirty-two steps separated the pavilion's corner poles, and in that span she counted fourteen rocks, six tussocks of sedge grass, a knot of periwinkle, two small anthills, and a sun-bleached shell dropped by a passing bird. Counting what she could touch, what belonged in the world of the living was more comforting than counting the myriad faces of the dead. It was enough that she could hear their voices.

Sing for us, the dead asked. *Sing us the song we heard in the night. Sing us into the light of God.* Étaín closed her eyes. She was the beacon of Christ. And as the living strove in blood and slaughter, she sang for the dead. Her voice lifted across the green plain of Chluain Tarbh, where the sea foamed against the shore. Her song tinkled like chimes in the soft breeze, a balm to the wounded who stood at the threshold of death, who cursed the unseen blow that stole their life away, who fretted over those still on the field, who cried bitter tears and pined for heather and hearth. Étaín sang for the dead; but she sang for the dying, as well, and for those who would bear the guilt for having lived . . .

As her song ended, Étaín opened her eyes to see two men rushing across the plain, a pair of the king's Dalcassians; between them, they half carried a third man: old Ragnall. They were all three hollow-eyed and blood-blasted, their limbs trembling and spent – though Ragnall looked as pale as a man who'd been bled dry.

The king met them. He took Ragnall's cold hand and sank down beside him as the Dalcassians lowered him to the grass. He had no wound upon his body.

'His heart,' Étaín murmured.

'Brian,' Ragnall gasped through lips gone pale and bloodless.

'I am here, my old friend.'

'My king.' The steward's fingers tightened around Brian's. 'The . . . The s-song of doom . . . the . . . the d-daughters of Odin! They r-ride . . . they ride for me . . . and for . . . for your son! Murrough . . . your son . . . Murrough . . . fallen! Murrough has . . . has fallen!'

The old Northman sank back in death, eyes glazing. A sob caught in the king's throat. Étaín saw the bulwark of his faith crack and crumble from the blow; she watched the light of his soul grow dim and his flesh crumple in on itself. 'No,' he whispered.

Étaín knelt beside the king and Ragnall; she took their joined hands in hers. Eyes fierce and unblinking, she looked past the living and into the faces of the dead. 'Tell me,' she said.

And they did. The dead sang to her. In the chanting cadence of war, they sang of a great beast made of flesh and steel that writhed across the field of Chluain Tarbh, twisting like a serpent in its death throes. They sang of Black Murrough of Kincora, resolute in his love of Christ Jesus, who strode fearlessly into the maw of the beast. The dead sang of his prowess and of his ferocity; they sang of the strife beneath the Raven Banner of Odin, where the blessed blade of Murrough cleft the heart of the giant, Sigurðr, and broke the spine of the great beast. But their praise song became a dirge as the dead recounted his last moments, breast-to-breast and dagger-to-dagger with a king's heathen son of Norway. The dead sang of the harrowed earth, salted with blood, which rose up to embrace the two fallen princes. Their song ended, the dead of Chluain Tarbh wept . . .

Tears fell from Étaín's eyes as she turned to look at the frail old king. Brian mac Cennétig bowed his head.

'It is as God wills it.'

6

As implacable as Death itself, the son of Bálegyr ranged the broken field in search of Bjarki Half-Dane. He did not stop to gloat over the flight of the Dubhlinn Danes, driven back to the Liffey Bridge by the axes of Hlymrekr and Corcaigh; he barely registered the fall of Maelmorda, rebel king of Leinster, who was torn apart by the wolves of the Uí Ruairc. He passed the death mound of corpses surrounding slain Prince Murrough without remark, and paid no heed when young Turlough of the Dal Cais caught Bródir of Mann in a death grip as the reaver fled for his ships, and vanished with him beneath the bloodstained waters of Dubhlinn Bay.

Nothing else mattered, save Grimnir's long-delayed vengeance on his brother's slayer. He returned to the site of their combat and combed through the wounded and the dead. Grimnir snuffled the blood-soaked ground, seeking the elusive scent of his prey. He found Bjarki's broken shield, but nothing else.

'*Faugh!*' he snarled and spat. 'Ymir take that piss-colored bastard! When I find him—!'

Near at hand, Grimnir heard a weak but familiar voice. '*Skrælingr,* I name you. Ch-Child of Satan.'

He crouched. From under a mound of dead Northmen and Scots, Grimnir spied the one-eyed visage of Draugen.

Clots of blood stiffened his gray beard, crusted his lacerated scalp; he had one arm free, and with it he struggled to shift the weight of armored dead pressing upon him. 'Christ-Dane,' Grimnir said, grinning. He used the point of his seax to ease the flap of skin off Njáll's scalp and examine the wound beneath. 'Should have taken your wretched head off, maggot.'

'Did you lie? Is . . . Is she alive? Is Étaín . . . ?'

Grimnir rocked back on his haunches. 'She lives. Where has Bjarki gone, Christ-Dane? Where has your master gotten off to, eh? Not back to Dubhlinn. Oh, no. The witch would never stand for that! Where, then?'

'His day is done,' Draugen replied. 'I have bled for him, and my oath is fulfilled. If he is to die, by your hand or by another's, he'll try to take Mac Cennétig with him. He hates the old king, body and soul.'

Grimnir stared back across the plain to where Brian's white linen pavilion stood on a slight rise, hard by the dark fringe of Tomar's Wood. 'Does he, now?'

'Where is she, *skrælingr*? You said she's alive. Where is she?'

'Where do you think?' Grimnir shook his head, chuckling. 'That foundling has a knack for getting in the way.'

Draugen clawed desperately at Grimnir's blood-slimed boot. 'Help me!'

'*Help* you?' Grimnir rose. He reversed his grip on his seax. 'Help you? Do you think me a fool, Christ-Dane?'

Daugen struggled. He turned his head so his one good eye could meet the hateful gaze of his lifelong enemy. 'You've won. I expect no mercy from you, *skrælingr*. If the Fates had written our end differently, with our places reversed, I would have no mercy for you, either. But if Étaín is with the king, then she is in danger. I swore an oath when I took her from England. An oath that I would not let her come to harm. I failed her once before. But, by Christ, I will not fail her again! I beg of you, help me! I am Draugen no longer!'

Grimnir snorted. He glanced again at the white pavilion off in the distance, then reached down and caught Njáll by the wrist. Grunting, he dragged him free of the clinging embrace of the dead.

Njáll rose on unsteady feet; though yet reeling from the thunderous blow he had taken to the head, he was otherwise unharmed. Grimnir bent and grabbed a long-handled axe off the ground. He thrust it haft-first into the Dane's hands.

'Go get your precious little hymn-singer and get her away from there. Your life is my gift.' Grimnir snatched a handful of Njáll's beard and dragged him close, red eyes boring into his like forge-gledes. 'But if you think to flout me – if you think this little bit of mercy makes me weak – then, by Ymir, you will watch me gut her like a fattening calf before I send you shrieking down to Hel!'

7

Bjarki Half-Dane crouched in the undergrowth at the edge of Tomar's Wood and glared at the pavilion of the Irish king. This morning he'd been nigh a king himself, with an army at this back and the world at his feet. And now? He was a tattered vagabond lurking in the shadows, penniless, with only a ragged hauberk and a notched sword to his name. Bjarki cursed the Fates that had brought him to this sorry state. He cursed Ágautr and his wretched omens, and he cursed his own useless pride. Chosen of Odin? *Pah!* He smelled the hand of a rat – and unless he was far off the mark, a cunning and perilous rat named Kormlada. Bjarki ground his teeth. *Should have killed the whore months ago!* Ah, no matter. Let that bitch revel in her little victory. He would be back, and he'd bring fire and steel to this green little shithole.

Bjarki glanced over his shoulder. Eight other men crouched behind him. Six were Norse mercenaries, blond giants in bloodied mail who had come out with him from the city; the last two were dark-haired Gaelic rogues, Leinstermen he'd picked up along the way, braggarts hot to avenge their fallen kinsmen. Nine of them, all told. *Odin's sacred number.* Bjarki snorted. Well, he'd come to this Hel-blighted land with less than this, and nearly carved an empire. Least he could do was leave it in ruins . . .

'That bastard, Mac Cennétig, is mine,' he snarled, drawing his sword from its sheath. 'Kill the rest.'

8

Étaín unfastened her cloak. Shaking it out, she draped the patched and worn garment over Ragnall's body like a shroud. The captain of the remaining Dalcassians, a clean-shaven man with the face of a boxer, came to the king's side and offered him an arm as Brian struggled to rise. The king nodded his thanks.

For a moment, the high king remained motionless; he gazed out over the trampled and blood-sodden field of Chluain Tarbh, where men yet strained and contended like yoked oxen. 'Send for a horse,' Brian said, quietly. 'It is time to call an end to the slaughter, time to care for our wounded and honor our dead. I must fetch Murrough home. Send to King Sitric, if he yet lives, and bid him do the same. Our differences can wait.'

The captain nodded. 'Aye, as you wish, sire.'

But, as the man turned to do the king's bidding, Étaín felt an eerie sensation tickling her spine. A spirit had joined them, grim and indomitable; she heard its whispered warning. '*Protect my father.*'

'Wait.' Étaín laid a hand on the Dalcassian captain's shoulder . . . and felt him quiver even as she heard the thudding impact. He half-turned, looking down in wide-eyed disbelief at the thrown axe that had suddenly sprouted from his breastbone. Breath rattling in his throat, the old

442

soldier crumpled without a word, his spirit suddenly free.

Étaín saw them, rising from the edge of the woods: six mailed reavers and a pair of traitorous Gaels led by a twisted giant whose sallow skin and *skrælingr*'s eyes marked him as Bjarki Half-Dane – and in the dark shadow of his soul, she beheld the one-eyed titan who hung from Yggðrasil.

'Protect the king!' she screamed, wrenching the bloody axe free of the dead Dalcassian's chest.

Amid incoherent roars and shouted imprecations, the blond-bearded reavers crashed into the king's remaining Dalcassians. And though they were old men, slowed by the weight of their years and stiffened by the stigmata of past glories, they nevertheless fought with the fury of their kind. Norse spears darted and licked; broad-bladed swords, blunted from the day's butchery, shattered Irish shields and the bones beneath. But the whickering axes of Dal Cais reaped a red harvest among the Foreigner.

The two Gaels, dark-eyed jackals of Leinster, skirted the fray and made straight for Étaín, their eyes aflame with lust. And Étaín did not shrink from them. All fear had left her, and the courage that put steel in her spine was her own – hard-earned and precious.

She leveled her blood-smeared axe at them. 'Know this, dogs of Leinster! I am a daughter of the Blind Witch of Lorcan's Wood! Harm me and her curse will be on you!'

One of the Gaels slowed – which was Étaín's intent – and glanced about him, half-expecting to see imps boiling from the ground at the mention of Blind Maeve. The other only showed a mouthful of blackened teeth as he grinned. 'We ain't in Lorcan's Wood, now, are we? You'd best come with us, girl, before these heathens go and get their feckin' hands on you!'

And as he reached for her, Étaín lashed out at him. Her

axe caught him high, between the brow and the bridge of his nose. Blood fountained, and the sickening *chook* of impact vibrated up her arm as the blade staved in the Gael's face. He toppled like a sapling, dead before he hit the ground.

The second Gael snarled. 'Witch's daughter or no, I will gut you, bitch!' He threw his axe down and drew a curved skinning knife from a sheath at the small of his back; he came at her with the wariness of a hunter stalking wounded prey, and she knew he would not fall quite so easily.

'Hold!' the king thundered.

The Gael stopped in midstep, cowed by the power in the old man's voice. The two remaining reavers ceased slitting the wounded Dalcassians' throats and looked up. Only Bjarki was unmoved. He stalked toward the king with murder in his eyes, a naked sword in his fist.

'You bring your leman to war?' Half-Dane mocked. 'Or is that one of your cursed daughters?'

'Let her be, spawn of Satan!'

A malicious grin split Bjarki Half-Dane's face. 'She can watch your end, ere my lads have their fun,' he said. 'Will you fight?'

'I cannot spill blood this day. Not even yours.'

Bjarki laughed. 'So be it. Your hymn-singers may have won the day, but their victory will be bittersweet! Odin! Look here! A last sacrifice! The blood of a king to assuage your anger!' And with a grunt, he brought his blade up and hacked into Brian mac Cennétig's neck. Étaín cried out as Brian sank to his knees, clutching at the wound with trembling fingers as though mere hands might stem the blood that sheeted down his front. Cursing, Bjarki struck again, and again, until the head of the high king came free of his body with the dull crunch of vertebrae. With a bark of triumph, he stooped and snatched it up by the hair, thrusting it aloft. 'Now let Gael tell Gael that it was by the hand of Bjarki Half-Dane that Brian mac Cennétig fell! I spit on their king, as I spit on them!' He turned to Étaín and gestured to her with Mac Cennétig's dripping head. 'Come here, girl, and kiss your father good night!'

She screamed her rage, her grief. She hefted her axe . . . and reeled as the wary Gael darted in and slammed his fist into the side of her head. Her axe thudded to the turf. Before she could fall, the Gael caught her up and held her tight, his knife pressed to her throat. 'Gotcha, you feckin' bitch!'

'Half-Dane!' a voice called out.

Through a blur of tears, Étaín saw a ghoulish figure emerge from the taller grass to the right, where the eaves of Tomar's Wood ran down into a low hollow. Though one-eyed and bloody, his beard more gray than chestnut, there was nevertheless something familiar about him – in the breadth of his shoulders and the way he carried the long-handled axe so casually in his fist. She struggled in the Gael's hard grasp.

'Draugen.' Bjarki laughed. 'Well, you've earned your moniker over and again, you bastard. Thought the snuffler killed you.'

The man touched his lacerated scalp. 'God loves a fool,' he replied; Étaín's breath caught in her throat. She recognized that voice, though she dared not look at him for fear of seeing only some cruel trick of Fate.

'Not our gods,' Bjarki said. 'Or did that blow knock you back on your knees with the rest of those useless hymn-singers?'

'It knocked a little sense back into my thick skull, is all.' Njáll turned to the two reavers. 'Sense enough to know it's over, mates. Time to start thinking about your own hides. These Irish are coming for blood, and you don't want to be standing over the corpse of their king when they get here.'

Bjarki's eyes narrowed. He tossed the king's severed head off to the side. 'What are you doing?'

'It's over,' Njáll repeated.

'Aye, it's over. But we'll skin out when I say we're ready.'

Njáll ignored him. 'You lads, I know you, and you're both good men. But if you follow this one's lead, all that will come of it are hard blows on the way to an ignoble grave. You deserve an honest gold-giver—'

Bjarki snarled. 'Gold-giver? I'll give gold to the one who brings me your mutinous tongue!'

But neither of the two reavers moved to do Half-Dane's bidding. They exchanged glances, looking from Njáll to Bjarki and back again, weighing what they knew of each man, what they knew of their reputations, on a scale of their own devising; suddenly the balance tilted. The older of the two Norseman, with a plaited beard and a torque of twisted Spanish silver, nodded to Njáll. 'You're an honest gold-giver.'

'No, lads. I got amends to make. Head inland – west for a day, then south. Keep your wits about you and you'll be knocking at the gates of Veisafjorðr in a fortnight. You'll find *jarls* aplenty, there.'

'Stand your ground,' Bjarki growled.

'Aye, stand your ground,' Njáll said. 'And if you keep standing it long enough the Irish will bury you in it! Go, I said.'

And the reavers did. Backing away slowly, they turned and vanished into the shelter of Tomar's Wood. Bjarki's face flushed with rage. 'Maggots! Filthy traitors! You think you can just put by your oaths to serve me? *Pah!* And you, you wretch, I'll tear your spleen out!' He jabbed his broad-bladed sword at Draugen. 'You're a dead man!'

Njáll snorted. 'Better than you have tried.' He hefted his axe, his gaze sliding to where the Leinsterman stood, Étaín still hard in his grip. 'I'll take the girl.'

'The feckin' hell you will,' barked the Irishman. 'I'm skinning out, too, and the bitch is coming with me!'

'No!' Bjarki roared. He gestured to the Gael. 'Bring her to me! Now! I want this little snake to watch while I joint her like a side of beef! You'll take this and you'll not take that, eh? *Pah!* You'll take my leavings, you wretch! Bring her, damn your eyes!'

In response, Njáll lowered his axe . . . and smiled.

That was warning enough. With a sulfurous curse, Bjarki Half-Dane whirled around . . .

. . . and bellowed as the handle of an axe crunched across the bridge of his nose. He staggered, blinded, blood sheeting from broken cartilage. 'Daufi,' he heard Grimnir chuckle, his voice like the grinding of stones.

Bjarki lowered his head and charged like a wounded bull; he swept his sword low, like a scythe, hoping to reap a harvest of flesh. Half-glimpsed through a haze of pain, Grimnir somehow danced aside, pivoted, and struck. The axe handle splintered on the back of Bjarki's skull.

And Bjarki Half-Dane, who had once made kings dance like marionettes, felt Fate's sharp blade sever the strings of his consciousness . . .

9

As Bjarki fell, the Leinsterman panicked and ran. He hauled Étaín back by her hair and dragged her along with him. His callused hands stank of blood and sweat and the filth of battle; his eyes gleamed with fear, and it made him reckless. He did not care anything for the kinsmen he had lost, only for the spoils now denied him. That was why he had fallen in with the reavers – the gold arm rings and inlaid sword pommels spoke to his lusts. He *wanted,* and in wanting he died.

Njáll crossed the interval at a run and struck the Gael with a thunderous roar. All three went down in a tangled heap. An axe hacked into bone; a man screamed. A foot caught Étaín in the hip; a body rolled over her, crushing her head into the dirt. The sharp edge of a pommel opened the skin above her eye. Snarling, she rammed her elbow into a groin. There came a wet grunt, and a spray of blood washed over her. And then . . .

Silence.

Étaín felt a gentle hand on her shoulder. She opened her eyes, felt a man's fingers wipe away the blood. She concentrated on the face staring down at her – bloodied, bruised, and much older but familiar nonetheless. 'I found you,' Njáll murmured. 'Almighty Christ, I found you.'

Étaín threw her arms around his neck and sobbed like

a child. 'It's been so long,' she said, gasping. 'So long! I thought . . . I thought you'd given up!'

'I almost had,' he said. 'Come, let's get away from here.' And cradling her to his chest, Njáll stood and limped away from the blood and the twisted corpses. He carried her across the green plain and down to the shore, where the waters of the Irish Sea foamed against the sand . . .

And when the Irish came up, weary and heartsick from battle, they found their slain king. They mourned and they railed and they swore vengeance before Almighty God, but they never found a trace of his killer.

10

A stream of hot liquid spattered Bjarki's face, rousing him from his stupor. He spluttered and groaned, flinching from the salt sting; a bitter stink filled his nostrils, recalling the bilges of the wolf ship where he'd spent his first years of life, scrounging through filth like a feral dog, getting pissed on by his father's savage crew . . .

Bjarki cursed; he twisted away from the gush of urine directed at him. Opening his eyes, he saw Grimnir standing over him, naked to the waist with his prick in his hand. Grimnir chuckled as he finished pissing on his brother's bastard son. 'Wake up, Daufi.' He turned away, fastening his trousers. Bjarki spat at his retreating back.

Like Grimnir, Bjarki was stripped to the waist, clad only in blood-stiffened trousers and hobnailed boots of oxhide. He lay on his side, bound at wrist and ankle with ropes of plaited leather. 'Where are we?' Bjarki muttered. His face was a mass of bruises, and the back of his skull felt like a smith had used it for an anvil. He glanced about. From the foreshortened horizon and the distant booming of the surf, he surmised they were on a headland, an upthrust spit of rock that was lifeless save for an ancient ash tree that thrived somehow on the thin soil and salt-heavy air. A scion of Yggðrasil, it had stood sentinel over the Irish shore since the Elder Days. The land around smelled of

450

burning, and of sea spume, and of a cold wind from the North; overhead, beyond a thickening veil of clouds, the Promethean sun brought fire to the western sky.

'Someplace quiet,' Grimnir replied. Muscles writhed and tendons cracked as he flexed his heavy arms, his ape-like shoulders, and his corded neck. Sinew creaked each time he clenched and unclenched his taloned fists. 'Will you not beg for your life?'

'Why?' Defiance burned in Half-Dane's eyes. 'I still have it.'

'Not for long.' Grimnir sat on a large stone, its surface pitted by the elements. 'Bugger all, but you might have made a trusty lad if only you'd remembered your place.'

'My place?'

'The bilges, swine. It's where we keep all the half-breeds and by-blows. But, no . . . you got so high-and-mighty by thinking you were something you're not.'

'And what is that, old fool?'

'One of us,' Grimnir snapped. '*Faugh!* Look at you! What *kaunr* worth his sand would follow something that crawled from between a slave-whore's legs? Hrungnir should have wrung your worthless neck.'

'But he didn't,' Bjarki said. 'And look where that got him! Dead by his own son, his own blood!'

'Aye.' Grimnir stood. He reached down, and from inside his left boot he drew forth a bone-handled dirk, its blade a foot of damascened steel with two razored edges tapering to a diamond-hard point. It was a noble weapon, snatched from the axe-riven corpse of a Norse captain on the plain of Chluain Tarbh. 'Too bad for you I'm not the fool my brother was. I should tie a stone around your filthy neck and throw you over the edge of the cliff.'

'But you've got something else in mind, eh?'

Grimnir's nostrils flared; his eyes blazed in the

451

deepening gloom. 'I want to see if you're as good a sport as your whore of a mother was!' He tossed the dirk down; it clanged and skittered across the ground, coming to rest hard by Bjarki's feet.

Grimnir stepped back. His rune-etched long seax hissed from its scabbard.

Half-Dane snatched up the dirk. He sawed through the ropes binding his feet, then reversed the blade and freed his hands. For a moment he crouched there, motionless, glaring at Grimnir through rage-slitted eyes. Then, with a wild and desperate laugh, Bjarki reeled up and hurled himself at his hated enemy.

Grimnir sprang to meet him. Bjarki was a head taller than he, heavier and with a longer reach; nevertheless, Grimnir's fury was the berserk rage of Fenrir, his cunning the sly craft of Jörmungandr. Under a blood-red sky the two foes crashed together, breast-to-breast, half a thousand years of poisonous hatred pouring into a bone-cracking orgy of violence. Steel flashed and grated; it darted and rang. Breath hissed and spatters of blood rained to the ground. Red blood. Human blood.

Cursing, Bjarki stumbled back; his left arm hung useless by his side, the thick muscle of his shoulder severed by a ripping blow of Grimnir's seax. The *skrælingr* raised the blade and licked a thin ribbon of gore from it. A slow serrated grin spread across his vulpine features. '*Faugh!* Red as that whore who whelped you!'

Bjarki snarled and swiped at the offending blood, glaring at it as if it were a badge of shame the Fates had saddled him with. He circled right, panting, now, and dripping sweat. Grimnir shifted, moving in unison to keep Bjarki from getting around.

'Trying to run? Oh, but we're not done yet, little fool! Not unless you're ready to beg.'

Half-Dane wrung sweat from his eyes and spat. 'No,' he growled, stumbling back left; he staggered, fell to one knee. The tip of his dirk scraped the stone. Rivulets of blood streamed from the wound in his shoulder, sluicing down his arm to drip off his useless fingertips.

Grimnir's smile widened. 'Maybe you are done, Daufi.' He stalked forward, reversing the grip on his seax. 'Beg, and I'll make it quick.'

Faster than his twisted frame belied, Bjarki pivoted at the hip and slung his dirk in a desperate underhand throw. Any other knife would have gone hilt-over-tip, or wobbled like a useless chunk of metal, but not this one. A master had forged it, and its weight and balance were as precise as that of a Frankish axe. It struck his foe in the face, point-on; Bjarki heard Grimnir grunt in surprise, and watched as his kinsman reeled and crashed to the earth.

'Ha!' Bjarki thrust himself upright. 'Who's so high-and-mighty, now, son of Bálegyr? Piss on me? By Odin! I'll piss on you, you dunghill rat!' Grimnir lay facedown on the cold stone of the headland; a puddle of black and stinking blood spread out from the left side of his head. Half-Dane staggered up and planted one hobnailed boot in his ribs. 'Black-blooded son of a whore!'

Nothing.

Bjarki laughed. He bent over Grimnir and seized him by his left arm, rolling him onto his back. 'Where's that fancy blade of yours, eh? That'll make a fine—'

Grimnir came around hard, hissing like a snake; his right eye burned like a seething ember of hate while his left was nothing but a blood-leaking ruin. The hurled dirk had gouged a furrow from the bridge of his nose, across his eye socket, and to his left temple.

The rune-etched blade of Grimnir's seax flashed up; driven by iron muscle, it thudded into Bjarki's right side,

453

sliding under the ribs to pierce his vitals. Bjarki Half-Dane's eyes registered shock.

'Got you, Daufi,' Grimnir cried, shoving Half-Dane aside. He snarled at the pain in his skull as he got to his feet. '*Nár!* Not as dead as I looked, was I?'

Bjarki writhed; he curled around the blade in his belly, unable to draw breath. Red arterial blood foamed in his throat. Grimnir snatched a handful of his hair and dragged him to the base of the ancient ash tree. He slammed Bjarki upright against the gnarled trunk.

Bjarki Half-Dane gasped for breath. Grimnir took hold of the gore-slimed hilt of his seax. 'Hear me, Sly One, Father Loki! Bear witness, O Ymir, sire of giants and lord of the frost! By this blood, I fulfill my oath!' A cold wind rose from the north.

With a howl of savage fury, Grimnir carved the blade across Bjarki's belly and ripped him open from right to left. Viscera tumbled out, loops of red and purple intestine, sacks of organs; blood splashed the roots of the tree, and the stench of bowel rose from the cavernous wound. Bjarki staggered, dragging his guts along. His mouth worked soundlessly.

Grimnir caught him by the scruff of the neck. 'Look here, Hrungnir! You are avenged!' Grunting, he hurled Bjarki Half-Dane over the edge of the cliff.

Tall rolling clouds sailed like titans before the rising gale, and the purple skies erupted in jags of savage lightning, the clean white light striving against the rage of darkness; thunder roared like the crash of war drums. Yggðrasil trembled, and Grimnir, who was the last son of Bálegyr left to plague the hollows of Miðgarðr, sat with his back to the bole of that ancient ash tree . . . and laughed as the heavens erupted in endless strife.

II

At the far eastern tip of the Howth Peninsula, on a rocky headland three hundred feet above the crashing surf, Étaín stood beneath the boughs of the gnarled ash tree and watched the sun rise through a veil of storm clouds. Days before, this had been a green and pleasant land where the wealthy *jarls* of Dubhlinn made estates and built mead halls, where slaves tilled the soil and *thegns* hunted for pleasure. All that was before Murrough's raid. Now, Howth was a wasteland of scorched fields and burned-out groves; the estates were heaps of ash, and the mead halls of the Danes were gutted skeletons that clung to hilltops. The green land would return, she knew. She could feel it.

With one pale hand, Étaín reached out and caressed the rough skin of the ash. Deep in its heartwood she heard the voice of its spirit. It was faint, but it sang . . . and she knew its song:

> *Away sprang Bálegyr's son, | across the Ash-Road*
> *With shoulders cloaked | in the skin of the wolf-father;*
> *The Æsir gave chase, | goaded by Alfaðir,*
> *And with him | came the Twilight of the Gods.*

Nodding, Étaín turned away. She had given her word that she would make an ending to his tale, but in her marrow she knew it could only be the ending of a stanza, part of a larger song . . .

EPILOGUE

In the days after the Battle on the Plain of Chluain Tarbh (known today as the Battle of Clontarf), Étaín of Wessex returned to the tiny cottage on the coast of Leinster where Blind Maeve lived and learned the healer's art; Njáll son of Hjálmarr joined her there, and with his help she composed a saga in both her native Anglo-Saxon and the tongue of the Danes. After Njáll's death, in AD 1017, she traveled the breadth of Ireland, healing the sick and bringing succor to the victims of war. She settled, finally, in the valley of the River Shannon, where the O'Brien kings of Kincora founded a nunnery in her honor. Étaín died in AD 1084.

During her long life, Étaín amended and added to the saga she had written with Njáll; at least two other hands added to the manuscript after her death and canonization. Eventually, it became part of a manuscript whose official designation is 'British Library, Cotton Vespasian D.VI,' commonly referred to as *The Rathmore Codex*.

Though Saint Étaín never gave her work a title, scholars today refer to it as the *Kaunumál* – though it is better known in lay circles as *The Death-Song of Grimnir son of Bálegyr*.

Author's Note

Every writer has *that* book. One born from the same soup of half-formed ideas and underexposed imagery as any other, but once conceived it digs in its heels and fights for life. It knuckles its way through your crowded subconscious, squalling in the din – it wants you to hear what it has to say, and it wants you to act upon it. That book doesn't care that it might be unworkable, or trite, or done to the point of cliché. It simply wants to *be,* and it leaves the details of how to the writer. For me, this was that book.

Since young adulthood, I've wanted to write a book about Orcs – those foot soldiers of evil first revealed to us in *The Hobbit* and *The Lord of the Rings* by J. R. R. Tolkien. I wanted to write it from the Orcs' point of view. And I wanted to *redeem* them. This was not a new idea, either. British fantasist Stan Nicholls had realized the same idea in 1999, with the publication of *Bodyguard of Lightning*; before that, in '92, Mary Gentle wrote the gallows-comical *Grunts,* wherein a company of Orcs discover a cache of modern weapons. Indeed, so common was this notion of the redemption of the Orc that before I ever put fingers to keyboard on the earliest drafts of *A Gathering of Ravens* there were already dozens of books out there featuring Orcs as protagonists – from Noble Savages to hulking Greenskins to classic Tolkien-inspired goblins.

But, damn it all, I had an idea for a book and it just wouldn't go away.

Alas, such are the vicissitudes of the writing life that what I called simply 'The Orc Book' got pushed onto the back burner as I wrote *The Lion of Cairo*; it fell by the wayside again in order for me to work on an ancient Greek tale called *Serpent of Hellas* (which was never realized), and it was finally put aside with the rest of my writing so I might become caregiver to my terminally ill parents. And yet, because it was *that* book I kept tinkering with it, creating a secondary-world Orc culture in terms and equivalences my history-wired brain understood: '. . . one part Vandal, one part Afghan tribesman, and one part Mameluke; none of the usual attributes: not inherently evil or blighted, no aversion to sunlight, and don't require a powerful non-Orc Will to guide them. They are not green, simple-minded, or piggish.' More importantly, however, this gave me something creative to do. It kept me sane, more or less.

My parents both passed away in 2011; when I returned to writing in 2012 I decided to do *that* book the honor of finally getting it written. But when I went back over my notes, my synopses, and my fragments of prose I discovered the whole thing had a decidedly pastiche air about it – a Frankenstein's Monster scavenged from the notebooks of Tolkien and his literary descendants.

I used to blog quite frequently, so I can look back and see that at least since 2008 I had questioned my ability to create a distinctive enough take on Orcs in the framework of a secondary world. It wasn't my forte. All my previous books were either pure historical fiction or historical fantasy (with an emphasis on the historical); did I dare try to chisel Orcs out of their accustomed milieu and mortar them into our own world – mixing history and myth à la Robert E. Howard's 'Worms of the Earth'?

That question elicited a great deal of conversation online, some pro but mostly con. It was the late Steve Tompkins of the online journal *The Cimmerian* who best elucidated the problem of taking Orcs out of their accustomed haunts. He wrote:

> To reconfigure them as an unlovely-but-arguably-racially-profiled warrior-race, unrestricted free agents looking for a destiny of their own is to risk losing the plot. It's precisely the fact that they were gengineered in the hells beneath the halls of a Dark Lord – 'And deep in their dark hearts the Orcs loathed the Master whom they served in fear, the maker only of their misery' – the tension between slavery and sentience that characters like Gorbag and Shagrat evince, that renders them so compelling.[1]

Steve was right, as he often was. Putting Orcs in any other context was risky, but inserting them into our own past? Perilous, indeed. Writing a novel is a precarious endeavor at the best of times, but here I was coming off a hiatus and into a scenario where my last book, *The Lion of Cairo* in 2010, had not lived up to expectations. Still, I wanted to do something different, something that might allow this book to stand out in that stellar crowd of Orc-themed fantasy already on store shelves. And so, despite some good advice to the contrary, in late 2011/early 2012 I went back to the drawing board. I played a little game of 'what if?' with myself. As in: 'What if Tolkien found his inspiration for Orcs in mythology?' and 'What if they had actually existed?'

[1] From *The Best of the Cimmerian*, 'Lonely Mountain, Crowded Expectations; Or, Prelude as Successor,' originally posted 2008.

What the answers to both questions had in common was what W. H. Auden referred to as Tolkien's fascination with 'the whole Northern Thing' – that confluence of Norse, Germanic, and Anglo-Saxon myth that informed much of the Professor's creation. Viewed through that same north-looking lens and filtered through the language of the sagas, historical parallels fell readily into place. The veneer of the Orc, popularized via fantasy literature, inexorably cracked and flaked away. What remained was the fabled *kaunar*. They existed, and their legend spread as the garbled re-tellings of an older cycle of myths that crossed multiple cultures – with a memory of them found in the creature Grendel from *Beowulf*, an echo of them in the Fomorians of Irish legend, even a parody of them in the *kallikantzaroi* of Medieval Greek fairy tales.

And this is the result. A book – *that* book – about a vengeance-minded *kaunr* whose DNA was laid down by Tolkien; an Orc who is never explicitly *called* an Orc – though the Anglo-Saxons might label him *orcnéas,* while the Danes might name him *skrælingr,* and the Irish will forever curse his name as one of the hated *fomóraig* . . .

Here, in the end, I can only hope I did as I intended and redeemed the Orc. But whether I did or not – or whether I fell flat and lost the plot entirely – I leave it to you, Gentle Reader, to decide.

SCOTT ODEN
DECATUR, AL
10 AUGUST 2016

Acknowledgments

Writing a novel is one of the few solitary endeavors a person can undertake that actually requires an army to pull off. And for this one, let me tell you, I had an army of champions watching my back. First, thanks to Mido Hamada, my friend and frequent sounding board, for suggesting early on that the young monk, Aidan, would be more effective as a young woman; to Steven Savile, for providing nudges of inspiration and for helping me understand Danish; to my cadre of editors and beta readers, who make sure I don't look like an illiterate ass in public: Louis Agresta, Rusty Burke, Tom Doolan, Ryan Wagner Flessing, Patrice Louinet, David Murray, Josh Olive, and Marcus Pailing.

A very warm thank-you to Robert Szeles, for giving my words an added dimension through the genius of his artistry; to Michael Mikolajczyk, Simon Walpole, and Jason Deem for their sketches of Grimnir.

Thanks, also, to my patrons, who kept me going when times were rough: David Murray, Rusty Burke, Richard Brown, Emily Delaney, Kenneth Apple, Amy Herring, Scott Hancock, Paul McNamee, Tom Doolan, Chrispian Burks, Charles Rutledge, Keith Rose, Doug Ellis, and Josh Olive. To Delores and Joe Morris, my second parents, who let me lean on them more than once. And a heartfelt thank-you to The Authors League Fund for their generous grant, which allowed me time to heal and time to write.

A grand thank-you to my cheering section – my myriad social media friends, who keep me energized, who urge me on, and who hold my feet to the fire when I'm slacking.

Thank you, as well, to the fine folks at Thomas Dunne Books/St. Martin's Press, who make me look spiffy and professional. And finally, to those three people who make it possible for me to do this, through their boundless patience, their expertise, their willingness to listen (and kick my ass when needed), and their bedrock support: my agent, Bob Mecoy; my editor, Pete Wolverton; and my lovely wife, Shannon.

To one and all, I thank you.

Men of Bronze

Scott Oden

Egypt 526 BC, and the kingdom of the pharaohs is dying, crumbling under the weight of its own antiquity. Across the expanse of Sinai, like jackals drawn to carrion, the forces of the king of Persia watch ... and wait.

Yet all is not quite lost. Hasdrubal Barca, a Phoenician mercenary feared as much by his own men as by his enemies, has vowed to defend Egypt against invasion. But the treacherous defection to the Persians of one of the Pharaoh's most able commanders sparks a conflict that will test Barca's military skills – and his humanity – to the limit.

From ancient Memphis to the parched wastelands of Palestine, Barca and his nemesis play a savage game of cat-and-mouse that will culminate in the bloodiest battle in Egypt's history. And there, in the hills east of Pelusium amongst the fallen of two great armies, Barca will face the same choice as those legendary heroes of old: death and eternal fame – or long life and obscurity ...

'Fast, tense and exciting ... the descriptions are terrific and the final, climactic battlefield scene is just brilliant'
CONN IGGULDEN, bestselling author of *Emperor*

God of Vengeance
The Rise of Sigurd 1
Giles Kristian

Norway AD *785. It began with the betrayal of a lord by a king . . .*

When King Gorm's men murdered the family of Jarl Harald, they made one fatal mistake: they failed to kill the jarl's youngest son, Sigurd.

With his kin slain, his lands seized, his people taken as slaves, Sigurd goes on the run. Hunted by powerful men, he wonders if the gods have forsaken him – and yet he has a small band of loyal followers and fighters at his side. With their help, and that of Odin the All-Father, Sigurd will have his vengeance – and neither men nor gods had best stand in his way . . .

'What elevates Kristian above the many pretenders to Cornwell's crown is the style and swagger of the prose. He is a modern *skald*, borrowing the old rhythms to create a brutal, absorbing tale'
Antonia Senior, *THE TIMES* 'Books of the Year'

'Unrelenting pace, brilliant action and characters. A masterwork'
CONN IGGULDEN

Pendragon

James Wilde

Winter AD 367, and in a frozen forest beyond Hadrian's Wall six scouts of the Roman army have been murdered.

It is Lucanus, the one they call the Wolf, who discovers the mutilated bodies. He knows the far north to be a wild place inhabited by barbarians, daemons and witches – a place where the old gods live on. It is not somewhere he would willingly go. But when the child of a friend is taken captive, he feels honour-bound to journey beyond the wall and bring the boy back home.

His quest will span an empire – from the pagan temples of Britain across the kingdoms of Gaul to the eternal city of Rome – and will ensnare a soldier and a thief, a cut-throat and a courtesan, a druid and even the emperor himself. And what it reveals will reverberate down the centuries . . .

From the bestselling author of *Hereward* comes an epic new historical adventure set during a time when the world faced a Dark Age and was in desperate need of hope.

'On the shadowed frontier between myth and half-imagined history, James Wilde paints a vivid and gritty picture of the genesis of one of the greatest legends of all time'
MATTHEW HARFFY, author of *The Bernicia Chronicles*

Dolphin's Barn Library
Leabharlann an Charnáin
Tel: 01-4540681